Sagheer Afzal, whose parents come from
Pakistan, was born in Harrow. He read Physics
at university and after years teaching IT he is
now working with school-leavers.
This is his first novel.

THE
RELUCTANT
MULLAH

BY
SAGHEER AFZAL

HALBAN
LONDON

First Published in Great Britain by
Halban Publishers Ltd
22 Golden Square
London W1F 9JW
2010

www.halbanpublishers.com

A catalogue record for this book is available from the British
Library.

ISBN 978 1 905559 16 9

Typeset by Spectra Titles, Norfolk
Printed in Great Britain
by MPG Books Ltd, Bodmin, Cornwall

The day, somewhere in the middle of July, was strangely wild. The wind howled and the walls of the Madrasah of Islamic Britons echoed with pulses of anxiety emanating from the devout inhabitants within. The elderly mused that such a sign heralded Judgement Day but the younger devotees, awash with science and weather forecasts, somewhat sardonically held responsible the frenzied applause of liberated Iraqis or jubilant Hamas Party members.

Whatever the reason, the looming sycamore trees which were too close to the north wing of the Madrasah repeatedly opened and closed their branches, revealing a window through which three young Holy men could be espied, buoyant upon a wave of electronic impudence. They were soon-to-be graduates of the Madrasah. Embryonic mullahs, they had memorised the Holy Quran but at that very moment they were indulging in that act of impish behaviour all first-time users of a webcam seem to enjoy, irrespective of custom, creed and culture: gesticulatory abuse.

The least enthusiastic participant, Musa, sat by the computer trying to configure a microphone, a webcam,

Yahoo messenger and a Windows XP operating system to work in unison so that his cousin in Pakistan (also a Holy man with awesome credentials) could hear and see him. His two comrades, Ali and Basto, crouched behind him, working their index fingers in a furious oscillatory motion.

"Assalaam-u-alaikum. Jahangir, can you hear me?"

"Waalaikum assalaam, Musa. I am hearing you wonderful, but I cannot make vision with you," Jahangir's clipped English crackled slightly.

Musa adjusted the webcam so that its elliptical window faced him.

"How is that, Brother Jahangir?"

"It is better with Musa, but I think there is great disturbance behind you. It looks as though it is raining fingers in the background."

Musa scowled and waved angrily behind him. "Hey, guys cut it out! Grow up would you?" oblivious to the fact that his one-fingered salute, given a few irate moments ago, had started the mother of all one-fingered salutes.

Ali and Basto stood up and chortled. Ali was Samson-like with his shoulder-length hair and immense physical strength. His craggy, haughty features were better-suited to a mountainside since mountains, according to the Quran, refused the privilege of emotion. Ali was the voice of hard realism in the group and he despised sentiment and slowness. For this reason he often fought with Basto, who by unspoken, common consent was the slowest of the three. But Basto wasn't bothered for he lived in a state of perpetual peace, a streetwise version of the Dalai Lama, aglow with his shaven head and cherubic face.

Musa tweaked the webcam again and slowly Jahangir began to emerge from the digitalised nebulae as a sombre-looking young man whose black hair was combed back in the manner of a 1930s' film star. His face filled most of the screen now, and the three young men were slightly unnerved by the stern eyes and the hard flat line that served as his mouth.

"Welcome, Brother Jahangir!" said Musa, as though he had just walked through the door.

"The welcome is mine, the welcome is mine, how are you?"

"Oh, fine thank you. How are Aunty and Uncle?"

"They are sending their most warm regards, Musa. Um…how is your sister?" Jahangir's voice changed into a more cautious mode, as though he were enquiring about the presence of landmines.

Ali exchanged a knowing smile with Basto. Shabnam was famed for her dazzling green eyes aflame in her pale complexion and notorious for her acerbic tongue which sadly did nothing to detract her many admirers on whom she lavished contempt and derision. She called Ali RGD (recessive gene dump) on account of his parents being cousins and his fiercely pronounced nose. Clearly, Jahangir had also been bitten by the Shabnam bug.

"Oh, the same, Jahangir. Everyone is trying hard to find her a suitable husband, but she treats each one like betel leaves: she chews them up and spits them out!" Musa laughed at the wittiness of his metaphor. All this, however,

3

was lost on Jahangir, whose eyes widened in alarm. Turning away he hollered a name, and after a few moments a more genial face filled the screen.

"Assalaam-u-alaikum Uncle," said Musa.

"Waalaikum assalaam, Musa," responded Uncle, leaning forward until his nostrils engulfed the entire monitor. The three Holy young men were treated to a surgical view of an enclave that might have been situated in the Amazon rain forest, filled as it was with green hairy vines.

"Why do you not recite to us your award-winning poem, son?" he bellowed.

"Uncle, you don't need to shout, we can hear you fine and why don't you lean back? We can't see you properly."

Uncle sat back and smiled with the expectant joy of a child about to be told that Santa will visit him tonight. Musa noticed the incipient yearning in his face and sighed. The event to which his uncle was referring was a poetry competition organised by the Madrasah. One night after Musa had eaten a halal burger that must have come from a toxic cow, he had stumbled into the common room, nauseous and unable to sleep. To soothe the tumult in his belly, he loaded a DVD of *Shakespeare in Love*. On that very auspicious night, the combination of intestinal acid and the wonder of love had inspired him to write a majestic poem which won the competition and now every dumb schmuck wanted to hear it recited.

Quite unnecessarily, Musa cleared his throat and inhaled a lungful of the oxygen which energised only poets. Basto and Ali's expressions slipped into a "not this shit again" cast.

4

In the cave that is our soul
The darkness is our desire for power.
Blind bats flee from our call
To nest in a sane man's tower.
Laden is the heart that seeks respite
From this world's deadly fight.

As always when reciting the poem, Musa's voice assumed a more refined, plummy, cadence. A passer-by might have thought himself privy to a newscast but across the cyberspace which separated Musa and Uncle, a chorus of angels sang.

"Oh…that is so nice and beautiful Musa. I am so proud of you. Who could ever think that the little boy who used to slide on his bottom whenever he wanted to move could write something so nice and pretty? Hold on one second, you must recite this to your aunty."

Musa sat still, exultant in the praise of his poetic prowess and his chest swelled. Ali briefly wondered if Musa's kameez would burst the way he had seen in the *Incredible Hulk*.

Aunty, like her husband, beamed her pride at her prodigious nephew into the webcam. The years had taken their toll and her face was jowly, but each jowl quivered with joy. Even the single streak of silvery hair that fell across her lined forehead seemed to swish happily.

"Hello Musa. Congratulations. This is a great moment for this family. I remember your father when he first left to come to England and…" she elongated the *and*, sounding like a boxing-match commentator, "he say to

5

me that after five years he will come back, but I say to him you must stay in England for the sake of your children and now…" her voice choked with emotion, "his son is talking English the way English people do!"

Musa tried hard to sound casual and weary. "Oh it's nothing Aunty, it's just inspiration. You know the way Allah inspired the bee to make honeycombs and the Prophet Noah to build the ark. It's…more or less the same."

Aunty smiled and nodded her head at each syllable, looking increasingly blank as she tried to unravel Musa's thread of modesty. Ali and Basto glanced at each other and shook their heads in disgust.

Musa recited his poem again and, as before, the reaction was ecstatic.

"Oh Musa that is lovely. It is like hearing…" Aunty's face creased as she struggled to think of a suitable comparison…"water rushing over a…a…waterfall. No it is much better than that actually. It is like hearing children singing in a playground or like a song sung by…by…a singer, you know what I mean don't you son?"

Before Musa could reply she hurried on: "Musa, could you recite the poem again slowly, so I can write it down and get my son Hosnaan to make a T-shirt with the poem on the front. He is getting very high in textiles you know!"

"Oh no, Aunty, there's no need for that. I mean it's just a poem," said Musa unconvincingly.

"Musa, it is my duty. Besides look at the rubbish people are wearing on their T-shirts nowadays." Aunty leant forward in the manner of someone about to impart a national secret. "The other day on the bus I see a young man with a T-shirt that said MR ZERO IS HERO, so I went up to him and asked: 'Who is Mr Zero?' and you know what he said? 'It's just a name, get off my case, mad woman!' I told him, 'If your mama had been on your case properly you would not be turning up like this.'" Aunty leant back, outrage plastered all over her face. "But it is getting like this now! Too many illegitimate children are using public transport! Anyway, please to recite poem again, but slowly please."

Aunty readied herself with pen and paper and Musa did as he was told, sounding distinctly unhinged. Ali nudged Basto and gestured towards the door.

Sometime later, after he had recited his poem to yet more relatives and had successfully fielded questions about his future with the ultimate in philosophical one-liners (he repeated "Live" to anyone who asked what he planned to do), Musa looked around and found that he was completely alone.

At that very moment, in a small dingy room in Scotland Yard's anti-terrorism unit, a young detective constable sat facing a giant screen covered with concentric green circles in the centre of which flashed a red light emitting an intensely irritating, electronic noise. The room was without windows and there was no ventilation apart from that emanating from Detective Inspector Harvey Edwards who sat snoring in his chair, his ruddy cheeks swelling ever so slightly as he let loose explosions of sound.

Paul Dearden looked dejectedly at his superior officer. How the hell could the man sleep so much? Throughout every accursed day over the past six months, ever since he had been assigned to the decryption unit, Edwards snored blissfully, waking only towards the end of the shift when he would burp, look foggily at Dearden with those huge blue eyes, run a trembling hand through his spiky ginger hair and, knowing full well how annoying his junior officer found it, he would say in a parody of a Yorkshire accent, "Awreet our kid. Owt been happenin'? No? Nowt? Let's have a yaw down the local then." He would then stand, shake his drooping gut, with both hands and march briskly out of the room. A *yaw* meant conversation and *owt* did not mean the conventional out but a*nything.* And *gander* meant *look,* and *tab* meant cigarette, and *ullet* meant owl, and *nark* meant annoy and that was the only fucking decryption he had done since coming to the unit: unravelling the vernacular of DI Edwards.

As his mentor snored on, Dearden stretched, smoothed the lapel of his jacket and gently pushed back his black hair, enjoying its reassuring thickness. Bored, he walked across to Edwards' desk, picked up his newspaper and rolled it up tightly. Then he whacked his superior officer on the head; he had done this plenty of times before and never once did Edwards wake up but the exercise did release a certain amount of frustration in Dearden. Glumly he fanned himself with the newspaper. He deserved so much better than this. A tall athletic graduate of University College London with a degree in Mathematics and a Masters in Algorithmic Operations, he should have been a banker or an economist but at the end of his studies he had decided, "I'm tired of being a bookworm. I want to experience life. Be an adventurer. I mean come on! How many girls have said I look like the young Sean Connery?' And so, despite his parents' fury, he had joined Scotland Yard and was immediately accepted on the accelerated Intelligence Officer course. But when he had emerged top of his class with a fantastic working knowledge of Aikido, what had he really achieved? How could he have known that he would end up in this shithole?

He jumped out of his skin when, shattering the tedium, a voice on the intercom announced, "Incoming Echelon alert. Level 4. Sending through now. Repeat, sending through now."

Dearden rushed to the huge Kyocera printer which churned out a single piece of paper containing that indecipherable code which he, only he, would crack, and that would herald his dazzling ascent through the ranks. And then the grey faces, those pompous officious jerks, would know his name. Yes, that was the way forward. That was the mistake he had made – it wasn't just what you knew, it was who you knew.

He picked up the sheet of paper, his hands quivering with eagerness, and stared at a poem…He frowned. Had a mistake been made? Echelon 4 signalled an imminent threat. Then he saw it – the name. It wasn't really that complex.

He would have to wake Edwards. This was too important. But how to bring this tub of lard to life?

Rummaging in the man's pockets he found his lighter. Once again he picked up the newspaper and rolled it into a tight cylinder. This he gently inserted into the large gaping mouth and carefully lit the end. Slowly, fire-rimmed ashes crumbled over the gigantic belly.

Edwards shuddered and sighed, "Maggie," but he did not wake up.

Dearden wondered who the hell Maggie was. Edwards was married to some hag called Lizzie. He had met her, briefly, at the Christmas party and remembered her strong handshake. She had caused a bit of a stir that evening as she went into a pinching frenzy after drinking too much although he himself had avoided her fingers.

He looked thoughtfully at the blinking screen. Something else from that insane party floated into his mind. He had been standing with a group of fellow officers and one of them, commiserating with Dearden, said what a relief it was that he no longer had to work with "that lazy sod". He added that the only way to get a reaction was to call him Billy Bunter.

It couldn't hurt to try. Dearden leaned over and whispered in Edwards' ear, "Wakey, wakey Billy Bunter."

Edwards immediately opened his eyes.

"Good afternoon sir. You will not believe what has happened. I've just cracked —"

Dearden never completed his sentence. A fist struck his jaw and knocked him over.

It was dawn. Musa smoothed his kameez and looked out of the window. The Madrasah was surrounded by a park now enclosed by high iron railings. The park had been the idea of the local council who thought that a large swathe of greenery would quell the turbulent spirit of the demonstrators who frequently marched through their area. The theory was that the young warriors would be distracted by the lush foliage and plentiful trees and perhaps be tempted to gambol through its sinuous footpaths rather than scream anti-establishment slogans like a horde of demented banshees. Sadly, the saplings were uprooted within the first month and any protestor fool enough to stop and admire the artistry of God was in for the same treatment. Now the view beyond the Madrasah was a rectangular dump filled with the conversation of the criminally active, along with snores of the sleeping vagrants for whom the park was a kind of retirement home. On the occasions when angry demonstrators did march through chanting, "Affordable housing" or "Free education" so incensed did the protestors become, that they would vent their spleen on the park dwellers. To prevent an escalation into violence, the council had erected the iron fence. Musa smiled sadly. It was all there in that gloomy canvas of suburban life: the desolate reality of this world.

He turned away from the window and noticed a partially open box containing what looked like a shawl lying on his bed. He pushed the lid aside wondering who it was for: a gift for Ali's rarely mentioned mother, perhaps? The buying and receiving of presents though was far away from Ali's nature. Musa lifted the scarf and underneath it was an abaya, a thin gown to cover the body from the shoulders to the feet. Underneath the abaya was a hijab to cover the head. All were made from the simplest black cloth. At the bottom of the box were gloves.

Musa, still holding the abaya, walked to the mirror. The room, like all the rooms in the Madrasah, was spartan and bare. The grey carpet was plain and when the room was warm it gave off a faint rubberised odour. The walls were an old, blistered white; even the mirror was covered in layers of dust. Musa gazed at his obscured reflection and then down at the abaya. The Sisters. The veiled entities who existed on the other side of the Madrasah. Always shrouded yet so full of presence. When they looked at you, even though you could not see them or the expression in their eyes, it always seemed somehow that their layered garments uncovered their silent appraisal. You felt the shadow of their opinions before you were aware of their silhouettes. What was it that gave them this aura of omniscience, wondered Musa? He looked back at the bed and then again at himself in the mirror. No…it was too crazy…but still it would be interesting, like an experiment, and no one need ever know. He'd have a job explaining it if he was seen, but even so…

The idea began to snowball in his mind: to hell with it, it was just a two minute job, nothing more. Musa quickly put on the abaya, just as he would put on a jumper. Next came the hijab. He placed it on his head and pulled it down. It was loose; clearly Ali's mother had a big head, just like her son. A thin piece of gauze, something he had not noticed before, fell from the top, covering his eyes. Then there was the shawl, all he had to do was to wrap it around his shoulders and that was all there was to it: he had crossed over.

Dearden no longer looked the suave scourge of terror that he imagined himself to be a few minutes before. His hair was dishevelled, he had trouble focussing and his jaw flopped around like a limp fish.

Edwards had helped him up from the floor and on to a chair. He explained that when his father was at school he was on the tubby side and was landed with the nickname Billy Bunter. When Edwards himself started school he too was a bit fat and history repeated itself, thanks to a friend's mother who had known his old man as a child. This gave him the jip and whenever he was called Billy Bunter he hit out.

"It got to be automatic if you know what I mean, so when you whispered in my ear…It's like a reflex thing. You know, like this –"

He struck Dearden on the kneecap and the young officer yelped in pain as his lower leg jerked forward. "See what I mean? That's a motor reflex thingammy. So no hard feelings, our kid?"

Dearden nodded, grimacing.

"Champion!"

Edwards grinned. "So what's all the palaver about?"

Dearden told him about the code he had cracked, explaining the flawless logic in his meticulous reasoning.

The detective inspector scratched his head thoughtfully as he read the print-out.

"The Madrasah of Islamic Britons. I was on the beat when it opened. Hell of a big do with a load of toffs. Back in Yorkshire I used to hang about with some of these

Muslim characters. At first I thought they were a right bunch of wing-nuts but after a bit I changed my mind. They're honest, mind you. With these guys what you see is what you get. Some of me mates back then were AC/DC, if you know what I mean. But them lot were stand up fellas; the whole lot of 'em. One time, I asked one of them if I could go to one of their talks and he says you're welcome, jus' like that. No push off, your face is white. No none of that. So I went to the talk for five days in a row. What an eye-opener! A scary-looking bloke with a big beard and big shoulders did the speaking and boy did he have a pair of tongs on him or what! He could've blown away any opera singer. But do you know the scariest thing? All he talked about for those five days in a row was Judgement Day and Armageddon; you know mountains crumbling, oceans boiling, angels giving you a proper hiding. It gave me nightmares but he was so excited.

"Afterwards I got to thinking that this lot are more serious about life and death than our lot. How many young people do you know that think about resurrection and heaven and hell and all that malarkey? None I'll bet. That's why they're so proper and formal. Not because they're unfriendly but because they got other things on their mind. Anyway, if we gotta go, we gotta go."

He looked sternly at DC Dearden.

"Are you sure you're up to this? Because if you don't mind me saying so you look like a right yogurt!"

Musa walked over to the mirror and studied himself. He sighed heavily and lifted his chin up. He didn't feel any different. Truth be told, it was uncomfortable as hell; and he smelt his breath each time he exhaled. He looked out of the window and surveyed the world from the perspective of a veiled Sister. The world tottered on, much the same as before. A few stalls selling vegetables and fish were being set up on either side of the road. Two elderly drunks lurched unsteadily along the pavement, their arms round each other's shoulders. There was however no sense of filter, no sense of segregation. Perhaps it was as they said, thought Musa, the real veil is behind the eyes.

He smiled sadly and prepared to disrobe just as Ali and Basto pushed open the door. He turned with the speed of a ballerina, then crouched and stuck out his arms as if preparing to hurl himself at the two intruders. Incredulous, Ali and Basto froze as they considered the bizarre spectacle of a Sister preparing herself for man-to-man combat. For a few minutes no one dared speak.

It was Ali who came to his senses first, while Basto timidly hung back.

"Musa, is that you?" he asked, warily.

"Who else, you dumb fool?" retorted Musa angrily.

Just as Ali prepared to launch into a tirade they heard a commotion downstairs followed by the sound of heavy footsteps heading towards the door. In strode Edwards and Dearden and a bunch of Holy young men with excited faces filled the doorway.

Ali scowled at them. "Hey you baboons! Knock it off!

15

Don't you have any manners? Did none of your parents teach you how to behave when visitors come around?"

He slammed the door and turned and glared at the two policemen. Dearden looked awkwardly at Edwards, who nodded.

"Good afternoon, gentlemen and... lady," he began awkwardly. "We are from the anti-terrorism branch and have some questions to ask you but first we must point out that we are not placing you under arrest."

He stopped, smiled suddenly, walked towards Musa and stretched out his hand.

Musa turned his face sideways and in a smooth fluid movement he slapped Dearden across the face. Still suffering from his superior's earlier attack, the police officer groaned but instinctively squared up to his assailant, momentarily forgetting Musa's assumed gender.

Edwards quickly stepped between them and frowned at Dearden.

"You can't shake hands with Muslim women. What do they teach you at university nowadays?"

"But it's not what you think!" began Basto. "He's not a woman."

Musa slapped him hard across his face too. Basto stumbled and fell backwards.

Edwards nodded towards Musa and said to Ali, "Cor! She's a feisty one."

"I suppose you could say that," agreed Ali. He caught Musa's eye and pointed towards the door.

"Leave!"

Musa shot towards the door but slammed into Edwards

who jumped in front of him. Musa fell back and landed on Basto. A combination of two intestinal sounds was heard as his head made contact with Basto's abdomen.

"What a carry-on this is!" Edwards chortled as he surveyed the struggling forms on the floor. "Let's start again," he suggested.

"Assalaam-u-alaikum. I am Detective Inspector Edwards. There are only two ways from here on. My way or the high way. My way is nice and easy. All you gotta do is just come with us and answer a few questions. None of you is under arrest. I will say that again for the record. You're not nicked. Like my colleague said, all we wanna do is ask a few questions nice and polite like. And all we want you to do is answer, nice and polite like. So are we ready or are we ready?"

Edwards smiled and gave a thumbs-up sign, as though he were a game show host ready to signal the start of some fantastic fun. Musa and Basto got up. Musa carefully arranged his veil. Ali shook his head in disgust and the three of them made their way out, followed by the dazed DC Dearden.

In the narrow corridor, the Holy young men waited.

"Hey where's Musa?" "Who's the Sister?" "What are the policemen doing here? Are you selling drugs?" "That's not Islamic you know!" "How come you gotta Sister in there?" "That's not Islamic you know."

Edwards placed himself directly in front of Musa and shouldered his way through. A few steps further and the number of inquisitive Holy men multiplied. Edwards made a sweeping motion with both arms looking as if he were doing the breast stroke in a sea of crazed Holy men. Musa was pushed up against Basto's back and his veil brushed against the sweat on Basto's neck. There was a wall of volume on either side of him that heaved with distaste and excitement. Basto, aware of the responsibility of his role as Musa's protector, grew indignant and raised his voice: "C'mon guys, give them a break! Ain't any of you got sisters yourselves?"

More laughter and more chuckles and more sneers. Dimly, Musa was aware they had reached the staircase but that did not alter their rate of progress. Even the stairs were packed. Where had the Holy men come from? He couldn't recall seeing so many people at breakfast or even prayer. But nonetheless they were all here, crucifying him with their venomous intrigue. Musa curled his gloved hand into a fist and prepared to strike at the mob but as he did so, he felt his entire body lunge forwards. Slowly, it dawned on him that his feet were no longer touching the ground: he was suspended in this bedlam of bedevilled Holy men. Like a dark angel, he wafted down the stairs held aloft by the rabble.

After they dropped him Musa realised they were in the foyer and at the far end of this sun-lit space was the main entrance. The rabble had momentarily calmed down but like a crazed swarm of bees they re-grouped and hustled Musa all the way to the exit. Dimly he was aware of Ali and Basto's furious protests as they fought, pushed and cussed their way out.

Relieved to be outside Musa prepared to take off his hijab, but reconsidered the action. It wouldn't look good at this particular moment: they might start thinking he was a transvestite and that would do irreparable damage to his reputation as a Holy man. That demented impulse he'd had to foray into the psyche of a Sister! It all seemed to be such reckless folly now.

Detective Inspector Edwards opened the door of a flattened, white Audi with a flashing revolving beacon and announced proudly, "Welcome to the bat mobile!"

Looking directly at Musa he asked, "You wanna go first, Madam?"

The anti-terrorist unit's detention room reflected none of the fabled goodwill of which its proprietors liked to boast. No more than a squalid cell it was lit with ferociously bright bulbs, their wattage so intense the mould in the corners of the room was obscured. Musa, Ali and Basto sat on creaky wooden chairs alongside a metal table. The door remained open although that in no way offered a possibility of escape for, wedged in the doorway, was a large, dour-faced policewoman.

"Do you think she's a lesbian?" Musa whispered to Ali.

"Dunno. I read somewhere that all senior people in the police are freemasons, and most freemasons are racists. And I remember hearing Imam Faisal say that a lot of racist people are gay," replied Ali, also in a whisper.

"So what does that make her? A racist, a lesbian and a freemason?"

"Does she have to be all three?"

"Maybe not, but even if you picked your best two we're still fucked."

19

Just then the policewoman moved aside for Edwards and Dearden who closed the door behind them. Edwards pulled up a chair and with a slow deliberate casualness leaned back and placed his right ankle on his left knee. He then placed his hands at the back of his neck and beamed at them. Dearden sighed heavily and did likewise, grimacing slightly as he smiled due to the large swelling on his cheek.

Musa, Ali and Basto stared at the pair with their brilliant smiles. They then looked at each other and, as if some telepathic conference had taken place, they put their hands on the table.

The detectives maintained their fixed smiles, a second became a minute and a minute became much longer until it finally dawned on Musa that the dazzling duo were expecting a reciprocal gesture. What would a Sister have done at a moment like this? He couldn't guess and briefly had the urge to remove the veil and bare all. There was the small chance that such a gesture would tickle the British funny bone to such an extent that they might forget why they were here in the first place. But to presume upon their sense of humour would be as wise as walking across the M1. He watched as a bead of sweat from DI Edwards' temple coursed down his face only to be diverted by a dimple on his cheek to the bottom of his lower lip.

Edwards undid the holster on the side of his belt and took out his pistol. He undid the magazine catch and slowly separated it from the rest. With great care he placed the two parts side by side on the table, the beatific smile still fixed on his face. DC Dearden followed suit, accepting that the finer mysteries of life would forever elude him. The two then leant back with their legs in exactly the same position as before, radiating goodwill through the glint of their incisors.

The dawn of comprehension at last broke in the minds of Ali and Basto and they leant back, folded their arms and smiled. Musa gave them a hesitant thumbs-up sign. DI Edwards' smile grew even broader and he chuckled in appreciation of this newly formed coalition of friendliness.

"You see, folks, we're not here to hurt you or to make you feel afraid! We're keeping the peace so we can increase the peace, if you get what I mean. We know you guys watch the news and think policemen are all bell-ends, they wanna lock you up and throw away the key! But it's not like that at all! Isn't that right?"

He turned to Dearden who gazed at the three and shrugged in a non-committal way. Edwards laughed. "Don't mind him. He's a joker and a half is this one!" He paused.

"There is something I want you to know. I was born and brought up in Yorkshire and some of my best mates there are Pakistani. Every time I go back they say to me, 'Harvey, you must have a pint with us.' Or, 'You must come down in your policeman's uniform and do a little talk in our mosque.'

"One time, honest to God, it's no lie, I found a girl crying on a park bench and I asked her what's up. She tells me that her mum and dad are putting pressure on her to marry her cousin who she hates. I ask if he lives in Pakistan but she says he lives next door! So I say to her, 'You just gotta give it time, love. Every relationship is like that. You hate someone and then you love them and then you hate them again. It's like that for all of us, black, blue or white.'

"I take her home and her parents are so pleased they invite me to have my supper with them. While we're eating I say to her dad, 'Don't force her! You gotta respect whatever she says. And if it's no, it's no'. And I says to the girl, 'Your mum and dad want what's best for you. They've seen more of life than what you have and moving next door is no big deal. You'll settle down in no time.'

"That was five years ago and every time I see her she's gotta little'un." His eyes softened. "So you see. We're all friends. I am not Johnny Westerner and you aren't Ali Pakistani. We're all the children of Adam and Eve. You get what I'm saying?"

Musa, Ali and Basto nodded their heads.

"Good. Let's get to it. DC Dearden, take it away!"

Dearden cleared his throat.

"Let me begin by reiterating the sentiments of my colleague. We all want a swift and amicable resolution of this matter. Now, a little while ago, we intercepted an electronic communiqué which contained what appeared to be a code. After some careful analysis I found the source of the communiqué was the Madrasah and on further analysis it was discovered that the mode of electronic transmission to Pakistan was a webcam which upon even further analysis led to the discovery that this communiqué emanated from your room."

"All we did was ask at the reception if anyone had a webcam!" interrupted DI Edwards.

Dearden gave his superior officer a disdainful look and carried on.

"Now, if I may, I would like to read aloud the first line of this apparent poem." He paused.

"'In the cave that is our soul…' I was immediately struck by the menacing tone of this first line, its deeply negative interpretation of a man's soul, equating it to a dark, forbidding cave. It struck me, as I am sure it must strike you, that these are the thoughts of someone who is essentially a loner, someone who is deeply entrenched in pessimism.

"Then the second line." His voice dropped to a whisper. "'The darkness is our desire for power'.

Musa, Ali and Basto fidgeted nervously.

"Darkness, power. Darkness, power. Darkness and power. The dark and then the power. The power that comes from the dark. Do you see how that follows on as an attacking blow? Now we see the psyche of a person who is empowered by the dark murmurings of his soul which he thinks is a cave. Then the third line.

"'Blind bats flee from our call'. At this point we see the desperate plight of someone who is trying to call out, trying to connect, but instead of finding sympathy and compassion, he discovers that everyone is running away and in his hatred he labels them as being blind because they cannot understand his distorted view of the world and himself.

"The next line. 'To nest in a sane man's tower'. Do you see now how suddenly the whole tone of the poem changes? Can't you feel the dark intensity of the metaphors? The person is now clearly distinguishing between himself and the sane man. He sees the sane man as someone far away in a tower, while he is languishing in his quagmire of pessimism and negativity. Then the fifth line…

"'Laden is the heart that seeks respite…'"

Dearden folded his arms and looked coldly at the three men facing him.

"Eh? There's summat a bit dicky mint about that line," mused DI Edwards.

"Dicky mint, precisely sir," replied Dearden. "Now if viewed in conjunction with the final line, 'From this world's deadly fight', an ominous pattern emerges."

"What's that?" asked Edwards excitedly.

"Cave – power – tower – Laden and then…fight," answered Dearden.

Edwards frowned. "Um…I don't mean to sound thick, but just what are you blathering on about?" he asked.

"Cave power tower Laden fight. Who do we know that lives in a cave and is known for an event concerning a tower and has the name Laden and calls for people to fight?"

"Osama bin Laden!"

"Precisely, sir." Dearden smiled. "Now which one of you is the author?"

The three young men were aghast.

Musa spoke first. "DC Dearden, you've got it wrong. It's a different kind of Laden. You see Laden in Osama bin Laden's name is pronounced Lah-den; whereas Laden in the poem is pronounced lay-den, meaning full up. You've got the wrong end of the stick!"

Dearden was curious.

"Did you write this, madam?"

Musa nodded warily. Ali and Basto cut a glance to each other, aware of the potential for further disaster.

"Why's that then?" inquired Edwards.

"Well, you see sir, the thing is I've always had a way with words. I like to read and I have a diary and I write things in that diary whenever I get the urge. It's just the way I am."

Edwards pursed his lips and looked appraisingly at Musa. His fingers drummed on the table.

"Are you a poet?" asked the detective inspector.

"I do my best," replied Musa modestly.

"And you can turn it on any time any place. Is that so?"

Musa nodded, not wanting pride to unmask his gender.

"OK doll. This here is what we are gonna do!" said DI Edwards.

He placed a sheet of paper on the table with a pen atop. Slowly he slid the paper across to Musa.

"Write some poetry," he ordered.

The two policemen, Ali and Basto leaned forward expectantly. Musa picked up the pen, stopped, looked up, and then put the pen down again.

"I can't do it with everyone watching," he said plaintively.

Edwards nodded: "OK. You've got a point. We'll be back in two."

After the pair had left Ali turned on Musa. "I can't

believe this is happening. We are in a detention room in Scotland Yard. Blue lights all the way down the M1. You are dressed as a woman and two fucking jerks think you're Shakespeare!"

"Cool it! Getting flustered will not help. We need to reason our way out of this."

"How're you going to reason your way out of your clothes when we get back? If we ever get back, I mean. What were you thinking? They can lock you up for that, Musa! I bought that thing for my mother's birthday. How can she wear it knowing a man has been inside it?" exclaimed Ali.

"She won't know," said Musa dismissively.

"Get your head out of your arse. We have been sweating like pigs. A sniffer dog would die from an overdose if he were to come near you right now."

"I hate to break up the party, but shouldn't you start writing something? They'll be back any second," said Basto.

"That's right, Musa. You'd better get going! Make it nice and fancy, not like the crap that landed us in here!" said Ali.

Musa thought hard and started to write rapidly. He was still writing when Dearden and Edwards returned.

"OK. Time's up. Let's hear it," said DI Edwards.

Musa handed the sheet to Ali who first read the poem to himself. He groaned and cleared his throat.

"'I went to the woods because I wanted to live deliberately. I wanted to live deep and suck out all the marrow of life. To put to rout all that was not life and not

26

when I had come to die discover that I had not lived.'"

Through his veil Musa saw only stupefaction on Edwards' face. At length the detective inspector turned to Dearden and asked, "Whaddya think?" but before the junior officer could reply Edwards suddenly grabbed the sheet of paper from Ali.

"See here, I'm no expert on poetry but I do know one thing: if it don't rhyme it's a crime." He smiled, tickled by his own wordplay. Do you see what I'm saying? OK, strike two. C'mon Dearden."

As soon as the door closed, Ali said to Musa, an anguished look on his face, "What the fuck are you trying to do to us! I said to make it good and you start stringing together some crap about living in the woods. What do you think this is? A camping holiday?" said Ali.

"But it was written by an American scholar. It's a famous poem!" exclaimed Musa.

"Who gives a shit who it was written by? Every poem you write ends the same way. Someone's foot gets planted up our arse."

"Why don't I have a go?" suggested Basto.

Musa and Ali looked at Basto, their minds whirring with the same thoughts. He was not renowned for his literary ability nor indeed ability of any kind. Entrusting this task to him would be a monumentally hazardous thing to do. What choice did they have? Musa passed him the pen and paper.

Basto began tapping the pen on the table, thinking hard. A couple of seconds later, he smiled and began to write. He finished just as the detectives came back into the room.

"Shoot!" said Edwards.

Ali took the paper from Basto and began to read in a monotone:

> *This is a crock of shit.*
> *We didn't do it.*
> *We have nothing to say.*
> *Please don't send us to Guantanamo Bay.*

All neural activity in the room came to a grinding halt. Synaptic pulses flickered with poetical portent and came to a shuddering stop. In that primal hypnagogic state everyone's consciousness hung like a guillotine frozen in mid-air.

Then an extraordinary thing happened. DI Edwards started to rap. He moved his neck backwards and forwards, his cheeks swelled as he expelled a tu-tu-too noise and with his head still rocking, he moved his hands up and down on the table and began to intone: "We have nothing to say. Please don't send us to Guan-TANAMO Bay. B-b-b-bay. B-b-b-bay, B-b-b-bay, B-b-b-bay." Dearden couldn't believe his eyes and wondered what the hell Edwards got up to when he was off duty. Musa, Ali and Basto felt nothing but relief.

"This is real good. Real g-g-g-good. G-g-g-good. This is street poetry Dearden. You know Ice-T and Ice Cube and Eminem and all that! She ain't no more a terrorist than I am. This here has been a huge misunderstanding."

He smiled benevolently at three exhausted Holy men.

"OK then. I'll drop you off at the Madrasah. Fixing on Musa he said, "Don't you fret, I'll make sure nothing bad happens to you. I'll have a word with your boss."

"No!" cried out Musa, Ali and Basto in unison.

2

Mufti Bashir, the chief elder of the Madrasah, readied himself for the dreadful explosion of noise that signalled the time for prayer. These days it seemed everything was said with too much exuberance, too much excitement, and too much disrespect. This he was told was the way it was now: the tide of change was a part of revolution, and revolution was needed to rekindle the ashes of the faith that made Islam so great.

Sure enough it came, the young muezzin mindful only of the need to impress upon everyone with the sonorous timbre of his voice, desecrating the rhythm of the call to prayer by compressing its syllables into a throaty screech. Mufti Bashir sighed and became aware of how slowly that reflex act of irritation occurred now. And how alien the breath his chest expelled seemed to him, like a stranger's cargo. He stared sadly at a large frame on the wall, which contained the oft-repeated phrase from Surah *Rahman*: Which of your Lord's favours do you deny? Now that phrase seemed to have a heavy inverse meaning to him.

Mufti Bashir spent much of his time in the Madrasah in a large attic room dominated by an oval window that stretched from wall to wall. The glass panels of the spotlessly clean window shone from above the thick alabaster wedges. As he looked around the room he noticed nothing. The distinctions between old and new, dust and dirt were gone. He was aware of objects and possessions as perhaps they truly were – inanimate and impersonal. The lacklustre light from a bulb that hung from the high ceiling illuminated the shiny gold and red stripes on the spines of shelves full of well-thumbed leather-bound books. He spent a great deal of his time poring over these tomes, not for the sake of acquiring knowledge but for that sense of connecting with something familiar. This vestige of reality had for him become very faint now. Even the air he breathed seemed like spoonfuls of a once familiar fluid.

He knew his time was approaching. This did not trouble him for he was by now a soul encased in a feeble infirm frame. The reverberations of his soul were the only pulses of life he felt. He heard a person's voice and knew what sort of a person they were and how deeply their shadow would cut. But voices very quickly faded away, he heard emotions more keenly, and this further increased his distance from others. That did not bother him. He no longer had any real interest in people and their companionship. Even when his five sons came to visit him with their terrified children, he was always glad when they left. Had his wife been alive, this might have been different but then he would have been different. She had died twenty-three years ago and it was her death and the subsequent renunciation of physical pleasure that had led to him being concerned only with the soul.

He had come to England grudgingly and at the insistent wish of his wife who like so many women was only preoccupied with the vanities and baubles of this world. He remembered with a faint smile what she had said when she first arrived, "Is it always this dark and cold?"

He too had felt the cold and darkness, not in the weather but in the slim young fellow Pakistanis who had come with him and who were lazy about calling their wives over. They were all like that then. Rakish in their cheap suits and slick with their shiny hair and boots, they were all fascinated by the white flesh and confident smiles of English women. He used to see some of them at weekends standing like guilty, excited children in a single line outside an empty house occupied by a busy woman who needed only one room.

In those early days, British Islam was still in its infancy. Mosques were few and far between and the attention span of those attending was minimal. They were more interested in worldly matters; working hard, making money, and sending money back home. On occasion, he would be invited to their houses where there would be as many as fifteen men, huddled together and stoking their companionship with debate and banal banter. He liked to sit with them in those days although he seldom spoke but they never seemed to mind that. A brown face was all the entry needed into their hearts. They were all so warm and friendly back then; their talk was alive with dreams and longing and their eyes were lit with greed as their wiry frames twitched at every window of opportunity. Some talked big and dreamed much but made little. Some were just content to live under the sway of events and let be what was meant to be. Destiny was a dark ocean which they all tried hard to conquer.

When their wives joined them the season of their lives changed. No longer was their laughter carefree. When their children were born they harried them with their ambition and rivalry. When their children grew older the season of their lives changed again and with that change came the unmasking of a harsh reality. Some tried to summon the ways of their forefathers and ripped apart the very fabric of their lives. Some were just content not to push against the prevailing norms. Then his mosque became full and his gathering listened as they never did before and they started to pray as they should have prayed. Long, long before. And they came to him with hearts like beggars' bowls and children like sacrificial lambs to be admitted into his flock, to atone for the sins he watched them commit when they were young, brash and so very bold.

Mufti Bashir gradually became aware of an insistent knocking at the door. He blinked and was annoyed to discover that they were moist.

"Yes," he replied querulously.

Hafiz Aleem entered the room and moved his hand to his temple by way of respect. Mufti Bashir watched him, feeling his arrogance, aware that the students had given Hafiz Aleem the nickname Adolf — the result of his relishing his primary role of reporting their misdemeanours.

"What is it?"

"There was a disturbance today at the Madrasah. Two policemen came and took two of our students and a girl with them, sir."

"Were they arrested?" inquired Mufti Bashir.

"No sir. Just escorted away. They told us they just wanted to question them."

"Who was the girl?" asked Mufti Bashir.

"We don't know," answered Hafiz Aleem nervously.

"Well, who were the boys?"

"Ali Akbar and Bastayazid Bihari."

Mufti Bashir considered this. Ali and Bastayazid were never noticeable but for their association with a third, Musa. A familiar topic for conversation among the other elders. At times, when he finished leading the prayer and turned to face the gathering, he would see him in the front row. Always searching with his eyes and wandering away with his mind but he searched too deeply and thought too little.

"There is no great riddle to solve. The girl was Musa," snorted Mufti Bashir.

"Musa? Are you sure sir?" asked Hafiz Aleem, momentarily stunned.

"Of course I'm sure! Have him brought to me when he gets back," said Mufti Bashir, already turning away.

He slipped into another reverie. Of a time before time, when he was young and supple and had shiny shoes to go with a suit chosen by a woman who was earthy and loud. Still suspended in his musing, he slowly moved over to his books and picked out an album. On the last page was a photograph which he told himself he must not see too

34

often and he had kept this promise to himself. His eyes became moist but this he did not notice, not even when a teardrop fell into the fold of a day a dreamy aeon ago.

Musa, Ali and Basto got out of the car, spent and weary beyond belief after another three-hour race north along the motorway. Inside the Madrasah once more they were told by one of the two boys on the reception desk that they were to go to the waiting area overlooking the foyer.

"What do you think they'll say?" asked Ali.

"What can they say? They might even think of us as heroes. How many people get taken to Scotland Yard and then escorted back! We could be on the cover of *Eastern Eye*!" said Basto enthusiastically.

"What about you Musa? What are you gonna say when they ask you why you are dressed as a woman?" asked Ali in the tone of someone making small talk.

Musa looked thoughtful. It was all so very embarrassing.

"Stand up straight, guys. It's Adolf!" said Ali urgently.

An intense, emaciated-looking Holy man with a perpetual scowl snarled, "You three have some explaining to do!"

"Easy Adolf, we've had a rough day," said Ali condescendingly.

Aleem's face reddened. He drew himself up as if his outrage was somehow able to elongate his scrawny body.

"You two," he pointed at Ali and Basto, "go to your rooms and you, Musa, are to come with me to Mufti Bashir."

Before they parted company Ali, unusually solemn, said

to Musa, "Be careful in front of Mufti Bashir. Speak from your heart but don't shoot from the lip. And don't be thinking he's senile because he doesn't forget what he's seen and he's seen a lot."

Ali walked away with Basto in tow. Hafiz Aleem watched Musa with an uncertain expression in his eyes.

"Ready?"

"Yes, let's go," said Musa.

They walked towards a winding wooden staircase. The stairs creaked and the banister moved as he placed his hand on it. As they began to climb Musa gathered his thoughts on Mufti Bashir. For a start he did not seem to like people. He kept his distance from every other living being in the Madrasah and his reluctant conversation was gnomic and terse. His main contribution to communal life in the Madrasah was the leading of the prayer, a duty which he had fulfilled every day, five times a day, for the past forty years. Sometimes Musa would catch Mufti Bashir studying him during the Friday sermon. The look in his eyes always troubled Musa for it was as though he was watching his life unfold and there was something in that trajectory that filled him with sadness.

They were now on the top floor and Musa's legs were beginning to ache. The pipes running above the skirting board were rusty and to Musa's surprise there was a proliferation of cobwebs.

"He's in there. Watch yourself when you speak to him," said Hafiz Aleem, pushing past Musa and making his way back down the stairs.

Musa knocked on the door. There was no response so

he tentatively stepped inside. An odour emanating from the leather-bound tomes greeted him as he squinted in the gloom. Facing the window stood Mufti Bashir, a photograph in his hand, seemingly in a world of his own.

"Who are you?" he asked without turning around.

"Musa…sir."

"Take off the veil," commanded Mufti Bashir, still with his face to the window.

Musa did as he was told. He rubbed a gloved hand over his sweat-streaked face, glad that it was all over.

"Who are you?" asked Mufti Bashir again.

"Musa," replied Musa nervously.

Mufti Bashir beckoned him to his side and Musa, his head bowed down, walked with small, hesitant steps until they were face to face. Slowly Musa looked up and met Mufti Bashir's eyes. One was light blue and the other dark grey. He had noticed this on the first day he arrived at the Madrasah when Mufti Bashir had placed his hands on his shoulders and gazed at him. Musa had stared back in wonder and he remembered seeing a ghost of a smile flicker across Mufti Bashir's face. Mufti Bashir had chuckled then, a wheezy, crackling sound. "Heterochromia, an abnormality inherited from my forefathers. It has stunned many people into silence."

He motioned to a chair. Musa sat down and Mufti Bashir also seated himself. Musa looked carefully at the chief elder of the Madrasah. What surprised him were his fresh even features, untouched by age or concern. Only his hands and feet were wrinkled and gnarled. And the eyes, they did indeed have a mesmeric effect. When looking at the blue eye it seemed that the thoughts of Mufti Bashir were hopeful and merry. When looking at the darker eye it was as if sorrow and regret were all that reigned in his heart.

"I have watched you for a long time now. You are eager to confront and question and less eager to listen and obey. I have seen you when you daydream and I have felt the flight of your dreams. You are drawn to the glitter of the outside world, are you not?"

"I don't know," said Musa, warily.

"You do know, but your heart is telling you to be careful. That is another trait you have, always following your heart, even if it leads you to ruin."

Musa sat silent, fighting the inclination to relax and talk.

"Tell me, why you are dressed in the clothes of a woman?" asked Mufti Bashir, without irony.

"Well sir, it all started like this. Ali had bought this outfit for his mum, and it was just lying there on the bed. And I suddenly started thinking about the Sisters. Not that I've got anything against them, because I don't know them and they don't know me. But it's like whenever they look at you it's like they know you and I've always wondered why that is. So when I saw the outfit, I thought the best way to find the answer to that question was to try it on. And you know when you get an idea in your head and it just doesn't go away, you've *just got* to do it! No matter what! So I put it on to see if I felt any different, if you know what I mean. It was like a sociology experiment, but then those blasted policemen came barging through the door, and everything went a bit crazy."

Musa held his arms open, dismayed by the fickleness of events.

Mufti Bashir considered Musa's answer. "How did you feel when you put it on?"

"Well at first I couldn't feel a thing. It was sticky and uncomfortable and when I looked in the mirror I couldn't sense anything. But later – Musa leaned forward excitedly – when I was in the interrogation room, I could feel the policemen treating me differently. But the strangest thing was when I was in there I felt protected by the veil, like I could look at them and react to them but they couldn't react to anything I said or felt because they couldn't see me!"

"Did you gain knowledge that you wanted?" asked Mufti Bashir, smiling.

"Yes sir."

"At what cost?"

"I don't know what you mean sir," replied Musa truthfully.

"You gained knowledge at the expense of your own dignity."

"I suppose so," agreed Musa reluctantly.

"Could you not have asked someone?"

"Well you see, the thing is sir, the alims and the elders don't seem to be all that approachable and I couldn't exactly go up to them and ask them about this sort of thing could I?"

"Why not? Are you not talking to me about it?"

"Because sir, no offence, but I've always got the feeling that you and the other elders and alims don't really like young people. You just want us to act like we're old," said Musa earnestly.

Mufti Bashir stood up and slowly tottered over to Musa. He handed him the photograph.

"Do you recognise me?" he asked gently.

Musa held up the photograph and stared at a black and white image of three young men wearing suits with very thin ties sitting on a sofa. The two at opposite ends of the sofa were English. Their expressions were assured, smiling, and they sat with their legs wide apart. The one in the middle looked proud and sat up straight with his arms folded and his knees close together. An English woman holding a baby stood behind the three and her eyes were tense and unhappy.

"The man in the middle," said Musa quietly.

"Yes. That photograph was taken forty-five years ago. When I was…like you."

"But how did you end…"

Mufti Bashir raised his hand to cut off any questions. He walked to the window and gestured to Musa to join him. It was now night and the street was empty. A pub, the Red Lion, had its sign illuminated by a flashing red light. Suddenly a figure emerged from the pub, an elderly white man. He walked unsteadily to the pedestrian crossing and looked up. Slowly, he touched the peak of his cap and Mufti Bashir placed his hand on the window in response. The old man smiled and started to walk carefully across the road.

"I have seen that person three times a week for the past twenty-five years. Always he greets me and always I return his greeting in the exact same manner, three times a week for the past twenty-five years. Yet I have no desire to know him or to communicate with him. Do you think it is because I do not like people Musa?"

Musa was silent, unable to merge what he had seen into his reasoning.

Mufti Bashir continued, his voice carefully even. "The lines of our worlds are very clear to me. I have no wish to push against that line. I have no wish to see beyond what I can see. But with you Musa, it is different. You hunger for the colours of experience and such hunger is like fire in your belly. All that you are is fuel for this fire. Do you understand what I am saying, Musa?"

"Yes sir, but I am not a bad Muslim."

"Islam is a religion of peace. If you are not at peace with yourself, how can you find peace in your faith?"

"Islam can give me all the answers that I need, sir. I believe that with all my heart," said Musa passionately.

"Yes, Islam can do that. But will it give you the answers that you want, Musa?"

"That depends on the question, sir," said Musa defensively.

"Yes, it does depend on the question." Mufti Bashir raised his finger and wagged it at Musa. "That my son is why you must leave the Madrasah. You cannot be a leader of men in prayer if you do not know what you are leading against."

Musa gazed at the elder: one eye knowing and sad, the other grey with meaning and purpose. He felt himself cast to a strange netherworld by the reflection in his eyes, a world torn apart by the tug of opposites; the sensation of leaving and the sensation of arriving; the unknown freedom and the secure familiar; the excitement and the ignorance.

"It is written in the Quran, 'God is the ally of those who believe: He brings them out of the depths of darkness and into the light.' Follow the light Musa. Follow the light so that you may become a child of the light and let your steps be as happy and carefree as those of a child," he said sadly.

Musa handed Mufti Bashir the photograph and took off his gloves, his eyes never leaving the elder's face. As he turned to walk away, Mufti Bashir laid a gentle hand on his arm.

"Know this also, Musa. With each step you take to the light, my prayers are with you. And should you step the other way, know that my tears shall lie in your footprints. For it is also written, 'For the disbelievers, their allies are false gods who take them from the light into the depths of darkness, they are the inhabitants of the Fire, and there they will remain.'"

Eunice Benton looked out of the window and scowled. As usual, clogging up the street and raising an almighty row were the Asian kids playing cricket and screaming like mad every time they connected with the ball. It was impossible to tell the difference between them, they all looked the same to her. Grinning brown faces with huge eyes and big white smiles.

Eunice was the oldest resident on her street. She and her Ernie (who had succumbed to one cigarette too many) had watched the arrival of the Pakistanis with just the faintest hint of disapproval. She remembered with a bitter smile her Ernie's take on it (he was known to dabble in a bit of philosophy now and then).

"Look love, since Churchill sent us to war killing them Nazis, there's no one here to do all 'em little jobs like sweeping the streets and such like. And I'm sure as hell not gonna do that. I've just come back from France and I'm still pissing gun oil. You watch love, soon as they make their five bob they'll be out of this street in a jiffy."

The problem was though they never did leave in a jiffy. They stayed and had wives who stayed, and worst of all they had kids who never left the bloody street. Feeling her radiation, the Asian kids stopped playing and recognising their old foe they made for her window, excited by what they were about to do. A few of the more adventurous started thrusting their hips towards her. The tamer ones made loud kissing noises.

"The dirty animals," thought Eunice. One time one of them had even taken his trousers down and bared his buttocks to her. When she complained to the local Neighbourhood Watch she was told (amidst many chuckles) that this action was known as a "moony" though it didn't look much like a moon to her at the time.

She frowned suddenly as an idea came to her. "Herbert!" she called, and at the sound of his name a large Alsatian came running towards her.

"Good boy. Good boy," she said, ruffling his neck.

She opened the front door and issued an order to the dog.

"Attack, Herbert! Attack!"

With his large, liquid, honey-coloured eyes, it was difficult to imagine Herbert attacking anyone but since Alsatians were German in origin they must have it in them to kill, reasoned Eunice.

Herbert looked at the Asian kids, then back at his mistress and barked.

Eunice smiled with the murderous delight of a huntress about to close in on her prey.

"Go boy go!" she said, pushing the dog out.

Herbert bounded across the street and was immediately met by a great cheer as his detractors rushed towards him and embraced him as one of their own. He barked and pranced about excitedly, euphoric in his newly found role as mascot.

Eunice sighed in disgust at her fickle canine.

"Maybe it's because he smells like them," she wondered out loud.

She noticed the old Pakistani who lived further up the road walking along with his head down. He always walked like that, like he just didn't want to know anymore. You could always tell him a mile off because unlike the others he didn't have a beard. He was a small neat man, with a poker face and small fierce black eyes. She watched him cross the road. He was wearing grey schoolboy trousers and a thin brown jumper that pushed against a huge shirt collar.

They were a strange family. She would often see the wife on her way to the supermarket. She had obviously been pretty in her time with a fair round face that dimpled every time she saw the kids playing on the street. Now and then she would walk with her daughter, who was a real stunner. Ernie (who never really got rid of his eye for the girls) used to like to watch her.

"She's a looker that one for sure, but she has a mean expression."

Eunice would glare at him and he would then grin and playfully smack her on her behind.

She knew there was a boy too. A young man to be exact, who seemed to come and go as he pleased, but there was also someone else. Every so often, when it was really late, a car would stop outside the house, a big expensive car that made no noise. It would stay for about five minutes and then drive away silently.

"You watch love, their kids are gonna be like us when they grow up," were the prophetic words of her Ernie but at the time she thought he was talking rubbish.

The old man whose family so intrigued Eunice and the late lecherous Ernie was in fact Musa's father Itrat, or Aboo, as he was known, and at that particular moment he was feeling the weight of the world on his shoulders – a most unacceptable burden at his age.

Aboo went into his home of thirty years and as always the crisp pungent aroma of his wife's cooking greeted him. This always soothed him: that odour had been one of the markers of his day for so many years.

Small to begin with, the house stayed small as Aboo was completely against the idea of extensions and now it was cluttered with over-large furniture. The front room had been the scene of many great and epic dramas and accordingly gave you the feeling that you were walking on a holy battlefield.

Overlooking all was a giant rug that hung on the wall. Inscribed upon it was the *Ayatul kursi*, a passage from the Holy Quran that was supposed to ward off evil spirits. Its effectiveness was debatable because a closer look revealed signs of damage from objects that had been hurled at it with great force.

Shabnam (Aboo's daughter) and Amma (his wife) were sitting in silence. Shabnam was idly flicking through a glossy magazine and Amma was stroking a strand of her long hair. She did this when she was upset about something and Aboo briefly wondered if she somehow knew the news that was erupting within him.

Shabnam looked up at him. He wished he could take pride in her beauty the way Amma did but instead he felt a dark sense of urgency whenever he looked at those large cold green eyes. At times he hated himself for it.

Because he felt the need to bark, he exploded, "What are you doing reading that trash?"

Amma spoke softly. "What's wrong?"

Aboo sat down in his red leather-backed chair, his one extravagance, his face drawn.

"Musa has left the Madrasah," he said, hoping to sound contemptuous and detached but failing.

"Why? What's happened?" asked Shabnam.

"They wouldn't say but I asked Abdul Jaffer as his son studies there as well and he told me quite a few things…" he spoke in a slightly accented though fluent English.

This time Amma spoke for she knew better than anyone how to draw Aboo out.

"What did he tell you?" she asked keeping her voice soft and calm.

"It seems Musa has created quite a name for himself over there. Always arguing and being cheeky. Abdul Jaffer told me that the boys even have bets on him. Every time he gets into trouble someone makes a lot of money." He shook his head disgustedly.

"He told me something about Musa dressing up as a woman and getting found out."

47

"Musa dressing up as a woman?" asked Shabnam in delight at the image she conjured up.

"No…No…I don't know exactly. All I know is they're sending him home," growled Aboo.

"Have you spoken to anyone at the Madrasah?" asked Amma.

"I phoned this morning and spoke to one of the alims. He said not to worry and try to think of it as a holiday for Musa. He said he needs to sort his head out."

Shabnam laughed. "Do you think staying here is going to straighten him out?"

Amma looked disapprovingly at her daughter and spoke sternly. "Shabnam, don't be stupid."

"What he needs is to understand that money doesn't grow on trees, and he needs to be showing some more respect for his father's hard work. He needs to have more fear of Allah and stop acting like a spoilt boy," said Aboo forcefully.

Through this noisy conversation a faint noise could be heard, the noise of a door handle softly turning and quiet footsteps that seemed to be able to contract their impact as they approached the room. The practitioner of this well-rehearsed skill was Suleiman, the second oldest son and Musa's elder brother. Tall with a thin wiry build and a full head of curly black hair, his inscrutable eyes were like his father's but the smooth dark complexion and the razor-sharp alertness that made him stand out as a child seemed to have come from nowhere.

Suleiman worked with some friends who had formed a company called Sharif Construction. What Suleiman did within the company remained undefined. Aboo, happy to be relieved of his role as provider for the family never asked. Whatever it was it gave Suleiman an edge of tension that never seemed to ease and made his life largely nocturnal.

Aboo gestured sharply at the sofa for him to sit down. Relishing his role as leader of the family, Aboo surveyed them imperiously.

"There is nothing the matter with Musa. He is just showing off his quick tongue and he is being given too much attention. When he gets excited people always think he has a point but they forget he's still a kid. Talking doesn't get you places. You have to bend your back and sweat and even then you can't be sure. Musa doesn't know this. He doesn't know life. All he does is daydream and I put up with it because I thought he was going the way of Allah. But if he is getting twisted I will straighten him out."

Amma looked up at Aboo trying to filter out the bluster in his speech.

"How you gonna do that Aboo? Musa's not easy," said Suleiman.

"And if he does stay here what's he gonna do? Just sit around, eat and watch TV all day. You know the kind of stuff that's on TV these days, it will drive him wild and that's not gonna do anyone any good," said Shabnam.

"He needs to learn what it is to work. He needs to learn responsibility and when he learns what it is to graft, he will understand that it is much easier to learn the words of Allah," insisted Aboo.

As Aboo's continual invocation of the Almighty's name obstructed any attempt to lighten up the situation, nobody bothered replying. Trying to get something across to Suleiman, Shabnam caught his eye.

"Do you want me to sort him out a job with the guys?" asked Suleiman.

"No," said Amma sharply.

"Why not?"

"Because black money makes people black inside," muttered Amma.

Though no one understood what Amma had said, everyone understood what she meant.

"Enough!" ordered Aboo irritably.

He settled back. "Dadaji will be coming in a few weeks. We can decide what best to do with Musa then," he said quietly, in deference to his father.

Dadaji was the family patriarch and the final source of authority. When the kids had been younger they had likened him to Don Corleone in *The Godfather*. After a while the analogy became too accurate to be funny as Dadaji was completely confident in the expectation that his sons would obey him at any cost. More often than not, the cost had been to his daughters-in-law whom he regarded quite unfairly as usurpers of his sons' loyalty and money. Dadaji was old, cold, and harder than any nail. He was also wise with eyes that were both eloquent and sad. He had endured the partition of 1947 and the aftermath of poverty and hunger with unbending principle and discipline. As a consequence he feared nothing and no one and his only enemy was disobedience.

Amma rose noiselessly and went to the kitchen and Shabnam would have pleased Dadaji greatly had he been able to observe her silent pursuit.

Aromas that seemed to encapsulate every mood abounded in that well-lit expanse and the pressure cookers whistled with a warm gust of welcome every time mother and daughter sought sanctuary. The kitchen was the largest room in the house and the best decorated. Aboo's thrifty nature had not been able to withstand his wife's insistence that her domain be bright and homely. This victory shone in the tiled walls which gleamed their pattern of a yellow vase of flowers and the floor was not covered with a dull fading carpet as was the rest of the house but was instead a more modern brown linoleum. All utilities and appliances were sheltered in matching wood; even the cooker glinted with expensive stainless steel. Overlooking a small garden was a set of double-glazed windows with gold-tinted handles, and long and heated had the debate been for their existence.

Shabnam began to peel potatoes into a large container. She did this quickly and efficiently, her mind on other things. Amma stood next to the cooker stirring a large pan. Now and then a great hiss would sound and the air would seethe with the smell of cumin and coriander. Shabnam noticed that the kitchen door was ajar and got up to close it. In the next door garden, their neighbour – a buxom woman – was hanging up clothes to dry with a fag hanging out of her mouth. Shabnam wondered if she realised that the smell would get into the clothes and ruin

51

them. She wondered again how Suleiman always managed to hide the smell of nicotine from his family. She smiled then, delighting in the craftiness of her brother. Amma looked across at her and understood why she smiled but did not smile with her.

She spoke to Shabnam quickly in Punjabi. "Do you know why Dadaji is coming?" she asked in a tone that almost answered the question.

"He only comes if someone is dead or dying or someone is about to be married," replied Shabnam.

"Be alert and watch what you say when he comes. He can pick up on what you mean like an eagle can sweep up his prey," warned Amma.

"Does it make any difference whether you watch what you say or not? He'll do whatever he likes and Aboo will go along with it," said Shabnam coldly.

"Your Aboo is not easy to talk to these days. You know he worries."

"Was he ever easy to talk to?" asked Shabnam.

"All I'm trying to tell you is that you can save yourself a lot of trouble by thinking before you speak," answered Amma patiently.

"OK. OK. Who's he trying to fix up? Me, Musa, all three of us at the same time?"

"Musa for sure…you two I don't know about yet." Amma's voice hardened. "In any case the time comes for all daughters and it has come for you now. It is becoming clear to everyone that you are not interested in your studies."

"I am as interested as any girl who knows she can study

all she likes but is going to end up in the same place," said Shabnam automatically.

"That place is no bad place. It is the place where all the women since Eve started from," replied Amma indignantly. "Building a home and raising good children is not easy." She stopped for a brief second. "You try and make it by yourself without your Aboo and your brother and you will realise what kind of people are out there."

Shabnam suddenly tired of this ritual argument and her indifference crested to deaden her eyes and silence her voice. That was how she felt most of the time, as if she was being shoved into a room only to realise she had never left it in the first place. It was true what Amma said. The subjects she was taking at college, Health and Social Care, and Psychology, did not particularly interest her. She did not struggle to understand but she struggled to connect, to find that spark that would get her head deeper into her studies. Even in the group activities and debates she would look around at her animated classmates and feel a slow steady surge of contempt at their enthusiasm for such mindless tasks. But if someone were to ask her what she would rather do she could not honestly reply. Some recruitment woman at college had once asked her that and became angry when she started laughing. She sensed that at home it didn't really matter much. Clever girls who were watchful and kept their mouths shut were not really any happier than the dumb ones who accepted everything and kept quiet. In other families girls were treated differently, as if they were glass dolls or something. Everyone rushed around to protect them and loved it when they were cheeky and confident. Maybe it was just as well her family was not like that. She was fairly certain she would have got bored with everyone kissing her ass all the time.

She wondered whether the arrival of Musa would change Aboo for the better, or would just make him more moody and irritable. Her brother's homecoming did not cause any great rumble in her heart. She viewed him the way she would view the traffic on the high street, noisy and always there, but not important enough for her to worry about. Sometimes she would look at him keenly, curiously, but she never really talked to him a great deal. When Musa was a baby, everyone had been delighted at his precocious babbling and this encouraged him even more. To her he just never made sense, then or now.

There was a change in him these days, for sure. In the earlier days, on the rare occasions when he came home he was so chirpy that it grated on her and she had to get busy with something or else she'd snap at him. But lately he seemed more thoughtful and, as was the case with all her three brothers, that meant more troubled. That was why Amma was so quiet these days, the unsettled tremor that had claimed her sons one by one was now gathering around Musa.

The empty sigh that escaped her then met with the vibrant sounds of duty buzzing in the kitchen and as duty has a way of doing, enfolded her and took away the name of her unhappiness.

★

The lights in the living room had now dimmed and the street was gradually withdrawing as commotion and noise dissipated into the fold of the night.

Suleiman stood outside in the cold inhaling his cigarette in exactly the same manner as he would have inhaled a cigarette six or seven hours ago. He was watching a young Asian guy talking to a young Asian girl. The guy was undoubtedly Pakistani and the girl was definitely Indian, maybe Sikh. You knew the guy was Pakistani because he was unsure how to do what he wanted to do and this made him tense and talk fast. He was wearing a blue denim shirt with all the buttons done up, jeans that looked almost black and trainers that must have come straight from the box. The girl was obviously Indian because she was handling the situation better than a Pakistani girl would have done. She was at ease in her dazzlingly white tracksuit bottoms and a Nike jacket. She was talking too, but in a relaxed easy way, and she was being kind to her suitor with her polite smile and the mechanical laughter she offered to his awkward sound bites. It was the arms that unmasked her lack of interest: they were folded tight across her chest while she nodded her head at the shit he was undoubtedly feeding her.

"You're sinking you dumb fuck and you don't even know it," thought Suleiman, putting out his cigarette and going back inside.

Aboo was listlessly watching the news. Images of war, hunger, and sectarian strife flickered across his face and as ever nothing registered. Suleiman sat on the sofa and waited patiently. He toyed with the idea of bringing the subject up but decided against it. Aboo was a card that you could never play no matter how well you thought you knew him. After an indeterminate amount of time, Aboo's chest heaved and he expelled air as if it was festering inside him. He then looked levelly at Suleiman, something he did not do in front of other people.

"Bring Musa back and sort him out a job with your guys. Something heavy and hard."

"Sure but Musa's not gonna last long with manual work. Why not get him doing something in the mosque like voluntary work with the kids. Teaching them Islam and all that stuff."

"I've seen people in the Zakaria Masjid. They sit there all the time talking, talking, and never doing any real work. Just sitting there like chickens waiting for their young ones to hatch." Aboo smiled briefly. "Sometimes they have problems with the missis and so decide to live in the mosque and talk about Islam all day long. Let Musa know what it is to work and suffer and then he will learn how much easier it was to learn about Islam. I don't want him becoming like those bloody fools in the mosque."

"I don't see how he's going to be any different," said Suleiman thoughtfully.

Aboo looked at his second son long and hard, mixing in everything he knew with everything he did not want to know. When he spoke it was in the whisper of his own father's voice.

"That's because to you there is no difference between cloth that has never been dirty and cloth that was never really clean in the first place. A son that has the mark of a true Muslim is a son that can make it easy for his mum and dad when their time comes."

"But that kind of son always fucks up the life of his own kids. Just like…" thought Suleiman to himself yet when he spoke he was as laconic and unconcerned as he always appeared to be.

"OK Aboo. Whatever you say. I'll bring Musa back tomorrow. Just go easy on him. He makes too much damn noise when he disagrees with something."

"Eat before you go," commanded Aboo as Suleiman rose to leave.

Suleiman obeyed as he always did and as always his obedience left no imprint in his father's vision, for Aboo opined in stone and Suleiman, through a circumstance completely beyond his control, always found himself bearing the hard-edged brunt of an undeserving estimation.

After dinner when the plates had been cleared and their children had left them alone, Amma sat heavily on the floor, cross-legged as was her custom, and looked up at her husband of forty years. She remained still, in patient repose, but the long black gown she wore spilt uneasily around her like viscous trouble.

Without fear of reprimand or consequence she spoke out. "Are you really aware of what is going on around us?"

"Of course. Do you think I live on the moon?" Aboo replied nonchalantly.

"The moon would be too good for us. At least then

your eyes would be on us for some of the time."

"My eyes never leave this family," said Aboo.

"Hmm. One eye back home and the other with us."

"You never get tired of saying that," he remarked dismissively.

"Day by day you seem more and more lost," said Amma desperately.

"Wrong Begum, wrong. I sometimes think if I could just lose myself, my mind, my conscience, my responsibilities, and become, as they say, senile, it would be a blessing from Allah. That way the trouble you get from thinking would just go. Perhaps that's the reason why English people drink. They want to forget and be happy."

Amma sighed knowing that no argument would ever penetrate.

"How long is Dadaji staying?" she asked quietly.

"I don't know. He thinks he can swing it all his way. Maybe he can. It's all simple from where he stands. I still need my father. Our children will never need me the same way. In any case his intentions about Musa are firm."

"Iram?" asked Amma.

"Yes Iram. Dadaji has stood watch over her all her life and he will never accept the idea of her marrying outside the family."

"Iram…is not pretty you know," said Amma as if troubled by her very acceptance of this fact.

"Pretty or not, what difference does it make? Pretty ones are more of a burden for their parents."

"Will Musa accept?" asked Amma hesitantly.

"Don't you know your own son? He will never accept

58

what is in front of him. He is someone who will dream of the stars while lying in the sun," said Aboo without derision.

"It was you who spoilt him," Amma retorted.

"All fathers spoil their youngest and all mothers spoil their eldest. I remember Dadaji telling me that when they were all young," said Aboo his voice soft and gentle.

Amma let her head drop.

"Don't do that. There's no point to it. We must have trust in Allah. Whatever happens is His will." Aboo stood up slowly.

"It's time for prayer," he said with more energy.

Despite her husband's admonishment Amma's head remained bowed even as he closed the front door, leaving for the mosque. But gradually her antennae of orderliness awakened her to the untidiness of the room. Quickly and instinctively she got to her feet and began to straighten displaced cushions. Everything seemed disjointed and this irritated her immensely. She went to the kitchen and took the vacuum cleaner from its cupboard and returned to the front room. She noticed that a picture frame was slightly lopsided, as if someone had taken it off the wall for a closer look and carelessly put it back. In the frame was a short composition written almost twenty years ago. Amma read what she had read a thousand times:

My family

My family is the best in the world because everyone has a shiny face.

I think my dad is the strongest in the world because he lifts me up. And puts me on shoulders and laughs like a nut case.

I think my baby brother Musa is the cutest in the world and he laughs. When I rub him on the back every time he does a hiccup. Whenever he cries Sally and me make funny faces to make him stop and laugh but he doesn't, only my Mum laughs.

I think my sister Shabnam is the prettiest girl in the world and people always look at her and smile when I have to hold her hand at the bus stop.

Sally is my bestest friend but sometimes he's a bit greedy and always wants what I have. Mum always sticks up for him and says it's OK he's your brother.

My Dad says because I'm the oldest people should listen to me.

I say because I'm the oldest my Mum should stop hugging me.
Javed

When he was in primary school Javed had won a prize for his effort. Aboo had laughed long and loud when he had read it, and eagerly showed it to all his friends.

Amma wondered who had re-read the composition. It was impossible to say for certain. She used to be able to tell when her children or her husband thought about Javed. A certain heavy quiet would settle in the room and she would look up and see disquiet on a face. But gradually Javed had made the transition from unspoken name to silent thought which as the years went became more like a whisper that you did not want to strain to hear.

Javed, her first born, left thirteen years ago and had never returned. Amma tilted her head slightly and closed her eyes as if trying to re-awaken the scent of him in her memory. She was surprised at how quickly and painlessly it all came back.

She remembered at the time that Suleiman and Javed, though only eleven months apart, had somehow found a different group of friends. Javed was then about seventeen and his friends were entirely English. He would sometimes bring them home and she felt they were all too informal and relaxed for their age. They lounged on her sofa with legs that seemed elastic, laughed for no apparent reason and smelling the cigarettes and alcohol on them she would frown disapprovingly. They in turn would grin in amused tolerance. Suleiman's friends were Pakistani and they were more respectful and watchful in front of her and this pleased her enough to ignore the smell of tobacco and alcohol on *their* clothes.

Javed became increasingly distant and brooded a great deal and even Suleiman seemed unable to talk to him. Every night he went out and did not return until the early hours of the morning. Then he disappeared for five days. After the sixth day she told Aboo who, instead of going to the police, went to look for his oldest son with his friends. He returned the following morning with Javed who had a black eye. He dragged him upstairs and threw him into his bedroom. When he came back down Amma asked him fearfully, "Who was he staying with?" but the outrage on his face answered her question.

That night Javed left for good. She had woken up with a start and heard footsteps creeping down the stairs. Without disturbing her husband she got out of bed. Javed and Suleiman were in the living room talking in low ugly voices. She steadied her trembling hand on the door and listened with her eyes closed.

"It's not your money, Jav. Put it back," said Suleiman.

"Stay out of it, Sal."

"Where you gonna go? You can't make it by yourself. Think, Jav. Think. That's all I'm asking you to do. Just think it through!"

"I'm tired of thinking, Sal. You can think all you like. But it ain't ever gonna get better. Not for you. Not for me. Not for anyone."

"Let me come with you, Javed."

There was a long pause and she felt in her heart the ache of one of her sons. Then she heard the reply.

"I'm not taking you with me. There's only room for two of us."

"You and…"

Javed laughed bitterly. "Yeah. Me and—"

"You can't even say the fucking name."

Then she walked in and saw Javed with his hand full of notes taken from the jar that she used to save up money for going on pilgrimage. He was bare-chested, wearing only jeans and trainers. His hair was spiked up and his face looked pale, unnaturally pale, and his lips were red and fierce.

She recognised her oldest son's expression. It was that of

a spoilt child who could never accept the word no from his parents. She never knew what was written on her own face in that moment, only that it was enough to stop Suleiman in his tracks and push Javed away from their lives.

Javed pocketed the notes, glanced at Suleiman and then walked past her with his head held high. The door closed and he was gone, taking a shard of innocence from all of them.

As Amma continued to stare at the composition she became aware of the presence of another son, standing very still.

"I didn't hear you come in," she said.

"No one ever does," Suleiman replied quietly.

More than three thousand miles away, in the village of Aima Ladian, a nightly ritual was taking place in an old ancestral home or haveli. Like most village houses in Pakistan the rooms surrounded a central pillared courtyard in the far corner of which was a small brick-lined space containing a stack of pots and pans. Nearby, stone stairs led to a spacious flat roof. Across the courtyard, from wall to wall, hung faded blue clothes-lines.

The three uncles, having finished their meal in silence, placed three string beds in the centre of the open courtyard. Their aged father lay back, propped up by cushions, on one bed, the sated brothers sat together on another and on the third sat their wives, the aunties. This was their daily opportunity to piece together the truth of the events shaping their lives. An old fan roared and turned in the corner, blowing cool air over them.

The younger children were in one of the rooms watching forbidden films. There was only one older, nubile child, Iram, and at night she sat at the edge of the courtyard, her head resting against a pillar, watching her star.

Sirius, the dwarf star, the brightest in the sky, is the jewel of the constellation and at night this giant ball of fire becomes the emblem of life for the whimsical few who still have an innate belief that within the stars rests the signature of their life. Every night when the uncles gathered in the courtyard, Iram would fix her gaze upon Sirius, and inhale the way smokers do when surveying the day.

Sometimes she imagined herself to be Sirius in human form, majestic and aloof, aware in the remotest possible way of the ramblings and idiocies of those below. She had once heard Uncle Tasin say that Sirius was mentioned in the Holy Quran and it fell every five hundred years. This she accepted passively as she accepted most things, but afterwards she wondered whether it was true. She couldn't imagine something so large and wondrous ever falling and how could it get back again? Uncle Tasin was not really known for his wealth of factual knowledge. He was talking now, leaning back and recalling his exploits of the day as he always did while his wife watched with a worried frown.

Iram loved the still and stealth of night. For her nightfall was her sanctuary, all those probing and prying eyes that watched her were dimmer. She hated the scrutiny. At times it seemed as if the unrelenting gaze of her grandfather, Dadaji, seemed to infiltrate the very air she breathed. Dadaji was the only one who was quiet at night; all of his sons were by contrast loud and boisterous. It was as if the effort of watching over her for the entire day had finally drained him and he relinquished this burden at night as eagerly as he assumed it first thing in the morning. An opinion voiced during the day would be met with harshness, and laughter would be silenced by an angry glare but when the uncles came back from the mosque after the night prayer, it was OK. She could laugh loudly and disagree strongly and no one would say anything. Not Dadaji or her uncles.

Her father returned late every night and when they heard the sound of his approaching motorbike, her two brothers would quickly get out their books. She wondered if it would have made much difference to their father. He always looked exhausted and exasperated and she knew why. It was the burden of being a man. All this manliness and strength stoked with displays of anger was submerged under the weight of that dreadful calculation: money coming in and money going out; money for necessity and money for vanity. Only Uncle Arshad was free from this burden. He had made it. Through enterprise and hard work he was now a wealthy man. The other brothers (including her father) hated this. All opinion now gravitated to him; his agreement was the rubber stamp of approval on family matters. His wife was the dignitary amongst the other sisters-in-law who acquiesced to queer fate and gave her the respect she so desperately craved in the days when she was just like them.

Her daughters, too, were luminaries in the family: Farzana, Fozia and Farrah were free from the drudgery of village life and above all they had never been harried by the attention of Dadaji. Together they laughed and shared with each other what they did and how they did it. They were a perfect circle. Everyone else orbited them but could never be a part of them, unless they were chosen. Thankfully, though, they had allowed Iram into their sanctum and through them she learned of a truth that she was certain she would have never known otherwise: that her uncles and Dadaji were troubled by her womanhood. Her security was a burden for them, not her physical security but the security that was always threatened by the gaze of young men and the careless whispers of people in the village. They did not know how best to protect her, how to control the slippery tongue of the outside world. They could glare darkly at her, maybe even shout and raise their fist at her, but beyond that they could do nothing. She was sure of it.

A sound came from the courtyard. A name. Musa. She turned away from Sirius and saw her family staring at her. The uncles looked away but Dadaji's eyes remained on her. In the time allowed her by her culture, she tried to take a sip of what lay behind his gaze. She quickly turned away, frightened.

Musa…Musa…The cousin from England. She had met him for the first time when he came to Pakistan a year ago. It was hard to sort out her impression of him then.

Every part of him seemed to demand attention. The angry eyes that looked through you, the fair skin which so pleased the women in the family. When he spoke he became excited, angry and then sad. Because he spoke without thinking, he was always in trouble.

Her mother and the aunties were silent. Uncle Tasin and Uncle Arshad were trying to speak quietly (which they could never do) but now and again Dadaji became agitated and raised his voice. They were talking about her marriage. To Musa. Iram's mother looked at her with the appraising eyes of a woman, not the soft eyes of a mother. It was at that moment Iram felt the mantle of womanhood and the emptiness of a woman.

She looked up at the star Sirius again and saw for the first time that it really was far, far away.

4

"Listen you wanna destroy a guy then first you fuck him up emotionally and then you fuck him up physically. And then when he's lying on the ground looking at you like you're the goddamn bad guy, you know what you do? You don't get all soft and mushy. You drag him to his kitchen and pin his woman to your chest and when you feel her dribbling on your shirt that is when you know that you have truly destroyed him."

Musa sat on the other side of a desk listening to a phone conversation and feeling as though he were an astral entity who had wandered into the wrong place at the wrong time. The first day of his new life had started at a frenzied pace. As soon as he had emerged from the bathroom, he had quickly changed into his first ever non-Islamic clothes: blue jeans that looked as if they had spun too many times in the washing machine, a big grey T-shirt which read Boss across the front and his most prized piece of attire – the Adidas trainers Suleiman had got him.

His brother had whisked him away in his car. No breakfast, no morning TV, no nothing. In the car Suleiman did not seem terribly inclined to elaborate and since Musa was still in a bit of a daze (as he generally was most mornings) he had not ventured to ask any questions.

Suleiman made a sharp left into an industrial unit of some sort. He pointed at Unit 1 and then left Musa alone with the words, "This is where we work and that's where Babarr is. Listen to him and don't give him no shit 'cos Babarr don't take no shit from no one," floating in the air like a pregnant cloud.

As Musa walked in, Babarr gave no sign of noticing him, engrossed as he was in his phone conversation. The room was large and modern-looking. A fax machine stood on the turtle-green carpet and in the corner was a small table on which rested a computer. Curiously, a poster of Confucius effervescent with wisdom hung on the wall. Light from the only window gave Babarr's heavy, bare desk a professional sheen.

Musa studied this magnificent physical specimen. Babarr was enormous but no adjective in the English language, and most certainly none in Punjabi, could accurately describe his gigantic torso. Larger than a Sumo wrestler and with pectoral muscles that gave his chest such incredible definition you knew without forensic analysis that the bulging veins of his forearms throbbed with steroids. His huge hands and hairy wrists were decked with more gold than a Dubai jewellery shop. Oddly, the only part of him that was not of macro proportions was his head, a small bald sphere with a forehead disfigured by a protruding vein that pulsed aggression into the air. He was still talking.

"Look bhaiji. You tell them motherfuckers that Babarr

ain't gonna kiss no man's ass. They got boys and I got boys. So what? You see me pissing my pants? I don't need no boys. Boys are for assholes. Hold on a second—" he turned to Musa for the first time and gave him a friendly wink. "Look time is money and I ain't got no money to waste. You tell them bastards that they wanted an extension, Babarr did an extension. They wanted a conservatory and Babarr gave them a conservatory. They wanted double-glazing and Babarr did them double-glazing. I charged them fair they paid me fair. And now those wankers are complaining that I scratched their skirting boards! What the fuck!"

Babarr stopped abruptly and his fingers started a menacing paradiddle. Musa could hear the caller's voice rising.

"That ain't the point. The point is respect. They go around telling people Babarr did this, Babarr did that, and before long I ain't got no respect. My market value goes down. People start talking and I don't get no work. And why? 'Cos I'm too much of a fucking nice guy. That's why."

Babarr slammed the phone down and turned his small green and very alert eyes on Musa. Softly he said: "Assalaam alaikum."

Enormously heartened, Musa replied: "Waalaikum assalaam."

"You look like shit."

"What?"

Babarr held up his hand – already wearied by the indignant invective of lesser human beings. "I've seen you around quite a few times. One time I think I even saw you talking to yourself when you were walking near your home. I saw you and I says the guy has problems. I ask Suleiman and he says we all have our issues and I say fuck you. There are only two issues your birth and your death. What do you say?" Babarr growled but his geniality was unmistakable.

"Well I suppose so," said Musa warily.

"You suppose so? You've been studying in a Madrasah for four years and all you can do is you suppose so?"

"Well it all depends on what context…"

"Don't you dare use that fucking word in front of me! I hear that word every day." Babarr cleared his throat and lifted his eyebrows in imitation of a type of person he truly despised. "In the context of this agreement I am not obliged to pay you this fucking amount. No Mr Khan we cannot grant you your rebate because the fucking context was different when we agreed it."

Musa shook his head in sympathy and thought briefly about smiling but decided not to.

"I know why you're here. But do you know why you're here?" Babarr lifted a chubby digit and pointed it at Musa.

"To learn what it is to labour and work hard and stuff," replied Musa lamely.

Babarr shook his head disapprovingly.

"No my friend, you are not here to labour. You are here to connect. You are here to learn responsibility by being honest. And there ain't no trade more responsible and honest than a builder's. There are lots of fuckers who always say I hired a builder and he never finished what he

71

started and when he left everything was in a mess. But they're lying fuckers, 'cos the truth is everyone wants to use builders. You finish one job they say do this and then they say do that. Then they say keep an eye on our kid while we go out socialising. And before long they start bringing their mates back to their house to show off their extension and then they say to you: 'Be a good chappie and make us all a spot of tea.' Fuck you and your spots, we're here to do a building job, pure and simple."

"Pure and simple" hung in the air.

"I understand," said Musa nervously.

"Good, because this ain't no business for philosophy and shit. Suleiman told me that you spend a lot of your time philosophising and that's OK outside work. I philosophise too sometimes. You ever read the collected sayings of Confucius?" he nodded towards the poster.

Musa, surprised, shook his head which pleased Babarr.

"Confucius was no bastard. There is a saying of his, which is very important for you to understand. One time he says, 'When you come to the last page of a book it is time to close it.'"

What else would you do? thought Musa avoiding his gaze but Babarr immediately caught on.

"I know what you're thinking. You're thinking it's a dumb fuck saying because what else would you do when you come to the last page of a book?" he smiled, tickled by Musa's folly. "The point is you have to move on even if you don't know what you're moving from."

Babarr settled back in his chair and was silent for a few moments, marvelling at this nugget of wisdom. "Get it?"

he asked, spitting the question with the ferocity of a bullet.

"Absolutely," said Musa.

"Good. Because with me there is only one rule. You listen to what I say and do what I tell you. You understand?"

"Yes," replied Musa, wondering if Babarr even knew how to count.

"OK, let's get started."

Babarr stood up and Musa noted with surprise the quality of his attire. A large polo shirt with even larger tracksuit bottoms were certainly not uncommon for a builder but the long leather coat that fell to his feet and the heavy gold chains that seemed glued to his neck were more appropriate for a thug. Still, thought Musa, what did he know of the dress-sense of the working world?

Musa followed him outside. The day was getting hotter and the sky was flecked with tufts of cloud. A lone bird circled the air and flapped its wings uncertainly, unaware of the envious scrutiny from below.

Babarr's van, darker than a Batmobile, gleamed. The alloys were painted with an image of a radial wheel of fire with flattened orange flames along the spokes. The tyres were huge and still had rubbery wisps at the edges. Most curiously, in large sloping letters that stretched across both sides of the van was an acronym:

B for Babarr

E for Extension

S for ?

T for Tidiness

"What does the S stand for?" asked Musa as he climbed into the front seat slightly taken aback by all the flashing gizmos on the dashboard.

"Whatever you like," answered Babarr proudly. "It's up to the customer to decide. If he gets it into his head that he wants his house to be like Buckingham Palace after a week of me working like a dog for him, then I say to him S is for simple. If the customer starts pissing me off then I say to him S is for shit. I don't take it and I don't give it. If I get another call from a customer who's gonna pay me top dollar then S is for sorry, I tell my other customers gotta skip town."

Babarr roared with laughter at the ingenuity of it all while Musa looked at the interior of the van. In one corner, stacked in an untidy heap were measuring sticks, tape measures, hammers and a shiny bag of cement. Two speakers hung without apparent support. For a moment he wondered why music wasn't playing but smiled as he realised the answer: there was a belief that the religious didn't approve of music and Babarr was afraid of generating the wrong impression in front of someone who was presumed to be one such. The charisma of the devout was hard to define – it was an aura that hovered around them – different to each and every beholder. Perhaps it was more to do with the person and how he believed what he was supposed to uphold.

"You're philosophising again aren't you," stated Babarr, disgusted.

"Not quite," replied Musa.

"That's OK. It'll take time to get rid of the old ways. Anyways Sajid will knock it out of you. If anyone can piss off a thinker he can."

"You mean Sajid as in Suleiman's mate as in the retard Sajid?" asked Musa horrified.

"Yep. Suleiman told me you two have a history."

Musa leaned back, dismay creasing his face. Sajid was a misshapen miscreant who Musa had despised since before he could walk. Small and dark, Sajid possessed a protruding lower lip that constantly quivered. Since he had been the first child after four miscarriages, the very act of his breathing was enough to sustain his parents' adoration.

Like the little Columbus that he was, he had managed to venture into unknown waters and had come up trumps, marrying his cousin Gulshan from Pakistan without question and without seeing her, thus cementing his position as a demigod among sons. Subsequently he strutted around town, giving lengthy lectures to any poor soul who stopped for a moment to listen.

"What does he know about building?" asked Musa incredulously.

"He don't know shit about shit but boy can that fucker work! You should see him mixing cement. He's like an ape on ecstasy!"

Musa sighed and turned his attention to the considerably brighter world outside. They were in a wealthy area now. The houses were large and detached, their front gardens vast and leafy, and the roads were filled with small white stones. Two or three cars were parked on each driveway – mobile monuments to money. No litter blew across these streets and no empty cans were lobbed into the next gardens by lager louts.

Babarr drove more rapidly than was necessary and his eyes flicked at the mini-palaces to his left and right. Incredibly, his pectoral and neck muscles seemed to swell in response to this vision of suburban wealth. Musa became aware of another bulging vein in his left forearm and realised that Babarr, the Confucius-loving, bullshit-hating, muscle-bound Czar of construction, was preparing for a confrontation.

"Who's the client?" he asked.

"Santosh Pandey." Babarr said this with disgust. "He owns a restaurant and several newsagents in the city centre. He is seriously loaded. He's been pestering me to do an extension to his house but the fucker won't pay me what I'm worth. It's his woman that's the problem; she is one clever bitch. Every time I'm speaking sense to the guy she butts in and then he looks at her and then at me and then goes, 'Oh, no, no, no,' and we're back to square one. It's like, you know, and what business is it of yours? How dare you fucking shove your oar in when two blokes are discussing business? It ain't like I'm asking to marry your daughter now is it? So today I'm gonna put it to him all nice and simple and respectful like and if he still won't agree to a fair price then I'm gonna burn his fucking house down."

Babarr motioned ahead: "There he is. Outside his house."

Musa saw two figures, one gesticulating wildly. That was the exasperating Sajid who was dressed in his usual clownish pair of navy-blue dungarees. To elevate his stature he wore leather boots with soles at least three inches thick. The van pulled up and Babarr sat still, watching his adversary from a few feet away.

Santosh Pandey was a wiry, bespectacled man with thick pomaded hair, neatly brushed to one side. His dark complexion was smooth, as if it had been ironed for business along with his dark blue suit, and he stood with his hands clasped, bowing his head politely at the fusillade of high volume babble coming from Sajid.

"Look Pandeyji. You gotta accept the fact that Kashmir is ours and even if it ain't why can't you lot give it to us? You've got the best batsman in the world. You've got ten billionaires and we ain't even got one. So let me ask you, brother to brother, is it gonna kill you to give us Kashmir?"

Babarr sighed and rolled his eyes upwards. He got out of the van along with Musa and briskly he cut short Sajid's eloquence.

"Shut the fuck up," he commanded and as if by magic Sajid fell silent. He looked at Musa and a sly ugly grin creased his ugly face. Musa knew what was coming next.

"Mr Pandey, sorry I'm late," said Babarr. He paused, flared his nostrils and inhaled deeply. The whole process made a distinctly unsavoury sound.

"Let's get it sorted, once and for all."

"Please come inside," said Mr Pandey, looking utterly bemused.

Sajid stretched out a hand and Musa shook it with as limp a grip as was humanly possible.

"Do you have any worries?" asked Sajid giggling.

This went back to a time when Musa, then a child, was ill. Sajid had asked what the problem was and Amma, misunderstanding the question had answered, "He worries a lot." Sajid had found this hilarious and had made a point of asking Musa if he had any worries every time he saw him, speaking in Punjabi since he was one of those patriotic people who always spoke his mother tongue to fellow Pakistanis. Musa had often racked his brain for a withering pre-emptive put-down but could come up with nothing more than a pseudo-friendly smile.

Sajid chuckled and as they followed Babarr into the house Musa noticed a curtain twitch. He looked up and glimpsed a stern face with huge glasses staring at him. Another twitch and she was gone.

They were greeted by a smell of burning incense. The spacious hallway was aglow with lavender patterns and on the wall facing them was a gold-plated clock. From the ceiling, a chandelier moved uneasily and cut dancing squares into the floor. To one side, a door stood slightly ajar and through it Musa saw a cabinet adorned by the large photo of a young man with familiar shiny hair proudly holding his degree.

Babarr led the way into the kitchen and Santosh Pandey, glancing nervously at Sajid, followed. Apurva Pandey, an imposing figure of a woman was waiting there.

Her long hair was tied back and she wore a plain, blood-red sari. On her forehead was a large red bindi. The combination was dark and brooding. She whispered in her husband's ear.

"Babarr," said Mr Pandey gently. "Though my wife and I respect your…honest talk, we both feel that your asking price is exorbitantly high and not proportionate to the effort incurred."

"Look Mr Pandey. You're asking me to extend your kitchen by four feet, redo your old one and tile it. All in three months. That is worth fifteen thousand."

"You must try to understand, ten—"

Babarr cut in. "You saw my van outside and you know what I stand for. You know how I work: I work tidy, I don't cut corners, I don't get pissed off, I don't rush the job, I work my balls off, night and day, day and night. You add all that up and it's fifteen thousand."

Babarr's proud defiant work ethic – combined with his simian forearms – seemed to jolt Santosh Pandey. He smiled a brilliant but nervous smile.

"I respect that Babarr and you must never for one second think that we do not value your professionalism and your commitment."

"Then pay me what I'm worth and let's get started," said Babarr wearily, his shoulders drooping as if this was by now a debate as old as the Israel/Palestine conflict. Mrs Pandey again whispered in her husband's ear. Musa could hear the final word of each sentence sounding like a bullet and ending in *che*.

"Oh, no, no, no," replied the chastised Mr Pandey, on queue.

He was about to continue but stopped as Babarr had raised his right arm. From where Musa stood, Babarr's triceps obscured the little bit of sunlight there was and for a few seconds the kitchen was engulfed in the darkness of his fury. He brought his fist crashing down on to the worktop. The resounding thwack stunned them all. After a few beats of silence Babarr raised his right arm and again struck the worktop. He took two quick steps to his left and swung his fist into the wall. A pause. Another blow. A trickle of plaster fell and Babarr swung again with the same methodical precision. At the fourth and final blow, large stainless pots and pans fell crashing to the floor, destroying the Pandeys' orderly world.

Musa noticed that Mr and Mrs Pandey had almost merged into one body and they now took large frenzied breaths of air together in perfect unison.

Noiselessly Babarr walked out of the kitchen to the stairs. Ashen faced, the Pandeys followed him with the hesitant footsteps of conjoined geriatrics. Astonished by the noise, a young woman, the face at the window, had left her room and now hesitated at the top of the stairs, staring down at them. Babarr stood still. The veins in his neck, engorged with fury, pushed against the array of gold necklaces. He gathered himself and jumped. The noise reverberated throughout the house. Testing the floor with his foot as if trying to determine a fault line he jumped up and down like an angry child.

"Do you see what I mean?"

"No…What do you mean?" asked Mrs Pandey terrified but curious.

"What are you trying to do to us?" asked Mr Pandey in a shaking voice.

Babarr looked sadly at Santosh Pandey and shook his head.

"You see Mr Pan– Do you mind if I call you Santosh?" he asked politely.

Santosh Pandey shook his head the way drunks do when trying to shake off the after-effects of a toxic stupor.

"You see, Santosh, this house has many problems. The floorboards have not been put together properly, the plastering is a joke and your kitchen was fitted by a complete asshole. That means whoever you hire is gonna start right from the very beginning.

"That's redoing your floorboards, cementing your kitchen units properly, doing the plaster so it's nice and secure. All that is gonna cost money. And I am giving it to you for fifteen thousand. That's it. I ain't trying to trick you 'cos that ain't my style. You and me were born under the same piece of sky, and when we die we're gonna be covered by the same piece of mud. That makes us almost brothers. And as your brother I'm telling you to get your head out of your ass and see the light...See the light brother," emphasised Babarr with the faintest trace of a new emotion entering his voice.

The logic of Babarr's sentiments began to make perfect sense to everyone. The Pandeys moved apart and Santosh Pandey with a new-found assertiveness, agreed.

"OK...it's a deal."

"Good, I'll go get the contract," said Babarr.

He left the house, beckoning Musa to follow him.

"You see Musa it's all about knowing what the customer wants. That's the secret of any good business," he said when they were outside. "It's just as well he saw sense 'cos if he'd said 'Oh, no, no, no,' one more time, I think I might have killed the bastard."

After the contract was signed, the Pandeys departed. Their final request to Babarr was to make sure that he cleaned up any mess after he finished, as their daughter could not tolerate untidiness. Babarr acquiesced wearily. The effort of his triumphant theatrics seemed to have silenced his body language: he now sighed every time he breathed and his pace slowed as he walked to the swish living room and slumped into a chair. Musa and Sajid followed, unwilling to leave their shepherd. Babarr reached into his pocket for a packet of Rizlas and then, delving further, he took out what looked to be a brownish-greenish wad of dried leaves. He placed this wad on to a Rizla paper and carefully prepared a roll-up which he lit up, put between his lips and inhaled deeply, his eyes glazed with thought.

Sajid, unburdened by the need for any such mental activity, sat down on a sofa and immediately launched into one of his monologues. Babarr nodded and as if soothed by the inane chatter sank further into the chair. At this point, whether by accident or divine intervention, a footrest sprang out, lifting his heavy legs, and he smiled like the child who has found a lost comfort blanket. With a barely audible voice he requested that Musa make tea. The request was probably a command but so faint and plaintive was Babarr's voice that Musa felt it would have been positively inhumane to refuse.

First cup of tea made by Musa.

Segment of conversation between Sajid and Babarr:

Sajid: "Babarr I'm telling you the future is in socks. One of my cousins was really clever at school and his mum and dad wanted him to become a doctor but he said no. Then they said become a dentist and he still said no. Then they said OK then become a lawyer and he didn't want to do that either. So then they got really pissed off and asked, 'What is it that you want to do?' You know what he said? He said, 'Mum…Dad what is it that doctors, dentists and lawyers have in common?' They said they all earn over 50K a year. He said, 'No, they all wear socks. I want to become a socks trader. And his mum and dad were like really really upset with him and his dad says, 'Look son, I didn't work all my life in a factory so my son would grow up and become a sock merchant. You'll ruin the family name. But he stuck to his guns, yeah, and now all them bastards that laughed at him, they're all wearing his socks. And he is sitting pretty, laughing his ass off. I'm telling you bro, socks is where it's happening!"

Babarr's response: "Um…"

Second cup of tea made by Musa.

Atmosphere in living room: cordial and relaxed.

Third cup of tea made by Musa.

Segment of conversation between Sajid and Babarr:

Sajid: "I'm telling you man I used to wonder, what is all this nonsense about Kashmir? Because if you ask me there ain't no reason why Pakistanis and Indians can't be like brothers and sisters. Remember Adnan and Sunita?"

Babarr nods slowly.

"Man, I'm telling you I ain't ever seen a couple so hot as Adnan and Sunita. Babarr, I'm telling you those two were always making out. In the park, in his dad's black cab, in her mum's kitchen, in our office. I ain't ever seen a couple like that. They never ever argued about Kashmir, they just got it on."

Babarr: "Yeah I remember them two…Yeah!"

Fourth cup of tea made by Musa.

Atmosphere in living room: a pungent but pleasing haze is beginning to form over the head of Babarr.

Fifth cup of tea made by Musa.

Segment of conversation between Sajid and Babarr:

Sajid: "One time I'm down a mosque in Birmingham and they're all standing in a circle. And in the middle there's this guy who's sitting in a chair with his hand out listening to his mobile. And all these people are taking turns to kiss this bloke's hand. So I says to the guy in charge, 'Why're they all doing that?' and he goes, 'It's because the guy is like, you know, really holy.' So I said, 'Who's he talking to?' and the guy is getting really pissed off with my questions and he says, 'Probably God,' and I go, 'Why doesn't he just pray? That way he can talk to him for free…' Get it. FREE!"

Atmosphere in living room: A brown smog has settled. Everyone present is very happy and even Musa has found that he is becoming reluctant to leave the room despite the conversation.

When, three hours after the first, the command came to make the sixth cup of tea Musa got up from his chair with surprising alacrity. The floor beneath him felt as elastic as a trampoline and he had an irresistible urge to jump up and down. He made his way to the kitchen and noted with surprise that everything was gently moving. The large tin containing the slowly diminishing tea bags seemed absolutely enchanting and for a few long moments he stared at it, entranced by its lustrous surface. A noise broke into his trance: the refrigerator was humming with the insistence of a demented choir. Displeased he turned his attention to the task at hand.

While waiting for the water to boil he opened a jar of cumin and laid a few seeds on the worktop: with a small spoon he smashed at them. A feeling of irritation had been let loose within him and before he knew it he was furious. Did he have a sign stamped on his forehead saying Tea Boy? Was this why he had been assigned to Babarr? Was this a requisite duty of all associates of Babarr? If so how come that asshole Sajid never made the tea? The shame of it all! What an ignoble task for someone who had memorised the Quran in its entirety!

When the kettle whistled he knew it was a call to arms. A shrill request for revenge.

As he placed the ground seeds in the cup, an idea came to him. He poured the boiling water into the cup and went to the refrigerator to get the milk. Wincing at the hum of the accursed refrigerator, he poured milk into the cup but not to the brim. No, another fluid would

85

lubricate the palate of Babarr. He cleared his throat, coughed and cleared his throat again. Musa then spat into Babarr's sixth cup of tea. A large gob of saliva settled on the surface but refused to sink. This was bad news. Looking at the cup of tea it was obvious that it was no latte. Disconcerted, he stared furiously at the part of him that bobbed on the tea's surface.

"Saliva is one point six times heavier than water and point five times heavier than milk. That's why it's not sinking," said a calm voice behind him.

Musa turned to see who the oracle of fluid density was and recognised the daughter. She was taller than her parents and held herself with greater authority. With her large spectacles and the tightly bound puff of black hair at the back of her head she was as prim as a nun. Yet despite the austerity of her presence there was a certain tropical lucency to her, as if in another life she had been a Polynesian virgin who danced in the sun with flowers strewn through her hair.

"How long have you been doing this sort of thing?" she asked.

"Just started today," replied Musa, intrigued and amused by the ambivalence in his answer.

She walked towards him and Musa noted with surprise that the customary compliant demeanour had somehow been waylaid. She was dressed in a formal black dress and high heels. He tried to smile but feeling himself beginning to tense up, he could not. She stopped and placed her hands on her hips. As they looked at each other he recognised her father's eyes, far-seeing and shrewd. The beat of the moments that passed were like the whipping ticks of a crucifixion clock.

"Are you with Babarr?" she asked brusquely.

"Yes…I am with him though I am not yet *with him*," replied Musa, finding it enormously difficult to keep a straight face at his marvellous spontaneous wit.

"I don't think you're all there," she said warily.

"I don't know where *there* is. That's why I am here," confided Musa.

"Are you one of these Pakistani boys who start talking shit every time he sees a girl?" she asked contemptuously.

"It's possible I suppose," said Musa thoughtfully.

Musa's timidity seemed to have a disarming effect and the daughter nodded slowly and appraisingly, gradually shedding her hostility. She surveyed him briefly and came to a quick decision.

"If you ever wanted to know my name, would you ask?"

"Never," replied Musa honestly.

The daughter smiled and Musa realised this was in response to his own smile and that where a smile begins and where it ends was to him an arc as distant as a winter moon, which amazingly was also a sign of Allah.

"My name is Armila."

"I am Musa," said Musa and felt immensely powerful for a few fleeting seconds.

"Uh-huh." Instantly Armila became businesslike. "You need to add a little more hot water to the tea because the heat will expand the bubbles in your saliva and make it disappear."

"I'll do that," said Musa gratefully.

"You'd better hurry. You wouldn't want Babarr to start jumping again would you?" said Armila and with that parting advice, she walked out of the kitchen.

Musa nodded for longer than was really necessary and then began to boil more water.

When he returned to the living room Babarr and Sajid were not easy to identify as there was by now a mist which seemed to open doors and present all manner of inhibited notions in a platter from heaven. But the noise of their uproarious laughter with its explicit sense of the absurd became a maelstrom that sucked him in and then spun him out. Musa laid the tea on the table and began to reel with mirth, unaccountably and for absolutely no reason. He took a few steps, brought his hands together and suddenly bowed down as if he had just heard the joke and realised how extremely funny it was. The thrall of that insane, comic moment diminished his fear so that in a peculiar way it rested in his heart like the globule of saliva at the bottom of Babarr's tea.

With shaking hands and streaming eyes Babarr picked up the cup and took a huge swig. For a few seconds nothing happened and Musa had the sense of travelling many miles. And then Babarr coughed and sent a gigantic spray of tea across the room. Sajid exploded.

"*Bastard!* What the fuck did you put into that tea?" exclaimed Babarr.

He stood up. Disgust had now returned his senses to the fore of his consciousness but Sajid sat with tears rolling down his face. Impatiently Babarr waved at the cloudy air in front of him.

"Guys…Guys what is happening to us? We're sitting on our backsides laughing our asses off like a bunch of monkeys. We have work to do. Come on now, shift yourselves."

With this angry broadcast he strode out of the room, lithe with purpose.

Musa awash with relief followed him into the garden, the sounds of maniacal laughter trailing behind.

The Herculean endeavour of building was mixing cement. This was not as easy as it sounded. For a start the bags of cement weighed a ton and when Musa lifted one bag with his arms clasped around it in the manner of a bear hug he was sure his knees would give way. Once he had laid the bag on the ground he had to grab a shovel that was heavier than two fat men and pierce it. Then with the shovel he had to lift the cement into the cement mixer which was already slowly turning after some kind of powder had been put in there. The problem was that you had to shovel quickly or else the turning cement mixer would erupt and fire its contents back at you.

It was the shovelling that unmanned Musa. For hands that had held nothing heavier than the Holy Quran were simply not the paws of a builder. And Musa struggled: struggled to shovel, struggled to lift, struggled to do it quickly, and struggled not to throw the cement on Babarr who lay in the garden watching with a mild mixture of amusement and derision.

"C'mon Musa. Take pride in your work. Remember each time you throw the cement you are making a place where a kid can walk and feel happy." All the while he fanned himself with the contract his employer had signed earlier.

Sajid stood watching Musa as though he were a two-headed dog.

"Do you have any worries?"

Musa put the shovel down and straightened his back. He searched for a cold cutting response.

"Fu...Fu...Fu...Fuck off!" he panted, dismayed by his lack of originality.

"Guys...Guys...don't act like kids now. Sajid, you take over from Musa for a little while. I'll start clearing up and getting ready to knock the wall down," said Babarr.

"Which wall?" asked Sajid.

"The one down there," said Babarr vaguely gesturing to the sky.

"Are you gonna get the bulldozer?"

"No. Bulldozers are for babies," replied Babarr contemptuously. "I'll use what Allah gave me." He raised a fist.

"Are you the next Mr Universe?" said a cold voice.

Everybody turned around and saw the daughter looking disapprovingly at them.

"Oh...Armila. How'ya doing sweetheart?" Babarr put his arms down and smiled sheepishly at her.

"I'll be doing a damn sight better once you start working and stop making such a racket," said Armila, unmoved by his Neanderthal charm.

"I know, baby…I know…and I'm really sorry but to build you gotta make noise," said Babarr apologetically.

"Yeah, but the noise is not coming from you lot doing any building it's coming from your gobs," replied Armila angrily.

"I'm sorry sweetheart. We'll be out of your way soon," said Babarr.

She shook her head with disgust: "Have you been smoking pot in the living room?" she asked, her eyes boring into Babarr's like a laser.

"No love. We don't do that sort of thing. It's all tobacco, love, just like the stuff you buy in the shops." Babarr smiled his winning smile in an attempt to charm.

"What brings you down here, love?" he asked, unperturbed by the vibes.

"I came to see what was blocking the sunlight from the window and realised it was your big ass," snarled Armila and stormed off.

Babarr chuckled as if he had received an enormous compliment. He turned to the others and said, "Feisty little thing, ain't she?"

"She's got more balls than her dad, that's for sure," said Sajid.

Babarr shook his head, still smiling. "Musa, why don't you go inside and take her on. Show her some of your education. You need a break."

The mixer turned and churned implacably and its call was now heeded by Sajid who picked up the shovel and began to feed it cement and gravel, grinning like a goon all the time.

As Musa approached the house a breeze blew and combed his beard, which hung limply from his face like a grass necklace. He noticed the crimson horizon retreating with an army of clouds. The day had changed. Damp with sweat he made his way through the kitchen. The house seemed different now that it had lost its novelty. Outside the living room, remembering the heady, heavenly aromas, he placed his hand on the golden doorknob and then quickly withdrew it – the doorknob was warm which meant that Armila was either in there or had been in there moments before. He could not enter.

The door to the room which he had noticed when he first arrived was now wide open. It was the room with the photograph of Santosh Pandey proudly holding his degree. Curious, he walked in. There were no furnishings save for two heavy cushions that lay on opposite sides. The light came from a row of panelled glass tiles that spread along the top of the room. Gingerly he touched the wall, feeling the indentations of a faint, faded design on the wallpaper. On one wall hung a life-size photograph of a woman embracing a golden-haired child.

Musa examined it closely. The woman's chin rested on the child's head. Musa knew without knowing how he knew that the embrace was one of comfort. In the photograph he saw a line of light across the woman's head that seemed to spread to illuminate her face and give radiance to her smile. And it was a truly beautiful smile, sad and strangely joyful at the same time. Yet it was the wisdom in the faraway eyes that mesmerised him, an awareness of hope that lay on the other side of sorrow. He had seen eyes like that before and frowned, trying to remember where.

He heard someone coming down the stairs and turned as Armila entered the room. Quickly and awkwardly he stepped away from the photograph.

"What are you doing here, Musa?" she asked quietly.

"I just saw the open door and wandered in," he replied nervously.

Armila nodded and looked at him intently.

"Sit down," she said and beckoned to one of the cushions.

Musa did so, noticing that she was barefoot. He found this strangely disturbing as if he was privy to a sight he should not have been exposed to. Armila sat down on the cushion on the other side of the room.

"You don't seem the type that would hang around Babarr and his crew."

"Well, I don't really hang around with them. I just listen to what he says and do what he tells me to," replied Musa.

"Why?"

"Because…because I have to learn what it is to work and be responsible and stuff," said Musa, frowning at the sense of repetition.

Armila laughed. "You sound as if you just came from another planet."

Musa struggled with the underlying truth. "Well, I came from a school. A madrasah. And I was there and learning stuff and I kept getting into all these rows and fights. Then all of a sudden I ended up here." He sighed glumly.

"Were you there to be more holy?" asked Armila gently.

"No…just more religious," said Musa, deeply troubled by the distinction.

Armila nodded again and Musa could feel the empathy of her understanding.

"So are you learning yet?"

"I'm learning—" Musa stopped and thought hard. "I'm learning that there are lots of different ways to say someone is stupid. You can say it as if it's a joke and you can say it as if it's serious. But each time you say it you feel a little bit special. I'm also learning you have to be stronger than I am to mix cement."

"You learn quickly," smiled Armila.

Musa thought very briefly about returning the smile, but decided not to.

"Um, who's the woman in the photograph?" he asked more uncomfortably than he would have liked.

"Oh her. That's Ammachi."

"What does that mean?"

"It's her name. She's a saint," said Armila proudly.

"What's she done?" asked Musa with interest.

Armila frowned as if displeased by the irrelevance of the question.

"She's been known to cure lepers and people with cancer. One time she even made a bowl of water have enough rice to feed the entire village. But none of these things really matter," she said impatiently.

"What does matter?"

"What matters is that she works twenty-two hours a day to provide homes for the poor and shelters for battered women. Every year she tries to build a thousand homes to give free of charge to poor families. That's why she's a saint."

Musa nodded his abashed agreement.

"Next year I'm going to India to queue up and meet her," said Armila.

"How long are the queues?" asked Musa.

"Miles long. She says she sees God in the face of everyone she meets. That's why I'm going to meet her. I want her to see God in my face and then when she hugs me I want to feel what God feels like," said Armila.

"But you know what your gods look like don't you? They've got four legs and four arms and they fire lots of arrows at the other gods," said Musa earnestly.

Armila's expression changed to one of contempt. "For a second you sounded like Babarr there."

"Oh, I'm sorry."

To avoid her gaze Musa got up and stood close to the photograph of Ammachi.

"There is definitely something about her. It's almost like, when you look at her, she's trying to tell you something. Like she's trying to say…" Musa stopped as he heard Babarr grunting outside. "…trying to say…" He stopped again as he heard something heavy and metallic.

"What? What's she trying to say?" said Armila with considerable annoyance.

"Fuck," said Musa as the combination of bricks, glass and Ammachi's photograph exploded from the wall, hitting him right between the eyes. He fell to the floor, dimly hearing Armila screaming, "You goddamn fool! It's not this wall you're supposed to knock down!"

Then he felt a soft tender hand on his forehead. He breathed in deeply, savouring the perfume of care, and then passed out knowing full well that on this first ever day of work he had more than earned his daily bread.

5

As Musa lay out for the count in the back of Babarr's speeding van, occasionally prodded by the fascinated Sajid, the course of his life was being pondered on nearly four thousand miles away.

In the dead of night, amongst people long gone, Dadaji the patriarch sat gazing at his wife's tombstone. The earth around Afiya's grave teemed with life: lizards busy with survival scurried about, their green coats prickling in readiness for conflict, fire-flies puffed light – microscopic shooting stars – the screech of rodents and insects alike combined with a sense of the presence of the dead and made the air hum with a hauntingly familiar note. To Dadaji their performance recalled the chorus of Quranic recitation which as a child he was made to do. Then, as now, duty was the weight that pressed so heavily against his heart. Then, as now, duty was the blood which cried through his mind and calcified the bone in his infirm back but now there were also differences. The family which he had built, nourished and sustained was altered. The unity between his sons which he had once forged was now as fickle as the wind. He was at a loss to understand how this had happened. Perhaps it was the division of wealth among his sons? Perhaps it was the wily whispers of their wives? Many were the possibilities but the ending he could foresee was one he would never want to witness: a world which no longer bore his mark. Fractious sons jarred and jolted by their greed and seduced by envy would disunite and erase the very purpose of his existence.

Yet he knew that flotsam flowed with the tide which, as it ebbed, began its journey to the sea from whence it came. He had seen the children of worthless men give worth to their fathers. He had seen the bounty written for the infant spread like a ripple and envelop the impoverished parent. So unity that would diverge amongst his sons could converge through his son's sons: unity through a union and with that unity a burden that was meant for stalwarts, all accomplished through the vow of marriage.

Dadaji smiled at the symmetry of his reasoning. Then, as with all things of joy, it slowly faded with the onslaught of reality. His sons he could command and in their devotion he was secure but the grandchildren were beholden to no one. Those of suitable age were Itrat's and they could not be herded with the arguments of old and the ways of their forefathers.

He took his rosary from his pocket. Ninety-nine beads for the Ninety-Nine Names of Allah. Names he had recited without fail for most of his life. His sons, when younger, had asked him why he kept on doing so so long past the duty of prayer and he had told them it was for the same reason he rubbed wood until it became fire. When

Afiya had died Dadaji had recited the names as a parrot would try to mimic the song of a lark and this had helped to stave off the black depression which threatened to swamp him. And that was when he stopped conversing and his thoughts became silent chants of the Ninety-Nine Names. As the years went by his instincts led him to the truth.

Closing his eyes Dadaji recited a name as he flicked a bead. The beads clicked rapidly and a vibrato of knowledge filled his mind with a rush of dark experience. He stopped, opened his eyes and started again but this time he focused on a face. The beads clicked and intuition was heightened by the truth and he saw chaos and passion, longing and innocence, devotion and rage, intellect and ignorance, all enmeshed in the heart of Musa. The clicking stopped.

Again, his eyes closed, he clicked the beads and this time he felt the crystal in Shabnam and the stilted fire in Suleiman. He smiled sadly and returned the rosary to his pocket, seeing the conflict between fantasy and reality. He felt the whisper of evil in the promise of the unknown. Behind his eyes he saw Iram and Musa, aspirants enchained by the same innocence.

Dadaji arose, his bearing proud and erect. His fierce bright eyes lingered on the words engraved on Afiya's tombstone, "Unto Him shall ye all return" and he realised his journey to England would be his last – he would never return from there to this place.

★

Lahore at night is unlike any other city in the world. Nowhere else is so completely claimed by the ebb of the working and the flow of the indolent. When darkness descends it is the bazaar that awakens from the sloth of commerce to become the den of friends and the rendezvous of the discreet and hopeful. One such is Anarkali bazaar and on this night it is indeed vibrant with occasion and poised to house the moment that will forever hold a glitter for posterity. It is perhaps for this reason that the customary melodies of the bazaar resonate the way its young long for love. The air is thick with the scent of burning wood and aromas of barbecued meat. Motorcycles roar and swerve through the crowd with reckless swagger, the riders laugh, their heads flung back, and their laughter permeates the ambience to become that thrilled flutter a child experiences when taken at night to a city with bright lights. Couples meet and talk and flash questions each time their eyes meet. Vendors, soiled by the day's labour, talk and chortle aloud, their brown faces glowing with perspiration and shining with the nightly zest that is known both to the careworn and carefree. An old man naked but for the long flowing cloth around his belly sits on his string bed, all the time crowned by a swarm of flies, and with doleful eyes watches the procession passing by.

Outside a neon-lit restaurant, Iram sits with her three cousins Farzana, Fozia and Farrah who are wearing identical silk chiffon outfits and neat hijabs: not a single strand of hair can be seen. Iram was once amused that the sisters always dressed the same but now she viewed their custom as perfectly sensible and a sign of good taste. Fozia and Farrah are speaking about someone they know and are engrossed in each other's opinion. Iram does not join in the conversation not because she is not curious but because Farzana, the eldest sister, does not participate. Farzana watches the bazaar without seeming to look at anything in particular even though her gaze is deep with appraisal.

Iram is much taken by Farzana, and those who know the younger girl well have noticed a slight haughtiness in her manner when the two are together but this is of little concern to her. The problem for Iram is that she lives in a village and her cousins live in the city: because she lives in the village it is considered that she might pick up village ways and that is why the cousins are rarely allowed to visit her. But Iram is stuck there and knowing this she concentrates hard on keeping herself on the same level as the three sisters. Through careful observation of her cousins she has come to know her own worth.

Tonight is a rare night for her. She has been allowed out of the village compound because Khalil the eldest, rarely-seen son of Uncle Arshad had been made a lieutenant in the army. In his honour Uncle Arshad had decided to throw a party and had booked a restaurant for the evening. Iram was glad of the welcome diversion from the family's attention. It had been three weeks since that conversation about Musa and there had been no let up. This was something to stoke the banter of the villagers. Looks and giggles pierced her like darts and each time she went to her mother to complain, her mother would smile indulgently and do nothing. Farzana and the girls had said nothing but instead now watched her the way her father watched her brothers when they were about to take their matriculation exams.

A Pajero pulled up, a door opened and out stepped Uncle Arshad, vanity deepening the pause in his movements. He always overdressed. No matter how hard he tried he always looked like a poor man who had gone over the top when buying clothes with his newly found money. Tonight was no exception and he looked silly in his cream, double-breasted suit and white shoes with black heels. He seemed agitated and the girls, sensing this, immediately stopped talking and looked down, all apart from Farzana who coolly looked on while her father started to berate the waiters for the lack of food on the tables.

More guests arrived and the noise rose to such an extent that it became difficult to hear what anyone was saying. When Khalil turned up he was instantly the tallest and most popular man in the restaurant. He wore a dark suit cut in such a way that it added to his natural air of refinement and that was something Uncle Arshad craved. In the dim glow of the restaurant Iram saw that he had clean square-cut features that were neither dark nor fair. He moved and laughed with ease and Iram felt the blood tie between them quicken. At their table Khalil bent down and his sisters passed proud hands across his back. Even Farzana smiled and spoke lightly to him about something which Iram could not hear. Khalil looked directly at her then and before she could summon the correct gaze, he unnerved her with the polite welcome in his eyes. Then he laughed in sudden delight as his friends crowded round and whisked him away.

Iram saw that though his smile seemed to come and go casually, his natural gaiety did not shift. She kept her eyes on him as he moved to the buffet but then her sense of propriety, powerful since infancy, made her turn her heard sharply. The cousins were all busy talking and smiling pleasantries to women who passed by, unaware of her indiscretion.

She often had trouble with that sudden feeling that was in no way appropriate or proper. Such feelings seemed so crude and village-like and she hated herself for not being able to smother them. The cousins appeared to be completely natural in their poise and in the way they could talk and sound clever. She thought of Musa then and closed her eyes trying to stir a sense of premonition, anything upon which she could base an instinct, something with which she could prepare herself. But nothing came, only the emptiness of a foregone conclusion. She opened her eyes and found Khalil standing at the foot of their table, perplexed with concern yet once more smiling at her. She frowned and turned away, displeased by the sudden realisation of her attraction to him.

6

Randy Andy made out like there was no tomorrow. He contorted his body around girl and sofa with such flexibility that watching him you felt he was a walking poster boy for the karma sutra. The girl whose lungs were being deflated remained out of sight. She was pinned to the beat-up sofa cushions and her only form of expression was a pair of uncertain hands that told voyeurs all was not what it seemed.

"How do you suppose they breathe?" asked Shakila.

"Dunno, probably through the nose. They don't look as if they're all that worried about it though," replied Shabnam who was sitting opposite the pair. Her answer was delivered in a shout. This mode of communication irritated her but since it was her first party she was bound to be peeved by some age-old rituals.

"It looks different when you see it in films doesn't it?" asked Shakila thoughtfully.

"That's 'cos it's rehearsed. This is what it looks like in real life," said Shabnam. "Like he's trying to catch a fish with an open mouth."

"I think if some guy did that to me I'd kill him."

"That's why no guy will ever do it to you!" retorted Shabnam.

"Sure they will. A Pakistani guy will do it to a donkey if he thought there was a chance of a settlement visa."

They both laughed. The party was hosted and arranged by Randy Andy, the most popular man in college who had slept with all ethnic minorities and true to his upbeat, no-regrets outlook managed to remain on good terms with both sexes. The party was proof of that. Everyone who had a social connection with Randy Andy's conquests was here: black men with braided hair and long leather coats, Chinese guys with Hawaiian shirts, English blokes who laughed the loudest and Pakistanis in their customary groups of four, all wearing black polo necks and gold necklaces. There were even those morons who dressed like they were vampires.

The lights had been dimmed and a great stroboscope gyrated from the ceiling filling the room with alternating hues of green and red. There wasn't a chair or sofa that did not have two people wanting to become one. The bittersweet smell of alcohol filled the air which was already turning brown from opiates. Music blasted from speakers in all four corners – deafening music was the signature of the party: as ever Randy Andy had something for everyone, Bollywood songs for the Asians, Bob Marley for the Afro-Caribbeans, and the Stones for everyone else.

"I can't believe I let you talk me into coming to this place," said Shabnam.

"What would you be doing instead? Cleaning the

kitchen? You can do that tomorrow!" said Shakila brightly.

Shabnam glared.

"Chill out for God's sake! Look every guy here is giving you the eye. Talk to a few of them. They don't bite you know!"

"What difference does it make if a guy gives you the eye? Is he gonna take you home? Can you take him home? Can he show you a good time and keep showing you a good time? Suppose you just have a one-night stand with him and you think yeah, this is great, I want more of this and then you start pestering him to give you some more. Before you know it he knows all your buttons and when he starts pushing them you're gonna run to him like you were his bitch!"

"Oh God," groaned Shakila. "You're off again aren't you? Look why don't you go get us a drink of coke or something? That way you can be my bitch!"

Shabnam extended her index finger but nonetheless got up and edged her way to the table which was laden with drinks. To blend into the cosmopolitan hive she had forsaken her traditional dress and wore new Levi's and a white Tsunami Relief top. The air warbled with the words "Shine like a star wherever you are". She guessed this to be a Jamaican song and shook her head in disgust at the idiocy of its proclamation.

Although she had only been at the party for an hour, people were definitely less sure on their feet and she had to change directions mid step to avoid men who moved unsteadily towards her. A tall ginger-haired guy with psychotic blue eyes asked if he could help her in any way and was promptly told to just fuck off. There was no path of minimum resistance. Assholes were everywhere. To the left she recognised Mauritius, a foreign exchange student, who was sitting in somebody's lap and having two bottles of a urine-looking liquid emptied into his mouth. To the right there was a Sikh guy with his legs wrapped around the waist of another Sikh guy: both were singing. In a corner Chinese guys were attempting their version of the Mexican wave. Only the black guys seemed to be aloof and in control of their dignity.

Shabnam sighed hopelessly but...but there was an opening...Dizzy Lizzy, a tall, buxom blonde, had just appeared and immediately dispersed the crowd quicker than a police warning of a bomb. This was because Dizzy Lizzy loved to talk and talk and talk about her endless relationships. Each time she did so she would sway her head to and fro and give vertigo to her hapless confidante. Hence the name. Shabnam began walking backwards as if in response to the sublime melody bellowing in the room. Some dozen steps and a well-timed one hundred and eighty degree turn and she would be by the drinks.

"Oh Shabs honey. Hi!" squealed Dizzy Lizzy. "Knew it was you! All you Asian girls got such big bums you can spot them a mile off. What you doing here love?"

Before Shabnam could continue she went on.

"Did you see that film *Yasmin* on Channel 4 last night? It was set somewhere round here. I was watching it with my Sebastian and I said to him I know a girl like that. Weren't that guy funny the way he wanted a quickie every time he came home at two o'clock in the morning?

Thing is sweetheart…" she bent down conspiratorially, "they're all like that, even my Sebastian. Don't think we got it any easier love. Men are men and they're all a bunch of fucking pigs if you ask me."

"Even your Sebastian?" asked Shabnam caustically.

"Even my Sebastian. You know the other day he said I think we should become exclusive. And I said, Sebastian just because we've been going out for one year that doesn't give you the right to trap me in a relationship. And then he goes, Liz I love you and I said to him just because you love me that doesn't give you the right to control me. Then he said, don't you love me and I said love is free and just because you love someone doesn't mean you can't be free. Then he goes, I need a commitment and I said to him in a polyfidelous relationship commitment is guaranteed. And then he goes to me, what's polyfidelous mean and I said it means faithful to lots of people and then he said you slut and then I said Sebastian I refuse to be abused and then…" Dizzy Lizzy went on.

After a short while Shabnam was able to escape to the drinks table. The music had changed to Bollywood and the heroine was loudly cooing the ecstasy of love. The goal was in sight. Two steps. Swerve to avoid pisshead. One step and then…The Asian Guys.

There they stood in a group of four, leering at her like a pack of dogs. Shabnam gave them a smile laced with the required amount of contempt.

"Shabnam, what you doing here? You're supposed to be a good girl," sniggered one of them.

"You're not here to find a husband are you?" said another.

"We're all available," said a third and they all laughed.

Pakistani men always acted like this. Full of macho bullshit. When they were at home they were dutiful and obedient, ready to do anything and everything for the family. Outside home, they strutted around like they were heroes with the world waiting to be theirs.

"Even if I was I'd rather kill myself and go to hell than marry any of you assholes," she snarled.

"Ooh!" replied the chorus of assholes.

"Instead of moaning like pregnant women why don't you all move out of the way?"

"What you gonna do if we don't?" one of them asked.

Shabnam laughed: "All I have to do is scream and point at you lot and every man here is going to come to my rescue. Do you know what's going to happen then? You're all gonna run with your tail between your legs!"

Shabnam threw her head back and cleared her throat. The Asian Guys quickly dispersed. One of them stopped to admire the sight of her lush flowing hair but was quickly pulled away.

Triumphant and victorious, Shabnam shouted after them: "That's why none of you will ever have a woman worth having! You're all just a bunch of cowards!"

Grabbing two of the coldest cans, Shabnam made her way back to Shakila. The air was now filled with a mist that felt as if it was pouring dirt into the pores of her skin. Shakila was almost impossible to distinguish and Shabnam cursed her for wearing her stupid black sequined dress.

She moved through the swimming crowd grimacing at the falsettos of the over-loud music. A shake of a head that rustled a black tress of hair identified Shakila deep in conversation with Hardeep. Or to be exact Hardeep deep in conversation with Shakila.

"Hey Lord Attenborough! Why don't you stop bothering my friend here?"

"Easy Shabnam easy. Nothing wrong with talking to someone is there?"

"And there's nothing wrong with pissing off out of my seat is there?"

Hardeep sighed and got up. "Well nice meeting you," he said politely to Shakila.

"Likewise," said Shakila brusquely.

"Can't bloody leave you alone for five minutes can I?" said Shabnam.

"Five? More like fifty. What took you so long?"

"Got held up by the Karachi Cops."

Shakila cast a disdainful look over her shoulder. "They look like a bunch of poofs with their moustaches and necklaces don't they?"

"They got no fucking manners that's the problem. They got no idea how you should speak to women…Here, drink up," said Shabnam handing her a can of Red Bull.

"Keep it cold for me." Shakila looked quickly and nervously at Shabnam. "I'm off to the loo."

"Don't let Hardeep see you," warned Shabnam.

She settled back into a smelly sofa with the cold cans in her lap and in a moment that was as long as a pang of guilt or a sigh of regret, she was the girl inside the home whose mark she so desperately wanted to shed. She was alien and she was alone.

The roar of the crowd around her and the frenzied antics of those who loved to have fun were as cryptic to her as the calligraphy inside a mosque or the speeches of her father.

Surveying the party around her and with an insight that comes through longing and scrutiny, she saw that there were those who laughed as though they had lived a little and loved a lot. They would become part of a greater spectrum within which men and women could look at each other and be happy and then live lives in which they were happy. And that was a life which she could not live, though there were many who looked at her and made a fragrant bubble inside their heads in which she floated. She knew then why it was she could never come again to a party, or any gathering of toxic innocence.

It was then, just then when the heaviness of certainty weighed heaviest that she looked up and saw that Randy Andy had gone and in his place sat someone who was watching her.

"Hello," he said.

Shabnam did not answer but she saw the kindness in his eyes and felt the blood in her veins settle.

A song she had heard many times before from *Dilwale,* an Indian film, was now playing. The lyric cut a swathe into her mind. "The illiterate mud of this village cannot read the letter from your heart." Mud…she remembered at school she had a Nigerian friend and how she once teased her about putting mud on her face. She smiled at how stupid it all was.

Pleased at her smile he said, "When I see a beautiful girl who's sad and shy I don't normally bother her. But when I saw you, I said to myself some rules were just made to be broken."

"Is that supposed to impress me?" asked Shabnam.

"No, no, not at all. I just know that life is too short to be sad. You got to start living before you start dying."

"Which one are you doing?"

"You can't talk in a place like this. Why don't you and me get all intellectual in a fine restaurant with good food and nice music in the background?"

Shabnam did not answer so he tried another tack.

Gently and politely he asked, "Can I give you my number?"

Shabnam then saw him clearly. With the velocity of an experience that was forbidden and new she could see the raw-boned strength in his body, the hardness of his jaw and the keenness of his eyes. Above all she heard the whisper of something free and the perilous dance between the seen and the unseen was in time with the furious beating of her heart.

"Yes."

He fished a card out of his pocket and wrote on the back. He smiled again and she felt the unexpectedness of his pleasure. Then he was gone.

"Hey girl," said Shakila arriving in a flurry.

"You took your time."

"Uhh-huh. What was that black guy saying to you?"

Shabnam noticed the time and knew that soon they would begin to expect her at home. "Nothing…come on, let's go."

7

The living room of Aboo's house had undergone a miraculous change. There was no clutter now. Along one wall was a sofa which could be made into a bed and on the floor was a long white cloth, a tattered old bag and, sitting on the cloth, an old man dressed in a simple white cotton tunic and thickly wrapped white dhoti. Around the old man, sitting on kitchen chairs were gathered his son, niece and grandchildren. Their current mood was varied. One was wryly amused. One was sycophantic. One was belligerent and resentful. One was fearful and apprehensive. One was feeling the sanctified presence of a Holy man.

Dadaji's expression was contemplative as he opened the bag and took out a rock, a plant in a small plastic case, a bottle of oil and lastly an orange. All were placed in a neat arc in front of him. He looked up and surveyed the astonishment. For the briefest of seconds everyone felt the untamed levity of a chuckle about to explode into the air.

"One of you children is like this rock, hard and tough, yet even so like all rocks it may be broken to become something that gives sustenance." Dadaji looked at each of his grandchildren. "One of you is like this plant – if nourished by the right hands it will produce great things but if neglected it will become like dust and fade away. And one of you is like this oil. It can bring relief or it can anger fire."

All sat bemused and spellbound. Then the laughter came and it was a rich earthy laugh, grizzled and with no harshness.

"Itrat, which of your three is the cleverest?" asked Dadaji.

Aboo silently pointed at Shabnam and her brothers almost smiled.

"Shabnam, tell me why am I here?" asked Dadaji.

"To marry us off." Her accented Punjabi rang with defiance.

Dadaji laughed again and the whiteness of his dentures flashed his amusement.

"And what is wrong with that? Marriage is half of faith."

"But none of us has any faith, except maybe Musa," retorted Shabnam contemptuously.

Dadaji looked at Amma: "Your lioness is no longer shy," he said gently.

He turned back to Shabnam, straining his small eyes, remembering something. He pointed to Javed's composition.

"He spoilt you first and then later you spoiled yourself."

Dadaji hung his head in silence, still bemused by his reverie and slumping slightly as people do in mourning. Then he raised his head and looked directly at Shabnam who suddenly seemed very unsure of herself.

"Every child leaves the mark of their parents in this world. Yet for some children their mark forever scorches their parents."

Though Dadaji's gaze was on Shabnam he spoke almost as if to himself and his eyebrows were raised as though surveying a calamity.

"Which of you three knows the most?" he asked.

"About what?" asked Shabnam, still the conduit.

Dadaji raised his hands in ambivalence. His eyes were now crafty and a faint smile flickered across his face.

"Musa knows the most about Islam. Suleiman knows the most about everything else," she answered.

Dadaji chuckled and looked at his son, sharing in his amusement.

"Who is the happiest then?" he asked.

The question rang with an ugly sound, and in that moment they felt for the first time Dadaji's clear-cut simplicity.

"We might all be happy if we were allowed to do what we want," said Shabnam.

Dadaji absent-mindedly fumbled in his tunic for a cigarette and lighter. With long tapering fingers, he held the cigarette, firmly depressed the lighter and drew from his cigarette. He exhaled deeply, considering what he would say.

"When you are young, you know no God other than your impulse. You will hear many voices but you will heed only one, the voice of Satan, and that voice will always tell you to do whatever you want."

His voice was quiet and determined.

"When I was your age," he pointed at Musa, "my father was paralysed. I fed him, bathed him and took care of him. When he wanted me to clean him he would poke me with a stick that had a nail at the bottom. And every night he would poke me and draw blood and I would lift him and help him to defecate and urinate and then I would collect his excrement and throw it away. Nobody asked me whether or not I was living the life of my dreams. I never wept knowing that other children led better lives."

"It's not the same thing," said Musa.

"It is the same thing. Do you think I or your father were not young like you once. Our hearts also told us to do many things. But we chose to listen to our parents and now we reap their blessings. What blessings will you reap?"

The passive sage no longer, Dadaji was now an angry and indignant old man.

"Our peace of mind is more important than their blessings," said Musa angrily. Shabnam looked at him sharply.

"Peace of mind that is purchased with our pain is no peace. It is nothing but rank selfishness," replied Dadaji quietly.

Musa felt the measured calm of Dadaji's words and had the eerie idea that he had calculated his each and every response to his questions.

"Of the three you are the most glib and yet the most searching. Yet you cannot see what is around you. You read the Holy Quran and yet the words of Allah still do not fall upon you," said Dadaji.

Everyone looked at Musa, expecting a fiery outburst but, strangely, he was struck dumb, unnerved by his unmasking.

Dadaji continued and as before it was not clear whether or not he was addressing himself or Musa...

"Reading the Holy Quran and learning the sayings of the Prophet (peace be upon him) does not make you any wiser than anyone else." Dadaji straightened and raised both his hands, his eyes intense. "Wisdom is on the other side of pain, not on the other side of a page. Wisdom is after experience. Relief is after hardship...Do you understand what I am saying Musa?"

"Yes Dadaji," replied Musa.

Dadaji shook his head in disgust: "No you do not understand. You cannot understand."

"What is it that you want?" asked Musa, very simply and very innocently.

"I want you to heed my words so that you may be saved. What is it that you want, Musa?"

"I want to be free. Free to feel what I want. Free to think what I want. Free to be happy. Free to be crazy. Free to love. Free to marry."

Dadaji nodded, far from surprised. He lit another cigarette and breathed deeply.

"Who can give such freedom?" he asked, knowing full well the answer Musa would give.

"Allah," said Musa.

Dadaji smiled at him, pleased with the confidence of his answer.

"Do you think Allah will grant you such things?"

"Yes."

"Why?" asked Dadaji, with an air of polite curiosity.

"Because the Holy Quran states that Allah is the guardian protector of those who have faith and will lead them from the depths of darkness to the light," said Musa, echoing the words of that gentler sage at the Madrasah.

"Do you think I am in darkness?"

"No, Dadaji, but I cannot see a way forward with your light," said Musa.

Dadaji threw back his head and laughed.

"So certain are you of light and darkness. A suckling from yesterday." He waved dismissively at Musa. "You are nothing but a slave to your own desires."

"I am a slave to Allah," protested Musa.

"Then do you trust in Allah?" smiled Dadaji.

"Completely," said Musa defiantly.

Dadaji motioned Musa to sit opposite him. He reached forward and handed him the orange.

"Let us each offer a prayer. I will pray that you marry Iram and you will pray that you find love and happiness."

Dadaji closed his eyes and raised his hands. Aboo and Amma raised their hands too then suddenly let them drop. And Musa's prayer, when written, became a little tablet of faith that he always carried with him, right until the very day he died. Creased and crumpled it would become but the naked hope would always remain.

"O Lord of the Universe, God of worlds. You are the most Beneficent. You are the most Merciful. To You I offer this prayer because I know that only You can understand my prayer. O Lord I want so very much to feel like I am safe and part of my family. I want so very much for that tear I saw from Amma to climb back into her eye and never come out. O Lord I want to find love and I want to marry a woman who is beautiful and kind. I cannot see her in my life so lead me to her. Surely this is not too much to ask for. O Lord forgive me for saying this but I cannot but help notice that these things fall into the laps of plenty of people out there, infidels and hypocrites, without them even asking. I know that I will never be happy with Iram and she will never be happy with me so spare us both from this misery. Surely we both deserve to be happy. Amen."

Musa finished praying and opened his eyes. He saw Dadaji looking at him and he saw his wet orange hands.

"If I had given you the rock to hold, would you have crushed the rock Musa?" he asked.

Musa did not answer but looked down at his hands, not remembering crushing the orange.

Dadaji continued, solemn and dignified: "Let us put our prayer to the test."

He reached into his pocket and took out his rosary.

"There are thirty-three beads on this rosary. I give you one month of days in the pursuit of love. If by the end you have not found love, you will marry who I tell you to."

He inched forward on the white cloth until his knees touched Musa's.

"Do you agree to this pact Musa?" he asked.

Musa sat deathly still and silent.

"If you trust in Allah, what have you to fear?" said Dadaji.

"I accept," said Musa.

"Let all bear witness to this pact," said Dadaji.

Slowly, he offered his hand to Musa. Crimson passion met with old earth as they shook hands. Life had just begun.

8

"What have you done?" asked Amma desperately. Dadaji looked at her crossly, annoyed as always by the theatrics of women. He lit up a cigarette and breathed in deeply.

"What else could we have done? Your son was already in the grip of rebellion."

"But still," said Amma.

"Still what? Have you learnt nothing from what has happened? Events control us. We cannot control events. All we can do is go with the wind and see what chance is available to us when it changes."

"How do you know it will change?"

"Events always change. No one knows whether for the better or for the worst."

"What about Iram?"

"What about Iram?" repeated Dadaji angrily. He put down his cigarette and glared at his niece. "Iram is not the worry. The worry is your son, who has committed the Holy Quran to memory. Upon whose piety you hope to gain entry into Paradise. If Iram is in his destiny then there is nothing you can do to prevent it and if she is not then there is nothing you can do to make it happen. The lottery of marriages is known only to Allah."

Amma fell silent. It was hard to say whether this was through chastisement or appreciation of the truth. Dadaji settled back on his sofa-bed and gazed out of the window which was what he usually did when alone.

In the days following the pact Musa and Shabnam became almost invisible. They would return home in silence, collect food from the kitchen and make for their rooms to eat alone. Only Suleiman appeared to be at ease in front of Dadaji. When he gave money to his parents or received orders from them, Dadaji seemed to look at him with a kindly eye. The biggest change though was in Aboo and this was what Amma had dreaded most of all. In front of his father and brothers he was always brusque and aloof towards her and now her importance diminished each and every day Dadaji stayed.

"I don't understand how any of this happened. I worked so hard for my children…so so hard," said Aboo plaintively.

Amma looked at him in disgust. That was another of his traits – maudlin self-pity in front of his father and emotional outbursts in front of his brothers. She knew Dadaji would become angered by this melodramatic remark.

"Don't be a fool," he said. "You have lived long enough to know that children come with their own dispositions and they live to make their choices not yours."

"Do you think he will be successful?" asked Aboo.

"Where he looks for the wives, there are no princesses to be found. All you can do is pray that he will realise that in time."

"What about Shabnam?" asked Amma fearfully.

"Shabnam will be less of a problem than Musa. Daughters are given to you to be raised. Nothing more. "

"I worry about Shabnam. Boys are beginning to look at her," said Aboo.

Amma smiled proudly to herself and Dadaji laughed at the menace in his son's voice.

"And do you think Shabnam is not aware of this?" Dadaji shook his head thoughtfully. "The wiles of women are indeed awesome."

"The Asian boys in this country are all up to no good. You see them hanging around together in their groups trying to be like black men. None of them work, yet they wear expensive clothes and drive flashy cars. These are the ones that bring pain to their parents," said Aboo.

"How do you know Suleiman is not like that?" Dadaji asked.

"Suleiman comes home and gives money."

"Is that all that matters?" asked Amma.

"It is important. He is the only son of ours that can support us. Musa will never be able to." Aboo shook his head glumly. "He is an investment from which we may never receive our reward."

Dadaji leaned forward, his eyes fierce and bright. "Musa can still hear the good in him though. He still likes to feel holy. As long as he has that your salvation is secure."

★

Seven miles away, in Babarr's office, another debate concerning Musa raged with greater fury and gusto, so much so that the fellow occupants of the Levenshulme Industrial Unit left their offices and stood listening in a perplexed huddle.

"Babarr you Neanderthal pig!! Wipe it off!"

"Where the fuck do you get off saying that shit!"

"Easy Shabnam! Every man's entitled to his own opinion."

"That's not the opinion of a man. That's the opinion of an asshole!"

Babarr stood at a whiteboard with a marker in his hand.

BOOTY + BEAUTY = PERFECT WIFE

"Babarr, just wipe it off. Anything for a quiet life hey?" said Suleiman.

"The only thing I'm wiping is my ass. My opinion is just as important as everyone else's."

Babarr was holding the floor and was in his element. With his blue dungarees and shiny leather boots he gave every impression that he was the Jack-in-the-box who was born for this task. With him were Armila, Shabnam, Suleiman and Musa; on the board was Babarr's succinct prognosis. They had gathered to agree on a plan, a way of progressing Musa's situation. Armila was there at Musa's request and she was fast becoming the most vocal member of the group. Shabnam had reacted with great surprise when she discovered that Musa had a female friend, and she viewed Armila with veiled distrust.

Suleiman sighed wearily: "OK people, just forget what Babarr has written and focus on the problem. And the problem is, how does Musa go about getting a woman? Best thing to do is this. Babarr you sit the fuck back down and anyone else who has an idea writes it on the board."

Suleiman's suggestion made perfect sense to everyone and Babarr reluctantly sat down. They looked at each other nervously, afraid of derision, afraid of showing their ignorance. Armila cast a furtive look at Shabnam's traditional clothes – an elegant green top and cream shalwar. Her own black dress felt wildly out of place. Nevertheless she had something to add. She strode to the board and with firm definite strokes wrote EDUCATION.

Babarr snorted in contempt but heeded Suleiman's warning glance and said nothing. Shabnam smiled wistfully at Armila as Babarr grabbed the marker and wrote LOOKS. Armila and Shabnam were enraged but they chose not to speak. Suleiman wrote DECENCY and then handed the marker to Musa.

"You have the final say Musa; make sure it's a good one."

Without hesitation he wrote PURITY.

For the first time in Musa's memory, Suleiman smiled affectionately at him.

"OK. We've got something now. We want to find someone who's got looks, decency and purity."

Babarr stood up excitedly: "I know someone like that Musa."

"Who Babarr, who?"

"Thing is Musa, I don't think she's got any degrees or anything. That OK with you?"

"No problem at all!"

"Well, she's got beautiful fair skin and long thick hair. She lives with her stepmom who's a real bitch and makes her do all the housework but she never complains."

"Who is she?" asked Musa enthusiastically.

"Another thing with this girl is she is pure and kind even though her two stepsisters make her life a misery."

"Who is she?" demanded Musa.

"Her name is…Cinderella. Yep, Musa, you got it, Cinderella is your ideal wife." Babarr collapsed in gales of laughter.

Musa looked at him with contempt but Suleiman smiled.

"OK you asshole. Cool it. Let's be serious now. C'mon I want to hear some real ideas."

Babarr regained his composure. "Look, this whole thing is a crock of shit. I mean no way are you gonna get a woman with all those things, man it's just too damn much."

"At some point Musa will have to compromise, but until then let's do what we can," said Armila.

"I agree. You never know what's around the corner," said Shabnam.

"Hip fucking hooray. We all agree on something. But what now?" said Suleiman.

"We need to start looking," said Musa.

"Yeah, but where?" asked Suleiman.

"On the internet," said Armila. "Loads of people I know find their partners that way.

"That's a good idea," said Suleiman and he wrote her suggestion on the board.

"What about agencies?" said Shabnam.

"What agencies?" asked Suleiman.

"You know, Muslim matrimonial agencies and that Aunty bitch on Zee TV. Stuff like that."

Suleiman nodded and wrote AGENCIES on the board.

"What about if we just asked around, you know like friends or girlfriends of friends or just girls…that sort of thing," said Babarr.

Suleiman wrote CONTACTS on the board and asked, "Anything else?"

Nothing else came to them. Contemplating the list, Shabnam shuddered at the coldness of such a clinical analysis. She turned to gaze at her younger brother and recalled something the guy she'd met at the party possessed in spades but which Musa did not.

"Everybody, I see a problem. Look at Musa," said Shabnam.

"Stand up for a sec," said Suleiman.

Musa warily did as he was told.

"Yeah I see it. Do you see it Babarr?"

"Yup."

"What is it? What do you all see?" asked a worried Musa.

"What they're trying to say is that you lack charisma," said Armila gently.

"You look like a pussy," confirmed Babarr bluntly. "To get a girl you gotta talk the talk and walk the walk," he continued. "Ain't no way you gonna get the woman the way you are now."

"What can I do to change?" asked Musa.

"Listen Musa, Confucius once said to whip ass in real life is to whip ass for the second time around. Once in your head, second time outside your head. You gotta make it real inside your head," said Babarr.

"How do I do that?"

Shabnam laughed. "Part of the problem is the beard. You've never shaved in your entire life. You gotta be clean cut." She put her arm around his shoulders. "And the dress. You gotta dress smart, not prehistoric. Suleiman, take him across to Haji's."

"You ready to lose the beard Musa?" Suleiman asked.

"Yes," said Musa.

"You absolutely sure Musa? There's no going back."

His beard, the mark of the mullah, the symbol of piety, would be gone. No more would people tag him with the label "virtuous". The facial appendage that had grown in spurts had for a long time been commensurate with his faith. Now one would go and the other would stay, perhaps. Mutely, he nodded.

9

Haji's Hairdressers, a family-run business, was started by Younis who by his own admission was no Vidal Sassoon. He was a barber and his repertoire was limited to just the one type of haircut – the skinhead look. The community had long despaired of explaining the demands of fashion to Younis; he would always listen to them politely and smile with tobacco-stained friendliness before proceeding to shave off their hair. Yet the customers still kept coming. This was partly due to his competitive rates but mostly to his zany anecdotal genius. The main source of mirth and banter came from the fact that Younis had two wives: one a cousin from Pakistan, the other a six foot feisty vixen from New Orleans, and the fact that they lived under the same roof multiplied Younis's reputation of virility and manliness. How could this wiry man of diminutive stature quell and control two such disparate entities? How was it possible to have such equable passion? It was noted that the children of the Pakistani wife called their mother Khala, or father's sister, and the New Orleans wife Mum.

The New Orleans wife had just one son Shafqat, and he

had followed in his father's small but energetic footsteps although he had inherited his mother's imposing physique. He it was who attended to Musa's beard.

"You OK then, boss?" said Shafqat pleasantly.

"Mmm," said Musa.

"You home for good then?"

"Nope, just the bad," laughed Musa.

"Thought you lot were never meant to shave."

"Times are changing Shafqat. Even mullahs have to change with them."

"Can you be a mullah without the beard boss?" asked Shafqat politely.

"Well it's all relative; it depends on who you ask and how much he knows about Allah."

"You come back to get a woman then?" asked Shafqat after a long pause.

"Yeah," said Musa wearily.

"You gonna get a Holy Jane type, you know the one that prays five times a day and all that?" asked Shafqat.

"Nope, most definitely not," said Musa.

Shafqat looked surprised: "Why not boss?"

"Believe it or not Shafqat, they're too opinionated. It's like they all try to be men or better than men."

"Nothing wrong with that boss, not much fun in them being women!"

"But you see that's where you're wrong. Women were created with natures that complement men's. They were made to be feminine and gentle just as men were made to be strong and fearless."

"You gotta lot to learn, you have," said Shafqat gravely.

"I know but at least I'm in a better place to learn it," said Musa.

"No arguing with that, boss," said Shafqat.

"You know something, since leaving the Madrasah, I hardly ever argue now."

"You're just like my wife. First time she came from Pakistan all she wanted to do was argue and talk shit. Soon as she gotta bit of responsibility it all went out of her."

"So what now? You agree to disagree?" asked Musa.

"No boss, she just shuts the fuck up because the kids are noisier."

"You ever wonder what it would have been like with anyone different."

"I'm not the wondering type boss. I just get on with it."

"Is that enough?" asked Musa, barely opening his eyes.

"If it ain't I sure as hell don't miss what's left," replied Shafqat.

Shafqat now began to cut Musa's hair. Musa relaxed. He remembered a talk given at the Madrasah by some guy who had a beautiful long white beard and who hated the clean shaven in his audience. At that time Musa's beard was in its infancy; a soft downy growth of hair covering the skin underneath his chin. He frowned trying to remember his name... Sheikh Farooqi...yes that was it. He remembered clearly now. Sheikh Farooqi was an asshole who had a degree in hotel management and was a conscientious manager of a hotel in Karachi. The story went that Sheikh Farooqi had taken pity on a pair of powerfully built strangers who carried gigantic back packs and had no credit cards but heavy money belts bulging with dollars.

After ascertaining that they were not homosexuals (apparently they were too shabbily dressed) he had allowed them to stay in a suite at single room rates. Later that evening, when the Sheikh was in his room on the first floor, a bomb exploded in the hotel. The hapless Sheikh fell through the floor and landed in the nightclub that, for the sake of propriety, was situated underground. As he lay on the floor among the debris and the remains of half-naked dancers, he renounced his profession and became a scholar.

Sheikh Farooqi was fanatical in his belief that the longer and more unkempt the beard, the brighter the spiritual light. At that talk he recalled a saying: every time you shave an angel collects your hair and on the day of judgement weaves the hair into a rope and strangles you. Musa smiled at that picture and for his own pleasure imagined himself picking up the Sheikh by his long beard and repeatedly smashing his head into the ground.

Gradually the rhythm of hammering the Sheikh's head became a lullaby. Shafqat smiled as he saw Musa's head drop. So like a kid, he thought. He noticed the copper-brown streaks in Musa's hair. Javed had hair like that. The old man, Itrat, took a great deal of pride in his first born. Javed had everything that everyone around him craved. He was handsome, charming and charismatic. Guys resented him but nonetheless flocked around him; and the girls were smitten. He looked at his sleeping customer; remembering the last time he ever saw Javed.

It was a very hot summer. Javed had walked into the shop carrying Musa and said, "Hey Shafqat. I need a massive favour. Can you take care of him for a couple of hours!"

"What! Are you crazy?"

"I gotta go somewhere," explained Javed.

"What about your family?"

"They've had to take Mum to hospital. I was left with this." He looked with annoyance at his smiling brother. "There's something I just gotta do."

Javed smiled and winked at him and Shafqat understood but did not smile back. Javed checked his wallet and quickly left the shop. Shafqat picked up Musa and he had smiled thinking he was going to be taken outside. He laughed and clapped his hands excitedly. Shafqat gently ruffled the copper brown curls. He was a cute, unspoiled child. Musa had then pointed to the door and said "Sally". Shafqat held him very close then.

When Javed returned his face was flushed and he smelt slightly acidic.

"Thanks Shafqat, you're a star!" He pressed a ten pound note into his hand.

"I only get paid for cutting hair man!"

"Take it. You've earned it. He's a noisy bastard."

"Hey, don't speak like that about your brother."

Javed winked at him, picked up Musa and sauntered out of the shop.

That was the last time he saw him. Suleiman would still come in now and then. Always quiet and always looking at everyone longer than he needed to...

"Wake up boss. You're done."

Musa yawned and opened his eyes, squinting at the blurry world around him.

"How long have I been asleep?"

"Twenty minutes boss. Turn round and have a look at yourself."

Musa swivelled the chair round and looked at himself in the mirror with a curious detachment. He saw someone with large, intense eyes flecked with sapphire and emerald. His eyes were drawn to the fairness of his skin now shorn of the beard and the cut of his jaw was smooth.

He felt a gentle hand on his head and saw Shafqat smiling at him in the mirror.

"You look good Musa." He did not add that his expression of innocence was striking.

"Thank you Shafqat. How much do I owe you?"

"It's been sorted."

"How come, when?" asked Musa.

"Sixteen years ago," replied Shafqat softly and before Musa could ask any more questions he added, "You'd better get going. They'll be wondering what happened to you."

Surprising himself, he embraced Shafqat and left the shop. Shafqat smiled sadly after him. Younis who had been watching from the back of the shop followed his gaze.

"He's an exact copy, isn't he? Do you ever think about him?"

Shafqat shook his head. "He was a no-good."

Back at the Unit, Musa stood before his detractors, still without a firm posture of manliness, yet there was a difference, an awareness. Babarr spoke first.

"You looked like a pussy before and now you look like a goddamn rent boy."

"Babarr! Cool it," said Suleiman. "I think he's got it. What's your view Sis?"

"Yeah…Most definitely he has something but I can't put my finger on what it is," said Shabnam thoughtfully.

"I think you look amazing, Musa," said Armila enthusiastically.

Suleiman rolled his eyes: "OK, so you're not an ugly bastard but that doesn't change the world any."

"That's very true. It helps but not by a great deal," said Shabnam. "Having a pleasing appearance doesn't give you much of an edge in this day and age. Girls want more these days. You gotta know how to use what Allah has given you. Lots of guys act like they got it when they ain't got shit and then they try to compensate by being too macho. Other guys know they ain't got it and try to compensate by trying to be too intellectual and too deep. You gotta find your own tuning frequency," said Shabnam.

"You gotta market what you got, Musa, 'cos the competition to find a good wife is crazy. Everyone is turning cartwheels to get the right woman but nobody knows for sure what to do," said Suleiman.

"How do they find wives then?" asked Musa.

"A lot of them get tired Musa. They make do," explained Suleiman.

"So what about me? Do I go on the internet or ask around or what? What's the plan?" asked Musa.

"The plan has gotta be for you to be confident in your

own shoes. Once you are we can try the other stuff," said Suleiman.

"That's right, Musa. You gotta walk your walk and talk their talk," said Shabnam.

"How do I go about doing that?" asked Musa puzzled.

"You have to learn by assimilating your own life experiences," said Armila.

"All of you is talking shit," said Babarr. "Confucius once said that the path of the lover begins like the path of the whore but finds its destination because of the guidance of the loved one."

"Babarr shut the fuck up!" said Shabnam.

"Titty Soups," said Babarr in reply.

"Titty Soups…Titty Soups…Genius, Babarr," said Suleiman excitedly.

"Who's Titty Soups?" asked Shabnam.

"Titty Soups is the guy that's gonna progress this."

"How?" asked Armila.

"You'll soon find out," said Suleiman. "Go on Babarr, you take him to see Titty Soups."

10

Babarr pulled up outside the fabulous Raj restaurant. "This is his joint. You go inside and I'll find a place to park," said Babarr.

The inside of The Raj was sumptuous to the point of excess. Chrystal chandeliers sparkled and sent patterns of coloured light across the marble floor. A waiter stood behind the bar adjusting his bow tie and clearly listening to a conversation between the owner of the restaurant and a young woman. Holding her hands the man nodded gently and rhythmically as he spoke.

"Look Rekha, you're crowding this relationship with your expectations. I can't fly solo with you right now baby. I gotta have my own space."

She whispered something inaudible, though her brimming eyes said it all.

The man appeared to be unmoved.

"You mean a lot to me baby but I can't give you the lease to my heart. It's too much right now. You gotta let this relationship grow on its own, sweetheart."

"Yo, Titty Soups you son of a bitch," boomed Babarr, barging through the door.

Titty Soups smiled broadly. "Hey Babarr! How ya

doing?" He was promptly engulfed in a great bear hug.

Babarr pulled him to one side and they engaged in a whispered discussion. Titty Soups laughed and threw his arm around Babarr's shoulder, and Rekha left the restaurant in tears.

Legend had it that when Titty Soups first arrived at the local comprehensive from Pakistan he had gone to the school canteen during the lunch break. On that particular day two of the girls were eating soup, and when he walked past them they were so awestruck by his good looks that their spoons missed their wide open mouths and the soup landed on their breasts.

The boys who witnessed this incident christened him Titty Soups, a name which stuck.

Babarr beckoned to Musa. "Shake hands with my man Titty Soups here."

Titty Soups gave Musa a critical once over. "Not bad. Not bad at all. The kid has it Babarr. He most definitely has it!"

"Is it enough?" asked Babarr.

Titty Soups grabbed Musa's arm and gently felt for muscle.

"He's got no body tone."

"What the fuck do you expect? He's spent half his life in a madrasah!" said Babarr.

Titty Soups shook his head. "Even so."

"Even so what?" asked Babarr.

Titty Soups grabbed Musa's buttocks and shook him fiercely.

"Ouch!" cried Musa.

"Sorry, kid," said Titty Soups.

He looked at Babarr: "Do you see what I mean? Do you see the waves? Women don't like that."

"Give the kid a break Titty. A month in the gym and he'll be sorted."

Titty Soups looked gravely at Musa. "You see kid. You know when they say beauty is in the eye of the beholder they're absolutely fucking right. If you've got it, you know it. You know how you know it?"

Musa shook his head.

"You get to recognise a certain look in a woman's eye. Only then do you know for sure that you have it. Guys spend half their lives in the bathroom looking at themselves in the mirror trying to see if they've got it. They never seem to get that they've got shit. You gotta know it for yourself kid. You gotta see that look on a woman. Everything follows on from there."

"But how do I tell the difference between a normal look and the kind of look that you're talking about?" asked Musa.

Titty Soups pointed outside.

"Out there on the street, at this time of the day, every Asian girl is walking around all pretty and dolled up. And every Asian guy is out there hunting and walking like he's got a rod jammed up his ass. But you my friend are gonna blow them all away. I want you to walk out of here exactly as you are and walk up and down the road. Every time you see a group of girls you make sure you get in their line of vision. Every time you see some guys you act like you're about to square up to them. Do that until you're about ready to drop and then come back here," said Titty Soups.

Titty Soups placed his hand on Musa's back and escorted him to the door. "Go get'em tiger," he said.

Musa made for the Shalimar shopping mall, famed for being the first shopping centre to cater solely for the needs of the indigenous Asians.

The mall was teeming with girls. At first glance, huddled in aimless groups of four or five, just like their male counterparts, they all seemed to be very glamorous and flighty.

Musa jumped on the escalator and took in the glitzy array of neon-lit advertising boards. Indistinct pop songs sounded across the mall, adding to the carefree ambience.

As he looked down he could see Asian couples larking around by the fountain, completely oblivious to custom or consequence. At the top of the escalator he stopped for a second deciding which way he would head. His eyes fell on a young girl who stood perfectly still. She wore a long black traditional outfit that made her look sleek and refined. Her face had that rich dark texture which is predominantly seen in Indian girls.

They looked at each other in a moment of shared existence and then she gave a nervous laugh and was gone. That was the look: a completely natural reaction of surprise and wonder that was utterly pure.

Musa stood there for a long time, trying to build a world out of that moment. A wonderful, crazy feeling came over him. Anything and everything was possible. What if he were to run after her and make something happen? It could happen! The force of what they had experienced could overcome anything. He sighed. Not now. He just did not have it within him but if he could arrest a girl's attention once, he could do it again…and again.

But how awful it was to meet someone like that and then watch them walk away: to experience magic but only in passing. Was marriage really pre-ordained? Could a man with will and hope carve a different path for himself?

He most certainly could, thought Musa. He smiled and started to hum as he walked. A man most certainly could and he, a Holy man, and a good-looking one at that, most certainly would.

Musa made his way back to the The Raj. Titty Soups was once more leaning by the bar, every inch the suave ladies' man.

"Hey Musa. How was it?"

Musa smiled.

"That good? Huh? Did you get the look kid?"

Musa nodded.

"Well, kid, the battle has just begun. Now you gotta get inside their heart and that's the most difficult thing. The greatest looking guy is the greatest asshole in the world if he doesn't have the right personality. You take Babarr. The first time you see him you think a condom stuffed with walnuts. You get to know him a little bit and you see that he pretty much acts that way. But even if you and me work out like crazy there ain't no way we could ever act that way because his personality goes with his appearance. If you pretend to be something you're not you become an asshole. If you try too hard you become an even bigger asshole and if you don't try at all you become even worse than an asshole. A loser. You gotta watch and learn Musa. Watch and learn.

"A girl's coming by soon. Her name is Neelam and she is hot, hot, hot! But at the moment she's going out with this loser Akhshay. Now I know Akhshay and there ain't no way a girl like that is going with a guy like that if you get what I mean. Now I gotta bit of insider info that Akhshay is coming on too strong and she don't like that.

"So all I gotta do is go softly…softly and then—" he suddenly brought his hands together in a tremendous clap, "Wham Bam Thank you Ma'am! Fast Titty does it in a jiffy!"

"What about Rekha?"

"Who?" Titty Soups asked.

Musa sighed as the door opened.

"Neelam sweetheart. How ya doing?"

"I'm fine Titty. Sorry I'm so late."

Neelam was all flowing hair. She had one of those rare faces that would have looked good on a man or a woman yet her appeal was not androgynous and she had a full flowing figure which she was obviously comfortable revealing. She threw her arms around Titty Soups and gave him a brief chaste kiss on the cheek.

"Who's this?" she asked, turning to Musa.

"He, my darling, is our waiter for this evening," said Titty Soups. He gave Musa a knowing wink.

"He seems a little strangely dressed to be a waiter," said Neelam.

"It's his first day," replied Titty Soups.

With the grace of a ballerina he placed a gentle hand on Neelam's back and guided her to a candle-lit table filled with steaming dishes. Musa stood attentively nearby, ostensibly waiting for any additional orders.

"So...how's life?" asked Titty Soups so softly it was almost a whisper.

Neelam, a woman weary of the injustices of life, raised a hand to her forehead.

"What can I say? He's so jealous."

Titty Soups' brown eyes saddened slightly as he began to shake his head.

"I could see it coming a mile off, Neelam. You see he's been raised in a place where love was rationed and all this has had an effect on him." A note of contempt had crept into his voice.

"You see Titty it's like this. I said to him Akshay I love you but I'm not in love with you and he just couldn't seem to get that. What is it with you men? Why do you always demand the impossible?"

Titty leant closer and gently began to stroke her hand. His touch was light and delicate.

"I just think he wants more out of this relationship than you, Neelam. It's Einstein's theory of relativity. You take two Asians who want a happy and fulfilling relationship. The bloke goes off to cloud-cuckoo-land and the woman keeps her feet on the ground. When the bloke comes back he finds that she's close to the finishing line in their relationship and he still hasn't moved past first base."

Neelam nodded at the inherent logic of his argument and smiled ruefully.

"Akhshay is no Einstein."

Titty Soups moved his chair next to hers and brushed her cheek with the back of his index finger.

"Baby, don't be so hard on yourself. Before you entered this relationship did you sign an agreement that stated you must take all the responsibility? Let's start eating," he whispered and helped her first to a dish of fragrant rice on which he heaped a little of each of the delicacies spread before them. They ate slowly, Titty gazing at Neelam all the while. He reached out and again caressed her cheek. Musa watched and became aware that he had stopped breathing.

Titty Soups, keeping his eyes on Neelam, gestured to the stairs with a nod of his head. She stood up and he quickly followed her. As he passed Musa he raised his hand in anticipation of a High Five.

"No peeking," he whispered.

Musa was greeted by the pungent odour of tobacco and the sound of the hookah bubbling slowly as its smoker chewed over his thoughts. Dadaji was still awake and Musa realised that he had been waiting for him.

"Come in *Barkhodar*." Musa smiled at hearing his grandfather call him respected friend.

Musa sat on the floor and waited for the patriarch to speak. Dadaji rested his head against the wall, dislodging his turban slightly as he did so. His eyes were narrowed with introspection.

"What have you seen? What have you lost?" he asked softly.

Musa sensed the underlying question. Most of Dadaji's questions were oblique; plain talk was not something he was familiar with.

"I saw many things. Some of them I may well forget others I will never forget."

"When the veil of the beard is undone, the things you see are not always what they seem. Shaitan casts his arrow hard and the first arrow is always aimed at the eye."

"Must it always come back to that?"

Dadaji leant forward, his face animated and amused.

"You have seen yourself exalted in the eyes of women, have you not?"

"Yes I have. How did you know?" asked Musa.

"You are filled with pride. I have seen such pride in women who know the power of their appearance."

"Are these women any happier because of their power?"

Dadaji settled back again. He seemed pleased by the question.

"Those who are born with physical beauty cause riots in the eyes of those around them. A riot in a person's eye speaks of passion in his heart."

"Doesn't passion come about because a person wants so badly to have those things which are not in front of him?"

"Can you see what is in front of you Musa? Only

yesterday you were a child so how can you tell the real from the illusory? A lie from the truth?"

"But why do you need to know these things? Why should every moment of life be a quest to seek hidden meanings? I am not a Sufi, Dadaji. Neither do I want to be. I just want to be me, Musa."

"What I am trying to tell you is that every time a woman looks at you with a lusty eye it is not a guarantee of happiness. It is not a doorway to Heaven."

Hearing the compassion in his voice Musa respected his grandfather but without thinking he replied in English, "Yeah but who gives a shit?"

Dadaji looked amused and Musa had the strange feeling that he had understood every word.

"What I am trying to say is maybe you're right. When a woman looks at you it doesn't always mean that the Angel Gabriel is going to come down from the seventh heaven and lift you up. And it doesn't have to mean that Shaitan is going to take you by the hand and lead you off to hellfire. All it means is that someone has looked at you and liked you. That someone could be a tramp or a princess. It doesn't matter. All that matters is that she looked at you and for a little while you flew. That's a great feeling to have Dadaji. To feel like you're young and going places that maybe you never knew you could go to. You don't always have to know the truth to be happy."

"You sound as if you are ready for your first day," said Dadaji.

"I think maybe I am."

Dadaji smiled and lay down again. He raised his thumb

147

and forefinger to the bridge of his nose, as if he were trying to recall something he wanted to say. But no words came. And Musa was too tired for any more soul-searching questions. Dadaji lived in his own world, and the view from his world influenced everyone else's. There was no denying his presence although Musa felt there was now little to fear from this frail, dignified old man.

He remembered the stories he had heard about him when growing up: the tyrannical overlord who forbade his pregnant mother from joining her husband; the ferocious father who pushed his baby daughter on to the floor when she was placed next to him; the violent man who beat one of his sons senseless and then refused to pay to send him to hospital. He had never demonstrated his concern yet somehow he commanded the devotion of all around him.

Dadaji's head fell to one side. Musa carefully spread the thin blanket over him, making sure that he would not be exposed to the uncertain cold of the night.

The motorway roared with the frenetic sounds of cars occupied by people maddened by their haste. The competitors for the greatest speed were infuriated by a silver Passat that motored along sedately in the middle lane at 52 mph and as they overtook the car, they horned their anger at the nonchalant driver who responded to their abuse with an index finger so casually flicked upwards he might have been drying his nail varnish.

A passenger in the backseat was becoming annoyed by the continual interruptions.

"Suleiman, do you think you could maybe drive faster or should I get out and run ahead and tell them we're on our way?" asked Shabnam.

"Calm down sis. If I drove any faster, you wouldn't have as much time to prepare Musa. Look at him, he's about ready to crap himself. Ain't that so Musa?"

Musa responded to the solicitous concern of his brother by raising his own index finger in a slightly more agitated manner. Suleiman chuckled and settled back, humming to himself.

Shabnam asked, "This Armila girl. Who is she? Why is

she going to all the trouble of surfing through the internet and registering with muslimbrides.co.uk and finding a bride for you?" she queried sharply.

"Calm down, Shabnam. Musa met her when he went to work for Babarr and they hit it off big time. They're always on the phone to each other," said Suleiman.

"When I answered and she told me that she'd found a bride for Musa, she sounded like she was my mum! She is one bossy cow!"

"Maybe you two have a lot more in common than you think!" grinned Suleiman.

Shabnam glared at the back of his head and then reached into her bag and pulled out a set of cards which she had prepared for Musa.

"OK Musa, let's start again." She cleared her throat. "Are you a man's man or a wussy good-doing mama's boy?"

Musa sighed and dutifully read out the response on the card.

"Unfortunately I have never taken part in any serious physical activity and I have never been involved in any punch-ups which is just as well because I would have been flattened." He was about to protest but Shabnam waved him on. "So in that sense of the word, no I am not a man. I do, however, have other advantages. I have memorised the Quran and am knowledgeable in other important areas of Islam. If you marry me I can perform the marriage ceremony for other people in your family and I can teach the Quran to our children and any other children in the family. You will never have to hire an imam and that means you will have more money to play with. And since I have no real concept of money, that money would be your money…"

Musa threw down the card. "I can't take this shit anymore!"

Shabnam promptly handed him another. "Come on now, just a few more. How do you feel about your wife wearing cosmetics?"

Musa looked puzzled as he read the reply. "I think cosmetics are the greatest invention since computers. Cosmetics make women look beautiful. I see no reason why men can't use light cosmetics. It is unfair that women should have all the pressure of looking good."

"Are you marrying this girl or Musa?" asked Suleiman contemptuously.

"Shut up Suleiman, concentrate on the driving. OK Musa, how do you feel about housework?"

"It is a duty and a privilege for a man to participate in it," read out Musa.

"Privilege my ass," muttered Suleiman.

Shabnam punched the back of the driver's seat. "All right Musa, now seal the deal."

Musa squinted at the final card. "I promise not to have more than two children. I promise to respect the moods of my wife. I will not make unreasonable demands and I will honour and obey her until death does me in. *Death does me in!*" he exclaimed.

"Yeah I know it sounds kind of common and plain but if I said 'Death do us part' it would have sounded too much like the way English people marry."

"We're coming off at this junction now. So get ready, we'll be there soon," warned Suleiman.

After a mile Musa saw from the window "Welcome to Nelson" written in faded black letters on a board that hung so loosely from its metal frame that it was about ready to descend on the next welcoming Nelsonion that walked past. He took a deep breath and brushed the front of his black tunic which he was wearing with matching black trousers and a jacket that had a leafy motif around its edges. This outfit had been chosen by Shabnam who wanted to convey an impression of simple elegance. She herself looked suitably attired for the occasion; hair neatly coiffed, green eyeliner to accentuate her eyes, and a white silk tunic and trousers.

Nelson appeared to be a hillier version of his own town. Grim terraced houses were wedged closely together and the streets were noisy. Children played football and laughed gleefully every time the ball ricocheted off a parked car. Elderly Asian women talked ardently outside their front doors. Midway through the terraces were alleys lined with overflowing bins.

"This is it, Carr Road. Parking is gonna be a son of a bitch," said Suleiman but he soon swerved the car into a narrow space between two battered minis.

"Musa, you get out now and get a feel for the place before you knock on the door," said Suleiman.

Musa did as he was told. He shut the car door and stretched his arms. The sun caught his eyes and he lingered in that posture, bathing his face in the warmth. He wondered if there was a prayer he could recite, but it probably wouldn't have made any difference. Aware of the overpowering odour of curry he smiled; he could have just as easily knocked on the door of a Pakistani family living in the street next to them and asked for their daughter's hand in marriage. He began to walk up the road, checking the numbers as he did so.

Back in the car, Suleiman scowled and turned to Shabnam.

"What was the meaning of all that nonsense?"

"I know. I know. It was over the top. But how else could I prep him? He doesn't know his ass from his elbow. You know what he's like. You may not believe this but yesterday I caught him watching some old movie, *An Affair to Remember* or something. You know those weepy films where the hero runs around and speaks in a posh voice and the woman just falls over herself. That's what he thinks this shit is gonna be like." Shabnam shook her head in disgust.

"OK but if you can, act supportive like an older sister is supposed to be. Don't be shoving the law into every man's gob. One day you're gonna go through this shit yourself."

Watching his brother he asked flatly, "What's the name of this little bombshell?"

"Dinah Hijazi."

"Well, let's go make it happen," said Suleiman.

He got out of the car and opened the door for Shabnam. Re-arranging her scarf around her neck, she paused for a moment and gauged her brother's clothes. Grey pin-striped suit with red braces, all very flash.

"You rob a bank?" she asked, almost afraid of the answer.

"You got your secrets. I got mine. C'mon let's go."

Musa, meanwhile, had found the front door open. He called out, "Assalaam-u-alaikum" but there was no response. He stepped into a narrow dark hall and heard a commotion upstairs.

"C'mon Musa, look lively. Don't just stand there gawking," said Shabnam sharply. She pushed past him and shouted out hello. Again, nothing.

"Isn't that pathetic? They knew we were coming. I'll go and find someone. You two plonk your asses in the living room." She nodded to her left and then strode briskly ahead to a door with no handle.

Suleiman suddenly seemed very uncomfortable.

"I'll go with Shabnam."

To Musa's surprise, next to a bulging bookshelf in the living room sat a stout, bearded man with pomaded hair who jerked his head as if avoiding invisible tennis balls. Gingerly Musa edged forwards and sat on a small sofa facing him. There was a metallic noise of something snapping and he felt his backside slam against the hard wooden base. His knees came together and his arms were pinned to his sides.

The bearded man jumped at the sound, and his head started to oscillate wildly. "Who's there?" he asked nervously.

"Um…Musa," replied Musa fearfully.

The bearded man's head became still.

"Ah, you're here to see Dinah aren't you?" His voice sounded odd, like that of a wheezy fortune-teller, prophesying gloom and doom.

"Yes."

"Excellent. My name is Tahir. I'm her brother." Tahir's head started to move up and down, in an approving manner.

"Hope we haven't kept you waiting too long, Tahir," said Musa, unconsciously moving his head up and down.

"Not at all. We were wondering when you would show up–" he paused and slowly turned his face upwards, his eyes half closed, as if trying to smell Musa's potential. "You're a Holy man right?"

At that moment Musa understood: Tahir was *blind*. He stared at him in fascination. He was certainly very well turned out: his brown checked shirt and corduroy trousers were clean and freshly pressed, and his suede shoes with black calf caps at the front looked new.

Pulling himself together, Musa answered the question. "I suppose so."

"You've memorised the Quran haven't you! That's wicked."

"What do you do?" asked Musa.

"I've just finished my PhD in chemistry. Unfolding of Proteins," he said proudly.

Tahir began to talk about his research, how his interest in the double-helix structure led him to the intricacies of protein, how he started to understand its ability to synthesise with all chemicals, and an image lofty enough to make angels swoon wafted to the fore of Musa's panic-ridden mind. Dinah Hijazi, that saintly sibling who cared for her brother, tied his shoe laces, ironed his clothes, and probably even went to the laboratory with him to inform him of that eureka moment when the protein finally unfolded. He could see it all now! His wife! That beatific personification of virtue. It didn't matter how she looked. In all likelihood she had that inner radiance from which all beauty gushed like a fountain of petals. And he would stand tall and proud at the apogee of this paradisal flow, bathing himself in the exquisite tenderness of her care. Unbidden the picture took shape in his mind. Coming home from the madrasah or wherever it was he would be working, she would be awaiting him with a warm soft smile of welcome. Ah!

Just then, the door opened and Musa's heart leapt.

"Is it OK to come in?" Such a cheery voice thought Musa. Could it be?

"Yes, come on in," answered Tahir.

"Is that her?" asked Musa eagerly.

"No. That's Samira, my other sister," replied Tahir.

With an effort, Musa got up. He saw a grinning face and he saw the footsteps, faltering and hesitant whilst carrying a tray of steaming tea. Samira put down the tray carefully and smiled in his direction. She had black frizzy hair, a dark complexion that shone with sweat and she too was blind. She, like Shabnam, was traditionally dressed but her pink woollen tunic and trousers looked as if they had seen one too many winters.

"Hello Musa. How are you?" she asked brightly.

"Oh I'm fine," he replied, trying to keep his voice smooth and his heart-beat steady.

"Tahir's not showing off is he? He can sometimes be a terrible show-off!"

"No, not at all, far from it. Um…excuse me, I need to find my brother and sister." Musa hurriedly brushed past her.

"Your brother's in the front room," Samira called out after him.

He found Suleiman holding a cup of tea but unable to drink as his face was just centimetres from that of a gaunt old man. The father, perhaps. Only the back of his head was visible and a few white wispy hairs stood out along that smooth round brown skull.

"You see my son it is like this. When I came to this country in 1964, I had nothing. Only a set of instructions of how to send money. And I think to myself, how am I going to support all my family. But then work was easy to find. And you know I worked eighteen or nineteen hours a day. No holidays. People said to me you need to be spending quality time with your missis.

"So one day I said to my boss that I wanted to take a day off and I told him why. He says OK, he was happy for me and all my mates clapped when I left work but when I got home, you know what my wife says? She calls me a lazy bastard. I say, 'I want to spend some time with you.' And she say, 'Don't try to fool me, I know. God gives you night-time for that, day-time you supposed to work. Go back to work. Don't be lazy. How do you think we will pay for the marriages of our two daughters if you don't work?' And I am very much surprised, but now I can see the truth. Daughters honest to God, they are a mercy but they are a burden as well?"

Before Suleiman could respond, the old man launched

into another monologue. Musa shook his head in dismay and went off in search of Shabnam. She was coming out of an upstairs room and was standing on the landing, a wide smile on her face and the rarity of this spectacle startled him.

"Shabnam, come here!" he hissed.

"What's up?"

"We have to leave. They're all blind."

"Don't be a schmuck. Sometimes it happens in families."

"What do you mean it happens? How does it happen?" exclaimed Musa.

"If the mother and father are related then the genes are too similar, if you know what I mean. Don't tell me you don't know people like that Musa?"

He scowled at his sister. "Let's get the hell out of here! I've got a bad feeling about this place!"

"There's no need to wet yourself. The girl you're supposed to see, Dinah, apparently she's as right as rain."

"Have you spoken to her?"

"A little…" said Shabnam cautiously.

"What about the mum? Have you seen her?" asked Musa.

"No and neither have they!" Shabnam laughed at the cleverness of her joke.

Musa gave her a contempt-laden look.

"No, seriously, she died a long time ago. The poor old father's been bringing up the family on disability benefits and his pension."

She suddenly grabbed hold of Musa and shook him as

if he were a flea-ridden dog. "Listen, don't be going to pieces now. Go to the bathroom and freshen up!"

Musa shook his head glumly and walked up the stairs. He tried what he thought was the bathroom door but it was locked.

"Just a minute!" called out a strained voice.

It must be Dinah! He quickly ran his fingers through his hair, and straightened his collar. That first encounter was imminent, that moment of which Titty Soups was a master. The door handle turned and out flew an apparition with long black hair. A hand waved in front of his face.

"Wouldn't go in there if I were you!" said a jovial voice.

Before he could even blink, she had run along the landing. Musa stared after her, not even aware that his head was cocked at a 45-degree angle, and followed her downstairs.

The house had become quiet and then he understood: they were preparing the girl to meet him. He opened the door of the living room and collapsed into the armchair where Tahir had been sitting earlier, aware of the hammering of his heart. An uneasy tight feeling was building up inside his temples so he tried to relax his neck and let his head hang back like a dead fish. Grimly he realised what he must do. When he was at the Madrasah, a brother had told him that if you were ever uncertain about marrying someone, all you had to do was recite a Name of Allah and the truth would slowly manifest itself in your heart. But what was that mystical Name? Ah...yes...he remembered now...*Al-Batin*, "the hidden" and you had to recite it an odd number of times.

Musa thought nineteen was a good choice as it was reputed to be a mystical number. He began reciting, his eyes closed and his hands clasped and a vision came to him. He was knocking at the bathroom door with two young children behind him. The children were wearing black shades and holding scented handkerchiefs to their noses. Musa suddenly sat up straight as if having woken from a nightmare.

He turned, bug-eyed, to see Dinah Hijazi coming into the room. She was bent right over with a long black cloth over her head looking for all the world like a submarine. Samira walked alongside, her arm around Dinah's shoulders and grinning like a maniac. She gave her sister an encouraging squeeze and then she was gone.

Immediately Dinah threw off the black cloth and jumped on to the sofa. Two hands shot in the air with their forefingers outstretched.

"Chill!" she grinned.

"Um…How are you?" Musa's voice was weak.

"Wicked!" That same brilliant smile.

"Err…I met your brother. He's quite a guy. To have accomplished so much in his condition. That's one hell of an achievement."

Dinah nodded emphatically and Musa, remembering the locomotion of her brother, shuddered.

"Yep! He is the dog's bollocks when it comes to books and stuff. He is like the Terminator when it comes to knowledge. What he don't see he remembers! He used to try and make me a bit clever when I was a kid, but I just ran away when he wasn't looking...Get it? When he wasn't *looking!*" She shook with laughter.

Musa found it difficult to observe her. She was a blur of perpetual motion. Her head bobbed from side to side making her hair fly around her shoulders and she constantly moved her hands. Her gigantic teeth were mesmeric and with every syllable she spoke her gums were revealed. She was wearing a black and white striped turtleneck jumper with blue jeans, pink Mickey Mouse socks and her slippers were those giant-sized furry monstrosities normally worn by children.

Eventually she managed to gain control of herself and wiped her eyes. "So Holy Man, tell me a bit about yourself. Were you born holy or did your dad tell you to become holy? My dad's always having a go at me to learn some of that jazz, but I just ain't got no time for it. I'll get into it when I get into it, like maybe when I'm old and stuff. But right now, it's like you can't be doing your head in with stuff that does your head in. You get what I'm saying?"

"I suppose so. It is written in the Quran, there is no compulsion in religion."

"'zactly. Big up to that. But you're obviously really into all this, no?"

"Well, I have memorised the Quran..."

"Wicked!"

"And I can understand a lot of the Arabic."

"Wicked!"

"And I know a lot about Islamic law and jurisprudence."

"Respect," said Dinah, with her hand raised in that curious gesture.

"So who looks after Tahir?" he asked.

"He does most of his own shit himself. Rest of the stuff, we get a lady from the council to help out."

Dinah folded her arms across her chest, staring at Musa. "You got a woman?"

"No," he answered, baffled.

"You ever had a woman?"

"No!"

"Are you batty?"

"No!"

Dinah raised her hands as if to placate him.

"So what are you looking for in a woman?"

Musa settled back, relieved at this new line of questioning. "Just someone who I can communicate well with. Someone with a good sense of humour. And also I would want her to be feminine but not submissive. Intelligent but not overbearing. Confident but not aggressive. I want her to have house skills but not be house bound."

"Bloody hell mate! Why not get her to do push-ups as well?" said Dinah, and then with a trace of a smile she winked at him.

"You wanna ask me anything?"

Musa shook his head.

"OK then. Later." She jumped to her feet and stretched out her hand.

Musa wondered at her impish smile as he raised his hand to shake hers. She suddenly pulled her hand back and wiggled her fingers in front of her nose.

"Gottcha!" and then she was gone.

"She asked if you were batty?" exclaimed Armila.

"They were all fucking blind!" exclaimed Babarr.

"My eyes! My eyes!" said Suleiman, with his head in his hands.

"I knew it! From the moment I laid eyes on that girl, I knew that this thing was gonna be a crock of shit." Shabnam shook her head despondently.

"You see the problem is that you people are not thinking logically," said Babarr. "Armila here finds a website called muslimbrides.co.uk. I mean come on! What kind of a name is that for a fucking matrimonial service! Can you really see respectable people with normal children saying to themselves, 'Look here love. The kids are getting older, we need to sort them out. Let's log on to muslimbrides.co.uk and that way all our problems will be solved. We can get a daughter-in-law and just chill out watching all those dumb fucking Asian dramas.' I mean does that make sense! Why do you think these assholes gave their details to a website like that in the first place?"

"Because they were probably already stigmatised in the local community," said Armila glumly.

"You got it in one sweetie. Only assholes with weird ass children use the internet to find husbands and wives. It ain't the normal way. If a girl is fit, that girl ain't ever gonna send her picture to some dumb-ass website. People on the street and the next street and street next to that fucking street are all gonna know there's a hot mamma in town. And they're all gonna be hitting on her like a train."

"Where do we go from here?" asked Musa wearily.

"Don't be disheartened Musa, this is a learning curve," said Armila.

"He don't have the fucking time to be going on any learning curves. He's only got one month and then after that his granddaddy is gonna stamp 'Mine' all over his forehead," said Babarr.

"Babarr is right. We all got carried away. No more websites. But what do we do now?" asked Suleiman.

"You know on those Asian channels, there's an advert that says 'Tired of being the bridesmaid and never the fucking bride? Call Aunty.' Well one time, just for a laugh I rang her up, and they make you go through all these options, but at the end I spoke to this woman who was really professional. I think that's an option," said Shabnam.

"What sort of questions did they ask?" said Armila.

"Do you want a professional with a degree? How far are you willing to travel? What height is ideal for you? Those sorts of questions."

"What about you Babarr, you ever hear about Aunty?"

"No, not personally. I know Titty Soups sometimes uses things like that for…erm…opportunities. I could ask him I suppose. But I have heard of people finding partners through proper registered agencies."

"OK, then, are we all agreed? Aunty is our next stop," said Suleiman.

"Fine with me. Can't do much worse," said Musa.

"Let's get busy then. Shabnam, you ring Aunty and sort it out," said Suleiman.

"One more thing, Musa; I'm dividing your day job into two parts," said Babarr.

"What do you mean?" asked Musa.

"You do some work with me in the mornings, in the afternoons you take it easy. Then in the evenings I want you to act as my man in charge of the Islamic Centre," said Babarr swollen with importance.

"What Islamic Centre?" asked Suleiman sharply.

"I'm opening an Islamic Centre on the high street. I bought the building a while back and tonight is the opening night."

"You've opened a mosque?" asked Musa puzzled.

"No, not a mosque, an Islamic Centre. It's like a youth community centre but for Muslims. It's gonna be mixed. So girls is gonna be there with boys. And everyone is gonna be learning and talking about Islam. Musa is gonna be my man for the boys and I'm gonna get someone for the girls."

"People are not gonna like it if you let boys and girls mix. You know how it is," warned Shabnam.

"It'll be OK. I'll get some of the old geezers to come along and I'll be there to make sure nothing happens. It's all cool," smiled Babarr.

"Since when did you get so interested in Islam?" asked Suleiman suspiciously.

Babarr's face became set in a cast of sincerity.

"I want to build something for the next life as well. Confucius once said—"

165

Everyone immediately stood up and began piling out of the room. "You're a bunch of assholes," Babarr called after them.

The Islamic Centre was buzzing. On the stage a young man, his brow heavily furrowed repeated, "Testing, Testing," at the same time gesturing furiously to some guys in the wings. Such was the importance of the occasion that Babarr had shed his weighty gold necklaces and was simply dressed in a black kaftan and white prayer cap. His demeanour was that of a man who knows it falls upon him to bring enlightenment to the multitude of degenerates around him.

A red-carpeted expanse that served as a seating area was adroitly divided into two halves: men on the left and women on the right. In each corner were bookstands that had perched upon them arrays of glossy hardbacks and paperbacks, cassette tapes, and DVDs. Behind the bookstands were animated, bearded young Holy men who were hawking their merchandise in a loud declamatory chorus.

Excited conversation charged the atmosphere with anticipation and every so often impish kids, infected by the mood of the adults, would jump on the stage and prance about, only to flee in terror when subjected to a violent description of their forbears by Babarr. On a row of chairs by the entrance sat several very old men with snowy beards and haggard faces. They looked inimically at the whole vulgar spectacle, flaring their nostrils at the inquisitive children who were intrigued by their spectral appearance.

Musa, as requested by Babarr, stood unobtrusively by the old men. The crowd made him feel uneasy and his eyes continually darted around the hall, deflected by all the excited faces. Their expressions filled him with a sad nostalgia and he cursed Babarr for the foolishness of his sentiments. His intuition told him that men like Babarr suddenly view the bleak terrain of their existence and crave for that something, that inexplicable something, that will make their very innards hum with purpose. They were all terrified of that encroaching abyss, known as "just too busy", which would somehow, some day, rob them of their opportunity to be noticed, to be praised, to be respected. And what better podium could there be for those who crave esteem than Islam, thought Musa. Mosques, Islamic centres, madrasahs abounded with such men. Pompous, self-righteous assholes who used their opinions the way little children used pumps to inflate the tyres of their bicycles. Petty bees buzzing in a hive of hubris.

Babarr strode to the edge of the stage and cleared his throat. He then raised the microphone to his beaming face – oddly he was still wearing heavy gold rings on each finger.

"Assalaam-u-alaikum. My dear brothers and sisters, I would like to welcome you to this opening night of the Islamic Centre. Now, I'm gonna tell you a little story. One time some friends of mine were staying the night in a mosque during the month of Ramadan. Suddenly they hear voices through the thin glass window and then a loud knocking. Two coppers are outside and they say,

'You're under arrest. This is private property. You can't be squatting here.' And my friends say, 'Officers, it's Ramadan' and one of the policemen goes, 'You come on out or I'll Ramdan with you.'"

Babarr threw back his head and laughed. After a brief silence, a faint ripple of laughter coursed through the crowd.

"Now afterwards I says to myself, Babarr why does shit like that happen in today's society? You know why?" he held out his microphone to the audience, inviting an answer, but before anyone could respond he continued, "Ignorance, plain and simple. People just don't know enough about our religion, the religion of Islam. You know why? 'Cos we don't know enough to tell them.

"Now me, I ain't ever been much of a book man. The only book I ever had was an *A-Z* of Lancaster when I was doing taxis. And even then I never looked at it because if I wanted to know about how to get to a place I would ask someone. So it seems logical to me that if you need to know about Islam you need to be asking someone who knows. And all of you know something different about Islam. And what one knows the other can share.

"Now there's gonna be two debating rooms here: one for the girls and one for the boys. Afterwards you can all chill out in the same place to drink coffee and eat biscuits and stuff. But remember boys, lower your gaze and keep your eyes and ears open to what's going on around you. Now for the important part –"

Babarr put his hands on his hips and gazing at the crowd, his eyes and his grin becoming wider by the second, he continued, "I would like you to big it up for the guy who's gonna be your supervisor, your point man. Ladies and gentlemen, brothers and sisters, give it up for Musaaaaaaa…"

The applause was thunderous as Musa joined Babarr on the stage. Putting his arm around him Babarr proudly announced, "This here is the brother who is gonna be the guide for the boys."

"Now, a guide for the girls. I want you to bring your hands together for a very special person. She has just finished studying at the Islamic School for Girls. She, like my man here, has memorised the Quran and upstairs she is like a library of knowledge." He tapped his head gently. "Let's hear it for our sister, Khadija."

With the microphone still in his hand, Babarr clapped gently and everyone else followed suit in a polite, respectful patter of hands. A figure in black emerged from the crowd and made her way up to the stage. She was unusually tall, almost the same height as Musa, and not only was she wearing the customary hijab but her face was veiled by a nikab.

"These two, Musa and Khadija, are here to help you. They will organise what you discuss and what you debate. You show them the respect they deserve because they have both been through a lot to be here. With their help everyone is gonna learn a little bit more."

Babarr began to clap again and the room was filled with the sound of appreciation.

Musa knew that the gaze of veiled girls was not bound by the same sense of propriety as their dress. As he faced

Khadija on the stage he could see that her grey eyes were flecked with deep blue streaks and her look was calm and knowing. As she appraised him he thought he saw a flicker of amusement and her scrutiny made him recall a time when he was perhaps five or six years old, and was taken to the seaside. As he had stared at the grey blue water, he became mesmerised by its serenity. Then suddenly there was a change and he was transfixed by a surge of a thousand furious waves. He remembered being snatched away but as he had looked back, he wanted the angry sea to return to its former glory.

Khadija left the stage and Musa saw that she moved easily and gracefully. That was a rarity with veiled girls. He felt a hand on his shoulder and turned to see Babarr smiling at him.

"Start mingling Musa. You're their shepherd now."

12

The men gathered at the Islamic Centre. Four rows of them, a small minority bearded, sat on plastic folding chairs.

As Musa gazed at his flock, he began to pigeon-hole them. This would make it easier to collate their responses if he was ever asked. The bearded boys, their expressions scornful, were undoubtedly fellow Holy Men. Those who lolled in their chairs with happy-go-lucky smiles could most aptly be characterised as rude boys and were becoming increasingly prominent at such venues. It was fashionable these days to be conversant in Islam, and they had come to the conclusion that their street credibility would multiply ten-fold if they at least knew what all the fuss was about with Muslims and Muslim countries. The remainder, who were quite clearly primed for intellectual debates, fitted the label "coconuts", a slightly derisory term for the Asians who excelled at school and loved such gatherings because it gave them a chance to unleash their highly polished English.

Musa cleared his throat and the room immediately became quiet. A couple of the rude boys winked at each other in a knowing way as if to say "An hour from now you're gonna be laughing your ass off." The coconuts sat up straight, their spinal cords tightening with the grandeur of the occasion. The Holy Men remained scornful.

"My dear brothers, I would like to welcome you to the Islamic Centre. Before I start on the topic for this evening, I would like to stress that this is a debate and not a battle. There are no victors or losers. Everyone's opinion counts. So please do not indulge in any games of one-upmanship. We are all here to learn about Islam through the eyes of others. All we want is to knock on heaven's door one day and be let in so we can stand in gardens through which rivers flow in the company of companions pure and chaste. Have I not just hit the nail on all of your heads brothers?"

Musa looked around and smiled. A few moments of silence followed, then those moments stretched to become minutes and he realised that the image had troubled them. He sighed; he would have to dumb down.

"OK. The topic I want to talk about is 9/11. And I know that everyone has heard too much about it but it is still worth asking ourselves exactly what impact it had on our faith. Did it distance you from Islam or did it deepen your interest?"

An array of arms shot up. Musa briefly surveyed them and decided it would be unjust to select someone and then describe them by their appearance or clothes as he had seen done on *Question Time*. He waved loosely at no one in particular.

"You there, what do you say brother?"

One of the rude boys stood up.

"I think them planes were empty."

The coconuts and the Holy Men were baffled.

"Honest to God, just think about it bro! Are you telling me that a bunch of guys with tin openers could just get out of their seats and beat up the air stewards and then force their way into the captain's seat? No way! Everyone thinks that all air stewards are fairies but that ain't so. Them guys are given training in ju-jitsu and all that shit. No way could they have done that. Them planes were remote controlled!"

"By who?" asked a coconut.

"By the CIA. Who else? Them guys trained him in Afghanistan! Think about it? America needs oil. They bust up a bit of their own yard and get everybody pissed off. Then they go invade Iraq for the oil. It's logical. This is what it's all about?"

"But what did it do for your faith?" pressed Musa.

The rude boy glared at Musa, angered by the interruption.

"Listen bro, I ain't the type that prays five times a day if that's what you mean." He held his hand in the air as if to deflect a torpedo. "One thing about 9/11 that pissed me off was all these guys telling me that I should start praying regular. Now that is a personal thing! No one ain't got any right to tell you what to do! I'm a Muslim at heart. And if your heart ain't pure you can pray fifty times a day and it won't do you any good."

The rest of the rude boys got to their feet and applauded their comrade. One of the coconuts then stood up.

"I'm sorry brother, but I think what you're saying is a load of tosh" – *tosh* lingered in the air like a chemical cloud acrid with contempt. "9/11 was a travesty and a tragedy but it gave birth to Islamophobia and I think it has been indirectly responsible for a lot of anti-Muslim legislation. Because of that day Muslims are treated as if they were Nazis. People do not seem to realise that 9/11 claimed the lives of British Muslims as well."

The coconut sat down and was immediately subjected to a storm of hearty pats on the back.

Then it was the turn of one of the Holy Men to speak.

"My dear brother, there is no such thing as a British Muslim. You cannot live in this corrupt society and be surrounded by all this filth and pollution and still call yourself a Muslim. 9/11 was an act of evil. But evil gives birth to evil. How about the number of Iraqi children that died every month because of UN sanctions? Is that not an act of evil?"

"Tit for tat killing is not justified in Islam," said Musa firmly.

"I know it is not. But we are standing on the wrong side of the fence. We need to tell this government to stop killing our fellow Muslim brothers. We need to make our voices heard!"

"We're getting away from the question. Did 9/11 change you as a Muslim?" asked Musa.

The Holy Joe shook his head wearily.

"I prayed five times a day before 9/11 and I prayed five times a day after 9/11. The only difference is that now I am uncomfortable about praying in public spaces. I would not feel safe. Non-Muslims look at me differently. They see my beard and think that I am a fundamentalist. But, my faith is stronger than ever. It seems to me you can't be both western and Muslim!"

This incensed the rude boys and one of them, his gold earring luminous, pushed back his chair and stood up. Musa recognised him; he was Urfan a neighbour's son.

"If you hate being here so much, how come you haven't left? I bet you've never done a day's work in your life. You say to people I can't get a job because my employers gotta let me pray five times a day and let me wear my tunic and trousers and when they say no, you cry Islamophobia. So why don't you go to places like Afghanistan or Pakistan? Shall I tell you why? 'Cos them places are third world countries and you've got so used to having it cushy here in Britain you can't stand the idea of going back! You lot claim benefits and then talk about Islam. I got news for you bro, when you claim benefits and don't even look for work, you are begging, plain and simple. And begging ain't in Islam!"

Now the Holy Men were enraged. "We all work brother but what we earn and how we earn it is halal. You people are the people of hellfire because you live amongst wolves and follow them like dogs!"

Musa, who had heard similar arguments in the Madrasah and feeling it necessary to restore a little equilibrium, intervened.

"You're going off at a tangent again brothers. The question was whether 9/11 deepened or weakened our faith. I think that watching you guys has pretty much answered the question. 9/11, a grand conspiracy, evil planning, call it whatever you want, didn't weaken our faith much at all because our faith was already weakened by Muslim fighting Muslim, arguing over the smallest thing to the biggest thing."

"I would also like to add something," said one of the coconuts. "Once I read a book by John Simpson, the news guy. In that book he mentions an encounter with Osama bin Laden when he was travelling through Afghanistan with some others. They suddenly get stopped by some people. Osama is with them and he tries to get John Simpson and his camera crew killed. Those around him say no, they are guests and they get the three days' worth of hospitality. Osama then tries to get them run over by offering to pay a truck driver five hundred quid. The truck driver says no and Osama gets so wound up he starts crying. Can you believe that? That is not the behaviour of a Muslim!"

"Who believes anything that the media say?" said a Holy Man.

"You can't trust anyone who ain't one of you!" said Urfan.

"But isn't part of faith based on trust?" asked Musa.

He pointed at a poster on which were printed Arabic words from the Holy Quran.

"Do you know what this means? 'This is the book that contains guidance for those who believe in the unseen.' Get that? To be a good Muslim we have to believe in the unseen. But if we can believe in the unseen even though we don't understand it, how come we can't make sense of things that we do see? Things all around us!

"I spent most of my life trusting what other people said because they were older than me and wiser and more religious but you can't use anyone else's roadmap when it comes to your own life. Who knows what was in the heart of Osama when he started crying because he couldn't kill John Simpson? Who knows if it was even him? Because to everyone else we are all alike."

He pointed to Urfan. "You may not think it is necessary to pray."

He then pointed at one of the Holy Men. "You probably think it's laughable that a person can call himself a Muslim if he doesn't pray. But the problem is, what you do affects what happens to us. I think that was one of the consequences of 9/11. It's only Muslims who draw the lines between us. To the rest of the world we're one and the same. Cut from the same cloth and we both dip into the same well to drink. I can't tell what's in your heart and you can't tell what's in mine. But until I know for sure the decent thing to do, the Islamic way is to assume you have nothing but goodwill towards me. Doesn't that make sense?"

"You're talking shit. There's plenty of guys that want to hurt us because we're Muslim!" stated a rude boy defiantly.

"Not everyone's like that. You're being narrow-minded," retorted a coconut.

"They're not like that if you talk like them and act like them, like you boys."

"But what is it to be ourselves? No one really knows how to act as if they like themselves. Seems to me that no one really fits into their skin. Everyone is trying to put on a new skin. Black or white. No one seems to want to stop and be themselves," said Musa.

"I know who I am!" retorted a Rude Boy.

"Yes, but do you like who you are? Are you telling me that no one around you wants you to be more than what you are? That's the problem guys. No one ever told us that it was OK not to be clever or rich and that the only thing that matters is that you are happy and healthy. All my life people have been telling me that if I want to know Islam and be truly happy I need to follow the creed of the great scholars, people like Abu Hanafi or Abu Maliki or Abu Shafi. No one ever said to me, 'Musa you need to follow your own creed because your life may not always be your choice but it will always be your responsibility.'"

After the debate ended and the men had left, Musa stacked the chairs against the wall in piles of four. He then moved to the lounge area and sank wearily into a comfortable seat. How much more at home he felt in these debates than in the company of women. With his brothers he knew what he had to say and there was a clarity to his thoughts. He tilted his head back and stared at the chandelier. One of its crystals seemed to have a life of its own, hiccupping light on to the cold floor. He heard a sound of quiet footsteps and a lonely shadow cut into the circles traced by his wondering eyes.

"Assalaam-u-alaikum Khadija."

"Waalaikum assalaam brother," she replied softly.

"Musa," he corrected.

Khadija, completely veiled apart from her eyes, stood still and Musa felt strangely troubled. He frowned as he pondered on the origin of his unease.

"Please, sit down," he said.

"How did your debate go?" she asked, sitting down in a chair opposite him.

"It went well... At first I thought there was going to be a punch-up because they were getting so heated! But they all had their say which is what I think they were worried about in the first place."

"Did you discuss 9/11?"

"Yes, but I didn't get a proper answer to my question on whether or not it deepened faith. I think they all enjoyed talking about it though. Strange...they all liked to feel they were Muslims when they talked about 9/11, but if ever they had the chance I think they would be tempted to run each other over!"

"Maybe you don't give them the credit they deserve...Musa."

He deliberately kept his eyes down in a meditative gaze.

"Hmm...perhaps you're right. What about you? What did you guys talk about?"

"9/11. Same as you."

"And what was the outcome?"

She sighed. "It was really hard work getting them to respond."

"Oh, why was that do you think?" asked Musa, intrigued.

"I'm sure they lack confidence. Lots of girls who haven't been to college seem to feel insecure in front of those who have."

"It's the same with the guys."

"But with men, it's different. All of you have an opinion, even if it isn't worth a great deal. Some of these girls are just not interested in 9/11 or in the repression of Muslim women and I think they're embarrassed by that."

"What are they interested in?"

Khadija considered the answer. She crossed her hands and Musa noted with surprise that her nails were manicured.

"They're interested in…enjoying life."

"They are? Just like us." Musa smiled.

Khadija stiffened slightly and got up.

"Or maybe just like me. Perhaps only me," he said loudly as she walked away.

Then he closed his eyes and sighed. It was so very tiring just being yourself.

13

Suleiman worked best in the dark. He sat in front of a large oak table wearing translucent surgical gloves. In front of him were two packets, a teaspoon, a beaker of water, gauze and a stand. Beneath the stand was an electric Bunsen burner.

Carefully he opened a packet containing granulated sugar and, using a teaspoon, he placed twenty-five teaspoons of sugar into the beaker of water. Now it was time for the other packet. He took a deep breath and opened the heroin. Using the same spoon he placed four heaped teaspoonfuls into the beaker of water. He then placed the gauze on the stand, the beaker on top of the gauze, and lit the Bunsen burner.

The granules of heroin danced crazily with the inert sugar that lay like the seabed at the bottom of the beaker. Cozened into life by the fury of the black particles of death the sugar began to rise like a graveyard ghost and swirl around only to be engulfed by a billowy blackness that at times seemed darker than night.

Sitting upright, his hands on his knees, Suleiman waited as pungent fumes began to arise from the beaker. In the twilight of the room the vapour hovered: a spectre of the unspeakable. His hair was now dank and as always the odour bothered him as gradually it became a part of him. On those occasions when he awoke in the night, cold but sweating, this was what he smelt no matter where he slept.

He walked to the window. The street below was deserted and littered with debris. In the moonlight, everything seemed draped with a deathly sheen. Giant bins reeking with uncollected refuse stood like sentinels warning away all who would enter his flat.

His mobile rang.

"You got any? I got someone who needs it. I can drop her by in five minutes."

"How many fucking times I gotta say this? I ain't dealing with anyone I don't know!"

"Look, I'll vouch for her. I will bring her and stay with her to make sure nothing happens. You can trust me, I'm a policeman!"

Suleiman had heard him say this dozens of times before and as ever it failed to make him smile.

"Is she a skank?" he asked contemptuously.

"Yes. Is that a problem?"

"Be here in five," said Suleiman. He snapped the phone shut.

Sergeant Bullock was a good asset even though he was expensive. Suleiman had known him for seven years but neither of them ever said more than was necessary to each other. In his line of work, people formed communities, but friendships often proved to be dangerous. No matter how much you laughed with a guy, and no matter how much you spent showing him a good time, he would rat on you in a second if it suited him. There were also guys who worked too hard and made too much money and then started going on stupid spending sprees, not having a clue how they could account for their wealth. Those guys were usually Asians who, when they felt the heat, ran like a bunch of rats leaving a trail of shit that led right back to them.

Ultimately it would catch up with him one day. He knew that. You could win battles but the war you would lose. It was inevitable. Some days you looked at the pile of money in your hand and said, This is it! It's time to go. But then the bastard world around you just wouldn't let up and you got to thinking one more deal won't hurt. It's not like you were committing a great sin because there were so many people now who were in on this game. Every neighbourhood had a supplier and if you didn't give the punters what they wanted, they could soon find another dealer. The truth of it was you got so that you didn't know how to do anything else, and after a while you realised that you didn't much want to either.

A police car pulled up and a dowdy looking woman got out. Suleiman sighed wearily.

The water in the beaker had now evaporated, leaving cut heroin, ready for use. From a drawer he fished out a little plastic bag, switched off the flame, picked up the beaker and emptied the contents into the bag. He then removed the gloves and switched on the lights.

Three knocks sounded on the door. There was a slight pause and then three more, another pause and then a final six knocks. Suleiman walked down the stairs, unlocked the padlock and opened the door. He was irritated to see that Sergeant Bullock had got back in the car leaving him to deal with the skank.

"What do you want? It's late!" he said gruffly.

"I need some stuff. Just enough to get me through the night."

Suleiman squinted at her. The moonlight and her long dark hair emphasised the pallor of her face behind crudely-applied make-up. She had the stench of unwashed linen. Suleiman's mouth tightened in disdain; she was a prostitute all right.

He climbed the stairs and after a few moments she followed him into the flat which he used as and when he needed it, sharing the facilities with others in his trade. He waved her in the direction of a chair, watching her with contempt. She wore a long black leather coat which was unbuttoned to expose a low-cut tight-fitting black dress with bits of gauzy fabric hanging around her breasts. Her long leather boots were zipped to the knee.

"Let's see the money. Count it slowly please."

She nodded and with shaking hands she quickly pulled out her purse and began to fish for money. Suleiman thought she was Latino and that she had been taking drugs for some time now. He could see that she had once been pretty; her high cheekbones and tumbling hair must have turned a head or two. But now her face had that emaciated look and pretty soon she would no longer find work as a prostitute. Some keys fell from her bag to the floor and as she stooped down to pick them up her hair parted at the nape to reveal a tattoo. A starfish.

Suleiman stood transfixed as he remembered.

He was in year ten at Compton High School, sitting in the row behind the clever group, the kids who were quiet when the teacher spoke and always put their hand up when they were asked a question. One such was Roopa Shah. She was taking her GCSEs a year early. Suleiman always sat behind her. For some reason he never tried to annoy her or even speak to her although he often threw screwed up bits of paper at the rest of the boffins. Roopa was very much the looker whose number everyone wanted. She had short hair and a Mickey Mouse watch he recalled. And on the back of her neck was a tattoo of a starfish.

"What's your name?" asked Suleiman.

She looked up and her eyes narrowed suspiciously.

"Why?"

"Don't worry I'm not gonna ask you for anything else."

She considered his response. Still wary, she replied, "Roopa."

"How did you get into drugs?"

No more than a whisper, his voice disarmed her. Her mouth opened and the hollows of her face widened in a mutation of what had once been a smile.

"My boyfriend used to give me them when I was feeling a bit down or when I was getting stressed. Then I started getting the habit."

"Where did your boyfriend get them from?"

"From you."

"Me?" exclaimed Suleiman.

"Yeah…Pedro."

Pedro Ramos. A tall man with shifty eyes and a perpetual half smile. Pedro, who asked no questions and was prompt with payment. He had realised that Pedro was not a user and was probably re-selling his drugs but that never bothered him. As long as he had his money, the chain of consequence and distribution was as flimsy as a spider's web. Pedro Ramos had used his drugs to turn Roopa Shah into a whore.

And now Suleiman, the pharaoh in his pyramid, stood looking at this creature that he had once admired from afar. She was now his own creation, his own vile, shameful creation, who reeked of semen and drugs.

"Can I go now?" she asked.

Suleiman nodded and Roopa took the packet with a sigh of relief.

He heard her close the outside door but he did not replace the padlock. He closed his eyes and raised a hand to his brow. It was coming. A vein in his forehead seemed to swell a little and throb. Something inside him was starting to become naked. It was slow and cold like someone peeling off the layers of his skin with an icy knife. It felt like his father's cold eyes boring into him and lacerating him with shame. The shame of children who are nothing in their father's eyes. The pain of grown men who know they can never be what they were meant to be. The awful truth of knowing who you really are.

If only he could make himself believe he was better than what he was. He had seen guys do that. They would make a little world inside their heads and become kings and strut around and talk loudly and brashly: he could never do that. But because he was a tough bastard and because shit happens and people get hurt, he knew there was no place for regret if you wanted to get on in life. That's what he often said to himself and some days it worked. Everyone knew he was a tough bastard and nothing and nobody could make him do what he didn't want to do. He was his own man. And that was something to be proud of, he convinced himself.

"My own man," he repeated aloud.

Suleiman checked his watch. His family would be expecting him home soon but first he needed something to pull himself together. He went to the fridge and pulled out a bottle of King Cobra. He downed the contents and reached for another, feeling the alcohol begin to do its work.

It wasn't his fault, really it wasn't. When Aboo got laid off work and told his sons to step up and take the responsibility that meant him. He was twenty and going nowhere. He had been no good at school, no good at those stupid courses they made him do after he left school. That was it you see. He was never any fucking good. He got a job but it didn't pay enough. Aboo needed money to send home. His mum needed money and he wanted Shabnam to have nice things so she wouldn't feel bad. And there were Musa's boarding school fees. Aboo was so fucking obsessed about wanting Musa to memorise the Quran and become a Holy Man and take him to paradise. So he had to do something and that was that. He was a whore just like Roopa.

And now he could not walk steadily. He would feel

ashamed if his parents saw him like this and at that moment a phrase his father often used flashed through his mind. "The best son is the son who has shame in front of his parents." Shame…look how much shame he had. How his father would be proud of him! The thought made him laugh uncontrollably. But just as the face of Roopa Shah had changed, Suleiman's laughter became ugly and hard. The torrent of shame ran through him anointing him with tears and crucifying him with truth. He became a martyr on that battlefield where sons searched for their fathers, who in turn searched for their sons, stumbling upon the corpses of broken dreams.

14

The rain beat down. At times like this the homeowners, men whose toil and strife had secured for them a stronghold against inclement elements, found themselves in desperate need to hear their own voice. Aboo felt this need keenly. Now, by the side of his father, the patriarch, he was compelled to hurl his weight at his family whilst awaiting the arrival of another prospective bride for Musa.

"Auntyji? Huh! This is what it has come down to. I spend my life trying to provide for you and educate you and in the end you go and ask this bloody woman to find a wife for Musa." He shook his head in disgust.

"Stop being such a drama queen, Aboo. We all agreed to help Musa and even Dadaji said it was OK."

The family, with the exception of Suleiman, waited in the living room. Musa deliberately sat facing the door as he wanted to be the first to drink from the eyes of his intended. Amma, worn with worry, noticed that her daughter for some reason had chosen to dress conservatively. Shabnam's attire was without adornment; just a simple dark blue tunic with a high stiff neckline and dark trousers and her hair was pulled into a tight bun.

"What exactly did she say to you?"

"How many times have I got to repeat this? I rang up and an operator asked me for some options."

"Options?" exclaimed Aboo.

"Yes, Aboo, options. Such things do exist when people consider marriage."

"And then what?" asked Amma.

"And then I specified that I was looking for a decent Muslim girl, who wants very much to live with her in-laws."

Aboo's mask of disapproval slipped for a second to reveal a pleased smile. "I said that she must be a practising Muslim who is suitably veiled."

"That's it?" said Amma incredulously.

"Pretty much. I had to pay her of course. I used your card Aboo." Shabnam grinned at her father's furious reaction.

"My card? *My* bank card? That card was only supposed to be used in emergencies! What has this blasted society done to you? You go off spending your parents' money on stupid things. Listening to what your parents advise is always better and cheaper but you will only realise that when you have bills and responsibilities of your own."

Aboo shook his head mournfully.

"What if it doesn't work out? Will we get our money back?"

Shabnam sighed. "No Aboo, this is not like shopping at Sainsbury's."

Amma's concerns were elsewhere and she wanted to get back to the subject of her future daughter-in-law. "What about her personality? Did they give you any details about her personality?"

"Well, Auntyji said she had found someone who was very pious, confident and proud of her identity as a Muslim woman. She felt she would suit our requirements."

"It is not good for a woman to be too confident. I have seen women like that," sighed Aboo. "They end up controlling their husband, and their husband's wage. Abdul Gafoor across the road is like that. One night when I came home from the mosque I saw him leaving his house and I asked him where he was going. He told me, 'I came home with ninety pounds and my wife said, Get back in your taxi and bring me another ten pounds.' I felt so sorry for him."

"Why didn't you give him the ten pounds?" asked Shabnam.

"Bugger that. I just felt bad for him." Aboo smiled grimly.

"Not all women are the same but sometimes it is good for a woman to speak her mind," said Amma.

"The tongue of a woman can be like the poison of a scorpion or the honey of a bee," remarked Dadaji as he puffed away on his hookah.

Aboo looked at him, baffled by his remark. A split second later, however, the light dawned and he bowed his head in agreement.

"Are you sure she really wants to stay with her in-laws? Girls in this country do not usually want to do that," said Amma.

"That's what Auntyji said. Apparently her own mother is arthritic and she gave up her job in London to look after her."

Amma smiled, settling back into the sofa and breathing a huge sigh of relief but Aboo was dismayed.

"She's not going to bring her here is she?"

"Don't be silly Aboo. She has a younger sister."

"Is she going to bring anyone with her?" asked Musa.

"Nope. She's gonna come here and talk to all of you. Auntyji said that she doesn't want to talk privately with you as that is not Islamic."

Aboo looked at Dadaji speculatively and the old man gave a wry half-smile.

"Maybe the Angel of Mercy has finally visited us. This could be the one!" exclaimed Aboo.

The prospect of a compliant, caring daughter-in-law no longer seemed like a fantasy. It was achievable! It was imminent. Aboo saw how silly he had been to mourn Musa's departure from custom. Why, girls in this country were every bit as Islamic and upstanding as those back home. In fact, more so! They didn't have the passion for gossip and intrigue the girls back home had. You didn't have to watch what you said or did in front of them for fear of it being broadcast. Yes! A mental picture was forming in Aboo's mind. An English speaking daughter-in-law who could be trusted with the management of the household and who could be relied on to care for them in their old age and not send them to an old people's home. Old people's home…Old people's home. Those three dreadful words. How deplorable it was that you could spend all your life caring and providing for your children and they – the worthless ingrates – would send you to an old people's home because they wanted to spend some quality romance time with their wives and in your home. And all because they couldn't afford to buy their own property with the way prices were now.

"Shouldn't she be here by now?" he asked. He touched his face and wondered if he had time to run upstairs and apply some of his aftershave.

"She's just coming. Look outside, her car has pulled up," said Shabnam.

Musa went to the window and saw a figure re-arranging her nikab as she stepped out of a silver car. He frowned.

"Hey Shabnam, her face is covered!"

"Yes I know. Normally she wears the nikab but once she is in the house she will take it off. Auntyji made sure that she would do that. Look sharp now Musa! Everybody sit up straight and get ready to smile." With that dictum Shabnam strode to the front door.

Musa heard his sister's voice, high pitched and welcoming.

"Hi! Assalaam-u-alaikum. Look at the rain! Come on in!"

A tall veiled woman stepped into the room. She wore a long white silken robe; her head scarf and nikab were also white, but her eyes were black and huge.

They fixed on Musa in deep appraisal and he at once felt ashamed. It was as though a sin he could not remember had been exposed.

"This is Habiba Al-Shahbaaz, everyone," said Shabnam brightly.

Aboo stood up and smiled with the simple humility of one who is truly honoured. He bent forwards a fraction as if he were about to bow.

"Welcome to my home, Habiba. Allow me to introduce myself. I am Musa's father and this is my most respectable father."

He indicated Dadaji who was staring at Habiba, captivated.

"And here is my wife." He gestured towards Amma who nodded at her prospective daughter-in-law.

"Whatever happens the will of Allah will decide everything so please be relaxed in my home. While you are here, you are like my own –"

Habiba reached for her nikab and took it off. Her face was proud, with wide delicate cheekbones, a firm purposeful mouth, a jaw that stood no nonsense and that flawless complexion which is unique to the women of Kenya.

Four sets of eyes stared at her and at Shabnam. Aboo's mouth opened but no sound came.

Dadaji stared at his gormless-looking son and then at Musa. He jerked his arms upwards and, beside himself with laughter, he screeched, "What is this?"

There was silence until, with great dignity, Habiba spoke, startling them all.

"Assalaam-u-alaikum everybody. May Allah bless this union if it is written in his decree. May the Angels shower their blessings upon you if not. May our entry into this meeting be one of honour and may my departure be one of honour."

The living room filled with venomous Punjabi in response to her solemn benediction.

"Shabnam what have you done?" exclaimed Aboo.

"The Day of Judgement has come! The Day of Judgement has come!" shrieked Amma.

"I did as I was told. You said a practising Muslim of good height and I got you a practising Muslim of good height. You've got no right to be annoyed at me!" retorted Shabnam.

"Look at her making eyes at Musa. I knew it. The girls in this country are up to no good. Wait till I get my hands on that Auntyji!" snarled Aboo.

"What if somebody has seen her coming in? That Shofiq woman across the road is always on the look-out," said Amma.

And then Dadaji began to laugh hysterically.

With an effort, Musa gathered himself. He stood up and motioned to Habiba to sit down next to Shabnam.

She waved a gloved hand towards Dadaji.

"It doesn't run in the family does it?"

Musa shook his head vehemently: "No…no…He's just getting old, that's all."

"It's just that I had an uncle who used to act like that before he got committed for drug-related schizophrenia."

Musa smiled politely. "You don't need to worry about that. The only drug my granddad uses is tobacco!"

"This place has stunk like a fucking chimney since he's been here!" muttered Shabnam.

Musa cut an angry glance to his sister and then turned back to Habiba, smiling cordially.

"I hope the journey was not too unpleasant, sister, I mean Habiba," he said softly.

"By the grace of Allah it was not too unpleasant. I had to get out of the car but that's about normal these days." Habiba beamed a brilliant smile.

"Oh, why?" asked Musa faintly.

"The problem is, brother, there is too much ignorance and Islamophobia in the minds of the white men. When they see a veiled woman, a Muslim woman, driving a car they give you dirty looks. And I ain't one for taking a dirty look lying down. When I was coming up here, there was a traffic jam on Stockport Road. A couple of men were in the car in front. They were looking at me in the rear-view mirror and laughing so I got out, knocked on their window and shouted at them, 'You ain't got no right to laugh at me. I ain't your slave woman and this here ain't your highway.' Then they started getting all aggressive with me. But I told them I been dealing with rude boys since I was three and that there was nothing they could do to me that I couldn't do back but ten times worse. That shut them up big time."

"Oh dear that sounds dreadful. You should have reported them to the police," said Musa.

"That was the second time, brother. Earlier some other guys started giving me some jip and then I start giving them some of my jip and then they ran away like a bunch of fairies. So I got in my car and went after them and then I get stopped by a policeman for speeding. So I said to the policeman, 'I have been a victim of Islamophobia and I am well within my rights to defend myself.'

"Then the copper gives me a mouthful and I give him a mouthful and then he pulls out a book and I pull out a book but his is a notebook and mine is the Holy Quran. And I say to him, 'I got the word of the creator and you got the word of the created. You want a head to head, I'll give you a head to head.' You know what the copper does? He just gives me a dirty look. So I invade his personal space and say, 'Bring it on sarge, I'll sue you for every kind of harassment there is!' You know what he does then? He legs it! So I go after him and shout out the verse from the Holy Quran, you know the one don't you? – When Truth confronts Falsehood lo! Falsehood turns and runs away! – I'm telling you brother. That is the greatest thing about being a Muslim. Every day you see your faith realised. In the tyranny of the police. In the ignorance of the non-believer. These are all little tests for us to become better Muslims."

"But my dear you are…you're…" Aboo's voice trailed off as he gawped at her.

"That's right sir. I'm a woman and I'm proud to be a woman. Most importantly I'm proud to be a Muslim woman. No disrespect to you sir, but we women have the toughest job in society. The future of Muslim kids is in our hands and it's about time we got the respect that we deserve. Ain't that so sister?" She elbowed Shabnam who smiled in polite but fearful empathy.

Habiba turned her attention to Musa.

"Can I ask you a question?" she asked belligerently.

"Sure."

She fished in her pocket for a piece of paper.

"It says here you have memorised the Quran?"

"Correct."

"And that you have spent six years in a madrasah?"

"Correct."

"So how come you don't have a beard?"

"What?" replied Musa, taken aback.

"You know that the Holy Prophet (Peace be upon Him) had a beard. And as Muslims we must all follow his example. If we don't follow his example in our appearance how can we follow him in our behaviour? Do you think you know better than the Holy Prophet (Peace be upon Him)?" she asked truculently.

"No, but you could argue that..."

Habiba pointed an admonishing finger at him. She seemed to be building up a good head of righteous anger.

"Satan also knew how to argue his way out of the Garden of Eden. You don't argue 'cos that's the devil in you arguing. You gotta hear and obey. Just like the angels."

"But we're not angels, Habiba. We're men. Our place in the scheme of creation is higher than that of angels."

"But the angels are flying higher than us," she shot back, defiantly.

"That's because they have wings. We just have our hearts," said Musa.

He turned his head to Amma, "She can speak her mind all right."

"She does nothing but speak her mind," snorted Amma.

"If her words came from my mouth you would all burst with pride," said Shabnam angrily.

"There is certainly fire in this one," remarked Dadaji, now calm.

Habiba smiled politely at this burst of rapid Punjabi and continued her interrogation.

"What school of thought do you follow?" Her voice was solemn as if this was a question of immense significance.

"How do you mean?"

"You know Hanbali, Maliki, Shafi and Hanafi? Who do you follow?"

Musa sighed. Clearly Habiba was bursting with Islamic knowledge. He had met girls like this before. They were addicted to verbal battles. No matter what he said, he was heading for an intellectual bruising.

"Well the thing is I don't really follow any particular school of thought. What I mean to say is that these guys were all great scholars in their time but I think that the best school of thought is your own conscience. And besides here in Britain people don't think about the beliefs of classical scholars like they do in a place like Iran or Iraq."

"What do people here think about?" asked Habiba.

"Money. Here Pakistanis think about money," said Musa. "How to earn more and be happier. If you say to them stop whatever it is you're doing because it isn't in the rule book of Hanbali or Maliki or whoever, they'll look at you like you're crazy."

Habiba considered this response carefully. She shook her head and looked speculatively at Aboo.

"You know something. It ain't your fault. It's the fault of

your parents. Your dad when he came to this country was probably as Muslim as the Pope." She winked.

"I bet you he was one of those guys that used to buy a bottle of whisky on the weekends and share it around with the rest of the tribe. Then when people started saying they were gay, they hit the town looking for the nearest English girl they could find. Twenty years later they get a letter from the Child Support Agency saying pay up or else your new and improved white family is gonna come knocking on your door."

Aboo's face turned red and he spluttered in outrage. Dadaji, his face alive with curiosity, prodded his son.

"What did she say? Tell me! Tell me!"

Aboo translated in a strangled voice and once more Dadaji rocked back in his seat, his frail body shaking with mirth. Habiba couldn't help laughing with him. United by faith and separated by perspective they cackled in unison. The cloud of matrimony darkened the horizon no longer but slowly dispersed into ether spawned by this sense of absurdity.

"She was a black woman?" exclaimed Babarr.

"Didn't you bother checking any of this out, Shabnam?" asked Suleiman who looked rough.

"No. I just did what I was told to do!"

"But wasn't one of the first Muslims black...Bilal I think his name was?" asked Armila who remembered this from her studies.

"Yes," replied Musa wearily. "Bilal ibn Rabah but some know him as Bilal the Ethiopian."

"And does it not say in one of your scriptures that all human beings are equal?" she pressed.

"Not in those words exactly, but that is true; Islam makes no distinction between colours," said Musa.

"So the only problem for your parents was that she was black. Are they ever likely to change their thinking?"

"No, never. Not until the camel will go through the eye of the needle," said Musa firmly.

"So any relationship with a non-Asian is doomed then?" asked Armila pointedly.

"What the hell is this? What do you think you are? An Indian Oprah Winfrey? Point is Musa, was she fit?" asked Babarr.

Armila and Shabnam were furious.

"Why're you girls giving me the evils for? All marriages gotta have a bit of that jazz. Confucius once said the ear of the loved one can steam the mirror that is placed next to it. So when you looked at this girl was there any fire down under?"

"No," said Musa huffily.

"Then what the hell is all this whingeing about. Remember folks, Musa has gotta find someone in one month of days or else he's gonna marry a yardie from back home. At this point, Musa, you wanna ask your granddaddy for an extension."

"This is not a loan repayment scheme, Babarr. It doesn't work like that!"

"If you could have married her Musa, would you have?" asked Armila. She leaned forward to catch the expression on his face.

"No…I don't think so."

"Because she was black?" queried Armila.

"No…she was too aggressive…too forward!"

"But you yourself said that you didn't want a doormat," reminded Shabnam.

"I know but this is different."

"Oh right! Shall I tell you the difference Musa? For all your Islam and knowledge you are just as racist and narrow-minded as Mum and Dad. If she was Pakistani and had brown skin you'd be doing a moony in front of Dadaji right now!" said Shabnam angrily.

"That's complete nonsense. It's just that I have an image of the type of person I want to fall in love with and it isn't her. That's not racism. That's just the way it is."

"Falling in love is not the same as marriage, Musa!" said Shabnam.

"That is so true. If everyone married for love, none of us would be sitting here right now. Confucius once said those who marry in love will repent in passion," added Babarr.

"You can go stick it with your bloody Confucius!" retorted Shabnam furiously.

"Calm down Shabnam. The point is where are we gonna go from here?" asked Suleiman.

"Perhaps we need to start looking at Pakistanis from Pakistan?" said Babarr. "Lots of girls from back home are looking for guys here. They want to live in a place with constant electricity and free education and benefits and shit like that! Titty Soups calls them the winter Pakistanis. They spend their summers here on the look-out. That

202

might be the best way forward. They're Pakistani so there won't be any colour clash and all they want is to marry a guy who can take them away from a third world country. I'll have a word with Titty and get something sorted out."

Babarr winked at Musa and Armila shook her head.

15

Khadija carefully placed a Quran and a neat pile of notes on a table and waited while the women filed into the Islamic Centre's library. They were a diverse bunch. Some of them were clearly working women. They had come from their offices, and were dressed conservatively in dark clothes that were suitably baggy to hide their figures but not so voluminous as to invite laughter from their co-workers. Khadija's veil hid her smile when she saw them. They were the sisters who were graduates and they came from families who cherished them as though each was a fragile piece of jewellery: as a result they were both confident and opinionated. Nowadays, it was fashionable for such girls to be conversant with Islam and have an informed opinion on controversial issues.

Others were sisters who walked proudly in their splendid Islamic outfits, looking every inch the radical women they thought themselves to be. Some of them were wearing veils as she was, others were not. But apart from that there was very little difference between them.

Finally there were the housewives; some were newlyweds and others had children. For the most part they wore colourful but slightly crumpled clothes. For them Islam was a means by which they could assert themselves, and a platform from which they could command respect and attention within the family unit.

Khadija waited some minutes before beginning. She noted that each group sat together and talked only among themselves; their preconceptions about each other stood like partitions and their opinions made opaque any reasons they might have for wanting to talk outside their circle.

Satisfied that no one else was going to turn up, she removed her veil. Instantly there was silence and as always when she revealed her face, she felt the air in front of her turn into a cold cupped hand that followed the line of her jaw and the set of her mouth. The feeling of nakedness hovered for a moment and then fell like a curtain to reveal her person. That sensation was strangely pure and it troubled her that there was no shame and it pleased her that she felt her eyes soften.

"Assalaam-u-alaikum my dear sisters. It is nice to see you all again and I am really pleased that so many of you have returned. However I was disappointed after our last meeting that not all of you responded with your thoughts and opinions. I really want every woman in this room to take part. This is not a competition and there are no winners and losers. Everyone's opinion counts: all of you count as Muslim women."

Khadija surveyed the faces of her audience. They stared back at her in silence.

"What I want to talk about today is the status of women

in our society. And to start off I will read to you. If you agree with what I say, put your hands up."

"Husbands should take good care of their wives."

They all smiled and waved their hands. Khadija, amused, continued:

"God has given to some more than others and with what they spend out of their own money righteous wives are devout and guard what God would have them guard in their husbands' absence. If you fear high-handedness from your wives, remind them, then ignore them when you go to bed, then hit them.

"Right sisters, tell me what you think of what I have just read?"

A radical girl called out, "I think it's a load of rubbish. I ain't ever heard of a bloke who just reminds his wife. They yell at you and say my way or the motorway. And I'm telling you straight, sister, if any guy tries to smack me one, I don't care if he's my husband, my brother or my father. That guy is gonna get a beating from me!"

Salma, one of the working girls, and a mentor at the local Women's Refuge, commented, "I think what you have read is the work of some chauvinistic Pakistani man. As for the issue of who has been granted more, it depends on the context. Ask any family who does better in school, the daughter or the son? Nine times out of ten they will say the daughter. Who's getting the higher paying jobs? It's the girls. Who's taking the responsibility for the children's education? It's the women.

"Do you know what Eleanor Roosevelt once said? 'Nobody can make you feel inferior without your consent.' That is exactly what's happening to Pakistani women. I see it every day. We are letting men think they are in charge of us and we are letting them dominate our lives. No man has the right to hit us. We are not slaves. We were created as equals. And should our obedience be taken for granted? Doesn't the husband have an obligation to his wife? If we have to be obedient then they have to be kind and supportive towards us. You can't have one without the other!"

The radical girls and the working girls applauded but the housewives were not convinced. One of them, plainly nervous, stood up to speak.

"What you say is true in this country but in Pakistan a girl has no future if she is alone. The only real life a girl can experience is that with her husband. It is the responsibility of the husband to look after his wife. So you see it is true that men are in charge of women. And you also have to look at it this way. In this country, if a girl is not happy with her husband she can divorce and move on but in Pakistan that is still very difficult, so she has to make the best of what she has got. Here, sometimes husbands do hit their wives, it happens, but you learn to deal with it. If a husband hits his wife too much then yes you must do something about it but in the end you must make peace with him."

This was too much for many of the women and they all began to talk at once. Khadija shouted above them and asked one of the radical group who seemed particularly angry to speak.

"Sister, that ain't you talking, that's your husband and

207

your dad. If you had more faith in Allah and in your religion you wouldn't be so afraid to stick up for yourself. You think your husband is the only guy that can look after and support you? Do you know why that is? It's because no one's told you that you've got a head on your shoulders. No one's ever said to you sort your own shit out and because of that you've gone running to everyone else. It may help you in Pakistan but it sure ain't gonna do much for you in this country!"

One of the working girls cut in. "I think you're being a bit harsh on her. It doesn't matter where you are or what you are. It is not easy for any girl to defy her family and culture. The only reason you're talking like that is because you know that there are a crowd of people around who will support you. What if you were in Pakistan? There are very few support groups for women there."

An older woman sitting in the front row asked, "Excuse me, Khadija, but who wrote those words? Where do they come from?"

"The Holy Quran."

The women were silent, uneasy.

"As you now know that verse comes from the Holy Quran, put up your hands if you agree with it," said Khadija.

The housewives put up their hands as did the radical girls, albeit reluctantly, but it was clear that the working girls would not follow suit. One of them, a tall girl wearing a beautifully tailored suit and whose name was Sofia, said imperiously, "One thing you seem to be forgetting Khadija is that the Quran was revealed fifteen hundred years ago. Circumstances for married couples were different and so was the status of women."

"Sister, the word of the Quran is true for all ages," argued one of the radical sisters.

"Are you then saying it was acceptable to beat your wife a thousand years ago?" asked Sofia.

One of the housewives broke in. "Listen sisters! Fifteen hundred years ago there were no divorce lawyers or marriage agencies. Marriage was meant to be for life and if something is for life you have to be prepared for everything, the good and the bad."

Khadija interrupted: "Before anyone answers, I would like to quote another verse from the Quran."

"'Men are the maintainers of women because Allah has made some of them to excel others and because they spend out of their property.' Could you please raise your hands if you agree."

Everyone did so. Khadija smiled, pleased by their unity, and went on.

"'The good women are therefore obedient, guarding the unseen as Allah has guarded; and as to those on whose part you fear desertion, admonish them, and leave them alone in the sleeping-places and beat them; then if they obey you, do not seek a way against them.'"

"I agree wholeheartedly with the first part. Men should maintain us and keep us. But they should never, never dominate us or beat us," emphasised a working girl. Turning to the radical group she smiled sardonically and said, "By the same token, I don't think it's a good idea for girls to try and dominate men."

"I ain't dominating no one sister. I just stick up for myself and for my religion," came the retort.

Khadija broke in with a gentle reminder. "Sisters, we're not living in a war zone and when it comes to Islam the best defence is not the best offence."

The calmness with which she spoke these words spiralled into the minds of everyone present like a vial of crystal reason.

"Let me read a slightly different version of the verse. 'Therefore the righteous women are devoutly obedient and guard in their husband's absence what God would have them guard. As to those women on whose part you fear disloyalty and ill-conduct admonish them first then refuse to share their beds, and lastly chastise them. Seek not against them means of annoyance.'"

"Refuse to share their beds – that's something the men need to be told!" said a housewife, and the others laughed raucously.

"That last bit's the same as before, where it says do not try to annoy your wives, I didn't know that was in the Quran," said another. "I swear to God, guys get mean when they don't get their own way in marriages. My husband deliberately pisses me off!"

"But where it says chastise them – that was different before – chastising a woman could mean something completely different to hitting her," said a working girl.

Khadija paused. "The interpretation is not the same. In the first version that I recited the translator commented that hit was just a single slap. So you cannot equate that to beating. Some of the greatest Islamic scholars such as

Imam Shafi say that beating is a symbolic act and it should be done in such a manner as not to cause pain. The Holy Prophet (Peace be upon Him) hated the idea of anyone beating their wives and was personally very much against it."

"I don't get this at all. If the Holy Prophet (Peace be upon Him) was so very much against it then how come men are instructed to beat their wives?"

"You need to adjust your concept of the word beating. Like I said, a single slap is not the same as beating," replied Khadija.

One of the radicals laughed: "If a guy is pissed off with his woman and slaps her you can guarantee it's not gonna tickle."

"It may not tickle but at the same time it's not supposed to cause any injury or pain. It's not supposed to be done in anger. And there are a number of stages that need to be followed prior to that act. You need to tell your wife off then refuse to share a bed with her. And also bear in mind that there are different degrees of intensity in a slap," said Khadija.

"But you still haven't answered my question. If the Holy Prophet (Peace be upon Him) was against the idea of slapping then how come it's in the Quran?" pressed the working girl.

"The Holy Quran was revealed to the Holy Prophet (Peace be upon Him), it was not co-authored with him. There's a big difference. You also have to consider the society in which it was revealed. The status of wives in Arabia one thousand years ago was not the same as the current status of women in England today. A thousand years ago women were not thought of as equal to men. What is perceived as unacceptable now was not perceived as unacceptable then."

"Women are still not thought of as equal now!" snorted one of the housewives.

Khadija had some more explaining to do. "I have read to you the same verse in three different translations of the Quran. One was from the internet, another was by an Egyptian born professor of Islamic Studies, and the third translation was made by an Indian-born Moslem, a brilliantly clever man who studied law in England and died here.

"The best way to stick up for yourselves and for your religion is to read what was meant to be a source of guidance for you. If you want to know the truth you have to be prepared to question what you believe and what you read. Just remember, for every answer that you like there may be an answer that you don't like but our questions have just one purpose and that is to strengthen our belief. If you're looking for a reason not to believe because it doesn't agree with the way you live your life then, my dear sisters, nothing you read in the Quran will ever mean anything to you. You have to want to be a Muslim to be able to understand the Quran. And having a brown face and an Asian name doesn't mean you will have the heart of a Muslim. That bit has got to come from you."

Musa sat on a battered swivel chair in Babarr's office in the Islamic Centre busily writing notes for his own session. Pausing, he studied the poster of Confucius on the wall. It was strange how oriental sages seemed to smile all the time whereas Hindu and Muslim wise men looked so doleful. Maybe it had something to do with the fact that Confucianism was a philosophy and not reliant on the concept of a god, he thought. No god, no accountability and no accountability meant freedom from the terror of the Day of Reckoning. That presumably meant you could spend your time focussing on the present and if you concentrated on the right things and overlooked the rest, it was possible you could be tranquil pretty much all the time. This notion pleased him and he rocked back and forth in his chair, smiling at the Chinese sage.

Suddenly he heard footsteps and turned to the partially open door. He glimpsed a figure in black – Khadija.

"Assalaam-u-alaikum. Please come in."

"Are congratulations in order?" she asked straight away, her eyes brimming over with levity.

"What? No, I'm afraid not." He frowned. "How come you're so familiar with my personal life?"

"You have some indiscreet friends, or friend," she answered.

"You mean Babarr?" Musa shrugged. "With him you have to take the rough with the smooth. Anyway, you seem to be in very good spirits." He pointed to a chair and Khadija sat down.

"I had a good session with the sisters. I really think they left feeling as though they learnt something."

Musa considered this carefully. He hadn't considered this after talking to the brothers as his mind was elsewhere.

"Are your personal commitments interfering with your duties?" asked Khadija, reading his mind.

"It's only natural I suppose. Marriage is half of faith so in the pursuit of marriage you must devote at least half your mind."

"That's a nice way of putting it. But is it getting you anywhere?" Her voice was soft.

"No," answered Musa glumly.

"Why do you think that is?"

Musa smiled at her curiosity.

"Maybe it's because I can't see what's in front of me. Only what's beyond me."

"I think men look for the wrong things when they are searching for a wife," she said thoughtfully.

"How do you mean?"

"You're looking for beauty and you think that's the same as purity," said Khadija.

"Beauty would be nice," he mused. "Beauty would most definitely be very nice but it's not just about the face. I think there is a kind of beauty which can travel from the heart and light up everything along the way."

"But that's just a fantasy, Musa."

He settled back in his chair. "I think everyone has a fantasy to help them through. Everyone needs something to believe in, something that can make tomorrow better than today."

"But if you have faith in Allah, why do you need to dream?" she asked.

"It's the way I am. I cannot change it. I'm not even sure I want to change it," he answered firmly.

"So you're going to keep dreaming that one day you will meet your beautiful perfect wife?"

"You sound as if I'm looking for a supermodel. I'm not. Sometimes when I close my eyes I can almost feel her presence. It's like I can sense her nature, her purity, her essence."

"How do you mean?" asked Khadija, controlling a rare urge to giggle.

His eyes closed, Musa rested his face in his hands and took a deep breath, "She's beautiful." He opened his eyes and looked pointedly at Khadija. "Sorry, but it's true. She's kind and gentle. She is patient but she can also be firm. She watches more than she speaks. She is sensitive but not emotional. She is brave but not brash. And when she smiles it's like you're seeing the sunrise for the first time. Does what I say make you want to laugh?"

Khadija stood up quickly, embarrassed. "No…I have to get going now. I almost forgot what I came here for." She picked up a folder which Babarr had left for her on the desk. "See you later."

Musa had closed his eyes again.

"Goodbye." His voice sounded slightly strained and far away as if it was struggling to catch up with his vision.

Khadija looked back through the office door and watched a dreamer float on the crest of his own fantasy while sheltered by his own hope. Saddened by what she saw she walked away.

16

Shabnam lay staring at her bedroom ceiling as she did so often when troubled and felt that the ceiling must be etched with the sum of her aspirations, thoughts and desires from adolescence to adulthood.

Leroy was getting impatient. She knew that. Their relationship had reached a critical point and she sensed that he felt supremely confident in what he was going to do from then on: all he needed was that one signal of physical compliance from her and then she would be treated to a luxury cruise of physical pleasure.

The thought of doing it...actually doing it with him was quite exciting, she had to admit, although she would have shot herself before letting Leroy know. There was something else though – a feeling of shame, of betrayal, of leaving a part of you behind, even though you didn't now want it to be a part of you. She could analyse that feeling until it became manageable and she could put it away into a little box to be kept in the back of her mind where all the anger and resentment lay, but it was still there, tugging at her like a slave chain.

Then again Leroy was her boyfriend and she was his girlfriend. He was attractive and sincere so it was only natural that their relationship should be consummated. They weren't going to spend the rest of their lives together but the time they had together should be enjoyable. It could even work out to her advantage when she did get married; she would be familiar with the territory. She wouldn't have to act all terrified and submissive like most Pakistani girls on their wedding night. She had heard how they put a scarf over their faces while their husbands climbed on them. Fucking ridiculous, at least she wouldn't be like that. She would have the upper hand. That's what mattered. She wondered if it would hurt – but hey, no pain no gain. She climbed off the bed, looked at herself in the mirror and went downstairs.

Dadaji sat cross-legged on his couch rocking to and fro gently as if listening to a divine mantra. As ever a cloud of smoke surrounded him, adding to his presence the way dry ice heightened the aura of a pop star.

Shabnam avoided him as a rule because he seemed to be able to see right through her. Sometimes she thought she could see sadness in his eyes when he looked at her, other times he would smile openly as if amused by her. Today there was no getting round sitting with him. She needed to get money from Suleiman and she would have to sit in the living room to wait for him as he came and went so quickly.

She tried to keep her focus on the job at hand. A strange notion came to her. What if she liked it so much with Leroy that she could never be satisfied by any other man? What if, when with her husband, she found her thoughts drifting to Leroy?

"The elixir of the forbidden has no equal."

Shabnam jumped. She looked up and saw that Dadaji was watching her as if he could see the play of her emotions.

"Its sweetness will mark you forever. Its memory will darken you forever."

"What are you talking about?" Shabnam was staggered that he should *know*.

"I have seen that look many times before. On the faces of other girls just before they enter the bedroom on their wedding night," said Dadaji gently.

"I don't know what you're talking about!"

"You, like your brother, are not led by what you know, but by what you feel."

Shabnam struggled with anger and shame. She raised an uncertain hand to her forehead and was angered to find it moist with sweat.

"Your heart is torn between the fragrance of the forbidden and the odour of shame. Remember, the fragrance will lead you to a jungle. Once you enter it, you will never be able to leave."

He dismissed her with an angry wave of his hand and an imperious, "Go now. What you do, do quickly."

Barefoot and dressed in a thin white T-shirt with blue boxing shorts that hung precariously on his hips, Leroy opened the door.

"Shabnam. Come on in!" he smiled. "It feels so good to see you here. Man I am telling you. This is…" he waved his hands in the air as if trying to summon the missing

218

adjective, "wicked! And it's going to get better and better!"

She could have predicted that Leroy would live in a stylish loft conversion. The thick carpet was a rich blue, the elegant sofas were a deep burgundy and a glossy oak banister led to a galleried bedroom. At one end of the room was a huge flat screen television.

Leroy picked up a remote control.

"Shall I put some music on?"

Shabnam smiled and nodded and straightaway Leroy began to move to the sounds of a catchy Latino tune, edging closer to her. When he was no more than a few centimetres away, he arched his back and thrust his pelvis back and forth in time with the rhythm of the mambo. Shabnam, alarmed, stepped back and Leroy stood still.

"Sorry. Do you know the music? It's by Tito Puente." Leroy pronounced the name slowly and carefully as if this were a personal favour to the great Latino composer. "Whenever I hear his 'Ran Kan Kan' something in the music takes over and, like, before you know it I'm like hot, hot…hot! You ever get like that Shabnam honey?"

He sighed when he saw her expression. If he were an insect she would have trodden on him.

"Look Shabs, I don't mean to embarrass you – it's just that every so often something comes over me."

"OK, OK," said Shabnam irritably.

"That's brilliant babe. You wanna eat now or…" Leroy's voice trailed off.

"Now would be good, Leroy. You must be tired with all those hot dance moves," said Shabnam light-heartedly.

He laughed in delight. Jokes were good. Jokes now usually meant making merry later. And not all that much later either.

"OK, please take a seat." He pulled out two small steel-rimmed, green-glass tables. He then went to the kitchen, opened the oven and carefully took out two steaming trays.

"All right, what I got us here is my favourite Italian dish – brassyolee," he called out.

"It smells great. What's in it?" asked Shabnam curiously.

"Beef can be used but I bought us some pork fillets and they are covered in minced garlic and olive oil. Very healthy."

Shabnam walked into the kitchen and gazed at the braciola. Instinctively she wanted to say that it was against her religion to eat pork but that statement in itself seemed stupid and shallow. Why refuse to eat pork and then have a bout of steamy rumpy-pumpy with a man you knew you were never going to spend the rest of your life with? If you were going to do one damnable thing, what was the harm in doing two, or even three or four?

"You don't like pork?" asked Leroy, stricken.

"No…no. I love pork. Pork comes from pigs and who doesn't like pigs?" Shabnam laughed loudly enough to disguise her anxiety.

"I don't like pigs. They keep arresting my friends!" Leroy snorted. "Would you like a pre-dinner drink?" he asked.

"Sure, I'd love one."

Leroy took a bottle of wine from the fridge and

pompously declared, "Pinot Blanc. Accept no other with pork."

He raised his glass, adoration in his eyes. "Here's looking at you kid."

Shabnam glanced at the liquid in her glass, took a deep breath and gulped it down but why was Dadaji looking over Leroy's shoulder with a wry smile? For once his eyes were clearly visible and were filled with an amused indulgence.

"Phew–"

The exquisite Pinot Blanc, which began life as a bunch of grapes in France and briefly spent some time in the mouth of Shabnam, ended up on Leroy's face.

He blinked several times in disbelief.

Shabnam was horrified at what she had done. Dadaji was no longer there. Only Leroy, sodden with wine.

"You never told me you didn't like white wine." He said this matter-of-factly, as if they were discussing the weather.

"Oh my God Leroy, I'm so sorry I don't know what happened. It's like I saw…"

She put her hands to the side of her head. Leroy, however, laughed as he wiped his face with his T-shirt.

"Ah well…shit happens. At least I won't have to wash my face tonight." He winked at Shabnam.

"Why don't we eat…yes…let's eat," she suggested nervously.

"Excellent idea. Let's get ready to party!"

He carried two plates of braciola from the kitchen to the two small tables and they sat on the floor to eat. Leroy cut a piece of pork and delicately played with it. The music had become a gentle soothing rhythm and he swayed his head, letting the moment fill with a lovely languid ease. He sighed happily and looked at Shabnam with a homely smile.

"If only every moment in life could be like this. A good meal, a beautiful woman and nice music."

Shabnam tried to smile as a thin bead of sweat began to trickle down her forehead. She pierced a piece of pork, sniffed it, opened her mouth and placed it on her tongue. She closed her mouth and exhaled in relief. Nothing had happened. The stress of the past few days had taken their toll, that was all, that was why she thought she saw Dadaji just now. She was not going mad. It was all going to be okay.

But no, there he was again. Dadaji was standing behind Leroy. He placed his hands on his hips and shook his head disapprovingly.

"Kachoom!" Out came the piece of pork but she managed to hide it in the folds of her shalwar. Leroy, immersed in the delights of his own cooking, did not notice. He had almost finished eating when he looked at Shabnam's ashen face.

"Shabnam honey, what's wrong!"

"I…I…I…" She pointed to the place where Dadaji had stood just moments before.

"You're not hungry. No worries."

He took her hand, smiling reassuringly. "Don't be afraid sweetheart. The first time is always scary. But then afterwards, it's just like riding a bike then you're on a motorbike and finally it's like you're in a Lamborghini. It's all good darling. I swear to you, it's all good."

He began stroking her hair and as he did so Shabnam came to her senses. She frowned at his caressing hand and opened her mouth to remonstrate but then she saw the piece of pork – surely Leroy would notice it. What could she do to save her embarrassment? She gazed at him, wanting to fix his eyes on hers. For Leroy the moment had come at last. Quickly and decisively, he pressed his mouth over hers and, moaning with desire, he let his tongue run over her teeth. She felt herself respond and closed her eyes. Catching their breath they paused and, as Shabnam opened her eyes, there was Dadaji again. This time he was watching them with an expression of polite curiosity. He raised a finger as if he was about to ask a question. Shabnam screamed.

"Oh my God. He was here. I saw him. He was right here!"

"Who, baby who?" asked Leroy looking about distractedly.

"My grandfather. I saw him. I swear to God I saw him."

Believing she was still nervous, he played the game and looked around. No one.

"I think it was a false alarm, sweetie!"

He took Shabnam in his arms and gently tucked a strand of hair behind her ear.

"Don't worry. Ain't nothing gonna stop us now."

"No…Leroy, there's something wrong. I keep seeing my grandfather. It's like every time we're together, he pops up from nowhere! I'm not lying I swear to God. Perhaps I'm going crazy!"

Leroy placed his hands on her shoulders and gently squeezed.

"I don't think you're crazy." His own voice surprised him. It was so hoarse and bashful.

"I know what to do! You wait here for a second." He quickly ran up the stairs.

Shabnam shook her head. It was all falling apart. Her carefully constructed schemes were all collapsing like a ton of shit around her. Maybe someone had cast a spell on her; she had often heard Amma talk about such things. It was that bastard Dadaji! Always sitting on his ass with that rosary clicking away like a fucking machine gun. He had definitely done something. She knew he had always had it in for her. He wanted her to be like a doormat so that every other Pakistani male could wipe their feet on her. She clenched her jaw. She would get her own way. She was going to do it today. She was going to give Leroy the ride of his life.

He came down with a scarf in his hands.

"Just close your eyes and relax, baby." Using the scarf as a blindfold, he gently covered her eyes and tied a knot at the back of her head. He then took her by the hand and led her to a sofa.

"Just lie back and open your mind. Let it loose baby."

Shabnam did as she was told and quickly her body became limp.

"That's it baby. You're getting the hang of it. Are you seeing your grandfather now?"

224

She shook her head.

"You see. I told you. Ain't nobody coming between us. Now I got a little surprise for you. Just wait here!"

Shabnam nodded, wondering if he was going to surprise her with another one of his stupid gifts. Sometimes he gave her bits of jewellery that were so expensive; she knew she could never wear them without attracting attention from her friends and family and so she would lash out at him for being such a thoughtless bastard.

"Just lie still now, baby. Let your mind go free."

Shabnam felt something icy at the base of her neck moving upwards and before she knew it Leroy had guided whatever it was into her mouth. She squawked and spat out an ice-cube. Enraged, she sat up, ripped off the blindfold and slapped Leroy hard across the face.

"What the fuck do you think you're doing?" she snarled.

"I'm kinda losing the mood here, Shabnam."

"I'm sorry I wanted this to happen today but something is wrong. Someone is fucking with my mind, or maybe my mind is fucked up. I don't know. But I swear to God I keep seeing my grandfather. You think I'm making this up don't you but I'm not I swear to you I'm not. I don't want to be like this with you. I don't." Her voice shook with tears.

Leroy grinned.

"I got it. You know what we can do. We can go down into the basement. Man, it's so fucking dark down there you can't even see your hand in front of your face, let alone your granddaddy. It's a little cold but hey at least we'll be together. Together forever, you get what I'm saying baby!"

Shabnam shook her head vehemently and wiped away the tears from her face.

"I am not a rat, Leroy. And I will not get down and dirty in any fucking basement. Not for you or for any fucking man."

"I'm sorry Shabnam. I just—"

She cut him off with a dismissive wave of her arm.

"I need to get going now. Do you mind lending me some money for a taxi?"

"OK, you win," he said dejectedly. He passed her his wallet.

Remembering that she had missed her brother she asked, "I'm a bit short so do you mind if I take £50?"

"Sure, not a problem," said Leroy. He suddenly felt very tired.

She blew him a quick kiss as she left.

Leroy looked mournfully at the door. As he bent to pick up the plates he felt his phone vibrate.

"Hello," he answered morosely.

"Wassup Leroy, you sound like shit!"

"Ah…Cupid has got his foot right up my ass."

17

Musa was preparing for a second session at the Islamic Centre and had spent the past hour preparing a PowerPoint presentation using a laptop borrowed from Babarr.

When the three groups of men were seated, he introduced the evening.

"Assalaam-u-alaikum my dear brothers. I am glad to see so many of you here again. Tonight the subject of our discussion is a very famous person who has done a great deal for Islam. Tell me, has anyone ever heard of Abdullah Yusuf Ali?"

"He wrote a translation and commentary of the Quran—"

"Correct. Abdullah Yusuf Ali was one of the first commentators of the Quran in English. Now brothers, I want you to turn your attention to the screen."

Musa pressed a button on the laptop and an image of an austere-looking bearded man with fierce eyes and a black turban filled the screen.

"Remember this image," said Musa. He pressed another button and another image filled the screen. That of a craggy Indian man dressed in a suit and tie. The man's eyes were sad and tired and he had a faint moustache. His

227

swarthy face seemed frozen in a gentlemanly effort to smile.

"Now brothers, I have shown you two pictures and one of them is of Abdullah Yusuf Ali. Can anybody guess which one?"

"Sure can bro. It's the guy with the beard. The other guy looks like one of them fifty years on," said one of the rude boys pointing to the coconuts.

There was some jeering and the raising of two fingers but one of the coconuts frowned and stood up. "I actually agree with him. The other guy just doesn't seem to be the Islamic type."

Musa smiled, "In fact Yusuf is this guy." He pointed to the picture of the man in suit and tie.

"He doesn't even have a beard. How can he be fit to commentate on the Quran?" asked an appalled Holy Man.

"Let me tell you some facts about Abdullah Yusuf Ali. He was born in 1872 in India. Does anyone know what it was like for Indians at the time of the British Raj?"

"It wasn't good," answered a rude boy. "We've all heard about General Dyer and the Amritsar massacre, and the way men and women were forced to walk about on all fours as if they were dogs."

"Yes, that is true. But what some of you may not know is that the British rewarded loyalty and Abdullah Yusuf Ali was amongst those who were intensely loyal to the British," said Musa.

This annoyed a coconut who asked, "How is any of this relevant? I mean where are you heading with this?"

"It's extremely relevant. Abdullah Yusuf studied law at Cambridge. He was one of the few Indians to be accepted into the Indian Civil Service, an organisation which basically ruled India. He also married an English woman who did not convert to Islam."

"He married an English woman! Any of our parents would kill us if we did the same thing. They would tell us to convert her or to get out," said an astonished rude boy.

"We know all about Abdullah Yusuf Ali. He was a white man in a brown skin. He did not lead the life of a Muslim and his commentaries should be burnt!" shouted an outraged Holy Man.

"That's where you're completely wrong," argued Musa. "At the time of the British Raj, there were a great many Muslims who were as fluent in English as they were in Urdu. And although there were a great many Urdu translations of the Quran, none of them explained or came close to explaining the truths in the Quran. But Abdullah Yusuf Ali was able to do this. Let me give you an example:

"'Man We did create from a quintessence (of clay). Then We placed him as (a drop of) sperm in a place of rest, firmly fixed. Then We made the sperm into a clot of congealed blood; then of that clot We made a (foetus) lump; then We made out of that lump bones and clothed the bones with flesh; then We developed out of it another creature. So blessed be Allah, the best to create.'

"If you read his notes on that verse, they mention the way the zygote cell, the fertilised egg if you like, grows by division, eventually becoming a foetus. That's the point I

229

want to make: at that time there was no other Islamic scholar who could use his knowledge of embryology to explain that verse. And throughout his translation and commentary, he does it time and time again. For example when the Quran tells us that Allah taught the bee how to make its home, Abdullah explains in meticulous detail exactly how that happens. Before him there was no Muslim translator of the Quran who did that."

"So the geezer had a library card. Big deal," said Urfan.

"Why should we Muslims owe him a debt of gratitude? Most people who read his Quranic commentary can hardly understand it, especially his notes!" said a coconut.

"Go to any mosque in pretty much any country and you will usually find his translation. There may be better commentators who were more fluent in Arabic than him, such as Mohammad Asad, but you are still more likely to see his translation," replied Musa.

"What happened to him, this granddaddy of coconuts?" asked a rude boy.

Musa sighed, "Ah…It was all very sad. His first wife, called Teresa Mary, had four children with him and then had an affair with someone called Obed Thorne. She had his child and poor old Abdullah Yusuf Ali had a nervous breakdown."

"Serves him bloody right. If he knew so much about Islam, what was wrong with him marrying one of his own?" asked a rude boy.

"You're missing the point again. At that time, the English way was considered to be the highway in life. So an English woman was supposed to be the ultimate. I bet he wet himself with joy when she agreed to marry him," said a coconut.

"What I have never understood is why he didn't bother to convert her," pondered a Holy Man.

"The brother just explained it. Abdullah Yusuf Ali thought the English were an inherently noble race. He thought that their natural instincts were Islamic instincts like compassion, kindness and tolerance. He even called the Royal family 'precious examples of purity'," answered Musa.

"Sounds like the geezer had a screw loose. What about that shit in Amritsar and all those Indians being made to walk like dogs? Didn't he see any of that?" queried Urfan.

"He most certainly did, but for some reason he was as loyal as a dog to the British," replied Musa.

"That's funny. A hundred years later and we're in their country but no one wants to be like them."

"You're wrong. There are plenty of guys that want to be like them. It's only Holy Joes like you that don't. Those that do just don't want to be Muslim at the same time," retorted a rude boy.

"That's right. And poor old Abdullah Yusuf Ali never did find any long lasting joy in the arms of a white woman. He married another English woman, Gertrude Mawbey who he called Masuma. They had a son, Rashid, but eventually they separated," said Musa.

"At least he was pulling them. You gotta give the guy some credit for that," remarked a rude boy.

"The only reason he was able to pull them was that he was probably more English than their own dads and spoke all posh and sophisticated. Women love that shit," smiled a coconut knowingly.

"Maybe, but whatever his personal life was like, he was the British Empire's number one man for representing their interests to Muslims. He travelled all over the world and everywhere he went he was treated like gold dust. He even opened the first mosque in Canada. But when the British left India he had no place to go," said Musa.

"What about his kids?"

"His children from his first marriage ended up hating him. When he died he left them nothing." Musa referred to his notes. "He wrote this in his will: 'these children by their continued ill-will towards me have alienated my affection for them, so much so that I confer no benefit on them.' Most of his money went to a fund set up in his name to help Indian students at London University."

"I can see why those children hated him. What the fuck did he expect? If you don't spend any time with your kids and go around the world acting like a hotshot white man, that's exactly what's gonna happen. He had no one to blame but himself," said a rude boy.

"Yes that is true. Children are your responsibility and they must be taught about their identity as Muslims," agreed a Holy Man.

"I'm surprised he didn't realise that. What's the point of a good education if you don't have enough common sense to see the obvious," said a coconut.

All three groups were in accord, Musa noticed. He continued, "I think you've hit the nail on the head, brother. One freezing cold winter poor old Abdullah was found by the police sitting in Trafalgar Square. His clothes were in rags and he had no money. They took him off to a council poor home. Shortly after this he got ill and he died in hospital. His death certificate stated that he was senile. Next time you pick up a copy of his translation you may want to say a prayer for his soul. Despite his intellect, his knowledge and his life experiences, he died without having a home or people around him that loved him. He knew so much about Islam and other religions but that didn't help him become a happier or better person."

After the session had ended Musa returned the laptop to Babarr's office. Khadija was sitting behind the desk, writing.

She looked up as he came in. "How did they take to the life and times of Abdullah Yusuf Ali?" she asked, amused.

Musa was taken aback at the realisation that she had been within earshot of the discussion. "How much of it did you hear?"

"A bit. You really felt for him didn't you?"

Musa nodded. "Yes I suppose I did. You see the sad thing was that he really tried hard to link his knowledge to his faith, but he failed. He just couldn't connect to the world beyond the page."

Khadija leaned back in the swivel chair and tapped her pen on the desk.

"It tells us that in the Quran doesn't it? 'This is the Scripture in which there is no doubt, containing guidance for those who are mindful of God, who believe in the unseen.' If you believe only in your own arguments and reasoning, then you will never get guidance. You're a good example of that."

"How so?" he asked tersely.

"Your quest for beauty. Would you ever agree to marry someone whose face you couldn't see?" Khadija's eyes twinkled when she saw how stung he was.

"No, most definitely not. But that's nothing to do with a lack of trust or faith in Allah. It's just a matter of choice. I believe that in certain situations the best veil is behind the eyes," replied Musa.

Khadija did not reply but looked at him as though he were a child trying on a cap that was too big for him.

"You're laughing at me aren't you?" asked Musa.

"No I'm not, and even if I was how would you ever be able to tell?"

"What about you? Would you ever show your face to your husband or to a guy you might want to marry?"

Khadija looked at her watch and gathered up her papers before leaving.

"No I would not and no I have not."

"How do you mean?" he asked

Khadija stopped by the door. "I'm engaged."

"Oh…Who is he?"

"Why ask when you will never get to meet him?"

"Was it arranged or was it a love thing?"

Khadija walked off, laughing.

Musa stayed where he was, lost in thought until an insight unfurled within his heart, bringing him out of his reverie. The drop of rain as it descended to the barren earth, the gradual reducing of a mighty intellect to an abject vagabond: all was caused by the agency of Allah. The mysteries of matrimony, the miseries of incompatibility, the riddle of aspiration; all were written in a decree. He like everyone else stood beside the shore of that mystic sea, forever trying yet never knowing just what it was that was meant to be.

18

Titty Soups lay sprawled across a marble slab in the steam room of the Asian Aqua Experience of which he was part-owner. His lean, athletic physique was naked apart from a flimsy white towel that just covered the taut mounds of his buttocks. The air around him was heavy with the tang of eucalyptus and birch, and antique brass lights lazily stirred columns of air, steaming the frosted glass windows.

A buxom masseuse of possibly Russian extraction pummelled his back, looking ravenously at the white towel. As she worked she pressed her fingernails into the top of his buttocks, causing him to wince.

"Ouch! Hey would you ease up bitch? You're not digging for gold!" complained Titty Soups.

"That's where you're wrong. She's after the family jewels all right," said Babarr with a leer.

"Fuck off!" grunted Titty Soups. He lifted his head and rested it on one hand and looked over to Musa and Babarr.

"What brings you two here?"

"I have been ringing you for the past four days but that numbskull of a receptionist you have did not seem to have a clue where you were. So I thought to myself, Titty's with a woman. But after two days I said to myself no way is Titty with a woman for that long. So I thought the Child Support Agency were after you again and you were lying low and then this morning I went to your restaurant and they told me you were here and so here I am!" said Babarr angrily.

"So what the hell do you want?"

"Some manners would be nice, you moody bastard! What's eating you?" asked Babarr.

"I went to a Diwali festival in Leicester, if you must know."

Babarr, startled by this announcement, asked, "What the fuck for?"

"I wasn't gonna convert if that's what you're thinking. I was there to eye up the cheese and plant a few seeds if you get what I mean." He winked at Babarr, looking for a second like his old self.

"But you don't need to do that shit. Enough women throw themselves at you."

Titty Soups settled his head down again.

"But they only want a way out of their low ceiling lives. They see a guy who's got the looks and the money and they think hey we got ourselves the dream. We don't have to live in our two by two rooms anymore. But that dream turns into a fucking nightmare when they get all clingy and then they start giving you the third degree every time you go for a piss and eventually you get so fucked off with them you want out. And that's when all the shit starts! Those girls don't let go without a fight. There ain't no heavyweight boxer in the world that can go the distance the way these girls can. They find out where you live and then they find out where your mum lives and where your grandma lives in Pakistan and before long you start thinking death is better than this shit."

"What do all these tramps see in you? I swear to God it beats the shit out of me!" mused Babarr.

"Dunno man. I was born pretty but I don't believe that's it somehow. I think lots of girls take me home with them inside their heads. You know something? This is no lie, but I swear to you that guys sometimes invite me around their house for dinner because they know their woman won't be able to take her eyes offa me and then afterwards she'll feel so guilty she'll give him a bit of night-time dessert."

Titty Soups lifted himself up on his elbows and looked gravely at Babarr: "I reckon I have indirectly fathered half the kids in this town."

Babarr chuckled and asked: "Is the sky blue in your world?"

"Kiss my red ass and tell me what you want."

"Some time ago you told me there's a family in your area that has come from Pakistan and they're on the lookout. What's the deal with them?"

"The Gafoors. So far as I know they're still looking. The girl looks OK. I could set something up if you like."

"Do that because my man here is running out of time. He's gotta find someone suitable and soon," said Babarr nodding in Musa's direction.

Titty Soups waved a hand at the steam as if trying to get a clearer view of him.

"But there is no such thing as a suitable wife. Any girl who is fertile can be a suitable wife. You don't want suitable, Musa, you want dependable and steady. Because believe me, girls nowadays have gotta dark past. You rattle their closet and nasty things will fall out."

The House of Gafoor, at the very edge of a leafy suburb, had a distinctly gothic quality. From the outside, it was easier to believe that the occupants were troubled ghosts and not frustrated Pakistani parents trying desperately to find a worthy match for their precious daughter.

Just as he was about to lift the heavy door-knocker, Babarr turned to Musa who was carefully dressed in a black tunic and trousers.

"Now before we go in there, remember you work for me. I pay you a salary of 37K a year and the promotion prospects are fantastic. You have already been head-hunted by several Arab institutions but you turned them all down because you want to provide a service for the community. You have an apartment at the Islamic Centre but you choose to live with Mum and Dad because they are elderly and you want to look after them. Got it?" he growled.

Musa nodded dutifully.

"Good. Let me do the talking. Remember, girls are attracted to men with strength so there is the real possibility that she might start giving me the eye. If that happens I will make it clear in no fucking uncertain terms that I ain't interested."

He paused. "If they ask you why you are dressed that

way I will say it's your preferred dress and then you say it's because that's what Saladin wore when he captured Jerusalem. If they ask how you know, go like this," he pushed his tongue behind his bottom lower lip and made a strange barfing sound. "Say you watched the film with that guy from *Pirates of the Caribbean* just like everyone else."

He winked at Musa before hammering at the door.

A small swarthy man, a servant of some sort, yet with a dignity acquired through proximity with wealthier men, greeted them.

"Hey buddy. We are here to meet the Gafoors. They're expecting us," said Babarr.

The faintest hint of a smile passed across the man's face as he beckoned them in to the house and in to a room furnished in a bizarre concoction of styles. Regency chairs stood at either side of a Victorian fireplace, now modified with phoney coals which glowed an intense red. A golden star-shaped clock, probably from Argos, hung on a wall decorated with deep-green flock wallpaper. Most curious of all, above a Land of Leather settee, was a large print of the *Mona Lisa*, the woman with the strange smile that reminded Musa of Imam Faisal, a travelling speaker who visited the Madrasah and spoke endlessly and bafflingly about states within states and the black house and the White House.

One time Ali had got hold of a bottle of ethyl-alcohol, a chemical which evaporated at room temperature and the resulting vapour had the curious property of freezing anything it came in contact with. Musa had told Ali to get rid of it by pouring it down the toilet but Ali refused to carry out such a menial task so Musa had to do it. As he left the toilet Imam Faisal walked in. Petrified Musa waited. He knew he should fear the worst but, when Imam Faisal emerged, he had on his face that Mona Lisa smile although he walked with a strange gait.

Just then, a sound of tinkling bracelets and rustling clothes was heard. With a regal flourish, a large woman in a psychedelic sari with short dyed red hair swept into the room.

"Ah…you must be Musa and Babarr. How delightful to meet you. Do sit down."

A fat hand with pink-varnished, pointed fingernails pointed to the sofa. "Ronnie! The guests have arrived." Her voice rose to a commanding octave.

She lowered her bulky form on to one of the regency chairs and smiled an impossibly charming smile. Size for size, she had a torso to match Babarr's. Her face was broad and her cheeks were pronounced in contrast to a thin, delicately proportioned nose. Most disconcerting of all her eyes, darting from Babarr to Musa, were almost feral in their keenness.

"So how was your journey?" she asked with legs crossed and hands resting daintily on her knees.

"Oh…it was fine. You know what they say about traffic these days. It's a bitch wherever you go."

Babarr chuckled jovially and in response the mother let off a round of tinkling laughter. Musa smiled politely. He wondered at the name Ronnie. Was he perhaps a convert to Islam? But then she didn't seem the type to marry a white man and then return to Pakistan. Normally it was the other way around. And her manner…too haughty…too authoritative…no, there was no doubt she wore the trousers and a corset too by the looks of it. Aboo was often known to rant against a woman who acted as if she was the man of the house. Such women were part of the hierarchy of Pakistani society. They danced within the parameters of their gilded lives, viewing the lower classes with a disdain that only the well-mannered among them tried to conceal. What could have made such a person leave the safe, secure waters of Pakistani gentility Musa wondered?

A tall, slim man walked into the room and sat in the Regency chair facing his wife, his posture ramrod straight. He was dressed like a member of the English landed gentry in a tweed jacket with a yellow pullover. Around his neck was what seemed to be some sort of handkerchief. His hair was neatly parted in the centre and he sported a thin symmetrical moustache.

"This is my husband Raja, but I call him Ronnie for short. Raja is such a mouthful you know," said Mother. She laughed as if this was the funniest thing she had said in years.

"So tell me young man. What is your connection to Musa? Are you related or are you a family friend?" inquired Mother.

"Well actually, I am a family friend. But I am also much more. I am his employer and mentor," replied Babarr importantly.

"Oh how wonderful! What do you mean exactly?"

Babarr settled back and clasped his hands together. "Well you see…Aunty, I've been a friend of the family for a very long time. And one day I get a call out of the blue from Musa's brother Suleiman. He goes, I gotta kid brother who's wetter than a dolphin behind the ears. Can you make sure he gets some life experience? I said no worries. You send him to me I'll make sure he gets so much life experience he'll wanna stop living!"

He laughed uproariously. This time however the Mother did not add her tinkling laughter and her face took on a pained pinched expression.

"And what is it that you do exactly, Babarr?"

"I'm a builder. Never spent a day on the dole. Never cheated anybody. All my life I worked hard and I slept good. Never done no hanky-panky with no chick. I give as good as I get and then some. There ain't nobody in this town that messes with me. Because they know that to mess with Babarr is a one way ride to the shit-creek of misery. Some blokes don't like what others do. All I say is that I ain't gotta answer to you on the Day of Judgement, so if you don't like what I say or what I do you can go to hell, because this baby ain't for turning."

The silence that followed Babarr's profile of himself seemed to suck the oxygen out of the air. Then came the sound of breath being drawn and good manners were restored. Mother smiled weakly and began to laugh again, but this time her laughter faded away.

"How…how charming." She frowned. "But we were told that Musa is an educator not a builder."

"He is an educator. You see I'm not just a builder of

243

homes. I run an Islamic Centre because I want to build something for the afterlife. I wanna get together some of the boys and some of the girls and make some noise. Because that's the way I learn shit. If you put a book in front of me, man, it's like toilet paper. But if you shout and scream, then I get it.

"That's how it all started. One day I was looking at this wall that I knocked down that I shouldn't have knocked down, if you know what I mean, and the guy starts screaming like a monkey and giving me all this jip and I suddenly realised that everything in life will be like that wall. Just a pile of dust. You can work hard all your life but what you got to show for it? A shithole with three bedrooms and kids who'll show you disrespect by running after every bit of white flesh they see. But with Islam, you can build something that will last. You get what I mean?"

Before anyone could answer, the servant entered the room carrying a corncob pipe. Ronnie opened his mouth as if in anticipation of a passionate kiss from Mother and the servant gently placed the pipe in his master's mouth. Removing a box of matches from the side pocket of his tunic he carefully lit the tobacco: Ronnie inhaled with great satisfaction, blew his pleasure into the servant's face and waved the man away.

Musa saw Babarr fixing Ronnie with a mean stare.

"Just how much do you earn Musa?" asked Mother. Her voice seemed to have a hard edge to it.

The servant stopped on his way to the door. Ronnie's hand froze in the air just as he was about to take his pipe out of his mouth while Musa pondered the question. He

244

had already forgotten the rehearsed answer and felt embarrassed. Then Babarr spoke.

"I pay him £37,000 a year," said Babar nonchalantly.

Mother nodded, her eyes flickering with calculation. "Is that net or gross?"

"Gross," replied Babarr.

"What tax code is on your payslip?" she asked. Her voice was tense and she now sat with her arms folded tightly across her chest.

"What…what do you mean?" Musa hadn't a clue what she was talking about.

"Do you have a K code or a BR code or an NT code or a DO code?" pressed Mother, urgently.

Befuddled, Musa turned to Babarr and whispered, "What do we do?"

Ronnie, mishearing the whisper, was immensely pleased. "It's a DO code. He's a high rate taxpayer."

Mother smiled approvingly. "What about prospects for promotion," she asked.

"Fantastic. If he keeps getting more people interested in Islam, I've promised to build a big five-bedroom house free of charge. That means that he'll be getting the salary plus he won't be saddled with a mortgage," answered Babarr.

Musa pondered on the implausibility of this promise and wondered if Ronnie and Mother had experienced a neural alert to Babarr's bullshit.

Mother, however, continued to smile. "This is all most interesting. I will phone you in the evening to let you know if we wish to pursue this matter."

Babarr frowned in annoyance and turned to Musa, who nodded eagerly.

"Not a problem Aunty," sighed Babarr.

"Bring down Rani!" commanded Mother.

Impassively, the servant nodded his head and shuffled slowly out of the door. Mother then turned to Musa.

"You appear to be a very quiet young man. What can you give my daughter?"

Before he could answer, Babarr spoke.

"I think you're coming from the wrong angle, Aunty. You should be thinking what your girl could do for my boy here. Because, let's be honest, why have you come to this country to look for a geezer for your gal?"

"Because we feel that England can offer our daughter certain things that Pakistan cannot. The situation in Pakistan is very unstable. Nobody knows what will happen from one day to the next," answered Mother.

"No. If you were so worried about the politics, you would have come to the UK years ago. That way your girl could have gone to university here and you could have made her into a doctor or something. The reason you're here, the reason why everyone from Pakistan comes here is because you want to go prospecting!"

"Prospecting?" asked Mother, puzzled.

"Yep, prospecting. The way guys in America used to go prospecting for gold back in the time of Clint Eastwood. They would take out a pan and dip it in the local river to see if they couldn't find any gold. When that didn't work out they'd try their luck in another river till eventually they hit the jackpot. Same thing with you guys. You can't tell me that you didn't try for a doctor or an army officer in Pakistan. That way you would have lived like kings there. You're here because your pan turned up rocks instead of gold."

Mother was indignant but before she could launch into a rebuttal, the servant was holding the door open for Rani. He flicked an amused glance at Musa, and then immediately cast his eyes down.

Rani's large hazel eyes swam in innocence. Her hair fell freely around her shoulders in a rolling black mass of waves and her smile to Musa spoke of the unbidden blossoming of shyness into courtesy. She was beautiful. As their eyes took in each other's appearance with pleasure, Musa felt such elation. She was the one: the emblem of his victory and the symbol of Allah's bounty. Nothing could match the majesty of this moment. It was a divine precursor to a life most blessed. The dreams he had hugged and cherished in the twilight hours of the morning would not now be sucked into the abyss of reality for fate had decreed.

A couple of hours after meeting Rani they were back in Babarr's office with the others. "What is taking her so long? And where's Shabnam?" asked Armila irritably.

"She had to stay at home as my mum was poorly," said Suleiman.

"I bet you a tenner it's a yes!" said Babarr, gazing at his mobile.

"You're on," replied Suleiman, taking out his wallet.

"Do you mind!" protested Musa.

"The girl was giving Musa the eye. I'm telling you man. She could not take her eyes off him," said Babarr.

Then it came: the digitised sound heralding the all-important text message.

"So sorry. Best wishes," read Suleiman.

"It's a no," said Babarr gloomily.

Musa hung his head.

"You set this thing up. What happened?" demanded Armila.

"How the fuck do I know? Titty Soups said they were a respectable land-owning family from Pakistan who were on the look-out for a respectable man from a good family," answered Babarr.

Suleiman laughed. "That's most definitely us."

Armila had devoted considerable thought to the enigma that was Suleiman. She gave him a quick once-over. As usual he was dressed in that long flowing leather coat over black nondescript clothes.

"Cheer up, Musa. There'll be other girls," said Suleiman.

"No there won't, not like her," said Babarr. "This girl was genuinely fit. Man she lit up that room. And she was all shy and pretty. You know the way a woman should be. Not like these mouthy slags you come across nowadays. Why can't more women be like that?"

"You weren't exactly honest with her. Telling her that Musa was earning thirty-seven grand a year!" said Armila.

Babarr stuck up his middle finger, his head still down. He reached into his pocket for his mobile phone and marched towards the door.

"Hey where do you think you're going?" said Suleiman.

"I'm gonna ring Titty Soups and ask him to come here. He'll know what to do next."

"Look, I think that you're gonna come across this a lot. It doesn't matter whether the girl is educated or not or whether she's from Pakistan or not. She isn't looking for decency and Islam, she's looking for a high-flyer – a guy with a flash car and a detached house who's his own man and is not afraid of telling his family where to go if they start interfering. That's what all the Asian girls here are looking for. If you say to them I'm earning thirty grand they'll say we'll be in touch and they'll put you on the reserve list and start looking for a guy who's on eighty or ninety. If you wanna be a player you gotta act like it's a game of poker where the guy with the biggest hand wins," said Armila.

She stood up and placed her hands on her hips and looked sternly at Musa. "Why do you think every Asian parent, Pakistani or Indian, is trying to get their son or daughter to be a doctor? It's not about prestige or respect, it's because they know these people earn a hundred thousand a year plus. That's the kind of money that gets you married. Musa is not in that league," she continued.

"Not everyone is like that. Are you telling me only doctors and dentists get married?" argued Suleiman.

"No, I'm not saying that. Let me put it another way. You gotta look at this thing as if it were a horse race. The doctors and dentists are the Arabian stallions. The graduates in the normal nine to five jobs, they're studs but not so hot. Everyone else is just a donkey," concluded Armila.

"Are you saying I'm a donkey?" asked Musa.

"Not quite a donkey but nowhere near a stud and most definitely not a stallion. But that's not your fault. You weren't raised in the right stable. And it's not the fault of the girls either. They have got mums who remember what life was like in the village and who don't want the same for their daughters. It's that simple."

"Stupid is what it is. People just don't realise that not every problem in marriage is about money," said Suleiman.

"You're so wrong," said Musa. "People follow their heart not their head. It's always been like that. I once read a poem by an English poet who was born more than three hundred years ago. He said the same thing. 'The ruling passion be it what it will, the ruling passion conquers reason still'. All it takes is that little moment inside your heart and then nothing else will matter. And when you see that in the other person's eyes, then you know it's forever. That's what none of you get. People never stop dreaming. It doesn't matter whether you're rich or poor, everyone wants a bit of wonder in their life. And they'll go on and on trying to find it. Maybe they'll cheat on their wives, maybe their wives will start living in a fantasy world, but they'll never stop looking. That's what it's all about; passion, not money."

The lights were on, meaning that they were still there. Thank God, thought Shabnam. She pushed the door open and saw a man she did not know sitting with his feet on the desk wearing a magenta and black striped shirt and

Armani trousers. It must be that bastard the girls called Stud Muffin and the men called Titty Soups.

So the rumours about him were true. "He looks so good and dresses so nice that at first I thought he was gay. But then afterwards when we went upstairs...girl I'm telling you he is a walking talking Karma Sutra," was typical of the comments she had heard.

"You must be Shabnam." He got to his feet and came round to the front of the desk. He studied her with his face tilted as if she were a rare breed of butterfly.

"Do you know your name means Morning Dew?" he smiled. "Your father must have seen a row of petals in the early morning before he named you. Suleiman has mentioned you before, but for some reason he plain forgot to mention your beauty."

"Maybe that's because he doesn't think with his brain in his trousers...*Titty.*" Shabnam said his name with acid precision.

Titty Soups laughed easily. "I see my reputation precedes me but don't believe everything you hear. I do have some flaws you know," he added in mock humility.

"Yes I know. One of my friends used to be one of your women."

"Oh...who would that be?"

"Rekha."

"Rekha? The name doesn't ring a bell, I'm afraid. But then it takes someone pretty special to ring my bell."

"Yeah...like anything that walks and has a pulse."

"You know you have a fantastic sense of humour. I like that in a woman."

"Your conversation makes we want to puke. I want to get out of here."

"I can give you a lift in my Alpha Romeo, if you like?" What a flash git Shabnam said to herself.

"I don't think so. People might think I'm one of your whores."

"Not to worry, the windows have smoked glass. We could stop at my place for a cup of coffee, if you want," he suggested.

"Fuck you," she said, leaving but as she opened the door, something made her turn to look at him. Titty Soups was smiling at her. She hated herself for the rest of the night.

Back in his flat Titty Soups reclined in the Casanova armchair he had bought at a substantial discount because of a certain down-payment the sales manageress had received from him. Shabnam obviously knew of him – that was the price of fame – although he was still unable to recall Rekha. His memory was not as good as it used to be. Perhaps he was getting on. There was no denying that the slide downwards from his peak had slowly begun. He had tried to live as if he were to die tomorrow.

He grimaced, Babarr was right. Going to that Diwali festival was a dumb idea. It was all getting to be tiresome. The thrill of the chase, the conquest, the brush off: you simply could not keep doing this shit anymore. Truth be told, the majority of women were beginning to bore him. The endless small talk, which he had perfected long ago, was beginning to sound flat and stale.

The eyes of a girl told you far more than was gained from thirty years of small talk. He focussed, trying to decide whether or not Shabnam had given him the look. She really was a stunner. Was there something when she first saw him, the moment when the look was at its most potent? Yes there was, although she had very quickly switched it off; sometimes girls did that because they did not like the feeling of overwhelming attraction – this was particularly so with married women. With her it was more to do with her personality, she was one feisty little minx all right. Her conversation was aggressive, perhaps too aggressive. But as she was about to leave, she quickly looked at him and turned away, very annoyed with herself. He smiled...that was it...undeniable proof. She had been bitten by the Titty bug, but not smitten. No sir, she was fighting it. Why? He had probably treated Rekha like shit but he bet his sore ass that if he were to ring her she would come running.

There was something else with Shabnam and he guessed she was going out with another guy. Yes, that was it; he had encountered that reaction from faithful girlfriends many times. Overcoming it was no real problem. He tapped his fingers on the arm of his chair. The time had come to settle down and do the right thing. He was Pakistani after all and they did say marriage was half of faith. Shabnam had the requisite qualities of a good wife, she was beautiful and ballsy.

His mobile vibrated in his pocket, it was a call from his latest. He dropped the phone into the bin. It didn't really matter; it was pay-as-you-go and he had made a decision – it was time for a more permanent tariff.

Dadaji was praying, his forehead pressed down on his prayer mat, but when he lifted his head turning to the left and to the right to salute the watchful angels, he became aware that he was not alone in the living room.

"Shabnam, there is still darkness behind your eyes," he said, without turning around.

She opened her mouth to deliver her well-prepared tirade but no words came.

"You are still a virgin," he said softly.

The calmness of his remark infuriated Shabnam.

"What business is that of yours? Do you think I fear you? Do you think you can control me like you do my mother and father?"

Dadaji chuckled as he struggled to his feet.

"You are a part of my mark upon this earth. Every step you make in your life bears my imprint."

"I have no wish to be your mark. I am not ashamed of who I am. I am my own person."

"What are you, Shabnam?"

"I am not a slave. I am not your puppet. I live my life by my rules not yours. I do not care whether you approve of me or not. I will do and say as I please."

"Is that all you are? A child that cries no to everything and everyone around her? If that is so then your pride in yourself is shallow. Just like your mark on this world."

"Who are you to judge me?" her eyes blazed with anger.

"Pain, hardship and sacrifice have given me my judge's robes. Do you have such robes? Yet still you judge. But you judge the way a spider builds a web. Not knowing how frail and flimsy his creation is, yet all the time imagining himself to be the most important thing in his world. You cannot stand tall in water, Shabnam."

"How tall did you stand when your wife placed your baby daughter next to you and you pushed her off your string bed and broke her arm? How tall did you feel when you beat your son till he was senseless and then refused to pay the doctor that treated him?"

Dadaji was silent for a few moments and Shabnam's heart leapt in triumph.

"Yes, I did these things...Sometimes a man cannot give that which he did not receive."

"Yes, that is so true, Dadaji. You made my father what he is. But maybe I am a better person than you because I would never treat any child of mine the way you treated your children and the way my father treated me."

"The bond between parent and child is mystical, Shabnam. Maybe my children feared me more than they loved me. But the fear of someone who fears only Allah will guide you far more than the love of any adoring father. That is why I command the devotion of my children. I am the one who gave them knowledge of right and wrong. I am the one who planted the seed of faith in their hearts."

"Your children never loved you!" cried Shabnam.

"You are wrong," bellowed Dadaji. "Fear did not make your Aunty, whose arm I broke as a baby, wash me and bath me when I was ill with malaria last year. Fear does not make your father massage my feet with oil every night. But what do you know of such things? What do you know of poverty and its stench? What do you know of raising six children when you have nothing? I am the blanket which shielded them from a world which turned the poor into beggars with rotten teeth and bent backs. As I have lived I have learnt. You! A brash babe with so much certainty! The world in which you reign exists only in your mind. In the real world, your path in life begins from mine. And while you are on this path, learn these things. Hate does not inspire devotion. Cruelty does not inspire obedience. Neglect does not inspire loyalty."

"It doesn't inspire mine," said Shabnam.

"You glory in your defiance and take pride in your argument. It is these things that caused the downfall of Satan."

"Are you saying I am evil? Just because I stand up for myself?" Shabnam laughed scornfully.

Dadaji shook his head slowly. "Within you there are the seeds of evil but there is also a strain of shame. As long as there is shame, decency will never be far away."

"Would you be saying this if I were a boy? Would you ever give this lecture to Suleiman?"

"Like you Suleiman lives in a different world. Unlike you, he is haunted."

"Haunted by what?"

Dadaji waved her question away.

"Listen. Who is there in this world who takes pride in your decency and grieves at your evil? No one but your parents, your family. As time goes on, purity is leaving this world. People no longer fight against the whisper of evil. Instead they long for its madness. Evermore people rush to their own destruction. People like you who crave illusions. The pearls of youth which you so desperately seek; excitement, adventure, these are nothing but cheap trinkets. You will weaken yourself if you try too hard to claim them. I know of the lust inside you. You long for its fire but you are afraid of its smoke. Fight it. For once you give in to it, it will forever stain your heart."

He paused for a moment and then added gently, "Construct your decency again, Shabnam. Once you have done this, your anger and bitterness will disappear. You will be clean again."

The gentleness of his voice began to disarm her and for a fleeting second she felt tranquil. But then the defiance which was at her core took over and she turned on her heel, slamming the front door behind her.

Amma emerged from the kitchen. "One day she will never come back."

Dadaji roused himself and looked kindly at his niece. "The path of every child follows back to their parents. They will all come back to you one day."

19

When they had last met in Babarr's office, Suleiman had seen something in Musa's expression – a certainty and an excitement which came from being listened to and understood. These were emotions that he had never experienced, not at home, not even in a mosque. As he walked down the street, he had never before felt so full of longing. A middle-aged woman smiled at him as she made her way into the local church and that moment of simple contact prompted him to follow her. He felt on edge, almost fearful, as he walked through the open doors into what appeared to be an empty space.

At the far end was a huge stained glass window which depicted a woman dressed in blue with white doves hovering above her. Pillars ran along either side of rows of wooden pews and between two pillars was a statue of Christ with one hand raised, his eyes both eloquent and sad.

Dadaji had eyes like that, he thought. And the raised hand. It seemed to say so many different things; an instruction to patiently persist, a command to resist, a warning to desist. He stared, spellbound by its inferences.

"Can I help you?"

A kindly voice with a distinct Irish accent broke the spell. Unable to speak, Suleiman stared at a small bespectacled man in a long black robe.

"Have you come for confession?"

Suleiman shook his head, not quite knowing what this meant.

"But you would like to talk to somebody?" The priest smiled.

"It's a bit hard to explain," responded Suleiman awkwardly.

"Is it to do with a woman?"

"Yes I suppose you could say that." Suleiman shrugged and continued in a rush: "No. I... buy and distribute drugs."

"That is a most heinous sin."

Suleiman wondered what heinous meant but guessed it wasn't good.

"If I stopped it, my family would have no money. They all need a lot of money from me."

"Do they know what you do?"

"My mum knows, don't ask me how but she knows. My dad knows I'm up to something but he turns a blind eye." Suleiman laughed.

"Why do you laugh?"

"Because he never really looks at me anyway. You kinda have to be there to get the joke."

"Are you a Muslim?"

"No, but I am a Pakistani."

"What does your culture say about narcotics? Do you

259

know of the evil they wreak?"

"Yes I do know. I know they take away a person's life. I know they will bleed self-respect out of a guy and I know that they turn women into whores."

"If you know this, then you must fight the evil in you that makes you distribute these drugs."

"What do you need to fight evil, sir?"

"You need only sorrow and courage. Which of these two have brought you here?"

"I don't really know. A few days ago I saw this girl that I'd turned into a whore. And it hurt to see her, so I got pissed. And once I got pissed I started to cry but then afterwards I felt clean inside although it didn't last."

"Is that why you are here?"

Suleiman struggled: "I remember my younger brother told me that one time he went to a mosque and the mullah turned off the lights and said that everyone should think of their sins and repent. My brother said that within minutes everyone was bawling their eyes out. So I got to thinking maybe they were all remembering a time when they were like me or maybe they were just bastards anyway. I don't know. The point is, when I cried and felt good inside afterwards, I thought to myself what does it take to feel like this all the time?

"And another thing, my brother has respect because he is holy and honest..."

"All you need is the belief that you can be different."

"Really?"

"Yes. Is that what you needed to know?" asked the priest gently.

"I think so…"

"Forgive me, my son, but why did you not go to a mosque?"

"I don't think a mullah would understand where I was coming from. I don't think he would be able to help me."

"And have I?"

"Yes, you have… Thank you."

Suleiman quickly walked away.

"Go with God, young man," said the priest from behind.

Suleiman turned and smiled. He raised his hand in farewell: an imperfect resemblance of the statue.

20

"However eagerly you may want them to, most men will not believe."

Musa read the passage from the Quran and waited for a reaction from his audience.

A handful of Holy men nodded sadly. Others gazed tellingly at the rude boys who stared back defiantly.

"Why do you think that is, guys? That verse is not an opinion, it's a statement made by our Creator. Do you know there is a saying of the Prophet – Peace be upon Him – that on the Day of Judgement, nine out of ten people will be thrown into hellfire. Think about that! Ninety per cent of everyone who was ever born will be thrown into hellfire!" said Musa.

"It is the way people are, brother. People will not recognise the signs of Allah. Everybody is too interested in chasing after money and material things," said a Holy Joe sorrowfully. He directed a question at the rude boys. "Why is it that you people do not believe? Why do you do things that you know are wrong? Chasing after girls and going out to nightclubs?"

"We do believe, geezer! Why would we be here talking about Islam if we didn't? Besides, having a good time and enjoying yourself when you're young is not anti-Islam. We still respect our culture and that's what counts. We ain't like them," he pointed in the direction of the coconuts. "They act like they're white and speak posh and look down on us even though we're the same colour."

Musa sighed. This was becoming a common digression in their debates. "But that's not what I'm asking. What I want to know is do you think that mankind was a failed experiment. In the Quran it also tells us the mountains were given the chance to have a soul and a personality, but they refused. Do you think they realised something that mankind did not?"

"It's all about free will. Men were born with the power to decide to do either good or evil. But to say that we are a failed experiment is a bit harsh. We do the best according to what we know. My father taught me from a very early age to respect education, to work hard and now I'm a barrister. Ultimately it all comes down to what you were taught when you were young," said a coconut.

"Are you saying that most men were not well taught when they were young, they were not guided properly, and that is what has caused their downfall?" asked Musa.

"The point is, brother, men are not taught to fear their Creator. Without that fear you will always be led astray," declared a Holy Joe.

"So you can only believe and have faith if you fear Allah? If that's the case, then that explains it all. People don't like to live as if they're scared shitless. In life you gotta be strong. If you act like you're afraid then you're gonna be the biggest loser there is," said a rude boy.

"Why do you bring your stupid macho shit into every answer? Your attitude is the reason why people don't want to believe in Allah. You think you know it all and can do it all and the harder and quicker you knock someone down the easier it will be for you to step over them and get to your final destination. It's not like that at all!"

Seeing the Holy man's fury, Musa stepped in with another question. "How many of you pray five times a day?"

Only the Holy Joes raised their hands.

"How many of you think about the afterlife or spend any time during the day remembering Allah?"

The Holy Joes kept their hands raised.

"Do you think that if there was a ladder which you could climb and see the heavens, would that make you pray five times a day and persuade you to remember Allah?" asked Musa.

This time everyone raised their hands.

"You're wrong. It actually states in the Quran that even if you were to have such a ladder on which you could ascend to the heavens, ultimately you would still not believe."

"That's rubbish! Everyone in this world, Muslim or non-Muslim, would believe if they saw something like that," yelled a rude boy.

"Not necessarily," said Musa. "People of all ages have craved for the mysterious and the wonderful. They demanded from every prophet that these cravings be fulfilled in order for them to believe. But once they received fulfilment, they began to rationalise, to explain, and once you have an explanation for everything mysterious and wonderful, the inexplicable no longer has any hold over you. In faith there is no fantasy. When you believe in Allah, you have to undertake a responsibility. The mountains knew how grave that responsibility was and they refused it. We accepted it and failed. We may be smarter than a mountain but for some reason we're all just as stubborn as rocks."

Musa was concerned that the groups making up his audience were becoming fractious. Each group seemed to pray on the insecurities of the other. No one, not even the suave coconuts appeared to be comfortable in their own skin. They either attacked or defended, and rarely did they seem comfortable with valid criticism. Perhaps the reason they all came back was that they were trying to find validation for their life choices and they wanted to be liked, even by the bullish rude boys. This need to be liked by those you spent most of your time attacking was so very strange.

He gently knocked on the partially open office door for fear of startling Khadija who he guessed would already be there. Sure enough she was sitting at the desk making notes. The room was filled with a warm ambrosial smell of leather and incense which cheered Musa.

"Assalaam-u-alaikum, Musa," she said with her usual steady calm.

"Sound travels in this building and I heard some of your talk. It was an interesting choice of topic. What made you think of it?" she asked.

"The mystery of belief intrigues me. Why human beings do not live up to their potential? Why our descent into evil is no longer in doubt but a matter of fact? Do you never think about such things?"

Khadija shrugged: "I liked what you said at the end."

"So what was your conclusion?"

"The power of free will: you should have mentioned something about that. The fact that people are born with the power to decide their own path in life. They choose the path that is easiest for them and that always leads them astray. Like Adam and his wife in the Garden of Eden."

Khadija opened her Quran and read from *Al Baqarah*. "'Adam, live with your wife in this garden. Both of you eat freely there as you will, but do not go near this tree, or you will both become wrongdoers.' But Satan made them slip, and removed them from the state they were in. We said, 'Get out, all of you! You are each other's enemy.'

"He was told to stay away from the tree. He disobeyed. Had he shown more firmness, the outcome for all of us might have been different. It's easier to follow an impulse than to resist it. That's why the vast majority of us are doomed."

"You can't blame Adam," said Musa. "I remember reading a story narrated by the Prophet – Peace be upon Him – in the *Hadith*, in which he recounts an argument between Moses and Adam. Moses said, 'It was your lapse that caused us to leave the Garden of Eden,' but Adam would have none of it and replied, 'Why do you blame me for an act that was ordained forty years before I was created?'"

"I'm not blaming Adam; I'm saying that disobedience is a path to destruction. It is better to be patient and obey and reap the rewards," explained Khadija.

The certainty in her voice troubled Musa. He was rarely obedient either at the Madrasah or at home.

"Did I touch a raw nerve?" she asked.

"Well…truth be told, I don't obey people much. I get into a lot of trouble for it. But you know blind obedience is just as sure a path to ruin. If your intentions are right and if the cost of obedience is too high, then it is better to be disobedient."

"What cost are you talking about?"

"Happiness. Everyone has the right to do whatever they can to be happy. Be they a Muslim man or a Muslim woman, be they a Pakistani man or a Pakistani woman. No one can take that right away from you. We only have one life to live and just because our focus is on the hereafter as Muslims, it doesn't mean that we should spend our lives here in painful obedience. Are you happy, Khadija?"

She remained silent.

"You see, you're not are you? If you were happy, you wouldn't be able to hide it. Same way if you were unhappy."

Khadija looked at him with the ghost of a smile.

"Were you always this passionate?"

"Yes, always. Every time I set out to do something or prove something I can almost hear trumpets sounding in my head. There is fire in my belly and that is a great sensation. When you feel the dream becoming life and you know for sure that it's because you're trying, that's what it's all about. Doing something so that tomorrow is better than today. You don't know what's written for you, no one does, but that doesn't mean that you can't do your utmost to make sure that it's just as good as the dream, if not better."

"Does it always work out that way for you?"

"Very rarely. But I never mind that because life is always better and richer when you're passionate. If you follow your heart and your heart is pure, then it doesn't matter whether you're being disobedient or rebellious. You may not know the ending but the journey is much better."

Khadija got up and started to pack her books away.

"You're leaving?" asked Musa, disappointed. "You always leave when it gets interesting."

"I have responsibilities. Not all of us have the privilege of being passionate dreamers."

"Were you ever young, Khadija?" he asked as she left the room.

21

Khadija let herself in. Upstairs a TV was blasting out the angry rhetoric of an impassioned speaker. Abdel, her brother, was obviously home and that was unusual. Normally he spent his evenings at a mosque in Manchester, returning in the early hours of the morning.

She took off her veil, leaving only her hair covered. A large mirror stood in the hallway but she never checked the way she looked. Her interest in her appearance had died soon after she took to wearing a veil. As always she welcomed the feeling of air on her face and she ran her knuckles uneasily across her jaw as she entered the living room, keeping her head down.

One side of the wall was the colour of olives and the evening sunlight gave the room the sickly sheen of a dying field. A fireplace flickered illusory flames of cobalt blue across the walnut-coloured vinyl floor. Her father sat in a white leather armchair resting his thick feet on a coffee table and, as ever, she tried to gauge his mood.

"Shall I bring you your food?" she asked in a voice just loud enough to be audible and low enough to conceal feeling.

He grunted, his customary way of expressing assent.

Khadija, with her head still down, quickly left the room. As soon as she walked into the kitchen she could smell drink. Abdel drank furtively and when drunk he exploded with rage against the Great Satan and his many disciples, and the fawning Muslims who were Muslims in name only, who paid mortgages and acted like they were English, in a voice so raw with anger that the slurring was hardly noticeable. It was ironic that in the midst of these tirades he forgot that their mother was also English.

Her father, however, was not given to covering shame with outrage and when he drank his stupor was more deadly than her brother's. He was mean and sullen and his tongue could lacerate more keenly than a surgeon's knife. It was strange, perhaps even laughably strange, that her brother and father both dipped into the same intoxicant to drown a hatred that was so similar yet so different.

Khadija opened the fridge. On the uppermost shelf lay a wrapped plate of rice. She placed it by the microwave and began to prepare the curry as her father liked it – too hot for most.

He never made any demands about food. He would eat a few mouthfuls and leave the rest unfinished, never noticing that it was recycled from yesterday's meal. She suspected that dinner for him and the manner in which it was served was a symbol, a way of connecting to a time long ago when he was a merry tyrant basking in the achievements of his educated wife, scarcely registering the tiny tots that were his children.

She opened a packet of cumin and sprinkled two generous teaspoonfuls into a stainless steel pan. She pressed a button on the cooker and a yellow flame hissed. As the cumin began to brown she added some butter to the pan along with a teaspoon of coriander. By now the kitchen had filled with an aroma that was the signature of an Asian family. Carefully she tipped the rice into the pan and stirred it, adding a teaspoon of ground ginger and chilli.

Always, no matter what the day was or how full or empty it seemed, she would think of her mother when preparing food. A reel of memories ran through her mind and lingered and faded away: infants too young to understand and, a little later, young children trying so hard to find their bearings. Her absence eclipsed them all, and ugliness had grown. Her father's gradual withdrawal into himself and Abdel's emergence as a fanatic were rooted in her mother's betrayal.

She remembered her mother as an energetic, tall figure with a warm smile. She remembered hearing bitter arguments between her parents and her mother's spiral into depression. Then time played a subtle trick and she was gone and the memory of her departure was gone. It could not be recalled, so smooth had been the transition, so clean the excision. When Khadija's father had told his children that their mother had left the family and that they must forget her and move on, she knew that she must assume part of her mother's duties. Only later did she realise that children who take on the burden of a responsibility they do not understand become entombed by sobriety. That was her mother's real crime: the theft of that certainty children have that life is carefree. Yet still her mother lived on in Khadija's heart.

The food was now ready and she carried it to the living room. Her father had taken his feet off the table and, as she bent down and placed the tray in front of him, he glanced at her, his face livid with rage.

Khadija walked upstairs to her brother's room. The door was open. The floor was a mess of unwashed clothes but in contrast stacks of anti-western videos lay in neat piles by the TV. Abdel sat cross-legged on the floor in front of the screen. Sensing her presence he turned down the volume and stood up. The urgency of his movements betrayed a need.

"Do you have any money?" she asked softly. He glared at her but quickly looked away. At that moment his resemblance to their father had never been stronger. But what a state he was in: his long hair had not been washed and smelt bad and his beard was unkempt.

Khadija reached into her abaya and pulled out a handful of twenty-pound notes, her accumulated salary from Babarr, and placed the money on top of the TV to spare him the embarrassment of stretching out his hand.

"Aren't you still signing on?"

Abdel shook his head.

She had guessed as much. Her brother had been out of work for a while now and the benefits people would have been pestering him about finding a job or going on a training course. Proud young men like him were known to tell such well-wishers to go to hell.

"You're going to have to do something."

"Allah provides sustenance to whomsoever he pleases."

"How can you be so sure that includes people who do

272

nothing for themselves?" she asked as she left him.

In her own room, Khadija switched on the lights. The walls were painted yellow and the carpet was a bright red. Everything was in perfect order. Her prayer mat lay diagonally to her bed, the corners neatly folded. Against one wall was a white desk on which lay her rosary and her Quran and above that was a bookshelf. From the window she had a view of the garden.

Khadija picked up her Quran and sat down on a chair by the window. Nowadays she rarely read a chapter from start to finish but preferred instead to browse through the surahs and focus on verses which would give her insight and comfort.

She flicked through the Quran randomly until a verse caught her eye. It was from Surah *Fussilat*:

"Good and evil cannot be equal. Repel evil with what is better and your enemy will become as close as an old and valued friend, but only those who are steadfast in patience, only those who are blessed with great righteousness, will attain to such goodness."

Repelling evil with goodness seemed to be a trait that had become extinct in the modern world. It was like Jesus instructing his followers to turn the other cheek or walking two miles if someone forced you to walk a mile. But in that instruction was all that was hateful to people with pride and self-respect, because everyone around her, especially her father and brother, had grown up with the idea that their worth as a man was judged by their strength in defending themselves, to answer with a brick anyone who pelted you with a stone. A person's capacity for exaggerating their sense of self was truly remarkable, she thought. Perhaps that was only natural though, because everyone craved glory in the silence of their hearts. She had seen brash vanity multiply in the worthless, those poor people wretched in the need for accolades in a world that spurned them of the sunshine, moments that came as easily as breathing to others. People like her brother, whose self-belief began to mutate as the instinct for self-preservation began to tick like a time-bomb. Pride and anger converged to give birth to a polluted ego. Goodness sacrificed at the altar of self-respect and dignity, mused Khadija, a strange bargain.

She frowned in annoyance; her brother had turned up the volume again. He did this whenever he heard something that incited him.

"Imagine you have a small knife and a monster is in front of you. The monster keeps sniffing you and turning away as if he can't stand the smell of you. But all you have to do is stab him in the neck until he bleeds to death. That is the first step: destruction of the enemies of Allah."

Telling him to turn the TV down would be futile; she could only try to block it out. She read the next verse in the Holy Quran.

"If a prompting from Satan should stir you, seek refuge with God: He is the All Hearing and the All Knowing."

She wondered anew at this verse. She had once discussed it with some of her friends who took it to mean that if ever you got an instinct to kill someone or steal something then it was most definitely from Satan and naturally should be resisted. But that was too simplistic. It posed that disturbing question, how could any person know whether or not the instinct to stick up for yourself and fight for your self-respect was a whisper of evil? It was easier to be angry. Anger gave you that feeling of power. With self-restraint there were no such illusions. But people who had been treated badly by others, near and afar, what were they supposed to do? You could say that their justice lay in revenge but their reward most definitely lay in patience.

The angry voice on the DVD next door blasted on.

"We have been forced to live inside a toilet and there are some who think they can shit on us and order us around in that toilet. And guess what? They are right! Because we are all under the boots of the non-believers. And that's where we are going to stay until we start fighting for ourselves. Because Allah created this world for the believers for us and us only!"

Khadija flicked through the pages of the Quran again, until she came to the last verse of Surah *Imran*.

"You who believe, be steadfast, more steadfast than others; be ready; always be mindful of God, so that you may prosper."

It always came back to that, the need to be patient and constant. The two opposing foes of intolerance and haste. But patience was not inborn. You had to reason it into existence and once there it was frail. But where was its reward? she mused. Would every long suffering soul be rewarded only in paradise? Were you meant to view this world with the eyes of an ascetic? Just renounce your earthly wishes and desires and keep your gaze firmly fixed on the hereafter. So what if the good things of life passed you by, you would find your treasure in paradise.

She frowned, annoyed with herself for letting bitterness creep into her thoughts. She looked at the title of another Surah – *Al-Anfal*, or Battle Gains.

Telepathically the angry voice next door roused itself again.

"If a non-believer comes into your land unless there is no peace treaty then he is booty. You take him to the market place and sell him. That is your right...'

She read the opening verse of the Surah.

"They ask you about the battle gains. Say, that is a matter for God and His Messenger, so be mindful of God and make things right between you. Obey God and His Messenger if you are true believers."

Khadija wondered at the raging speaker on the other side of the wall. Her brother was probably oblivious to everything except his message. And he was not alone; she had begun to realise that only recently. Young men, disillusioned and bitter, who ten years ago might have taken to vandalising cars, were now finding deadlier outlets for their seething rage. She had often spoken to the mothers of such men and they all assured her that it was just a passing phase, a transitional period of upheaval in a young man's life. Once they got married and had a bit of responsibility it would all fly out of the window, they said.

She turned several pages and found in Surah *Ankabut*, The Spider, a familiar verse steeped in personal meaning.

"Can they not see that We have made [them] a secure

sanctuary though all around them people are snatched away?"

A secure sanctuary…Khadija had read this verse a thousand times, from childhood to adulthood. As a child she had envisaged the sanctuary as a physical place made of bricks and mortar, the holy city of Mecca, perhaps. Then, when she was a teenager and started to wear the nikab, she saw the sanctuary as a veil that guarded her from the insanity of male desire, a fortress through which she could view people unseen and a place of comfort where she could seek solace.

As she had grown to maturity, however, she saw that what was for her a fortress was for others a dungeon which held their minds captive. But although she was alone, she realised she need never be lonely. For the secure sanctuary was not bound by the dimensions of her veil; it was as broad and open as the skies and guided by the mercy of Allah. This for her was the real test of her faith. To learn that sorrow was transient and that it was, after all, the creation of a divine will that was forever in a state of flux. Too many times she had tried to find the source of joy and tragedy but now there was no confusion. She had come to know the wisdom in surrendering herself to the divine will and relinquishing the ownership of her life. There was in this surrender a supreme and sublime peace which she could summon at will.

22

"Look Musa, you ain't got that long left. It's May Day. Every breath you take, every step you make, has all gotta be for one thing. You gotta get a woman. Confucius once said, 'To choose is to refuse and to refuse is to choose.' Meaning get your head out of your ass and get moving. You get what I'm saying bro?"

Musa nodded wearily. Babarr wondered if it was the kind of weariness men display at times when they know they are cornered by the force of argument of someone superior in wisdom, or by plain depression.

"Who are these people? How long have you known them?" Musa asked.

"The girl's name is Shagufta and she's the sister-in-law of my mate Raza. He's a mechanical engineer at some power plant. Now I ain't ever seen Shagufta but I know his wife Rozia. Now Rozia is a good woman and since her mum and dad spend most of their time in Pakistan she's had to take charge. I'm telling you it's a good family."

He stopped the van. "I get why you're pissed off but you still gotta keep trying. You can't give up. All you gotta do is go in there with an open mind. You go inside and speak to the girl and just see how it goes. How's that sound?"

"Aren't you going to come in with me?" asked Musa.

"Not this time kid. I got stuff to do. I'll pick you up in an hour or so."

Musa nodded his agreement. He got out of the van and inhaled deeply. It was time to go through it all again. He knocked on the door and it was quickly thrown open.

"Hiya. I'm Rozia. Shagufta's sister. Come in."

"How are you?" asked Musa.

"Oh busy. I've hardly got time to breathe these days, with the children so little. I'm always chasing after them. They're just like their dad, they've got so much energy!"

She showed him into a dark room where the scent of air freshener lingered. The carpet was covered with a white cloth.

"How old are they?"

"My youngest is a year old and the other one is two. Having kids close together takes it out of you. I've got no time for nothing now. Still at least I won't be old when they're older. But you know what, the second you have kids, you change. You stop being a girl and start being a woman…" She gestured to him to sit down.

Musa gazed at her as she continued talking about the woes of motherhood. Rozia was attractive. She had a fair face with large hazel eyes and her long brown hair was plaited down her back. As she talked her face morphed from one smile to an even bigger smile and then her eyes would widen as her voice dropped. She was animated in the way few girls in his culture were. There was no reserve and no formality. Her conversation was not guarded or contained, just simple and commonplace. He tuned in to her conversation again.

"So afterwards I thought to myself our elders know more than us, innit? They been there and done it all and we should listen to them. And besides Raza was always out and about and I was getting a bit bored around the house. Especially with…" she pointed at a photograph on the mantelpiece "him and his wife. They were like so strict. They never told me to do anything but they just kept giving me the evils all the time. Then as soon as I had Bilal, they were OK. Before that I was just hired help. But what about you then? Raza told me you were in a madrasah and you know the Quran off by heart. You're not one of them strict types are you? 'Cos Shagufta likes to have a laugh. She ain't gonna be happy with a fella who tells her she can't wear make-up or go out with her friends and stuff. Because you know in Islam we have a lot of respect. But all them imams just wanna keep us down, like we're women back home. Is that what you're like?"

Musa blinked. "No not at all. I fully believe that women are empowered with the same rights as men. And I'm not looking for a doormat." He stopped suddenly. He had said this before. "I'm looking for someone who will be my companion. My soul mate as it were. One of the reasons that I didn't go for the veiled option is because I don't want to come home at the end of a long day and just talk about Islam."

"You know, you speak dead posh. You go to a private school or something?" asked Rozia.

"No, not really. I only went to a proper school up until year eight and then I went to a madrasah."

Rozia nodded. "I'll go and get Shagufta. Are you all right chatting to her by yourself. You're not one of them geeks who gets all shy in front of women are you?"

"No, I don't think so."

"OK then. You wait here a tick and I'll go get her. When's Babarr gonna be back?"

"In an hour."

Rozia rolled her eyes upwards. "He's probably gone down to the local. You can't keep men from their drink."

"No I suppose not," said Musa courteously.

Some minutes later he heard a gentle knocking on the door.

Shagufta walked in and sat down with her hands tightly clasped and her back bent slightly. She wore a tight-fitting hijab and a long black shapeless dress and had obviously dressed to suit the occasion.

"Assalaam-u-alaikum. Wa barakata ho," she said carefully and correctly.

"Waalaikum assalaam," replied Musa.

They gazed at each other. Shagufta's face was wide and round and with two dimples that deepened when she spoke. Her eyes were not hazel like her sister's but amber.

She was heavily made-up and her lips shone with gloss.

"How was your journey?"

"Oh it was fine…thank you," replied Musa.

"I understand you're a Hafiz. You've memorised the Quran," said Shagufta.

Musa nodded.

"That must have been really difficult. I mean really really difficult. You must be really brainy to have done something like that. I could never do something like that. I reckon that's why I was never good at school. I just couldn't get stuff into my head. But you must be born clever. Was it really hard?" asked Shagufta eagerly.

"At times, yes."

"But once it's inside, it's never going to go away. That's the important thing isn't it?"

"Yes, that's true."

Shagufta thought hard. "So where do you think Osama bin Laden is?"

Musa was startled. "I don't know. They say he's somewhere in Afghanistan."

"Do you think he did all those terrible things?"

"Well considering he confessed to it, it's difficult to deny it," replied Musa.

"But you know the thing I can't get my head around is that he's really well off. His dad left him about three hundred million quid. I mean if I had all that money I'd go and spend it on some nice things. Maybe do a bit of travelling. You get what I'm saying. Better than being cooped up in a cave all day long. I couldn't stand that. I hate being stuck in one place all the time."

"What do you do now?" asked Musa.

"I've done a course in Nursery Nursing. But my parents won't let me get a job. They say I've gotta be settled first."

"That seems a little unreasonable."

Shagufta sighed.

"It's the way they are now. They never used to be like that when we was all little. But when my Dad got ill, he starting hanging around all these religious people and they kinda got into his head and he started acting all differently. He started looking at us different. He used to look at me and my sister like we'd done something wrong all the time. He was really strict with Rozia, but soon as she got married, he was OK."

"What happened to your father?"

"He had a heart attack and then he had to have a bypass. He's OK now. He and my mum spend all their time in Pakistan. They come back just once a year to tell us off. My dad's got no control when he's angry...I'm telling you Rozia was lucky. They didn't have to look too hard for her. People were always asking for her. Raza's family were asking for her a long time. They said no at first because he's too old but they kept pushing and in the end she said yes because he's got a good job and a big house.

"He was really sweet on her at first. He was always taking her out and buying things for her. Then when she had her kids, she got busy with them and he got busy with his work. That's always the case, innit? When people get married, they got no time for nobody. Not their mates, not their sisters. All my mates are married now as well," she added gloomily.

"What are you looking for then?" asked Musa, his voice controlled.

All of a sudden Shagufta was animated and chirpy.

"Well you see, I'm not like clever at books and all that. But I know how to cook and keep the house really clean and stuff. And I ain't into expensive clothes but I'm into my religion and all that. I'm not stuck up like some of these educated girls are. I'm into respect and culture and all that. And the other good thing about me is…"

As she extolled her virtues, Musa knew. She was a decent enough girl who wanted desperately to be like her sister. She wanted to be looked after and she was not choosy about who she wanted as a husband. Any man would do as long as he was a good man. He smiled at her and her eyes shone with pleasure and she talked more eagerly. Her world was so simple. She was completely content with whatever was before her and her horizon never moved beyond her grasp. The thought that she could be so easily happy in a way that he never could disturbed him.

As she rambled on Musa drifted off to a place where everything was shapeless, where there were too many people like him constantly searching across a changing terrain for a beautiful face or a means of escape. He saw a microcosm of a world where people flew past each other in their search for some glorious object of desire, a world where their paths never met. There never was an end point, a place where hope and desire finally met.

"She was OK and she was wearing all the proper gear. I really thought this one was going to be a winner but all he told me when I picked him up was that she's a nice person but not the one for him," said Babarr.

"What the hell did he mean by that?" asked Armila.

"It was probably his way of trying to get out of it because she was a minger! You would not believe what a guy will do to get out of that kind of situation," said Shabnam.

"But that's just the point. She wasn't a hottie like Shabnam," Babarr ducked as she threw her shoe at him, "but she wasn't a minger."

"Something weird is going on inside his head. He's not thinking straight," remarked Suleiman.

"Musa is sensitive. He has a lot of poetry in his soul," Armila mused.

"Fuck poetry. The fact is that he has hardly got any time left. After that, he's gotta marry his cousin. No two ways about it. And he won't be able to back out because he agreed to the deal in the first place. Then you know what's gonna happen, she's gonna walk all over him and he's gonna spend the rest of his life as a doormat. Chicks from the homeland respect a guy who is strong and who don't take no shit from no one. Musa just ain't like that!" said Babarr.

Suleiman walked to the office window. It was getting dark and the parking lot was almost empty. Across the unit he could see people in the insurance office. A balding man with a big belly in a colourful suit was talking excitedly to a couple of laughing secretaries.

"Time is running out. He's coming to the end of the road. If we know it then he's gotta know it as well," he said.

"It's just like that Sinatra song," said Babarr. He strode to the middle of the office, put his hand in the centre of his chest and began to sing – badly.

"And now the end is near.
And so I face the final cousin.
My friend I'll say it clear.
I'll state my case of which I'm certain.
I've been to muslimbrides
I've travelled to each fa–mi–ly
But more, much more than this,
I did it my way.

Regrets I've had a load.
Too much to fucking mention.
I've had my fill, my share of losing
and now I'll have some more.
I did it my way!"

Babarr bowed and the others cheered, jeered and pelted him with whatever they could find.

Musa, meanwhile, had taken himself off to the Mosque. A child sat in one corner of the prayer hall rocking his head as he learnt the words of the Holy Quran phonetically. The pulpit seemed to Musa to echo a lament to bygone times when all woes could be addressed by the imam and when prayer would cool troubled eyes. The significant moments of his life were etched within the walls of the prayer halls of the Madrasah but since he had left the place he had begun to notice a change in the fabric of his life.

Back then his moments of being had swung from the splendour of humble worship to the discipline of resisting the whispers of heady youth. Now it was all different, he too was bound by the same contours of ambition and fear. He could summon nothing, no memory of insight, no knowledge of the Quran, to aid him. Before he had prided himself in knowing that the luck which all people craved was not chance but penned by divine will and the ink was dry the instant life began. Now such knowledge was empty and futile: it did not instil calm in him when colliding with an unwanted reality.

Musa focussed on the verse from Surah *Rahman*, The Lord of Mercy, engraved over the pulpit: "Which, then, of your Lord's blessings do you both deny?" He smiled, remembering Mufti Bashir and his attic room in the Madrasah. The distance his vision had to journey to unravel such wisdom was so much shorter than the journey he had to make in the physical kingdom. He had once asked an imam why the verse was repeated so many times in that chapter and he was given the answer that because mankind was slow in learning to accept the truth, it had to be repeated.

If he could not find what he was looking for in the short time he had left, would he forever read that verse and think like an ingrate or a victim of hapless fate? Either way the truth of the verse stood taller than the obstacles that faced him. The agreement he had reached with Dadaji seemed at the time to be a test of his faith, a challenge to his certainty that Allah hears the calls of all who cry out to him. And he had cried out, he remembered that very clearly. So what had gone wrong? Why now, after all these encounters, was he faced with the bleak prospect that his prayer had gone unanswered? He did not want a phenomenon. That was the strange thing about it. All he wanted was to find a woman who was beautiful and pleasant, someone with whom love could unfold within a modest life. That was it. Something simple and ordinary, granted a thousand times a day to others on this planet.

He would not find the happiness which eluded his parents. He would have to marry as his father had done, in blind subservience. But he knew this much about himself: his life was only worth living when he was in the pursuit of passion and that passion would never subside. His journey would continue in flights of fantasy until the tie that bound him snapped and he would run barefoot, through hell if necessary, to find his little piece of heaven in this world.

23

" Assalaam-u-alaikum sisters. I am very glad to see you here and welcome to any newcomers. Tonight's topic for discussion is the veil. Before I put forward the Islamic viewpoint, I would like to hear your own thoughts."

As Khadija expected, the women fell silent. She wondered who would be the first to break that silence. Probably it would be the one who felt the most insecure about the issue.

"Do you mean the hijab or the nikab, sister?" asked someone she hadn't seen before.

"Both."

"The fact is, I don't wear the veil," said one of the working girls. "I don't have any shame in saying that. I go to the gym three times a week and I look good. As you can see I have long black hair that I'm very proud of and I don't feel the need to cover it up. There's no shame in taking pride in your appearance. I think that Muslim girls here should not have to follow Taliban-type rules of a country thousands of miles away!"

"So you feel that the veil is a symbol of repression?" asked Khadija.

"Yeah, I do, but I think Islam allows us women to make choices for ourselves and the choice not to wear a veil is one of them."

"Are you telling me, sister, that you are happy having men stare at you with their eyes popping out of their head and thinking dirty thoughts?" demanded a housewife.

"Just because I like to feel all right about myself by making sure I look good don't mean I'm some kind of slut. That's not you coming out with those words, sister. You've been brainwashed into thinking that a woman is an object of sin. I don't cause any man to have dirty thoughts about me. That's his problem. You have been taught to think like a slave and that's why you wanna dress like a slave!" came the defiant reply.

"I am not a slave sister. I may not have your education or your money but I am not a slave. I wear the veil out of respect for my husband. My beauty is for his eyes only," retorted the housewife.

Now it was the turn of a radical girl. "I am not married, sister, but that don't make any difference to me. I wear the veil because I want people to look at me and say to themselves, 'She's a Muslim'. And I am one hundred per cent proud of that."

"So to you, a veil is what? A symbol of modesty or empowerment?" asked Khadija.

Another radical girl continued the theme. "I don't wear the veil to cause arguments but because I want the world to know that I take my religion seriously. When I wear the veil, I know that thousands of Muslim sisters around the world dress in the same way and it makes me feel good to know that I am a part of them."

"But you see that's all wrong. You're not wearing the veil because you want to be modest but because you want to be part of a tribe. That's not what it's all about!" said a working girl.

"Who are you to say what the veil is all about sister? Do you pray five times a day?"

"The fact that I don't pray doesn't mean that I'm not a Muslim and it doesn't mean that I don't have the right to an opinion," said the working girl.

"But that's all it will ever be! Just an opinion," said the radical girl triumphantly.

Khadija intervened. "That depends on what your opinions are about sisters. I don't think it's unreasonable to say that women who live their life as practising Muslims have more of an insight into what Islam is really all about than women whose only connection to Islam is their culture."

"But wearing the veil is about female modesty. Every female has the right to have their say about their modesty," said another working girl.

A housewife got to her feet. "When I was in Pakistan, I never wore the hijab. When I got married and came here, my thinking changed. Before marriage, I used to like it when men would look at me. Which girl wouldn't feel happy knowing she is attractive? But all that changed after I married and, like my friend here, my beauty as a woman is for my husband only. I chose to wear the veil out of respect for my husband."

"If that's the case why don't you wear the nikab – that way no man alive will be able to see you," shot back a working girl.

"You would be surprised at the impact the hijab can have. It does diminish the impact of a woman's appearance," remarked Khadija.

"I have a confession to make," said one of the radical girls who hadn't spoken before. "I never wore the veil until after 9/11 when I saw how Muslims were treated. I wanted to be a visible Muslim because I wanted people to know that I am proud of my religion and culture."

"Again that has nothing to do with modesty. You are wearing the veil as an act of solidarity not as an act of modesty!" said a working girl vehemently.

"But that is not contrary to the spirit of Islam. Isn't empathy for your fellow Muslims just as important as modesty?" asked Khadija.

"Look at me sisters," said a working girl. "You can see I have long black hair, fair skin and big green eyes. Every man I pass in the street gawks at me. Now I'm not stuck up about that because ultimately the way we look has nothing to do with us but it is part of who we are and everybody should be proud of who they are. When you wear the veil or the hijab or the nikab you know what you're doing? You're agreeing to put a chain around your neck. When you're in the home the man will tie you to the kitchen sink and when you're outside his way of tying you down is the hijab. Think about it! Does the man have to do anything to protect his modesty? Isn't Islam supposed to be a religion that's equal for both men and women? Do guys wear long beards to stop women looking at them or have you ever heard someone say, 'My son used to eye up women all the time but since he grew a beard he stopped doing that'? No. In the end there's only one way of looking at it. The hijab is just a piece of cloth on top of someone's head."

Khadija studied her carefully. She was indeed beautiful and her willowy frame seemed to grow taller as she spoke. There was something strangely familiar in the way her eyes shone as she developed her argument, the way her voice started low and ended up high and strained. A housewife cut across her reverie.

"But if you think about it sister, every woman is a slave. Look at yourself. You can tell a mile off that you're starving yourself to keep thin. Doesn't that make you a slave to fashion? Western women who pride themselves on how liberated they are are really slaves themselves! They eat nothing and exercise all the time so they can show off their trim bodies!"

"I would like to explain why I wear the nikab," said Khadija. "I don't consider myself to be a slave or to be repressed in any way. I choose to cover my face because I believe that Islam is about our relationship with our creator. You cannot, in my opinion, separate your person from your appearance. I choose to conceal my appearance for the sake of my spirituality. In Islam, seclusion and spirituality go hand in hand."

A pretty girl stood up. "My brother told me that there is an Islamic saying that the best veil is behind the person's eyes. That's what a lot of people don't realise. I've seen plenty of girls who wear the hijab or the nikab and they're in your face, you know really aggressive. I don't see how that is acceptable. If you wear a veil for modesty then shouldn't your behaviour be modest as well?"

A housewife spoke excitedly. "I absolutely agree with you. There are so many women who wear the veil just so their voices can be louder. The tighter the veil the louder they are. I've seen girls wearing the nikab with tight jeans. What the hell is that all about? These girls take that bit of Islam that makes them feel as if they're important and forget about the bits that don't suit them."

"But a lot of Muslims do that. Men and women," said her neighbour.

"Do you know that the Quran forbids women from drawing attention to themselves by jingling their jewellery?" Khadija asked. "So if a woman is wearing an anklet and others hear it jingle, that would be considered a sin. The solution is not to ban jewellery or to stop women from being in the same room as men: the solution is to think about the principle behind the commandment. And the principle is one of modesty. Muslim women have a code of conduct. There's nothing restrictive about that as long as you realise that no code can be absolute. The code of modesty must always be an individual one and it must always start from a personal choice."

"How do you mean?"

"If you are brought up in an Islamic environment then the desire to wear a veil will be as natural as lowering your gaze. Covering your face would be a natural step in the evolution of your identity as a Muslim woman.

"If you have lived your life as a liberal Pakistani who only has a loose connection to Islam, maybe you'll never want to wear the veil. But if you then decide to wear the veil you've got to remember, as the sister has just said, that the outer veil enhances the inner veil, the veil behind your eyes. That requires not just a change in appearance but a change in attitude. And that's something that can't be done very easily but, if you can change your attitude you can change your life. It says that in the Quran: 'God does not change the condition of a people unless they change what is in themselves.'"

The meeting came to an end and, as the women prepared to leave, Khadija made her way towards the beautiful girl with green eyes. She put her arm around her shoulder and said, "Change is never easy. Wearing the veil may mean something to the world but it means nothing to Allah if you are not willing to make that journey to change yourself. As in all journeys we may sometimes lose our way or even forget the reason why we started it but as long as our intention is to become a better person then eventually we'll reach our goal. That's the promise of our creator and you can only trust in that promise."

Khadija returned to the office, absent-mindedly arranging the veil across her face as she went and wondering if anyone would still be in the building. She had found out by chance that late in the evenings Babarr helped the elderly caretaker in cleaning the Centre and she guessed he would be mortified if this became public knowledge. She smiled to herself.

The door was open but it wasn't Babarr who was sitting behind the desk.

"Assalaam-u-alaikum Musa," she said softly.

He tilted his head and looked into her eyes which she considered inappropriate.

"Waalaikum assalaam Khadija," he replied after a moment's silence.

"Another meeting with another prospective bride?" asked Khadija.

Musa nodded dismally.

She sat down and asked, "What happened this time?"

"Nothing. Another non-starter."

"Why?"

"The family was good. But…"

"The face didn't fit the dream," finished Khadija.

Musa flinched.

"You need to let go of this fantasy. You need to grow up," she said firmly.

"It's not about growing up. It's a life choice. I want to make the one that suits me. Everyone does."

"In the real world people compromise. I don't think you understand that. You can't cling to a dream, hoping it will become real. You think you're the only one out there who's looking for the perfect face with a matching personality? Everybody starts out like that. I've spoken to plenty of sisters who were looking for Mr Right in the exact same way. They wanted handsome and rich but at some point they grew up and realised it's what's inside that counts and money comes and goes. They took a few knocks, learnt their lesson and after that life was much better for them. Why haven't you learned your lesson after the knocks you've taken?" Her eyes blazed as she spoke. "I'll tell you why not Musa. It's because you think it's giving in, but it's not a war."

"It's always a war," he disagreed.

"Then you're fighting the wrong battle. If you'd put all the effort you have spent in defiance on making the best of what's in front of you, you'd be a happier man. Does it not say in the Quran that a hundred people, patient and persevering, can overcome a thousand? That's what you have to be, patient and persevering."

"But what if you don't know whether it's worth the effort? There is no prescribed way to change people. Change can only be effected by Allah. There are plenty of broken people in our community who wasted their lives waiting for their husband or wife to turn over a new leaf. If you were to ask them whether they would have made a different decision if they could go back in time, would they have taken a risk and gone against the tide? I bet you many of them would say yes."

"You have this idea that there is something great and glorious about disobedience and rebellion. That's the whisper of Satan presenting you with an illusion that all things wonderful happen to people who go it alone. That is not true. Your father's displeasure is the Lord's displeasure; you must have heard that saying before. If those words were not true, they would not have been uttered by our Holy Prophet, Peace be upon Him," said Khadija.

"Here's a different saying: 'The Son of Adam became

decrepit and corrupt. All that remained in him were hope and avidity for life' As long as you have those two things, you do what you have to do."

"Which is what exactly?" she asked.

"I don't know."

"You don't know but you are certain that it involves you disobeying your elders?" queried Khadija.

Musa sighed and shook his head. He walked out of the office.

Khadija gazed for a long time at the empty chair. Musa, crazed by his chase, was a fireball consuming all that could relieve him but she knew that no such fire rages forever. Like happiness and sorrow, it roared and spluttered and then died out.

Dadaji slowly lifted his head from the prayer mat. With his eyes still closed, he moved his head right and left, still deep within his trance. He remained still for a few moments until slowly he felt the presence of the physical world return.

Aboo opened his mouth to speak, but Dadaji raised his hand and in peace he took out his rosary. Aboo and Musa listened to the sounds of Dadaji's meditation, seeing him with mindsets a generation apart and both seeking clarity in a troubled time.

Dadaji broke the silence. "Musa, your journey has cut across many paths. With each crossing you have bled."

"Yes Dadaji, I know."

"You have tried so hard to carve your path among the stars that dazzle you, yet they have swerved not at all for you."

Musa hung his head, unable to reply.

"And your time draws closer. All that is to happen shall happen."

Dadaji rose to his feet and looked down at Aboo.

"Call Iram here."

Khadija sat on a prayer mat, her head bowed and her face covered to hide any evidence of expression from her father. Abdel sat cross-legged on a prayer mat next to her. His face was proud and angry for no reason other than that was the way he was in front of his father. Khadija felt pity for him. So empty, she thought and so much of their father in him.

Their father sat facing them. He gave Khadija a sideways look and slowly stroked his beard. He often did this but today there was a difference, there was something ugly in his appraisal and she was terrified at what he might say. At least he could not see her terror.

"Khadija, next week you will go to Pakistan. You are to marry Zahoor and you will stay there for one year. That will make it easier for his visa to be accepted. Understood?"

"What about me?" asked Abdel.

"You will also attend the wedding but will return with me."

As their father began to intone a prayer, Khadija focussed on a practice she had perfected: the calm induced by the words of the prayer slowly changed to indifference. She had no power over events but she did have the power to control herself and it was this self-control that so frustrated her father. He longed for her to show some outward sign of terror. He needed that. He always had. She was sure it was the reason why her mother had left when she was a child.

Khadija knew he hated her because she resembled her mother and she thought how strange it was that hatred was accepted among the threads of family ties. Part of his hatred for her came from a loathing of himself. For her father was teased by the flesh of the women he so passionately denounced. In the presence of women she would see him become strained as though he was inwardly savouring a lusty memory.

Khadija had learned to recognise lust in his eyes when she was a child. Just after their mother had left he would have that look. Then he would disappear at night, returning the next day. When he discovered Islam, his appetite for women and alcohol changed into one for terror and power. Abdel was the first casualty.

She was distracted by sounds in the street. When the weather was good an elderly neighbour would sit on a bench and play catchy tunes on his mobile phone, his head bobbing to the rhythm. It was absurd she thought, an old man so happy, enjoying the tunes of the young. Trusting in the mercy of Allah just as a bird would. That was what it said in Surah *Mulk*, only the grace of Allah holds the birds in the sky. Why couldn't that same grace be available to her? What if she were to leave now, taking nothing but the clothes on her back?

And for the first time in her life she cried, she who had withstood her mother's desertion, had raised her baby brother by herself and who had endured the loneliness and fear without shedding a tear. Her father stopped praying and was satisfied at last. Her brother stopped pretending and was frightened. The loss of her calm had unearthed the truth. Khadija had so wanted to be like her mother and now she knew that she was.

24

The reflected sun lay at the centre of a white quilt embroidered with flowers covering a huge bed. Shadows radiating outwards formed dark spokes that led to four cousins united by concern about the future of one of them, Iram.

Crickets were vocal in the glare of the fierce sun whereas the intense heat drowned the village in slumber. Men and women slept fitfully under a torrent of warm air that spewed from the blades of unsteady fans. The cousins, however, were safe from the oppressive heat and rickety electric appliances. Cool draughts of air circulated the room, powered by a generator that hummed quietly.

Farrah spoke first, her small eyes flashing with anger.

"Who does he think he is? To summon you for marriage as though you were an animal selected for breeding!"

Iram was pleased to hear the ire in her voice.

Farzana, her tongue sharp and her eyes sly, asked, "Why do you think he has waited until now to call for you? He went to England to arrange your marriage and he could not get everyone to agree with him. People in England are not like us, they argue with their elders."

"Why don't they keep on arguing then? Why stop now? Have they suddenly learnt respect and decency for their elders?" asked Farrah indignantly.

Farzana settled back on her cushion and scowled as her mother often did when declaring an edict.

"People over there have no moral values. They have no character. No principles. They can easily be persuaded. All Dadaji had to do was to use emotional blackmail. He probably said something like, 'If you don't agree to this I am going to die' and they fell for it."

"It is a pity he does not die. He has too much control over people. This is why Iram has spent her life in this…this toilet. It is only by the grace of Allah that she has not picked up the low habits of village women. The problem is that Dadaji sees her as a village girl. Here in the village girls are so simple. They will do anything without even asking why. He is probably telling them in England that he already asked you and you said yes." Fozia was by nature stolid of mind and leaden of heart.

The cousins contemplated Iram's disagreeable future.

"They think we are stupid and obedient like our aunties, that all they have to do is to shout at us and we will faint. We are not like our aunties, however. We have education. We have class and intelligence. We can do things they cannot do," said Farzana.

"All you have to do is to say no, Iram," said Farrah sternly.

"No!" said Farzana sharply. "That is stupid. All the blame will fall upon her if she says no directly. Then her parents will forever be angry and upset with her. She has to be cleverer than that."

"How did you feel when you saw Musa?" asked Fozia.

At the sound of his name Iram felt an ominous shiver of unease seep into her skin and could say nothing. She had begun to tire of the idea of him. The girls, especially Farrah, seemed to view him with contempt and she wondered what he had done to anger them so.

"When he came to our house he would have lunch with the servants instead of Mother and Father. He has no class. No etiquette. Everybody praises him because he has fair skin. That is so typical of village people," said Farrah scornfully.

"Still he is…" Fozia's voice trailed off uncertainly. Iram looked up at her, displeased at their mutual realisation. "Nothing."

Farzana shot an angry look at her younger sister and Fozia looked down sheepishly.

"What is Musa? He is nothing. He has no qualification or standing. What can he give to Iram? Besides, her hand is to go to Khalil," announced Farzana with authority.

Iram's heart leapt and she blushed. Her cousins grinned at each other, amused by her girlishness.

"Have you spoken to Mother about this?" asked Farrah enthusiastically.

Iram struggled to remain composed.

Farzana shook her head. She focussed on Iram, her eyes shrewd. "You will need to show that you are worthy to be an officer's wife. You will need to show your intelligence and courage now."

"How do you mean?"

"What are you going to do or say when you get to England?"

Iram's face reddened with desperation for she could think of nothing clever to say. Her cousins would have been able to reel off something ingenious without a second's thought and she wasn't surprised that Farzana gave her some advice straight away.

"A woman can get a man to do anything if she knows how. You must use your eyes to give the message of your tongue. When you meet Musa, you must let him know what he means to you without ever saying so. He will try to be sweet to you but you must not respond. Eventually he will become angry and try to force you to give a signal. All you have to do is to remain silent and he will understand and walk away. Something else you have to understand Iram, boys in England have no control over their bodily desires. He needs you more than you need him. He has probably had plenty of girlfriends. You are his way of becoming respectable," said Farzana.

"But he is a Hafiz!" said Fozia.

"What difference does that make? Putting books on a donkey's back does not make the donkey any wiser!" replied Farzana with asperity.

"Try to get Shabnam on your side," suggested Farrah. "She has a lot of confidence for a girl. Dadaji is probably trying to marry her off as well so she will know how it works. Watch her and learn from her."

"Remember Iram, if nothing else works you can still say no," said Farzana. "If they threaten you then remember that we are their honour. If we have a single hair out of place they will lose their respect; they would rather die than live through that. Nothing can happen to you if you do not let it."

As the intensity of the mid-day sun lessened a little the village slowly came to life. The muezzin heralded the call for the afternoon prayer and men slowly walked to the mosque with disgruntled faces. Iram sat on the veranda watching the shimmering blades of grass that stretched as far as the eye could see. Nearby, a buffalo stood with a long wooden pole stretching from its neck to a borehole within the well. An emaciated farmer wearing a dirty stained cotton shalwar kameez raised a stick and flicked it at the buffalo causing it to move forwards a few steps. Drenched with perspiration the farmer whipped the buffalo until it began a weary circling of the well and water started to fall from a rusted iron pipe.

Iram saw a parallel between her life and the buffalo's and was angry. Of all the sisters, Farrah was most prone to harsh observations. She did not have the unnatural wisdom and maturity of Farzana who was only a year older but, nonetheless, her portrayal of her plight hurt. All the boys in the family would have been involved if their marriage was being decided so why was that privilege not extended to the girls? Nobody had the right to map out her future. She would put Musa in his place. The way she did it would not be pleasant but that was a small sacrifice for the future she deserved. He probably thought that she would be as easy to conquer as one of his girlfriends. She would not be herded like that buffalo. She did not have her cousins' education but her wits were sharp and she listened and learnt from the talk of others. She was a lot like Farzana in that respect. Iram smiled proudly at the thought – essentially she was one of them.

How her heart had lurched when Farzana had said that she would be reserved for Khalil! For a moment she was alarmed that she might have done or said something improper that had revealed her attraction to him. But no, she had been clever there, keeping her eyes down whenever he was near her. All she had to do was to continue to be clever and she would become the wife of an officer in the Pakistani army. She would live in the best houses and have servants. She frowned, her lack of English would be a problem as they all spoke English in the army, but she could take a course – she would worry about that later.

25

"You can use this place for a while. My parents have only just bought it but at the moment they're too busy to organise finding a tenant. You're safe, no one will ever know," said Armila.

The flat was no more than a large white cubicle, the bed folded into the wall and a tiny kitchenette led into the bathroom. A painting of floating heads and arms hung on the wall.

"Who painted that shit?" asked Shabnam.

"It's a copy of a Picasso," replied Armila.

"He must have been a nut," remarked Shabnam as she flung her shoes off and sat down heavily on the one small sofa.

Armila shrugged. She pointed at the fold-up bed and said, "Listen, you and Leroy need to be careful. If you bounce up and down too much that thing will fold and you'll both be slammed into the wall."

"Shut up!" retorted Shabnam indignantly.

"You gotta start considering these practicalities when you're in a physical relationship. Attention to detail is always important," Armila grinned.

"What makes you such an expert on relationships and how do you know it's physical?" asked Shabnam.

"If it isn't yet it will be soon. You're stupid if you haven't realised that yet. Why do you think he's still hanging around?"

"You're gonna think this is crazy. But I think he has real feelings for me. I think he maybe even loves me."

Armila burst out laughing. "Oh come on. You know what he wants. You are going to have to stamp your authority on this relationship because once you're between the sheets you're going to want to stay there," stated Armila.

Shabnam groaned. "Why don't you focus on Musa like you used to? Give my brains a bit of a holiday."

"Now there's someone who is almost as messed up as you are!"

"He's not with it just yet. He wants…"

Shabnam suddenly sat up straight and squealed delightedly.

"I've got it. I've got it! I know who should marry him!"

"Who? Tell me who!" demanded Armila.

Just then the doorbell rang.

"Who the fuck is that?" hissed Shabnam.

"I don't know. Did someone follow you?" asked Armila.

"No I don't think so…I don't fucking know. I didn't exactly keep looking behind me."

"Do you see what I mean? Attention to detail. In a clandestine relationship, taking precautions isn't just—"

The doorbell rang again.

"We'd better open it otherwise the neighbours will start complaining," said Armila.

She peered through the spyhole and whispered

excitedly, "It's the guy my parents bought the flat from. He is such a hottie. Wait until you see him. Your eyes are gonna pop straight out of your head!"

She opened the door, taking in the visual feast before her.

"Hello Armila. Sorry to disturb you. I wonder if I might come in?" asked Titty Soups courteously.

Armila beckoned him into the flat. He was dressed in a three-button suede blazer with a white Rafaello shirt and denim trousers. His black Italian leather wingtip shoes gleamed.

"Good evening Shabnam."

"How the fuck did you get here?"

"I drove by to pick up some letters. You cannot imagine my delight to see you here with Armila. We have some important things to discuss so perhaps now would be a good opportunity."

"The only thing we're about to discuss is how you are gonna get your bony ass out of this place," snarled Shabnam.

Titty Soups smiled and for a second Shabnam was unnerved by how perfect and natural his smile was.

"Shabnam, your fire draws me in closer and closer like a helpless moth until I just know I'm going to get burnt. And do you know something? I don't think I would mind it one little bit."

Shabnam gritted her teeth. "Just what the fuck is it that you want?"

"May I take a seat?"

Without waiting for a reply he sat down on the sofa.

"As you know Shabnam, our culture is very unforgiving to the unmarried. Now I'll be honest with you. I've never really been the marrying type. I've always thought that marriage is for the elderly. Stupid huh?"

He winked at Armila.

"But lately I've kind of got to thinking that maybe my time has come. Now when I'm with kids, I'm not worried about whether or not they're going to puke over my shoes. I'm thinking whether or not someday I would want to have them. And that led me on to consider the qualities I would want in a wife. Once I would have said the normal things: she's got to cook, she's got to be respectful to my parents, bazookas a bonus, but my thinking has changed. Now I don't want those things.

"I want beauty and fire. That's it. I couldn't give a shit about the cooking. And I'm not too fussed about the bazookas, they'll come with the kids. Just beauty and fire. Fire and beauty. Fiery beauty. Beautiful fire. You get where I'm coming from?"

He winked again at Armila.

"Basically it's like this. You are one lucky girl because plenty of girls tried to get me to say this but you beat them all to the finishing line. Shabnam, you have the honour of being my chosen, my intended, my wife."

A little vein swelled on Shabnam's forehead.

"You…You…You arrogant fucking pig," she gasped.

Titty Soups raised his hand in a comforting gesture. "Yeah I know…I know. It's a shock to me as well. But hey, we all gotta take that step sometime. I thought I should tell you before my parents and then we can arrange that first informal visit."

"Shabnam is committed," announced Armila.

"I can see that!" chuckled Titty Soups.

"No, I mean she has given her heart to someone," said Armila in annoyance.

"You mean she actually has one?" Titty Soups shook with laughter.

"Listen asshole. I have a man. And all I gotta do is call him and he'll rip you in half," snarled Shabnam.

Titty Soups stopped laughing.

"Oh…who is he?"

"What do you mean who is he?"

"Your man," replied Titty Soups. "He does have a name doesn't he?"

Shabnam glanced at Armila, who frowned.

"His name is…La…Le…Liaqat," she replied lamely.

"Really? And I suppose it always takes you three attempts to pronounce his name. Come on, stop bullshitting. What's his name?"

"His name is none of your business; it's confidential, so fuck off."

"Why is it confidential? Are you ashamed of him?"

Shabnam struggled. "If you must know, the reason why I won't give his name is to protect our privacy. He's…non-Asian."

Titty Soups stared at her in amazement. "You're going out with a black man!"

"How on earth did you know that? He could be white," said Armila.

"Standard Asian response. If a chick wants to tell you where to go, she will always give you the name of her man. If they've been together for a while, she'll give you his height and chest size as well. But if she don't do none of that shit it means she's hiding something. Now a chick who's hiding something is going out with either a black man or a white man. If Shabnam were going out with a white man, then she wouldn't be looking like something the cat dragged in. She'd be looking like someone who's enjoying the secret and having the time of her life, because she's saying fuck you to the rest of the world. But Shabnam ain't doing that. You can see that she's also wearing a Donna Karan watch and she has a crocodile leather handbag. So the poor bastard is spending money on her but she's still got a bug up her ass. That spells black man who's still knocking on the door."

He checked his watch. "Well ladies. Sadly I must bid you goodbye. I'm late for an engagement, a dinner engagement."

"The day I agree to marry you is the day I take a knife to my throat, you bastard," grated Shabnam.

Titty Soups smiled fondly at her and said: "Love is my sin and thy dear virtue hate. Hate of my sin, grounded on sinful loving. O, but with mine compare thou thine own state."

With that, he bowed deeply to Shabnam and hummed his way out of the flat, grateful at last to his English teacher.

26

Awoozy Suleiman lifted his hand to his head and touched a bandage caked with dried blood. In front of him, like a flickering candle, the statue of Jesus glowed and he saw again the eloquent yet sad eyes and the gentle smile. All somehow familiar. He frowned as he tried to understand that strange sense of recognition.

"How are you feeling?" inquired a kindly voice.

"Oh, not too bad. Did you put this bandage on my head?"

"That I did. I am well versed in the art of bandaging."

"Thank you."

"You're welcome, my son. I did not want to call an ambulance because no doubt you would have had some unwelcome questions."

Suleiman nodded.

The priest smiled at him. "Thank you for what you did. That took courage. I thought they were going to kill you, but then they seemed to recognize you. Is that right?"

Suleiman nodded again, but felt awkward, unaccustomed as he was to receiving any kind of praise, and embarrassed also by his association with the gang who had jeered at the priest for refusing to hand over the cash they demanded. He remembered what he had shouted at the youths, how they had turned on him instead and, as he felt himself lose consciousness, he had heard running footsteps and a voice shouting at the gang to stop. That voice resonated in Suleiman's mind and suddenly he knew who it was. He winced.

"Here take this." The priest pressed a small flask of brandy into his hand.

Suleiman filled his mouth and swallowed. He closed his eyes as the burning in his stomach intensified, numbing the pain. Settling back into the chair he breathed deeply and easily.

"It was a very good thing that we arranged to meet today," the priest laughed. He paused and then asked, "Do you feel up to talking now?"

"I do. I'm still bothered. You see I don't wake up every day and think today is going to be the day when I figure it all out. You learn to stop thinking when you're in my line of work, you have to, otherwise you will get fucked up. Not thinking has become a habit. Maybe it's because I've come to realise that there's no point. What's done is done. You are what you are. Shit happens and you gotta deal with it."

He paused. "When I was a kid there was this family that my mum and dad used to visit. They had a son called Parvez who was brilliant at school. Never got into no trouble, a kind of perfect kid, you know? My dad used to drive me up the bloody wall going on about Parvez. He's like this and you're like that. Now I never met this Parvez.

"He went to a private school and his mum wouldn't let him hang around on the street with us guys. I used to pray for that family to leave. And when they did I thought I would never hear of Parvez ever again. But do you know something? Parvez wasn't the problem, it was that feeling that you're small and not up to much. Every time my dad would talk about Parvez, I used to get that feeling. If I think too much, that feeling comes back again. I think everyone has gotta Parvez somewhere inside of them."

"You need to be proud of who *you* are," responded the priest.

"Proud of who I am?" Suleiman's voice echoed through the church. "I'm not clever. I was never any good at school. I don't make an honest living. What have I got to be proud about?"

"With the eyes that I have used to observe the world for more than sixty years, I see a fine young man who is brave yet troubled and who has both the courage to realise the truth about himself and the decency to feel ashamed."

"What do I do, Father?" asked Suleiman.

"What you did just now. Confront that which you fear the most."

Suleiman stumbled through the door. Drinking brandy on an empty stomach and the after-effects of the beating he had received made him very unsteady. The lights were too bright. Everything was just too bright. He knocked over the hall table and steadied himself. As he did so he brushed against the plaque which had hung in the hallway for years and which was inscribed with the words

316

"Consider the seeds you sow on the ground — is it you who make them grow or We?" Their meaning was crystal clear. He had caused something malignant to grow inside him that took away all warmth. Whatever it was that made the priest shine when he smiled, he had none of that in him. He was a creature from a different jungle where all you needed to know was that you were tough enough to handle anything life threw at you. You took no shit and you took no prisoners. He touched the plaque gently. These were words written for people outside the jungle. There was no Allah in the jungle. There were gods and demi-gods instead of simple everyday people. There had to be a way out but the problem was that beyond the jungle, the world was no kinder. Twilight was safer, moving in darkness was easier.

Suddenly he heard a door open. His father, dressed in a string vest and white dhoti, came down the stairs. His thin frame trembled with fury as he grabbed Suleiman and shook him.

"You come to my house stinking of alcohol! Have you no shame? Coming to my house after you have been fighting in a pub! Piss off, bastard! I say piss off!"

"Aren't you going to ask what happened to me, Father?" Suleiman laughed hard at the irony.

Infuriated, Aboo closed his fist and struck his son hard on the chest. Suleiman, already deprived of his sense of balance, fell back against the front door, still laughing.

"You are a curse to this family. You have turned my honour into mud! Get out of here and never come back! You are a disgrace to me and your mother!"

As Aboo raised his hand to strike him across the face, Suleiman did not flinch.

"Itrat, that is enough!"

Aboo froze and slowly let his hand drop. Dadaji stood at the foot of the stairs. He looked past his son at Suleiman and severity melted away from his face.

"Leave us Itrat."

Aboo nodded and returned to his bedroom, his head down, and Dadaji beckoned his grandson into the living room. He took off his white shawl and placed it carefully around the young man's shoulders and then sat down cross-legged on his prayer mat, motioning Suleiman to sit facing him.

"Why did you do that?" asked Suleiman in slow halting Punjabi.

"You are naked."

Suleiman nodded slowly in understanding.

"On your face are the marks of fear and anger..." he reached forward and placed his hand on Suleiman's heart, "and here are the marks of hate."

"He has always hated me," replied Suleiman.

Dadaji smiled: "No he has not. And it is not the scar of his hate you carry. It is your own."

"I know. I have done bad things. I know I am a bad man."

"Suleiman, listen. A man dirtied by his own evil will continue to do evil. His face will become black but still he will go on. Then that day may come when he looks at his hands and sees what they have earned. He feels ashamed and wishes to be pure. In that instant he sees that his hands are clean and his face is radiant. Such is the mercy of Allah."

"Dadaji, today someone said I was a good man, a brave man."

"No man is chained by their deeds, Suleiman. Those who do evil have hearts that are harder than rock. Allah in His Mercy has softened your heart. The pain that you feel is the burden of truth. Only decency can ease that burden."

"What is decency Dadaji? Obeying your elders? That did nothing for me!"

"Decency is fear of Allah; kindness to your family, helping others in need, acknowledging mistakes, confronting evil. Decency is a hard path."

"What do I do?" Suleiman again asked the question which he had first put to the Catholic priest.

Dadaji stood up and told Suleiman to do likewise. He placed his hand over his grandson's heart and felt a seed sprout within as blood flowed anew, constricted no longer by memory but flowing to a chamber where the light, although dim, was increasing.

"You have already begun what it is that you need to do. You have made the first step. No one can ever despair of the Mercy of Allah which embraces all creatures on earth and today you too have become a part of it. Go now and live in peace."

As he left the room Suleiman did not notice that his grandfather was smiling proudly after him.

The kitchen door opened hesitantly and Amma, seeing Dadaji alone, asked anxiously, "What has happened?"

"One of your sons has come home."

27

Musa woke when the day was hovering between the ether of the possible and the realm of the real. For as long as he could remember this had been his favourite time. Even at the Madrasah, while his brethren continued to sleep, his eyes would open and he would finger the furry warmth of his quilt and rejoice in his snug state of being. Then his eyes would close and he would summon some choice fantasy or refine a curious whim. A blissful foray into his own inner world that would only be shattered by the call of the Muezzin for the morning prayer.

But now he could no longer slip into that place of peace. Things were different. As Khadija had said, no one had control over what happened to them, there was no master plan. It was all a game of chance. And he had woken with sweat on his forehead, the consequence of a dreadful nightmare.

As his eyes adjusted to the dawn light he realised that he was still in the Central Mosque where he had gone to offer the prayers made between the twilight and dawn, the Tahajjud prayers, and then had fallen asleep.

There was a loud banging on the main door. It was too

early for the imam and as he was alone in the Mosque, Musa opened the door to a tall, powerfully-built black man dressed in a grey vest and white running shorts. He was drenched in sweat and his face shone with vitality as he brought his hands together and bowed.

"Assalaam-u-alaikum…brother," he said carefully and slowly.

"Waalaikum assalaam." Musa smiled at the man's deference.

"May I come in bro?"

Musa nodded and led the man through to the main hallway where the shoe racks were stacked. Two chairs stood outside the entrance to the prayer hall. Musa beckoned him to sit down and then did so himself.

"How can I help you?"

The man, clearly agitated, began.

"You see, the thing is bro, I got a bit of a problem and I can't get my head around it. It's driving me up the wall so I decided to find out if someone here could help me get a handle on things. If you know what I mean?"

"What kind of problem?"

The man flashed him an embarrassed glance. "I'm in love bro!"

"You're in love?"

"Sure am," replied the man proudly.

"Do you want advice on how to convert to Islam?" asked Musa.

"Oh no, none of that stuff. I ain't the type to convert. But I'm in love with this beautiful Muslim girl. When I say beautiful, boy do I mean beautiful! She is like a

Supermodel. She is like…man….she like walks into a room and everyone's tongues are around their ankles. And when she gets in a strop, oh man, it's like you're seeing fire but you don't wanna run away from it. You just wanna get in closer and closer. And when she cusses you…it's like someone's giving you an ecstasy pill. You cannot imagine what this girl does to you. It's like being on one of them roller coaster rides. You just feel you're on a high all the time!"

Musa could see that although his eyes were alive with excitement and hope his voice was strained: he was trying to reach for the stars. Just like Musa himself. A great feeling of compassion came over him.

"Listen my friend, I understand what you're feeling. Do you want me or someone at the Mosque to talk to her or her family about the prospect of marriage?"

"Nah, not yet anyway. What I need from you is an idea of what makes her tick. Because to be honest fella, I don't have a bloody clue. I can't tell what she's gonna do from one moment to the next. I ain't saying it isn't exciting because it is but you get to the point where it drains the shit out of you. That's kinda like where I am."

"May I know her name?" asked Musa.

The man looked wary. He twisted his hands awkwardly.

"I don't mean to be rude but I know you lot are into marrying your first cousins and all of that. That suggests you are all related somehow or another. So if I tell you her name, you might know her. And I promised her I would keep it all confidential. No offence."

"None taken, but you have to realise how lucky you are.

You waited for the fantasy and now fantasy and reality have become one." The answer came to him straight away. "The best thing I can do is point you in the direction of someone who, unlike me, has vast experience in these matters."

"OK. What's his name?"

"No, don't ask…Only he can tell you how you can get your woman to do what you want."

Babarr looked speculatively at Shabnam and Armila's eager faces. Swivelling around in his chair he put his meaty hands behind his head.

"It could work. It just might work. What do you think Sal?"

His head still aching, Suleiman nodded gently.

"I'll see if I can set something up tonight," replied Babarr.

"Can you arrange it so that we can be there as well?" asked Armila.

"Are you out of your mind? What do you wanna do? Hide under the table?"

"You're forgetting the two-way speakers, Babarr. Don't you remember you connected them to all the rooms?" reminded Suleiman.

Babarr tensed his arms.

"I get the feeling that something serious is gonna happen tonight. All of you be here at ten."

Leroy was wearing a dazzling single-breasted white tuxedo with shiny black trousers. In his hand was the bunch of notes that he had written while Titty Soups was giving him a tutorial.

He smiled. That Titty guy was one hell of a nice bloke (even though he was definitely gay, what with the way he dressed and all) to have spent as much time as he had carefully explaining everything he had to do.

Leroy had not wanted to reveal Shabnam's name but Titty was such a charmer! He got him feeling so relaxed that her name just slipped out. True, he was a little put off when Titty Soups suppressed a laugh but as soon as he recovered his composure he was as nice and helpful as before. No, he was even nicer. Very carefully he had told him exactly what he had to do to win Shabnam's heart.

He looked at his watch. Where was she? Perhaps she was expecting him to pick her up? That would be it. He left the restaurant in a hurry and jumped in a taxi.

Within ten minutes he was at the flat. Armila peered through the spyglass and whispered, "It's Leroy."

Shabnam looked blank. "You know, Leroy your boyfriend. Have you even told him that he has a rival?"

"No, I keep meaning to but it went straight out of my head, what with Titty Soups and all. Leroy left me a text message saying that he wanted to meet me at eight. I texted back saying that he had to book us a nice restaurant because there was something important I wanted to discuss. He was over the fucking moon."

Armila looked at her watch. "It's now nine o'clock."

"Oh…shit. Does he think I'm one of those people who have photographic memories and can remember everything? I mean come on!"

The doorbell rang several times in quick succession.

"So what do you want me to do?" asked Armila urgently.

"This is going to be one of those fucking days. Let him in."

Armila opened the door. "Good evening Leroy. Come in. Do make yourself at home," she said hospitably.

"How do you know my name?" he asked.

Armila grinned. "Shabnam just doesn't stop going on about you. Twenty-four hours a day. Seven days a week."

Leroy laughed delightedly before giving Shabnam a smile that had more wattage than the National Grid.

"Listen, Leroy, about tonight, I'm really sorry, I only just remembered."

Leroy raised his hands in the air as if to say "shit happens".

"You know, Shabnam, while I was sitting there in the restaurant musicians started playing and all of a sudden I felt myself floating to a place where it was just you and me. It's like I closed my eyes and you were there. Then do you know what happened? I opened my eyes and I was smiling like I've never smiled before. Then one of the musicians comes over to me and do you know what he says? The cheeky bastard says to me 'I'm really glad you're still smiling because your lady has obviously dumped you.' I wanted to hit him.

"But do you know something? I don't care one little bit. Do you know why?"

"Because you're itching to get inside her p—" Armila did not complete her sentence as Shabnam, with tremendous force, smacked a cushion into her face.

"Go on."

"Um, where was I?"

"You were trying to get—" interrupted Armila again, giggling, and as before she did not complete her sentence as Shabnam smacked the cushion into her face with even greater force.

"Just what the hell is going on?" asked Leroy.

"Nothing. You know how girls love to play fight. Carry on," said Shabnam. She glared at Armila.

"The thing is the reason I didn't care is very simple. It's love."

He sat on the arm of the sofa next to Shabnam.

"Do you know what I want to do now?" he whispered.

This time Armila remained silent and Leroy began to read from his notes.

"My ancestors came from Uganda. They were from the tribe of Alur. The tribe of Alur have a custom amongst the men. When they see a beautiful girl, they go crazy.

"I have decided to do what my ancestors did whenever they saw a hot mama and will prove my love to you by doing something you will never experience again."

Shabnam groaned. "Listen, Leroy honey, now is not really the time. I have got to be somewhere in about forty-five minutes."

"It will have to wait. Because I am telling you, I can't wait. Baby, this is Runyege-Entogoro, the ritual of love, the marriage dance."

He stood up, his face a study in concentration. Slowly he unbuttoned his tuxedo and threw it by the door. He undid his trousers and let them fall to the floor. With one powerful movement he ripped off his shirt and threw it in the corner. He then took off his moccasins and socks and kicked them away. He was left standing in a pair of bright red boxer shorts covered with little hearts. Shabnam and Armila stared, spellbound.

And then Armila broke the spell. "I knew it! That's what I was going to say before. All you want to do is get naked."

"Shut up!" said Leroy fiercely.

He threw his arms in the air and began to swivel his hips. His head began to jerk violently from left to right and then from right to left. Shabnam and Armila watched the bobbing boxer shorts as they slipped down a centimetre. Leroy lunged backwards to such an extent that he was almost horizontal and the boxer shorts moved up again. He leapt into the air, his muscular body glistening with perspiration and a devilish smile on his face. He finished the dance by rolling head over heels and standing up. In his hand was a gleaming diamond ring.

"Shabnam I would like you to do me the honour of being my wife. You are the most beautiful thing on this planet. I want to spend my every waking moment with you. My sun sets and rises with you."

Seeing Shabnam's alarmed face Armila decided it was time to take charge. She ran her hand through her hair.

"Leroy, you can't just propose to an Asian girl on the spot and expect an answer. It doesn't work like that."

"Why not?" he asked.

"Because of our culture. It has to be done through the family. We can only say yes to marriage after long consultations with our family."

"Are you telling me that I have to do this again in front of her mum and dad?" he exclaimed.

Just picturing that filled Shabnam with horror but before Armila could reply the doorbell rang.

Leroy opened the door.

"Titty! What are you doing here?"

"I've come to talk to Armila about one of our friends."

Leroy frowned. He then threw his arms wide open and said, "Welcome to the party. It just got going. Come on in. I'll introduce you to the girl I was telling you about."

"Can't wait!" grinned Titty Soups.

"Shabnam this is my friend Titty Soups. Titty this is my fiancée Shabnam."

Titty Soups inclined his head politely. "Let me be the first to congratulate you."

"How is it you two know each other?" asked Armila curiously.

"We met through mutual friends."

Leroy gave Titty Soups a high five of the greatest goodwill.

Shabnam was speechless.

"Listen Leroy, why don't you and me go outside for our little chat?" said Armila, tying her hair into a bun.

He nodded his head and as soon as they had left the flat Titty Soups doubled up with laughter.

"You bastard," hissed Shabnam. "You put him up to this. You humiliated him just to get at me."

"I did no such thing. He asked me the best way forwards and I told him. You're the one who humiliated him by standing him up at the restaurant."

"You took advantage of him!" shouted Shabnam.

"And you haven't? You knew from day one that it wasn't going to work out with him. But you liked him making a play for you didn't you? You liked the attention and the money and the presents. You used him because you were angry at the way your culture and your family treat you. He is just one way of saying fuck you to your parents."

"Who are you to judge me?" she snarled.

"I'm not judging you. I'm telling you the way it is. Listen, there is no parallel universe where you and me can live the way we want to and not suffer the consequences. You can have your fun just like I've had mine but at the end of the day you've got to accept who you are and make do with what's in front of you. And at this moment I am in front of you. You hate your life and I can take you away from that. I'm the future. Leroy is revenge. And you should be ashamed of yourself for the way you've treated him."

"You're a fine one to talk," sneered Shabnam. "How many women have you treated like toilet paper?"

"It's not like that, Shabnam. It's a game. Boys chase after girls. Girls chase after boys. There is no girl who would not dump her guy if she found a better option. The same goes for the guys. There is no loyalty. I played that game just like you did."

"I hate you and I never want to see you again. Get out of here!"

Titty Soups looked at her tear-streaked face and smiled.

"Go easy on Leroy when you end it. Apologise and admit the things you've done. If you don't it will gnaw away at you forever. I'll leave you to it."

28

Musa was surprised to find the place empty. Suleiman had ushered him into the car telling him that Babarr urgently needed to see him at the Islamic Centre. He had noticed Babarr's van outside so he must be around somewhere.

"Musa, what are you doing here?" asked Khadija coming through the main door.

"I was supposed to meet Babarr. Why are you here?" asked Musa feeling distinctly uneasy.

"A girl rang me at my home and told me that she wished to convert to Islam. She asked if I could meet her here. She said Babarr had given her my number."

"Armila," Musa said to himself.

Hidden in a room at the far end of the Centre, Babarr, Armila, Suleiman and Shabnam stood around a table on which had been placed a speaker with a flashing red light.

"What makes you think it will work?" asked Suleiman.

"Khadija did. I went to one of her debates and she gave me the idea. Be quiet! Musa is saying something!"

"You're upset. What is it?" asked Musa.

"Don't you ever find such questions inappropriate?"

"Well no, not really. I've never really been a great one for propriety to be honest."

"Does that make you feel proud?"

"No, not at all. But you're evading the question. Why have you been crying?"

"How do you know I've been crying?"

"Your eyes are very expressive, Khadija, more expressive than most. That may be a side effect of having worn the veil for so long. Something is making you unhappy."

Khadija made as if to say something but knowing that she might break down she remained silent, her turmoil perceptible.

"I'm sorry. I didn't mean to intrude," apologised Musa.

Khadija snorted "Of course you meant to intrude. That's why you asked the question in the first place."

"My apology was not meant to anger you. It was just meant to placate you."

"That's even worse. How many times a day do you apologise Musa? Do you never stop to think before you act or speak?"

"Not much. I can't change the way I am and I don't much want to. I prefer it this way. Say what you mean and mean what you say. Nobody does that anymore. What is not being said always has more potency than what is actually said. In our culture you have to learn to read the sub-text and I've never been any good at that."

Khadija did not reply and guessing the reason for her silence Musa felt compassion for her.

"I know what's the matter with you. It's always the same

331

isn't it? No one can ever be free to make their own choices. We are all imprisoned by the same things. It doesn't matter how much we know about Islam or how little. It doesn't matter how much education we have or how little. The ache in your eyes is the same as the ache in my heart. You're trapped and there's no way out. No little door through which you can run and find the light. Do you remember the verse in Surah *Hadid*, the one before the last?"

Khadija nodded.

"Recite it," he asked gently.

She shook her head.

"Please. Just this once!"

Khadija began to recite: "Believers, be mindful of God and have faith in His Messenger: He will give you a double share of His mercy."

She hesitated and Musa saw that she was near to tears. He finished the verse for her: "He will provide a light to help you walk."

He paused and then asked, "Where's the mercy? Where's the light? Isn't it strange that people like us can't see the light or feel the mercy any more than the rest? Sometimes you come to a point in life where you can't see ahead and you need a light. But there is no light. And you feel so afraid. You want so badly to feel a blanket of mercy. But it doesn't come does it?"

"It does come," replied Khadija. "You just have to be patient."

For the first time Musa smiled at her.

"How long can you be patient? How much of your life

332

can you be expected to sacrifice in patience? There is a puzzle in all this, Khadija. What does each one of us deserve? Do you deserve what is happening to you?"

Khadija struggled.

"You're scared aren't you? Some bastard is doing this to you and there's nowhere you can turn. It gets to you after a while doesn't it? Endless patience but no reward. But the crazy thing is that it's not patience. All you're doing is tearing up the part of you that keeps hoping. If you lose that part, you won't ever get it back. You will live a *life of quiet desperation*." Those words of some American whose name he couldn't recall had hit home when he had first read them and they did so now.

Khadija began to weep. Her body shook with fear.

Musa knelt down and stretched out his hand, tentatively.

Khadija saw his heart in his eyes.

"Take my hand. I'll never let you go, Khadija."

Khadija placed one hand in his and with the other she removed the veil from her face.

Musa saw her then: here was his dream.

A great cheer erupted. Babarr pounded the table and whooped and Armila and Shabnam hugged each other. Suleiman, full of joy for his brother, ran out of the room to find him. When he walked in on Musa and Khadija they were only momentarily surprised, aware that he must have been part of the plan. He laughed in delight at seeing Khadija unveiled and put his arm around his brother. "You fool. She was right in front of you the whole time."

29

Dadaji lay on his bed with his arms folded across his stomach. The rays of a brilliant moon cut through the window and he smiled to see its beauty. Aboo came in and sat down by his side.

Without turning his head. Dadaji said, "Itrat, read the verse of light to me."

Aboo took the Quran from the shelf and flipped through the pages until he came to the correct place. "'God is the Light of the heavens and earth. His Light is like this: there is a niche, and in it a lamp, the lamp inside a glass, a glass like a glittering star, fuelled from a blessed olive tree from neither east nor west, whose oil almost gives light even when no fire touches it – light upon light – God guides whoever He will to his Light: God draws such comparisons for people. God has full knowledge of everything.'"

As Aboo read, Dadaji recalled a time when he had fallen under the sway of devotion through his holy friend. Their companionship was marked by a rivalry to outdo one another in prayer and remembrance of Allah. They would both arise before dawn and walk in silence to the mosque and there they would worship with all the zeal and vigour of one mired in filth seeking to cleanse himself. Then, when the darkness began to ebb away, they would walk in bashful bliss to the minaret and together they would watch the sun rise under the command of Allah and the awe of that moment would douse them with the awful nearness of the final day.

Dadaji knew that his holy friend was a disciple of Baba Pir-E-Shah Ghazi, the Great Sufi Saint of Mirpur, and when troubled or anxious he would make the journey to see him. Often he had asked his holy friend that he too be accepted as a disciple but the reply was always the same, "He will choose you, you cannot choose him." So Dadaji waited.

Then his beloved wife Afiyah fell ill and the village doctor told him that her time had come. He and his children gathered around her bedside weeping and chanting prayers. He remembered her face, ashen and grey. He had been afraid then and he walked away lest his terror unman him in front of his wife. That very night he had a dream and in that dream he saw an ancient man dressed in white with his head covered with a scarlet cloth. A light brighter than the sun radiated from behind him, obscuring his face in its brilliance. The ancient man had raised his hand and beckoned him and there was in that gesture an authority so imperial that no man could refuse. When he awoke, he set off, travelling some seventy miles by foot. To this day he could not recall the journey nor what had sustained him. All he knew was that the heavens and the earth beneath him seemed suspended and the air was filled with a musk-

335

like fragrance and music the like of which no one had heard before.

When he met the Great Saint, Dadaji had felt his eminence flood him and wash away all sense of self. The Saint had said: "To sit at my table you must prostrate your soul. When you are ruler of yourself you shall again hear my call. Begin the fight against the devils that try to waylay us all. Read the Quran as it was revealed to Our Prophet (Peace be upon Him) and pray as though the final day awaited you behind the veil of the night. Read the blessed verse of light and you shall be within my sight. Restrain your anger and unclench your heart so that mercy and compassion may once again flow. For the light of Allah shall not fall upon the hard of heart and the harsh of tongue."

When Dadaji returned to the village, Afiyah was ill no more and he rejoiced in this first boon. He busied himself in duty and devotion but try though he may his mind would race like the wind when in prayer and his anger would not subside. His children would quail as his steely eye fell upon them. He cursed himself for his weakness and vented his fury upon his long-suffering wife.

Slowly he felt his piety disappear and so he read the blessed verse of light and the Great Saint came to him in a dream and pointed at a lamp that lay on the floor. The Saint told him to pick it up but when he approached the lamp a furious storm burst into the room and the lamp hurtled from wall to wall, cracking but never breaking. Dadaji tried in vain to retrieve it but whenever he bent down the wind jostled him away. The harder he fought, the stronger the wind and the angrier he became. His sense of burning shame grew. In despair he looked at the Great Saint who smiled, calmly walked against the howling wind, picked up the lamp and vanished. When he re-appeared he was in a niche in the wall, the lamp in his hands still against the might of the storm. He looked towards Dadaji and said, "Stand tall and firm. Become the niche."

Then Dadaji understood. He persevered and in time he no longer summoned his anger to give him power. He discovered that all that separated him from calm was the control of an errant thought and gradually he felt the tranquil lull of prayer: when he prayed he was aware of nothing more. As his self-awareness began to fade he felt an inner eye open and his instincts heightened. But its vision was blurred and its perception clouded. The Great Saint came to him again in a dream and in that dream he held the lamp but the glass was dirty and stained. He said to Dadaji, "Cleanse your mind of all thought other than that of Allah and glorify him. Praise him for each breath you take."

And Dadaji did so. He seldom spoke but to recite a name of Allah or to pray. His sense of self was no more. As he toiled upon his land, he would see the earth and the people around him in shades of light and dark. His inner eye began to consume his physical eye and now its vision was pristine and bright but there was no horizon. His inner eye could focus on one thing only: the Great Saint of Mirpur. He was aware of his existence alone.

The Great Saint came to him a third time and in his

hands was the lamp but the glass was now bright and luminous. As Dadaji looked closer he could see that the glass was a brilliant star, a luminary of a world supernal, radiant with the light of Allah. When his consciousness returned to him he felt at one with the light that suffused all creation. His physical eye could now look at a person and relay the voice of their heart to him.

The Great Saint came to him one last time. Dadaji stood by the foot of an ancient olive tree, its branches interlaced with an intricate and unending symmetry. The Great Saint raised his hand in which he held a seed brighter than the sun. "This is the germ of the tree. Its form cannot be contained in the intellect of man. As you walk under the shade of this tree, some truths will be revealed to you and others will remain hidden."

The years rolled on and as Dadaji walked under the shade of the olive tree, he came to know of many things. He learnt of the mercy embedded in adversity. He saw the play of destiny and desire. He came to understand the myriad branches of choice and fate and he marvelled each time at the harmony of Allah's will and how it encompassed the mortal symphony of anguish and joy. He smiled as he saw the allocation of Allah's bounty in the enclave of human endeavour but his heart was sorrowful when he witnessed evil queer the path of the decent, a vagary of divine will that he could never understand.

After death claimed the Great Saint, Dadaji continued to dream about him. He saw that from the fruit of the olive tree came a luminous oil that flowed like a river and every ripple was a flame of a heavenly fire with radiance enough to dispel all the pain and darkness since time began.

The day before he left for England he dreamt of the Great Saint and his Holy Friend travelling on a raft upon the sacred river, heading towards the ultimate light. Their raft had come to a halt and they were hailing him. He walked towards them but stopped suddenly for the entrance to the ultimate light was darker than night. That way was his death, from which he knew there was no reprieve.

30

"Well here we are!" said Armila. She waved at the sofa. "You two make yourselves at home while I make some coffee."

Khadija, after a moment's pause, removed the veil from her face. Her astonishing almond-shaped grey-blue eyes were unusually large and her complexion was white.

"Why are you so fascinated?" she asked Shabnam.

"You're English, aren't you?"

"My mother is English, if that's what you mean."

"You know, without that thing covering your face, you're a completely different person."

"It's just a veil. It doesn't make you a different person, it just changes the way people react to you."

"What are you gonna do about Musa?" Shabnam asked.

"I don't know. I want to tell my brother first and at some point soon my father will have to be told. The longer we leave it, the more awkward it will be."

"Hey that's really good you know!" said Shabnam. "You're already thinking we."

"So can you if you try. I'm sure some of your unhappiness comes from the fact that you think too much about what you want and how you can make people do what you want. And you're so angry. I noticed that when you came to the debate. Is there really so much wrong in your life?"

Shabnam shrugged. "What can I say? Pakistani culture and Pakistani parents. There's no known cure for those two diseases. The world will end before they find the cure."

"Why is it always about your culture and never about you? There is a difference you know. Not everyone is defined by their culture or even their religion." She picked up her veil. "I wear this veil. It does not wear me. You don't have to be owned by the things you hate. That's one thing I've learnt from your brother."

Just then Armila arrived carrying three cups of coffee on a tray. "Here we are," she said brightly.

Khadija smiled and said, "Thanks very much but first I need to offer my morning prayers. Is there somewhere I can go?"

"Sure," answered Armila. "Just outside the front door on the left there is a quiet alcove. No one will disturb you."

As Khadija left the room, Armila handed a cup to Shabnam.

"So what are you going to do?"

"About what?" sighed Shabnam, knowing full well what she meant.

"You know the triangle, Leroy, Titty Soups and you."

Shabnam's face darkened.

"Who does he think I am?" she said crossly.

"Who? Leroy or Titty Soups?" inquired Armila.

"Titty Soups. I hope that scumbag burns in hell!"

"But he does have a point," said Armila. "You have to keep your eyes focussed on what's in front of you rather than always looking to the horizon."

Shabnam clenched her jaw.

"Do you know what gets me about you, Miss Goody Two-Shoes? You were born with a bloody silver spoon in your gob. Guess what? I never had it so lucky. Mummy and Daddy never sent me to a posh school so I could be all clever and educated. Mummy and Daddy never took me to restaurants. Your parents brought you up so they could be proud of you. My parents brought me up so I could be their slave and then, when the time comes, they can marry me off to some prick so I can be his slave as well. You don't know shit about my culture! You don't have a clue about what I've been through! You got no bloody right giving me your wisdom!"

Seeing Armila's face, she realised she had gone too far. "I'm sorry, I didn't mean to take it out on you."

Armila hugged her. "Don't worry about it."

Khadija re-joined her friends and after they had finished their coffees, Armila said, "Listen I need to go. I promised my parents I'd meet them. Can I give you a lift Khadija?"

Left alone, Shabnam sank into the sofa and slowly let her head fall back. It was true, it was too much to be pissed off all the time. But nobody ever seemed to get where she was coming from. Everybody had their own theories and opinions about what she needed to do in her life but none of it made any sense to her. She had never really considered marriage, believing it was more fun being a girlfriend. And then Leroy had got all serious.

Recalling last night's events made her smile. When Leroy got desperate all sense just went out of his head and he did the first thing he was told. Titty Soups must have picked up on that, the arrogant stuck-up pig. But he was right, she had to end it with Leroy, she knew that.

God, that Titty Soups was one sly son of a bitch. He knew exactly which buttons to push. The worst thing about it was that he was spot on. There was only one door in front of her and he was on the other side of it. If she could get Leroy eating out of her hand it shouldn't be too hard to get Titty Soups to do the same. It was just acting and that was something she had being doing for a long time, acting like she was respectful in front of Aboo and acting like she agreed with Amma. It was no big deal to do the same with Titty Soups and she had an ace up her sleeve. She knew instinctively how to keep a guy sweet.

She thought of Leroy and again felt shame at the game she had played. She would have to lose someone kind and good to gain what was meant for her.

Armila walked into Babarr's office carrying an envelope.

"Khadija is staying with me and she asked that you deliver this letter to her brother. She said you know where he usually hangs out."

"That I do, princess. That I most definitely do. He hangs around with them losers outside the Central Mosque."

"Losers?"

Babarr snorted in disgust. "They talk religion all the time but act like they want to mug every person that walks past. Dole layabout trash!"

He opened the envelope.

"Hey, that's private. You can't do that!" protested Armila angrily.

"Pipe down, darling."

He read the letter and chuckled.

"What's so funny?"

"This is what they call a letter bomb."

Armila was not amused and stormed out just as Suleiman arrived. Babarr showed him the letter and repeated the joke.

"What about her father? What's he like Babarr?"

"A huge hairy bastard. About six foot six with a really long beard. The guy gives me the creeps. He never says anything, just looks at you out of the corner of his eye like you're a bug that he's about to squash."

Suleiman groaned. "An asshole who got religious and became a bad ass. I seen plenty of them."

"This guy ain't your garden variety bad ass. He really freaks you out. He is gonna be a problem."

"What can we do about it? If the fucker wants to take Musa on, let him try. I'll show him some of my own freakiness," said Suleiman.

"Yeah well, we can cross that bridge when we come to it. What about your parents? What were they like when you told them?"

"They were OK. Aboo did his parent-who-has-worked-so-hard-and-then-been-let-down-by-his-son act. But that's his standard response to every crisis that involves one of his sons. And they've fixed up to meet Khadija. After that Dadaji will give the final say. I've gotta go and pick her up this evening and Shabnam's coming with me." Suleiman grinned. "I wonder if she shares Musa's curse?"

Babarr laughed. "It's not a curse it's a law. Whatever can go fucking wrong will most definitely go wrong."

Musa and Khadija walked through the park together. Cedar trees filled the air with a sharp wet smell that seethed with magic and hope.

"Musa, I am due to visit your family tonight. Isn't there anything you want to tell me?" she asked.

She was so gentle and modest. He felt a strange lightness when he walked with her as though the aura of her nearness unshackled him from the gravity of all earthly fear. He smiled and walked on.

"Musa!" said Khadija, annoyed. "What is the matter with you? You have to tell me what to expect."

"They expect you. Only they don't know it yet," replied Musa.

"Tell me about your parents."

"Well, Aboo is mostly quiet and keeps himself to himself but he loves to give orders and throw his weight around and he is a bit of a drama queen. A lot of a drama queen actually. Amma is patient, long suffering. She's cleverer than Aboo, but she keeps that to herself."

"That's it?" asked Khadija.

"Not quite. Above everyone is my grandfather, Dadaji. Everything rests on his word. He is the one person who will tell it the way it is. You'll never have met anyone like him."

He held out his arms and whirled around.

"You need to take things more seriously." said Khadija, laughing.

"It's not the time to be serious. You know, there comes a moment in life when you are so happy that you can almost walk on air. That time for us is now and we have to enjoy it while it lasts. Do you see those roses over there? They suffer the burning heat and the violent wind and then the bounty of Allah arrives and they revel in their good fortune. For now, let us do just that. Events are like waves. They can lift you up high or smash you down. Well, now they are carrying us up high and soon we'll be home. Let's enjoy the ride."

"What do you mean by home?" asked Khadija.

"Home in every sense of the word. Our home in this life and our home in the hereafter." But that does bring us to an important subject: our marriage. When do we get married? We can have a Nikah ceremony at the Central Mosque. Babarr and Armila can be witnesses. Let's do that soon. And next year we can perform the pilgrimage to Mecca together and the year after that we can do Iraq and see the shrine of Imam Al Mahdi and then we can go to Qom."

Khadija laughed: "What about enjoying the moment? In any case your plan, like many of your plans, is rash. First, your parents must be reconciled to our marriage."

"What about your father?" Musa asked anxiously. "Will he listen to reason?"

"Never."

"Is he educated?"

346

"He was a major in the Pakistani army before he came to England."

"Have you ever heard of Khalil Gibran, Khadija?"

"The poet?"

"Yes, the poet. He wrote something about parents and their children. I can't remember it exactly but he said something like, 'You may give them your love but not your thoughts. You may house their bodies but never their souls. For their souls live in the house of tomorrow which you will never visit.' Write a letter to your father with those words."

Khadija laughed. "You're insane."

"Sometimes, Khadija, insanity is a necessity if you wish to enjoy all that life offers you."

Khadija shook her head. "You need to start thinking like a provider instead of a poet. How are we going to make ends meet? What are you going to do for a living? That sort of thing."

"I have been raised to be a Holy man. A cleric. The salary of a Holy man is not much. But there are the benefits of a life simple and pure, graced by Allah, like Adam and Eve before they were expelled from the Garden of Eden. They had just one goal and that was to earn the pleasure of Allah. Their chemistry must have been unique, just two people, innocent and trusting. Completing each other and complimenting each other. No power struggles, no debates over who wore the trousers because they were content with the way they were. That is what our life will be like, happy and pure. Secure in the knowledge that we have nothing except that which is given to us by Allah."

31

Shabnam held down her kameez to prevent it flapping in the wind. When her scarf flew from her head, she gritted her teeth in exasperation. She thought wearing this outfit would help her in what she had to say but it was becoming an unbearable pain in the ass.

Leroy was waiting and her sense of guilt increased when she saw how pleased he was to see her.

"Hey Shabnam, am I glad to see you. Listen, if this is about last night, don't sweat. You don't have to give me an answer straight away. You take your time because I know what a big step it is for you. I know I went over the top but when I see something I want I go all out trying to get it. I didn't mean to embarrass you, honest."

He looked her up and down. "What's up baby? Why you dressed in them things? You always said you hated women who dressed like that. And why are we meeting here in the park? I don't see you as the outdoor type."

"Do you remember when we first met at Andy's party?"

"Sure I do. You looked like a real hot number then. Plenty of guys were heading towards you but they all got stuck in traffic." He laughed at the memory.

"That was the first party I ever went to and while I was

sitting there I said to myself that was the last I'd ever go to. All those people drinking and laughing. I just couldn't be like them. And it's not because I didn't drink. It's because when I looked at them dancing I got the feeling that they all looked like they were on the moon and I was watching through some telescope. That was when I met you.

"And you talked shit to get me to go out with you and all I was thinking was that you were like a racing car. You know some guys are like that. They got this vibe about them like they know where they're going and they're getting there damn fast. Funny thing is half the time them kind of guys don't even know they've got it going. At that party there were Pakistani guys and they were all trying to be like you and they were hitting on me as well. When I looked at them I saw a bunch of fucking losers but with you I felt like a winner."

"You are a winner," said Leroy earnestly.

"No I'm not and I'll tell you why. One of my friends once asked me about you. One of these veiled Muslim-type girls that we used to laugh at? And I couldn't tell her much. Do you know why?"

Leroy shook his head.

"I don't know how many brothers or sisters you have. I don't know where your parents live and what they do. I don't even know what you do except that whatever it is you make a lot of money. Did that never bother you Leroy? That I never asked you any of these things?"

"No! It never even once crossed my mind. And to tell you the truth it wouldn't have mattered much to me anyway. I ain't ever seen my father and the less I see of my mother and brother, the better. The only thing I could think about when I was with you was you."

"But didn't it matter to you that I stood you up so many times? That I got you to give me money? There must have been some part of you that said this isn't right?"

"No. I used to stand girls up a lot. The money ain't no big deal. If you got it spend it. You're my girl, Shabnam. Spending money on you goes with the territory."

"Doesn't me wearing these clothes tell you I'm on different territory?"

"They're just clothes," he said quietly.

Shabnam tried to explain. "The reason why I wore them is to... Do you know I fucking hate them half the time but I still wear them. I hate the things around me but they are still a part of me. I don't want to be at war with myself. I want to make peace with the things that I hate because I can't throw them away like they're a bunch of clothes."

"What things?"

She sighed. "My culture, my fucking religion, my dad and...myself."

"What you saying Shabnam?"

"When we used to go out I felt excited and happy because you were paying me so much attention and I liked the fact that I had this power over you. That I could treat you like shit and you would still come running. Did you never wonder why I didn't let you drop me off at home?"

"Because of your folks," replied Leroy.

"Yes, Leroy. That's it. My folks. I can't stand them and I don't ever want to be like them but I would hate myself if they think less of me. I hate my fucking culture but it would kill me if someone said to my mum I saw your daughter with a…with a man. I don't want to lie to myself anymore.

"Men look at my face and their hearts stop. I've been getting that from men for as long as I can remember. I used you and sometimes I humiliated you and it kills me that you don't realise that because all you see is my face.

"My brother told me that only Allah knows best what a man deserves. And you don't deserve someone like me, I'm not decent. You deserve someone decent and you're gonna find that person and make them feel special just like you did with me. You must hold on to her because not everyone can be happy like that…"

Titty Soups burst into Babarr's office.

"Hey Titty! Someone's looking pleased with himself. Who've you pulled this time?"

He pulled out his mobile phone, opened the flap and showed it to Babarr.

"Yes I will marry you you bastard. Shabnam."

"Man you actually did it. You actually went and tamed the tiger. I can't believe it. I really can't."

Titty Soups shrugged modestly. "It was a challenge, but not an impossible challenge. I just let her play herself out. You know, beneath all that fire and fury, I think there may be a sweet girl. I'm surprised that you doubted me, even for one second," said Titty Soups.

"Doubted you? Man they should erect a statue of you some place. Or carve your face into a mountain. You're the bee's knees!"

Titty Soups bowed with a flourish.

"What you gonna do now? You can't tell me you're actually gonna marry her!" said Babarr.

"Of course I'm going to marry her. I'm not gonna throw this fish back into the sea."

"She ain't no fish," warned Babarr. "She's a shark and when she starts hunting you had better start running!"

"It won't be like that," said Titty Soups with a dismissive wave of his hand.

"What will it be like then?"

Titty Soups winked at Babarr, "It'll be a whole new game…"

32

Khadija had thought long and hard about whether or not to veil her face. Armila had strongly objected to the idea saying it wouldn't help in front of people she needed to win over but in the end she decided that it would be more effective if she let her words convey the needed impression rather than her face and so had opted for the veil.

She sat in Aboo's leather chair facing Musa's parents. She thought his father looked sad and his mother weary. They viewed her in silence for a time and then Musa's father began to laugh.

"What is the matter?" asked the mother.

"I was just thinking, we never saw Musa for what he is and now his choice is in front of us and we cannot see her for what she is."

"It is just a veil," said the mother.

"What is clearer without the veil? And what does it matter? We no longer have eyes that can see the world around us," remarked Aboo. He pointed towards the door which led to the kitchen. "My father is through there. You must go to him."

Khadija nodded and walked through the kitchen into

the garden where the old man sat on his prayer mat on the grass. One hand was raised and he moved his finger as though tracing the line of the moon. She felt an immense sense of awe as she watched him.

Dadaji brought his hands together.

"You are the choice, are you not?"

"Assalaam-u-alaikum," she said nervously.

The old man pointed at the grass next to him and Khadija sat down. He turned and peered at her with his shoulders hunched. Khadija kept her head bowed, waiting for him to speak.

She had met many aged men who were renowned for their piety and learning. Normally they were disdainful of women and had little or no personality but this old man had an overwhelming presence. As he watched her, she felt as though he was reaching into her heart.

"What is your name?"

"Khadija. And you are Dadaji?"

He nodded slowly and smiled.

"Tell me of Musa," he whispered.

"Musa is…Musa is himself. He is not owned by any fear of what other people may think. He often speaks without thinking. He is passionate and he is excited by life. His dreams lead him and…" Her voice faltered.

"Does he bring you peace?" asked Dadaji.

"At first he did not. Now he does."

"How?"

"He is innocent and so like an innocent child in the way he is excited by life. When I am by his side I feel as though my footsteps are lighter."

"Innocence is not the same as purity."

"Yes, I know, but we can make a life together that will be pure and simple," said Khadija.

Dadaji smiled: "No one owns the life they lead."

"I know. I told him that but I don't think he understood what I meant."

"Knowledge will not always lead you to the truth."

"I don't understand what you mean, Dadaji."

"The will of Allah will unfold through pain and joy. Have you surrendered to the will of Allah or to the whispers of your heart?"

"I don't know."

"Had you been obedient, you would have been assured that Allah is with you. Now you have lost that certainty."

"We have committed no crime, Dadaji. To love someone is not a sin."

"But the passion of such love can often lead to sin."

"Dadaji, as Allah is my witness, we will live for His approval and good grace. There is no evil in our hearts."

"Yes, I can see that is true."

Dadaji laid his hand on Khadija's head and said, "In your eyes there is pain and in your heart there is a great weariness but your footsteps are steady and the light in your eyes is the reflection of a greater light. Be happy for as long as the will of Allah allows you to be. Go in peace and return in joy."

Khadija smiled shyly and stood up. Though Musa wasn't by her side, as she went back into the house she felt as if she was walking on air.

★

355

Abdel stood just inside the front door. His hands were clammy and his heart raced. He thought about leaving the letter, yes that was what he would do; he would leave the letter and come back later. He took it out of his pocket along with his keys which dropped noisily to the floor. As he bent to pick them up his father screamed his name and he froze.

His father walked heavily down the stairs and stared at the letter in his son's hand.

"Where is she?"

Abdel's terror deprived him of speech.

"Where is she?" His father smacked him hard across the side of his head, knocking him sideways.

"Where is she?" he repeated in quiet fury. He dragged Abdel to his feet, pushed him against the door and placed his huge hand against his throat, moving his thumb to the side of his son's neck and pressing gently to feel his racing pulse. He trembled with excitement as Abdel began to beg.

"No, no, no, please, no."

His father struck him repeatedly with his fists. Abdel was dimly aware of falling to the floor and trying to cover up his face but it was no use. The kicks began and finally he escaped into unconsciousness.

Blood stained his sister's final words which their father now read. And her words were simple.

Father

I am relieving you of a burden just as I am relieving myself of a burden. You will probably think I am just like my mother and in a way you are right. That is why you never gave me your love. And now I ask you one last request. Abandon the God that you pray to. Your God asks too much in the way of sacrifice. You have given your humanity but I will not give my sanity.

Khadija

A daughter's words swallowed up in a father's rage. A daughter's truth lost in an ethos where ignorance was crowned.

33

Aboo knew he had been in the wrong about Suleiman and that he had to make peace with his father. They were alone together waiting for the rest of the family to gather for a meal; Shabnam and her mother were in the kitchen and Musa and Suleiman had yet to arrive.

He brought his hands together in a plea for mercy and said, "Please forgive me, I feel I have brought shame on you."

Dadaji smiled, "In my time a father planned and his sons obeyed. In your time a father plans while a son dreams and a son plans even while his father dreams. In every age for every plan and for every dream the plan of Allah shall always reign supreme."

After Musa and Suleiman arrived and had greeted the two women in the kitchen, the doorbell sounded.

They heard voices and Shabnam came into the room.

"There's someone to see you, Aboo. Shall I let him in?"

Aboo sighed wearily: "Now is not the time but yes, let him in."

Musa, standing in the kitchen doorway, recognised who it was at once although he did not know how. It was something to do with the way he walked in, just like the young man he used to see when he was a toddler, always coming and going and walking around him. Musa felt a latent memory of dislike.

"Javed...my son." Aboo began to weep. Amma and Suleiman stood transfixed.

"It's been a very long time," said Javed. "You've grown up Musa, you probably don't even remember me. And Shabnam, you're beautiful..."

He fell silent as they gazed at him.

"Why are you here?" asked Shabnam angrily.

Javed smiled nervously. "I'm a father now and I want my daughter to know her family. Liz said that I should make the first step."

"Liz. An English woman!" gasped Aboo.

"A father," exclaimed Amma. "When did you marry?"

Javed laughed uneasily.

"What do you do?" asked Musa suspiciously.

"I have an import and export business. Tiles and jeans, mostly. I've been doing that for a long time now. I have two shops in the city centre."

"You've been living here all this time!" exclaimed Amma.

Suleiman laughed quietly. "Well, Aboo. What do you think now? Musa has betrayed the family by refusing to marry Iram and now your son has a child with an English woman."

"What is done is done. There is no point in going over the past. He has come back and that is the most important thing."

"No it is not," said Amma. She walked over to Javed and slapped him hard across the face. The she grabbed him by the lapels and was about to spit at him when Aboo came between them.

"Have you lost your mind?" he demanded but Amma ignored him.

"Thirteen years! You have been gone for thirteen years. We didn't know where you were, or what you were doing. We didn't know whether you were dead or alive. And all this time you are living in the same city. Did the thought of your mother never come to you? Or your father? Do you see that, Javed?" She pointed to his poem. "He never let me take it down. After every morning prayer, he looks at it. Every day for the past thirteen years he looks at it. And you come here now after all these years!"

She turned on Aboo, angry tears streaming down her face. "Do you remember how you hit him when you found out that he was sleeping with girls? Do you remember the day he left? Your beloved first born who you could never be bothered to find all these years. You said I spoilt him and made him the way he is." She pointed an angry finger at Aboo, "It was you who spoilt him. It was you who could never say no to him. It was you who became angry whenever I tried to punish him. You made him what he is!"

"Stop, Amma!" shouted Suleiman. "He doesn't understand a word you are saying. He doesn't understand Punjabi any more. Ain't that so, Jav?"

In one fluid movement, Suleiman grabbed Javed by the lapels of his jacket and yanked him forwards so that their faces were almost touching.

"You can understand me now can't you? Listen to me very carefully before you call me Sal. Five years ago you were walking with a guy through the fish market in Hayworth. I was right behind you. You walked and then you stopped and then you turned your head a little and then you walked on. Is that true or is it not?"

Javed nodded, his eyes wide in his red face.

"Did you fucking see me or not?" roared Suleiman.

Javed averted his eyes and Suleiman shook him and pushed him hard against the door. "Answer the question. Did you see me?"

"Yes…Yes…I saw you," said Javed. "Look, I was a different person then."

"Shut up. You lying piece of shit," hissed Suleiman. "Do you know what I did that day? I followed you. You lived with a guy in Roxbridge Gardens. And you were there for a long time. I used to watch the men and the women go into your flat but you never saw me did you? You were having the time of your fucking life. The same old Javed, screwing everything that moved. Do you know why I stopped watching you? Because I realised what a pathetic bastard I was, waiting for you to notice me."

Suleiman pointed to Musa. "Do you know what he used to feel like when he was a kid wondering why you never played with him? I should have told him then that his eldest brother was a worthless bastard. And outside the church, when I was beaten up, you came charging in to help me but then you ran off, leaving me on the fucking ground."

His voice cracked and Shabnam took his arm.

"Sal, it's OK."

"No, it is not OK." Suleiman glared at Javed and pointed a trembling finger at Aboo.

"Every time he laid eyes on me, he was thinking of you. Everything I ever fucking did or said was compared to you, the bastard who ran off."

Suleiman turned to his father. "I stayed Aboo. I took your shit and I never left. I grew up without you ever talking to me. I did everything you asked but it never made any difference. He comes home and you accept him without question and say what is done is done and there is no point in going over the past. But you buried me in the past, Aboo. You buried me the day he left. I came home drunk and hurt and all you did was swear and hit me. You never bothered to find out what happened. I wanted to leave that day but I didn't because of Dadaji. He's been more of a father to me in one month than you were in my whole life."

"It will be different now, Suleiman. I've changed. I know what I did was bad but we can put it all behind us and I want my daughter to know her family. We can all move on," said Javed.

"I've already moved on, Javed," said Suleiman, leaving the room. Musa and Shabnam, wiping the tears from her face, followed him.

"Where are you going?" asked Javed.

"We're going to see if our brother is OK. Don't ever come here again." Shabnam closed the door behind her.

34

Dadaji sat surveying all before him with a wry smile. It was the day before Musa and Khadija's wedding and Aboo and Amma were talking excitedly while Shabnam and Suleiman were for once happy just to sit and listen. Musa and Khadija sat on the floor by Dadaji.

"Is it all settled then? Everything is ready?" asked Dadaji. At first there had been considerable opposition from Aboo and Amma when Musa and Khadija said that they did not want to be in separate rooms for the Nikah ceremony. In the end the mullah, a gentle young man, convinced them that their being together was perfectly valid. And then there were endless arguments about where the ceremony would be held.

"Everything is ready Dadaji," said Aboo. "We have sent out the invitations and made preparations for the reception. Everything is as it should be."

"That must be a first," remarked Suleiman. "Khadija, have you heard from your father and brother."

"No, I haven't heard from either of them. I've asked one of my friends if they could get hold of my brother but he's nowhere to be found. Nobody is answering the phone at home," she said anxiously.

"Let it be. Leave that battle for later. No point doing your head in about it now," said Shabnam.

Amma nodded her agreement.

"Babarr has done a poster letting people know about the wedding. He's put it all around the Islamic Centre so a lot of people are going to turn up," said Suleiman.

"How many people can the Medina Restaurant take?" asked Musa.

"About three hundred," replied Suleiman.

"I want one nice picture of us as we are now," stated Amma.

"Dadaji does not approve of pictures," said Aboo pompously.

Dadaji disagreed. "Take one photograph of me with Khadija. Then do as you will."

Aboo looked stunned and then shrugged his shoulders. Suleiman took the camera from the book shelf and handed it to his father as Amma began to fuss.

"Where will Khadija sit? She cannot sit next to Dadaji." "Do you want to take off your veil, Khadija?"

Khadija shook her head firmly.

"It is not within you to be immodest. Remove your veil and sit at my feet Khadija," ordered Dadaji and she did as she was told, embarrassed by the curious looks from the family.

As Aboo fiddled with the lens, she tried to focus on the camera but found it impossible to hold her gaze. She looked at Musa and seeing those intense eyes and that lion's mane of unruly hair she smiled and Dadaji felt her serenity. He followed her gaze and in the face of his grandson he saw the beauty of his hope and he felt in his heart the humble majesty of his grandson's victory. A tear welled in his eye and coursed down his cheek.

The camera's shutter clicked. A light flashed. A teardrop froze in its path and a portrait of dignity and decency was born.

A couple of hours later Suleiman was in the Medina Restaurant kitchen bossing the cooks.

"Don't use too much oil; I don't care how pretty it makes the food look. And the sweet dishes, you can go for broke when it comes to them. Put in as much sugar as you like. What are you preparing for the vegetarians? And what about the fish? It must be fresh. Where did you buy the lamb? Are the spices freshly ground?"

In a large conservatory at the back of the restaurant Babarr was planning the layout for the Nikah ceremony.

"Now you gotta make the stage somewhere in the middle. And remember they're not too hot on the idea of sitting next to each other. Make it really nice so that they are going to think this whole shebang cost a lot of money. And we need some music before the ceremony, something romantic, but it's gotta be loud enough so that the two can't talk to each other."

Babarr then addressed the waitresses he had taken on for the wedding and who stood nervously to one side. He had heard they were good at what they did; they were certainly very pretty, and they were all white.

"Right ladies, you will each be paid extremely well for the work that you are going to do tomorrow. This won't

365

be like no other wedding you've worked at before. This is an Islamic wedding. All of you are going to be under a lot of pressure because there's going to be guys, young and old, who are going to be giving you the eye. At the same time they will look as if they despise you for tempting them. And then their wives are going to hate you because they think you are flirting with their husbands just by walking past them. If the old guys have to wait for their food and you don't come running every time, they'll click their fingers. On top of that there's going to be a few people who hate you because they think you've got no place being at an Islamic wedding but I'm sure you'll be professional."

On the temporary stage Shabnam was busy instructing a smitten camera man.

"Now remember. People are going to be watching your video carefully to see if they can grab a wife or a husband so what you do will have an impact on a huge number of people. You gotta make sure that you spend equal time on the men and the women. Zoom in on anyone who looks about thirtyish. Don't give any camera time to anyone with kids. Some assholes will play up for the camera. Give them what they want and then afterwards delete the bastards. No close ups of my brother and his fiancée. When people start eating, zoom in on their jewellery not on the food. Follow me around and you die."

35

That night Khadija dreamt vividly. The clouds were billowy balloons of red and blue and from them fell purple rain. Across a courtyard she saw a turbaned figure who sat gazing at a valley below. As she watched chaos left the rain and droplets fell in straight noiseless lines. She walked through the rain spinning in giddy joy until she came to Musa. As she laid a gentle hand on his shoulder, he turned to look at her and she saw Dadaji, smiling and humble.

"Dadaji, where is Musa?"

"He will be with you in the blink of an eye," he replied.

Subsequently a stench of scorched earth swept across the courtyard and she felt only terror. Dadaji disappeared but then she saw Musa, his eyes filled with love. She stretched out her hand to him but as he stepped towards her a furious wind pushed against him. He struggled, his eyes burning with passion as he strained against the merciless wind. She could not bear it any longer and tried to run to him but could not. Again she heard Dadaji's voice.

"Let him be. It is his destiny."

And then she woke. She was in Armila's flat and today

was the day of her wedding. Beside her bed were her wedding clothes, given to her by Musa's mother. She laughed out aloud.

Khadija's father picked up the telephone and as he waited for an answer he stared at the splatters of Abdel's blood staining the floor and door.

"Mukhtar Travel Agents," said a voice.

"This is Major Nawaz. Is everything ready?"

"Yes, Major. Your ticket for Islamabad is waiting to be collected."

"Good, I'll be there shortly."

"I will not go," announced Dadaji.

"You must come. Please!" urged Amma.

"I will not go. That is final."

"Then I will stay here with you," said Aboo.

"No!" replied Dadaji firmly. "You must be there at the Nikah ceremony. Go now!"

Musa smiled sadly. He knew why Dadaji was refusing to come. The idea of anyone marrying against his wishes still rankled. He had consented but his fierce proud nature forbade him from rejoicing in his grandson's victory.

"Let Dadaji be," he said to his parents.

Aboo shook his head.

"So be it. Let us go," he said.

As they were leaving Musa heard Dadaji call his name. Telling Aboo and Amma that he would not be long he returned to his grandfather. In his white sherwani and baggy white trousers, he knelt at his side.

Dadaji placed his hand on Musa's shoulder.

"Musa. Heed what I say."

Musa nodded and saw pain on his grandfather's face.

"There is never enough justice for all the injustices in this world so do not seek to find it. There is never enough pity in the human heart to compensate for all its cruelty so do not lower yourself to gain it."

"What are you saying?"

Dadaji forced a laugh.

"You must go now Musa. Khadija awaits you even as she awaits me."

The glass doors of Medina Restaurant sparkled. Garlands of sweet-smelling flowers were strung around the walls and music was playing as the many guests arrived. Musa and Khadija's romance had been the subject of much discussion within the community. Each and every guest rejoiced with them for in their hearts they loved a tale that had a happy ending.

Titty Soups and Shabnam were sitting on a table with Armila and Suleiman. Titty gestured to the platform and said to Shabnam, "That will be us one day soon."

"I curse the day you came into my life. I curse the mother who brought you into this world and I curse your asshole of a father," she replied and Titty Soups roared.

Shabnam gritted her teeth. Nothing seemed to fluster him. No matter what anyone said or did, he would take it all in his stride.

"Well, look at Confucius," laughed Armila as Babarr strode on to the stage wearing a gold brocade jacket with a mandarin collar and red buttons over snowy white pyjamas and black cotton shoes.

"Assalaam-u-alaikam. Welcome to the wedding we've all been waiting for. My brothers and sisters, respected elders, I would like to tell you the story of how I first met Musa. It's less than a year since Suleiman told me his kid brother had been chucked out of a madrasah and he needed a good kick up the backside. Could I help? Well, I said, bring him down and let me have a look at him. I can still remember the day he walked into my office and I thought nothing doing. But as soon as I got to know him, I realised that he was strong, he believed in his dreams and always backed himself to win no matter what the odds. And that is what sets Musa apart from everyone else. Now Musa soon had a mission. He wanted to get married to Snow White, he wanted the impossible, but he stuck to his guns and he has found his Snow White in Khadija. She is pure and decent and she respects herself and her religion. On top of that she's got class and courage. You ain't ever gonna find a better couple than them two. As soon as they walk in I want everybody to please jump up and start clapping. They're gonna remember this moment and cherish it for the rest of your lives. Here they come!"

An explosion of rapturous applause sounded as Musa and Khadija entered the restaurant and walked slowly to the stage. People stood up and whistled and showered them with red petals. As the petals rained down on them, Musa turned to Khadija. She was decked in red and gold and she wore no veil. Her eyes shone with an unconcealed happiness that filled him with wonder.

The mullah began to recite from the Quran: "And it is God who has given you spouses from amongst yourselves and through them He has given you children and grandchildren and provided you with good things. How can they believe in falsehood and deny God's blessings?"

He nodded at Khadija. She cleared her throat but when she tried to speak no words would come. Musa gently took her hand in his and she began again.

"I have given myself away to you in Nikah on the agreed gift." Khadija looked at Musa in alarm and whispered, "Wait a second, I haven't received any gift!"

"No gift?" asked the mullah.

"No gift?" echoed Musa.

Babarr swore under his breath and carefully lifted a gold chain from around his neck and handed it to Musa. Surprised at its weight, Musa gave the necklace to Khadija.

"Good," smiled the mullah, nodding at Khadija again.

"I have given myself away to you in Nikah on the agreed gift, the *mahr*," she said slowly and shyly.

Musa's eyes filled with tears and he spoke the words which he would remember for the rest of his life.

"You are proof of the Mercy of Allah. You are the reason that I was made…I accept the Nikah."

"Congratulations," said the Mullah.

Holding hands, Musa and Khadija stepped to the front of the stage. Everyone in the restaurant jumped to their feet and this time the applause was deafening. Khadija felt a light envelop her as tears of joy ran down her face. And then everyone fell silent and, bewildered, she looked up at Musa. He was staring in horror at something or someone behind her and in that instant she knew. She turned and saw her father with a pistol in his hand, the pistol that she had so often seen him assemble. Hope diminished and her life began to abate as she felt the dart of her father's hate.

Major Nawaz ran. He would return a hero to his tribe in Pakistan, the upholder of his family's honour. So much honour in the midst of such madness, so much honour and yet such misery filling the lives of his children. So much contempt from a father so base.

Musa gently held Khadija in his arms.

"Everything's going to be OK. We'll get you to a hospital. Everything's going to all right. Just hang in there," he sobbed.

"This is as far as it was written for you and me." She touched his hair and he raised his head. "I'm going to wait for you, Musa. Because I am your wife and I will be your wife in that world too. Only I have to wait for you a little bit. And you must wait for me too."

"No, no, please no!"

"Musa…listen to me…It's no one's fault. Really it isn't."

Musa's eyes blurred and he could see her no more. He buried his face in her neck and felt her pulse weaken.

She clutched his shoulders and moaned. "Musa…Can you hear it?"

He blinked for indeed he could hear the words from the Holy Quran that were sounding in her mind. "Go in among My servants; and into My garden." He could see the grey-blue eyes that for so long had been tinged with sorrow now filling with peace.

"I won't live without you, Khadija. I can't."

"Yes, you can. Don't you see Musa? Wherever you are I will be there too. Don't let hate come inside you. You must go on being you. That was what made me love you, Musa. I'm a part of you now. Promise me you won't lose me."

In that instant their world of hopes and dreams split apart at the seams. A future yet to be born blew away as faintly as the breath of a dusky dawn. His passion, so great and glorious, departed and left no trace; no memory of joy, not even a smile to light up his face. As he had not heard the screams, he did not now hear the sirens: his bride was dead.

Dadaji lay on his bed. Out of nowhere a butterfly swam into his sight. He stared at the flutter and flurry of its wings. So delicate was their play and so magical was their dance. The pretty butterfly spiralled slowly down towards him and as she flapped her gossamer wings at him, he felt his life unravel. The song of his life played to the tune of those ethereal wings.

"I could have been a better man," he said.

But the butterfly let him know that at the time the angels had blown life into the womb of his mother then was written the sum of his deeds. He was all that he was meant to be.

Hesitant and awed, Dadaji slowly raised his finger and touched the pretty butterfly and the ethereal wings stopped beating. The world ceased its motion and there opened before him a path to a mystical river. By the shore of the river was a raft on which sat two old friends and a beautiful bride. Dadaji's hand fell with the heaviness of a burden that could no longer be borne. And the pretty butterfly beat her wings once again and flew away, quivering in the trail of her forgotten song.

36

Distraught, they gathered together in Babarr's office but Musa was not with them.

"Did she have any family?" asked Armila.

"A brother who nobody can find and a father who's on the run. That's all she had to call family," answered Babarr.

"Musa was looking for his dream and for a moment he found it in Khadija. He really did. Some people have got memories they can always hold on to. He doesn't even have that," said Shabnam sadly.

"Musa brightened things up," said Babarr. "He was so like a kid. We all got such a buzz helping him out. I don't get it. It just doesn't make any sense. What he wanted was no big thing, it was so simple. But he couldn't get to the finishing line."

Suleiman shrugged, unable to speak.

"What's he going to do now?" asked Armila.

"Do you even have to ask?" said Shabnam. "He'll go back to the place that makes him feel safe and secure. He won't ever get that here."

"So he'll just become another Holy Man, preaching the same sermon every Friday?" said Babarr gloomily.

"No he won't," said Suleiman. "He'll be different from

the rest of them and he'll be better than the rest of them. His heart has been cut into little pieces and that will bring him wisdom which he'll pass on. Musa was born to be wise, just like Dadaji, but that doesn't mean he'll be happy because I can't believe the truly wise ever are."

Musa sat leaning against a pillar in the prayer hall of the Central Mosque. In the middle of the hall was his bride's coffin. Weeping women, her sisters in Islam, walked around it.

His eyes fell on a phrase from the Quran etched on the inner wall of the dome, a phrase he had remembered seeing not so long ago. "Which, then, of your Lord's blessings do you both deny?"

Musa stared at words which seemed to be filled with a heavy inverse meaning. That chapter was said to be the most sublime in the Quran. It spoke of the fruit of the earth which sustained all creatures. It spoke of the setting of the sun and of scented herbs and of the pearls and corals that lay at the bottom of the sea, all the while asking that same question. "Which, then, of your Lord's blessings do you both deny?"

But, Musa thought, it is not enough to rejoice in the setting of the sun and in the bounty of the earth. It is not enough to delight in the beauty beneath the ocean. Not when you knew that you could have lived your life with a beautiful and pure woman.

And what claim, after all, did he have over the bounties of Allah? He was raised to be a servant of Allah. All his knowledge had just one aim and that was to deepen his sense of servitude. The sun and the moon were perhaps content servants because they had no passion. It was his passion that had led to his distress and his folly was to seek an answer to a question without meaning. For there was no meaning to the puzzle of what he deserved. The angels who said we hear and we obey were better off; it was better to be made of light than to be filled with darkness.

He remembered talking about the Garden of Eden with Khadija. In that place the boundaries were clear. Here everything was blurred. Nothing made sense, and he did not have the tools to understand. All he had was enough faith to keep bitterness at bay but not enough to fill the emptiness or take away the pain.

Those by the coffin would at some point wipe their tears and walk away. They would look back in regret and move on and the lessons of their lives would fill their days and nights. But he, Musa, would forever carry the coffin of his wife in his nights.

He tried to stand up but was unable to. He was crying but that was OK. The tears would end and he would get up and go to the place from whence he came. And he would let it all go. He would be like a wave in the sea. In time, he too would be content with the Creator's decree.

Epilogue

"Who is going to be leading the prayers today?"
"Old misery guts. The man who never smiles."
"Mufti Musa?"
"Who else?"

Musa opened his eyes and stared into the darkness for a few minutes. His wife slept peacefully beside him. The sound of her breathing at the time of dawn had grated on him when they first married as it intruded on his special hour of reminiscence. Now, though, he found it strangely comforting.

He got out of bed and walked over to a photograph of Dadaji, a teardrop on his cheek, and Khadija. He gently touched the teardrop, his first ritual of the day.

"Will you have your breakfast now?" asked Iram.

Musa shook his head and she cursed herself for forgetting that whenever her husband turned away from the picture he was incapable of speech for a few minutes.

He strode across the prayer hall and nodded to the group of people who stood up as he passed. He saw Mufti Bashir watching impassively from the first floor. The elder was now wheelchair bound and a stroke had robbed him of his speech, but the different coloured eyes had lost none of their steel.

378

Ali and Basto stood in the front row. They too were muftis but were much more popular than he was with the youngsters. Musa was pleased to see that the hall was full as he began to recite the obligatory Surah *Al Fatiha* followed by the Surah *Hadid*, the Iron.

"No misfortune can happen, either in the earth or in yourselves, that was not set down in writing before We brought it into being – that is easy for God – so you need not grieve for what you miss or gloat over what you gain..."

He stopped, unable to continue. Those in the prayer hall shuffled awkwardly and Mufti Bashir's eyes filled even as Musa's tears began to flow. Alarmed by his distress Ali and Basto broke their prayer and stepped forwards, placing their hands on Musa's shoulders.

He nodded his gratitude and continued in a choked voice. "God does not love the conceited, the boastful, those who are miserly. If anyone turns away, remember that God is self-sufficient and worthy of praise. We sent Our messengers with clear signs, the Scripture and the Balance, so that people could uphold justice: We also sent iron, with its mighty strength and many uses for mankind, so that God could mark out those who would help Him and His messengers though they cannot see Him."

Musa bowed and, placing his hands on his knees, intoned, "Glory be to my Lord the Great."

He then rose and said calmly: "Truly Allah is powerful, almighty."

"Allah is powerful, almighty," came the response.